RECLAMATION

DEMON FALL TRILOGY
Book Three

S. USHER EVANS

Sun's Golden Ray
Publishing

Pensacola, FL

DEMON SPRING TRILOGY
Resurgence
Revival
Redemption

DEMON FALL TRILOGY
Reawakening
Resurrection
Reclamation

Demon Art by Ashley Gonzales, Zeefa Studio
Line Editing by Danielle Fine, By Definition Editing

Sun's Golden Ray Publishing
Pensacola, FL
www.sgr-pub.com

For ordering information, please visit
www.sgr-pub.com/orders

RECLAMATION

Other titles by S. Usher Evans

THE RAZIA SERIES
Double Life
Alliances
Conviction
Fusion

Empath

THE MADION WAR TRILOGY
The Island
The Chasm
The Union

THE LEXIE CARRIGAN CHRONICLES
Spells and Sorcery
Magic and Mayhem
Dawn and Devilry
Illusion and Indemnity

THE PRINCESS VIGILANTE SERIES
The City of Veils
The Veil of Ashes
The Veil of Trust
The Queen of Veils

DEDICATION

To WinnieBot
For keeping me on track

CONTENTS

DEMONOLOGY	9
Chapter One	17
Chapter Two	25
Chapter Three	34
Chapter Four	44
Chapter Five	54
Chapter Six	63
Chapter Seven	72
Chapter Eight	83
Chapter Nine	93
Chapter Ten	104
Chapter Eleven	112
Chapter Twelve	121
Chapter Thirteen	131
Chapter Fourteen	141
Chapter Fifteen	151
Chapter Sixteen	160
Chapter Seventeen	170
Chapter Eighteen	180
Chapter Nineteen	188
Chapter Twenty	190
Chapter Twenty-One	198
Chapter Twenty-Two	207
Chapter Twenty-Three	216
Chapter Twenty-Four	226
Chapter Twenty-Five	236
Chapter Twenty-Six	245
Chapter Twenty-Seven	256
Chapter Twenty-Eight	264
Chapter Twenty-Nine	268
Chapter Thirty	276
Chapter Thirty-One	284
Chapter Thirty-Two	293
Chapter Thirty-Three	302
Chapter Thirty-Four	312
Chapter Thirty-Five	323
Chapter Thirty-Six	332

Chapter Thirty-Seven	340
Chapter Thirty-Eight	345
Chapter Thirty-Nine	355
Chapter Forty	366
Chapter Forty-One	374
Chapter Forty-Two	383
Chapter Forty-Three	392
Chapter Forty-Four	401
Chapter Forty-Five	411
Chapter Forty-Six	423
Chapter Forty-Seven	425
Chapter Forty-Eight	433

DEMONOLOGY

The following is a brief introduction to the five kinds of demons found in the human world. The International Coalition for Demon Management (ICDM) is charged with protecting humans from unwanted demonic transformation, but we can't do it alone.

Learn the signs of demonic coercion and don't become a victim.

ATHTAR

First Seen: 1500 BC, Syria
Magical Element: Void
Original Sin: Pride
Original Demon: Bael

The oldest and rarest demons, Athtars live in the Underworld and appear during Demon Spring. They have the ability to manipulate time and space. NOTE: With the death of Bael in the Great Demon War, athtars are thought to be extinct.

ELOKO

First Seen: 400 AD, Democratic Republic of the Congo
Magical Element: Earth
Original Sin: Envy
Original Demon: Biloko

Eloko demons use the sound of a bell to hypnotize their victims
into a false sense of security. If you think an eloko is trying to
coerce you, stomp your feet or clap your hands to disrupt the
magic, then run away.

KAPPA

First Seen: 600 BC, Japan
Magical Element: Water
Original Sin: Greed
Original Demon: Mizuchi

Kappas mostly live near water, and will create an illusion of a house or structure. When the victim enters the illusion, it will break and the human will be drawn underwater, given the option to transform or drown. When near bodies of water, familiarize yourself with existing structures, and watch for others coming in and out.

LILIN

First Seen: 200 AD, Germany
Magical Element: Air
Original Sin: Lust
Original Demon: Freyja

Lilins use a mixture of pheromones and glamour (illusion) to lure humans into sexual intercourse, then transformation. If you think a lilin is trying to coerce you, pinch yourself or think of something unsettling, then run away.

NOX

First Seen: 1500 AD, Mexico
Magical Element: Fire
Original Sin: Anger
Original Demon: Mot and Xo

Nox demons use the human's innate fear of demons to construct terrifying nightmares, and the human agrees to transform to cease them. To combat a nox demon, take a deep breath and remind yourself it's only a vision.

PROTECT YOURSELF

If you encounter any demon or supposed demon, contact your local US Division of the International Coalition for Demon Management right away to report the incident.

UNITED STATES DIVISION
INTERNATIONAL COALITION
FOR DEMON MANAGEMENT
#demonspring

CHAPTER ONE

Bael, Master of the Underworld, Lord of the Mountain, emperor of all he surveyed, the original athtar demon, stood still as stone, watching the events of the past two years unfold before him in fast motion. He had a lot to catch up on, after all—since he'd been dead for the past year.

He wasn't resurrected, necessarily. More like given a wonderful gift from his beautiful Lady of the Mountain. He'd seen her traveling through the time river before, first alone, then with the nox prince Lotan. It had been surprising; the only athtar who'd ever known about the time river was Diogo, and his power limited him to a few minutes in the past. Bael had kept his distance for the most part. But when he'd seen his beloved Anat in the river once more, watching their daughter Asherah, he knew he had to speak to her.

It was unique to see his own magic in someone else's body,

to look at Anat and not feel her emotions through their connection. But there had been something else as well, a whisper of a hunch that if he held onto her magic, he might be able to skip over his fate and land in her time. In the future. And he, of course, was right.

His first order of business was to orient himself. As he'd always predicted, his demise had led to a chaotic future. The balance between humans and demons had been completely upset. A *nox* of all people (not even a nox belu, just a regular spawn), had thought he could take Bael's place as king of the demons. And poor Anat, too weak to do the hard thing.

Knowing the present, Bael had gone back to the past, viewing the events that had occurred. Time continued to flow as if he'd never left: from the moment Bael had taken Jackson Grenard, to Anat spawning with Camilla Macarro and their romp through the Underworld. The buildup of the war that would eventually end his life.

It was heartbreaking, to say the least, to watch Anat pick up Sharur, the sword he'd given her, and use it against him. For thousands of years, he'd considered Anat more than an ally. A lover, a partner. The mother of his child. The other half of his soul. But with one swing of that bejeweled blade, she'd ended any illusion that she felt the same. She'd been poisoned against him, listening to falsehoods and lies spouted by that human, Jackson Grenard.

Bael wasn't a vindictive man, and it hurt him just the same to watch her struggle after returning to the human world. Her human wasn't of any help; he had no idea how to manage Anat's mood swings and dark places the way Bael did. Her downward spiral continued until she reached a dark place even Bael had never seen her go.

Then something changed. The nox prince Lotan had been stolen by his own pack, and while Jack was gone with his human partner, Anat had been given a gift. The knowledge that an athtar was still alive.

Bael watched her absorb the magic with a little pride—at himself. Even in death, his plans could not be stopped. Diogo had retained his magic, just as Bael had always intended, and had been the one to guide Anat to the Underworld to retrieve the belu magic. And now, it seemed, his plan had come full circle. For had she not been the one to retrieve the magic, Bael never would've been sitting in this bustling cafe in the human world after his own death.

But that world was no longer his. There were anti-athtar talismans everywhere, which had proven useless against an onslaught of angry demons who'd wreaked havoc on hundreds of cities. Anat had managed to quell the riots by moving the demons back to the Underworld, but it was a temporary measure. The humans would want revenge, the demons would want their own, and poor Anat was in over her head.

Bael was the only one who could bring order back to this world. And if everything went according to plan, his beloved Anat would rule by his side once more.

Elonsi was dusty, and never a place Bael enjoyed visiting. Now, of course, it was filled with eloko demons, many of whom were still confused as to how they'd ended up here. Perhaps a day ago, they were fighting in the streets, massacring humans. The next moment, they were here. Undoubtedly, quite jarring for them.

Their belu, Biloko, was in the middle of a crowd of shouting demons, doing his best to calm their fears and promise he would return them to their homes as soon as possible.

"I will speak to the belu athtar," he said, waving his hands to try to keep the elokos calm. "I'm sure she can be reasoned with."

"Or perhaps you can speak with the *real* belu athtar." Bael's voice rang out across the group, and it pleased him to see his memory hadn't been forgotten. Every eloko seemed to wear the same mask of disbelief and fear, and Biloko himself paled five shades.

"B-Bael?" he croaked, taking a hesitant step back. "What are you doing here? *How?*"

"I'm just returning to see my old friend," Bael said, walking through the parting crowd. "We are still friends, are we not?"

"This isn't possible," Biloko breathed, shaking his head. "Anat killed you."

"So she did," Bael said. "And you did nothing to stop her."

"I was—"

"Hiding in your hut like a scared little boy while your spawn fought your battles for you?" Bael said, his voice low and even as he came closer. "It is a shame that I placed my faith in someone so cowardly. What might've happened had you been there to help?"

Biloko swallowed hard. "I meant no disrespect, my lord. You asked me to steer clear, so I was merely following orders."

Bael had no idea whether that was true or not; he'd skipped over the more boring parts immediately preceding his death. But it didn't matter. The time was near for a cleansing.

Bael turned around, gazing out across the elokos and searching their faces. He didn't care for the powerful among them, not when the balance was about to shift completely. He was after something else.

"I need to know who amongst you will swear fealty to me," Bael said, his voice carrying across the silent land.

"W-what?" Biloko began, but Bael froze time around the belu, leaving him motionless—and more importantly, quiet.

"I have seen what the humans have done in my absence," Bael said, walking out amongst the crowd. "They have abused their powers and killed innocent demon lords. Upset the balance of power in this world and theirs. My poor Anat cannot seem to do what needs to be done." He smiled. "But fear not, my friends, your king has returned."

Nervousness rustled through the crowd, and Bael saw hearts turning in his direction.

"Whoever amongst you will swear yourself to me before Biloko, step forward."

"And what if we don't?" a rather short man in the front asked.

"Then you shall remain here, with your belu," Bael said with a smile.

The crowd murmured, but a few brave souls stepped forward.

The first to reach Bael fell to her knee. "I swear my fealty to you, Lord Bael."

"Then you," Bael said, reaching down to lift her to stand, "shall be my first."

The numbers were not as great as he might've hoped; perhaps twenty elokos pledged themselves to Bael. But really, he only needed one.

"Very well," he said, when there were no more cries of support from the crowd. He nodded slightly. "This is where I take my leave."

The world slowed around Bael and the twenty elokos, and the woman who'd spoken up first inched closer.

"My lord," she said. "What would you have us do?"

Bael turned away from them, concentrating on the space between the threads of time. As if pushing aside a curtain, Bael opened a portal to a timeless zone. A space where time would cease to exist. He stepped through to the other side and beckoned the elokos to follow.

"You will be safe here," he said with a warm smile. "And I will return in time with a precious gift."

Bael returned to Elonsi, leaving his twenty loyal elokos behind. Time resumed its pace in the Elonsi world for the rest, including Biloko, who blinked three times before pulling his spear from his back.

"You are not welcome here, Bael," he said. "Not if you will be usurping my powers."

"They're yours because I gave them to you," Bael said with a smile. "And since you no longer swear fealty to me, I will have to take them back."

Bael felt the tug of the eloko's magic pushing him from the lands, so he stopped time once more. Taking the eloko's own weapon, Bael struck him in the heart, then used his sword to decapitate the belu.

As the belu's head fell from his body, the magic he'd held for thousands of years came to the surface. Bael reached forward to take it in his hands, careful not to want to take it for himself. He'd learned that lesson many times. It was not for him but for him to give.

This time, he would give it to those who would know and appreciate the gift. And who would do his bidding unequivocally.

As he stepped back into the time portal, time resumed once more, and the land of Elonsi collapsed on itself, taking every treacherous eloko and the dead Biloko with it.

He closed the portal, finding his twenty reverted humans collapsed on the ground, their powers gone with their belu. Bael walked to the one who'd spoken up first, the ambitious woman he'd selected as Biloko's successor.

Gently, he roused her, smiling as she blinked heavily at him.

"Who are you?" she asked in a language Bael hadn't heard in a long time, but still understood. "Where am I?"

"I am Bael," he said softly. "And I come with a gift from God. But first, I demand your loyalty to me."

She slowly nodded, that spark of ambition back in her gaze. "I will be loyal."

Bael took her hand and helped her to her feet, walking her back to the bright orange magic waiting for her.

"This power is ancient," he said, resting his hand on her shoulder. "And if you take it, it will make you one of the most powerful creatures in existence."

"What would you have me do with it?" she asked.

"Build me an army," Bael said. "Starting with the rest of the humans here. And then we shall begin our work."

CHAPTER TWO

What had she done?

Anya paced the living room in Ath-kur, chewing her fingernails to the quick and finding no solace. At least Cam, Lotan, and Jack weren't there, probably back in the human world to help with the clean-up and aftermath of the attack. She wasn't sure what she'd say to them—she wasn't even sure she knew what to say to herself.

Time travel was supposed to be just viewing. She'd traveled back in time and watched events over and over again. She hadn't even been corporeal there. Just a shadow of herself.

So how the hell could she have brought Bael back?

Running her hands through her hair, she walked to the window, waiting for him to make his appearance. *This* Bael was from the era just after she'd left him again, when he realized she was falling for Jack and turned even more vindictive than she'd thought possible. Surely, there would be some punishment in store for her.

No. Things were different now. He was no longer the all-powerful monster who'd found her outside her village thousands of years ago. She had the same power, theoretically equal to him in every way. He couldn't take it away from her even if he wanted to.

She would keep repeating that until she believed it.

Some small, perhaps hopeful, part of herself tried to convince her she'd imagined things. That in her sadness of seeing Asherah again, she'd dreamed all of it. But she'd become accustomed to believing her own eyes, and even that little candle of hope snuffed out.

What it all meant, she had no idea. She searched the human world and Underworld for any sign of him but couldn't See him. Whether because he was hiding himself or because in some place she couldn't find or…

Her spiraling panic quieted as the connection between her and the only person who would truly understand lit up. Diogo was on his way to her. She'd slowed time to keep Jack or Cam or Lotan from finding her, so Diogo had taken some time to prepare and arrive in the Underworld.

"My lady," Diogo said, appearing in the living room. "I'm sorry it took me a moment to arrive. What is the crisis?"

Anya looked at her reflection, unsure how to explain the situation or how far back to start. So she just came out with it. "Bael has returned."

Diogo's face was clear in the window, and he took a step backward in fear. "That's...not possible."

"It is," Anya said, turning around. "I went... I went back in time. One last time..." She shook her head, not wanting to go into the reason. "And he was there. Not as the man he was, but another version. Perhaps the Bael from just after the last Demon Spring."

"My lady, you aren't making much sense," Diogo said.

Anya exhaled. "I think...somehow... I managed to find a version of Bael in the time river and he used me to come to the present."

"As a vision or—"

She shook her head. "He was living. Breathing. Whole."

"Are you certain you aren't just..." Diogo licked his lips, clearly not wanting to continue that train of thought. "I don't believe this is possible."

"Perhaps not with a human or another demon," Anya replied. "But you said yourself we'd only scratched the surface of the time river. If two belu athtars meet in the same moment of time, one can, I suppose, hitch a ride to the present."

Diogo's eyes lit up with understanding. "So you're saying that Bael, the belu athtar from some time before his death, is now in this world? In this time?"

Anya nodded, pressing her back against the window. "He knew things. He knew about Jack. But he didn't know how I'd killed him..." She shivered, recalling what he'd said about planning his own death.

"Where is he now?" Diogo asked.

She shrugged. "I can't See him. I have no idea."

"Does this mean… I have resumed being his spawn?" Diogo asked, a little nervously.

Anya shook her head, offering him the only smile she could muster. "Our connection is still strong. He's merely a demon in the wrong time. But a demon as powerful as I am."

Visibly relieved, Diogo joined her at the window. "So…what do we do about it? You should inform your human compatriots."

Anya flinched. The last words she and Jack had shared weren't very…compatriot-like. After Yaotl had led riots in human cities around the world, Anya had moved nearly every demon back to their respective worlds as a stopgap measure to avoid any more bloodshed on either side. But it hadn't been enough for Cam, who'd demanded Anya give up her athtar powers to keep the demons and humans separated for good.

Jack had agreed and Anya had somewhat lost her temper. But after coming to realize that they were right, that the temptation to become what Bael had been was too strong, she'd made the decision to become human once more—after she traveled back in time to see her precious daughter Asherah one last time. To remember her voice, her cherubic face, the way her hair bounced when she ran.

And that was when she'd come face to face with Bael.

"My lady?" Diogo said, breaking her from her trance. "Shall I fetch your friends for you?"

"No," Anya said. Cam was already distrustful. Lotan didn't even know who he was anymore, and when he *did* get his memory back, he'd side with Cam.

And Jack…there was no way to explain this to Jack that he'd believe. The words he'd flung in her face in Lisbon still stung.

"You're still enamored with Bael and his magic, and you always will be. I will never be enough for you."

They'd come so far since that day. She could still feel his lips on her skin from the night before. But she couldn't risk ruining that any more than she already had. The only thing she could do was protect them from Bael until she managed to put him back where he belonged.

"I need you to do something for me," Anya said softly.

"Anything."

"I need you to convince them to wear anti-athtar talismans," Anya said, slowly. "I don't care how you do it. But this Bael knows Jack, knows how I feel about him. And by extension, Cam and Lotan. Until I can contain him, they need to be protected."

"Or you could just tell them what's happened," Diogo said slowly. "Then they would be protected because they would be by your side."

"Do as I say," Anya snapped, giving him the most dangerous look she could muster. "And do not question me."

Diogo took a step back, all his misgivings gone, and bowed at the hip. "As you please, my lady. I will find a way."

He disappeared and Anya exhaled, pressing her head to the

window again.

"Such a loyal foot soldier. It's a shame he never felt that way about me."

Anya would never get used to hearing that voice so clear, not when it had haunted her dreams for all these months. She lifted her gaze once more to the window, seeing Bael's reflection mere inches behind her. He gave no magical signature she could detect, perhaps because his magic was equal to her own. Or he was doing a good job of hiding it.

"Oh, my beautiful Anat," he said, sliding his hands down her shoulders and rubbing slightly. She hated how she trembled at the weight of them. He was absolutely *real*. "It pains me to see you so troubled. What can I do to ease your mind?"

Anya spun from his fingertips, forcing herself to remember she was just as powerful as he was. "Don't touch me."

He smiled. "So you still hate me."

"Why would I not?"

"I have seen your journey since my death," Bael said. "You struggled as a human, you struggled as an athtar belu. My arrival should be a blessing to you. Finally, someone to give you guidance."

"I'm not in need of guidance," Anya said, hating that she didn't sound convinced. "But if you'd like to return to your time, I would be happy to oblige."

"I don't think so," Bael said, with a knowing smile. "I find that this world is much more in need of care than the one I left."

Anya licked her lips, unsure if she wanted to ask him more

but unable to stop her curiosity. "So does this mean that the Bael I remember, the one I killed, is no longer dead?"

"No," Bael said. "Time is funny. The moment we met, I became part of your future. Your past remains unchanged. The events as you remember them remain the same."

That made no sense to her, but very little did at the moment. Bael smirked and left her in the living room, venturing to the kitchen and the bottles of wine Cam had left on the counter. He opened one and poured himself a glass, tasting it before pouring one for Anya.

"You see, once you enter the time river, all the normal rules stop. Your body physically remains in the present, as you know. It's merely an extension of yourself that travels to and from." He handed her the wine, and she took it, if only to keep him talking.

"And does your past self, the one who sent you, see what you see?"

"Who knows?" Bael said, bringing the wine to his lips. "This is my first time traveling forward in time."

Anya didn't drink, staring at him and racking her brain for more questions, but all she could do was watch him, marveling at the sheer *aliveness* of him.

"Are you pleased to see me?" Bael asked.

"What will you do now that you're here?" Anya asked instead of answering his question.

"Oh, I have plans," Bael said with an enigmatic smile that boded nothing well. "This world is in disarray. I don't blame you, of course. Your heart is far too soft to do what needed to be done. There is only peace through obedience. Now, my love, you understand why I forbade the use of those deadly talismans."

Anya brought the wine to her lips but didn't drink. "So they affect you as well?"

"Of course they do," Bael said. "But fear not. You don't have to tattoo the symbols on your lover Jack or his friends. They do not play into my plans."

She nodded. *If they affect him, how was I able to stop time in Geneva?*

"Then what will you do?" she asked again, her voice quiet and contemplative.

"That, my love, will be revealed in time." He stepped toward her, and before she could stop herself, she took a step backward. Thousands of years of fearing him was a hard habit to break, it seemed.

He leaned down to kiss her softly, and she was struck by how different his lips felt from Jack's.

Jack.

The memory of Jack in Bael's castle, of how he'd hurt the man she loved, broke the trance, and she yanked herself away from him.

"I told you not to touch me," she whispered fiercely.

"So you did," Bael said, his eyes capturing hers the way they'd done a million times before. "But perhaps one day, my love, you might change your tune."

He disappeared.

She hoped that he couldn't See her, because the wine slipped from her hands, and she slid down the windowsill, hot tears spilling down her cheeks as she held herself. She could've been the most powerful demon in existence, but with Bael, she reverted to the thirteen-year-old girl every time. Trapped in his gaze and believing every word he said.

"My lady!" Diogo was back, and she hated that he'd seen her in such a state. "My lady, what is it?"

"Nothing," Anya whispered, not wanting to upset him. "Did you do as I asked?"

"There was nothing to be done," Diogo said. "The humans have encamped in Geneva, which is still covered in talismans. I was unable to get closer."

"Then it is your job to make sure they stay that way," Anya said, looking up at him. "I want to know if they set one foot outside the protection zone."

He nodded. "You have my word. But Bael—"

"Leave him to me," Anya said, wiping her cheeks. "He's my problem. And I will solve it myself."

CHAPTER THREE

Jack Grenard tossed and turned in the twin bed, trying to find a comfortable spot, before recognizing it wasn't the mattress's fault. There would be no rest any time soon, not when he couldn't stop replaying his last conversation with Anya.

"Anya, this…staying athtar… It's not necessary. You would only be doing it to suit your own desires."

"It was necessary when I saved your life just now."

"But the danger has passed."

"There will always be danger—"

"Not if the demons can't reach the humans. You said yourself you're the only way they can get between worlds, so if you no longer have magic… You don't need it anymore, Anya. It's not who you are, and it doesn't define you."

"Then you clearly don't know me at all, Jack."

He stared at the ceiling, wondering if there was some other

way he could have phrased it, perhaps some other angle he should've taken that might've landed better. Or were they just destined for this inevitable parting of ways?

Cam was still fuming and had insisted they return to the human world since Anya wasn't interested in helping, which seemed a little unfair to Jack. But Geneva was in dire straits. Jack guessed ICDM had lost at least half their staff in the attack, and even more of their security forces. Backup was nowhere to be found, as most cities were dealing with their own aftermath.

More than that, Frank would've wanted him to step up.

He sat up and walked to the window, opening the blinds and looking out onto the side street in Geneva. Here, far from the chaos in the center of town, it was easy to forget that the world had been turned upside-down. Though no one was on the street, the coffee shop across the way had its doors open.

Was Frank a regular, and would they know that Jack was his grandson? Had they even heard he'd died?

Jack walked back to the twin bed and made it up, remembering how Frank would get onto him that one summer Jack spent shadowing him as a teenager. There were no maids in the US Councilman's apartment, so cleanliness was on the two of them, Frank had explained.

Jack dug through the hastily packed bag he'd brought from Ath-kur for a change of clothes and frowned at it. Things had moved quickly, and he'd been too distracted to take any care in stuffing his shirts and jeans into the bag. Now everything was wrinkled. Not exactly the picture he wanted to present when he went back to ICDM, but it would have to do.

His stomach grumbled, so he grabbed his wallet and busted phone—reminding himself to purchase a replacement on the off chance Anya decided she was done pouting—and walked out into the living room.

Lotan was already there, reading the paper with a steaming cup of coffee. It was so strange to see the former nox prince looking so…human. Some of his perfection had waned, and his hair wasn't quite as shiny and perfectly curled as it had been, but he was still too gorgeous for his own good.

He looked up at Jack and offered a genuine smile. "Good morning! Jack, right?"

Jack couldn't help the flinch. "So your memory hasn't returned."

"I remember…" He smiled sadly. "I remember my parents. Very clearly. I remember Cam, well…" His smile turned a bit bashful. "I remember how much I love her. But the details are still somewhat fuzzy."

Jack had to smile. If he lost his memory, he'd want to remember his parents, Cam, and…

"Why don't we head across the street and pick up some food? There's a cafe over there that looks inviting."

Jack led Lotan across the way, amused at how the former nox was fascinated at literally *everything*. He pointed to a croissant and announced loudly that he knew what it was, earning some odd looks from the old man at the counter. Jack thanked the clerk in his best French, and carried the bag and three cups of coffee back to the apartment.

Sugar, chocolate, and butter were what the doctor ordered, and Jack had two of the croissants in one bite while Lotan took his time, savoring the food as if it were the first time.

"Do you…think your memory is better than yesterday?" Jack asked. "Or better at all?"

"I think…" Lotan looked down at the cup of coffee. "I do remember the taste of coffee. It's almost like awakening from a dream. Experiencing things feels like…what's that thing when you've experienced something before?"

"Deja vú." Jack smiled.

"Perhaps there are things I don't want to remember, anyway," Lotan said, looking out the window. "I'm not the man I was. Perhaps it's a good thing to start clean."

Jack shook his head and took another long sip, following Lotan's gaze. From this side of the apartment, the plume of smoke coming from the wreckage of the ICDM headquarters was still visible. They would have their work cut out for them getting it back up and running—and protecting them from any unseen threats that still lurked out there.

"What do you want me to do?" Lotan asked.

"It might be best for you to lie low for a while, just until we know for sure what we're dealing with," Jack said. "We don't know if any of the noxes survived with their powers intact, and you'd be a target."

Lotan nodded. "I don't understand most of what you said, but I'll stay put if you think it's best." He smiled. "Will we be seeing that other woman again? Anya?"

"I don't want to think about it," Jack said, finishing the rest of his coffee and walking to the sink to leave the cup. "I'm going to headquarters. Tell Cam I'll see her later."

The closer Jack walked to the center of town, the more the ghosts of the previous day's attack haunted him. The sheer number of dead would take some time to work through, and identifying who'd been the aggressor and who a victim even more.

"I saw that demon about to kill you and I guess I just... did it. I was able to stop time completely and..."

The memory of Anya in the square, the sight of her wet, green eyes drinking him in, was seared in his memory. She'd seemed so breathless, so proud of herself for accomplishing the impossible. She'd cried over Frank then gently tended to Jack's wounds—he didn't even have as much as a scratch on him today. They'd made love, forgetting about the world on fire and just being together. Until the world came crashing back in.

A desolate laugh came from his lips. It was pretty par for the course for their relationship. Just when things were good, when the sun was rising and the world seemed to be settling, something else came up. He supposed he should be grateful it wasn't Bael this time.

And yet, he kept coming back to the sight of her in the square, and how no matter what happened between them, his heart still skipped a beat when he looked into those eyes. Perhaps he was just a masochist. Or stupid.

His internal deliberations ended abruptly when he arrived at the scene of the chaos. ICDM headquarters was a husk of itself, the initial explosion taking out the front half of the building. What was left was jagged rebar and concrete, a grotesque view into the innards of the offices, with desks overturned and wires hanging from the ceiling.

The Swiss military had moved most of the bodies from the square, but dark stains still marred the stone design on the ground. There was a heavy presence of armed guards milling around, waiting for the next attack. Jack hoped they'd been equipped with more than human weapons, but it would take time.

He was stopped at the first checkpoint, but after showing his ID and getting checked by the main security staff, he was allowed through. On the other end of the square, a large green tent had been set up as a command center of sorts. He nodded to the two guards out front, but they must've recognized him from the day before, because they let him through.

Inside, there was a flurry of activity. A mix of ICDM and military leadership gathered in clusters, all wearing the same exhausted, yet determined, looks.

Jack spotted María, Councilwoman to Mexico and Central America, and also Cam's great-aunt, standing to the side. She locked gazes with him and beckoned him over. Her forehead had a few stitches and her face was bruised, but she didn't seem bothered by it.

"Morning," she said, giving him a once-over. Probably wondering what happened to his battle wounds. "I was hoping we would see you."

"Frank would want me to help," Jack said, before swallowing hard. "Speaking of—"

"We have already made arrangements to have his body, and the bodies of his staff, flown back to Charleston," María said, speaking without emotion. Jack would've gotten mad about it, except that she probably had no emotion left in her.

"Thank you," Jack said with a nod. "What can I do to help?"

María gestured at him to follow her out the back flap of the tent, perhaps so they could talk in private. But there wasn't much privacy, not with all the armed guards floating around.

"Do you have confirmation on the location of the demons?" María asked. "The ones who disappeared?"

Jack nodded. "Anya moved them to the Underworld."

"And there's no way for them to come back?"

He didn't want to go into details just yet about Lotan. "The only way in-between worlds now is Anya."

María quirked a brow. "And you don't think that's a problem?"

"I do, actually," Jack said. "But unfortunately, right now, there's nothing I can do about it."

"What does that mean?"

He hated how often his personal relationship got muddled in ICDM business. "I asked her to give up her powers so that the demons would remain in the Underworld, and she declined."

"Give up her powers? Is that possible?"

Jack pinched the bridge of his nose. "It's a long story."

"I have time."

Against his better judgment, Jack told her what Lotan had done, and what it meant now that the nox belu no longer existed. She listened intently, asking no questions until he was done then nodded slowly.

"So if we were to kill the belus, all the demons would go?"

Jack cleared his throat. Typical María. "Yes. For now. But the magic would remain in this world. Eventually, another human would find it, then we'd have a new crop of demons."

"How soon?"

"I don't know. Could be tomorrow, could be a thousand years from now. But considering the belus are in the Underworld, I don't think it's a good plan of action to think about offing them right now."

María nodded slowly. "Thank you for telling me. There is still the matter of the topside demons to deal with."

"How many?" Jack asked, grateful for a change of subject.

"We are still gathering intelligence from our divisions around the world. A fraction of those who were here before, to be sure, but perhaps enough to be concerned about."

"You will have to get them to sign a treaty without the belus, then," Jack said. "Frank said—"

"Our plans have changed," María replied, lifting her gaze to meet his stonily. "After what we've witnessed, there is little appetite for any demon to remain in this world. The remaining

Council is coming together to put together an agreement for complete eradication." She looked at Jack. "I need to know if your demonic friend Anya will stand in the way of that?"

Jack stared at her. "Complete eradication? So even the demons who weren't involved in this attack will be killed?"

"They didn't exactly lift a finger to help us, either," María said. "Thousands of humans have been massacred, perhaps even hundreds of thousands. It's unheard of." She sighed heavily, looking at the soldiers standing mere feet away. "If we do not show that we are taking action, someone else will take it for us."

It took most of the afternoon for Jack to find a cellular store that was open, and another couple hours for the technician to retrieve his SIM card from his busted phone and put it in a new one. Once the device lit up, he found several missed calls from his parents and Cam's mother, but none from Anya.

He swallowed and found her number, punching out a text. *We need to talk.*

A moment later, the response came in. *Stay in Geneva.*

Jack frowned, looking around in indignation as if she were there herself. Stay in Geneva? What the hell kind of response was that?

It's important.

No answer.

ICDM wants to move against the topside demons. I need your promise that you won't do anything to interfere.

No answer.

Jack nearly threw his phone across the street. She could be petty when she was mad, but this was more than that. She couldn't be this juvenile when she was the one holding the key to the door separating demons and humans.

Anya, please.

Finally, he saw the cloud of dots indicating she was typing.

Stay in Geneva.

"Fine," Jack barked at the phone, earning him a look from the tech. But if Anya was going to be that way, he would just have to assume she wasn't going to help. Which made their jobs a lot harder.

CHAPTER FOUR

Cam heard Jack get up and leave, and the muffled conversation between him and Lotan. To be honest, she wished she'd gotten up and left with him. At least then she wouldn't be alone with Lotan.

Or the man who looked like the love of her life but barely remembered his own name.

He hadn't even wanted to sleep in the same bed with her the night before—not that she'd really asked him to. They were tiptoeing around each other now, or so Cam felt. She was being a coward, but she couldn't allocate any energy to being brave. Not when there were so many other pressing matters crowding everything else out.

Anya had disappeared, presumably to continue her life as an athtar and leave them to clean up Yaotl's mess alone.

ICDM's global headquarters had been decimated, and many

of its senior staff had been killed, including Frank.

The entire world seemed to be in a state of shock.

Certainly, her memory-less boyfriend problems could wait.

Footsteps echoed down the hall, and she tensed as the door opened, revealing Lotan's beautiful face. It was the same, and yet…different. There was less definition in those cheekbones. His eyes had dulled to a softer brown. But the smile on his face, that still elicited the same magic in her bones. She couldn't deny she loved him. Especially when he brought her caffeine.

"Good morning," he said. "Jack's left, but I thought you might need some coffee."

"Thank you," she said, taking it from him. "I should probably get up and join him. I'm sure it's chaotic out there."

She expected Lotan to argue with her, but he nodded supportively. "What do you need me to do?"

"Lie low—"

He chuckled. "You've been talking with Jack."

"Did he say the same thing?" Cam asked. "Then doubly so. We have no idea what's still out there, and who might have a bone to pick with you now that you're human."

"Was I really so hated?" Lotan asked, looking at her with a sad curiosity.

"Not hated." Cam took a sip of the coffee. "Just…when you gave up your nox magic, it caused a ripple effect across the world. Every demon who had the nox magic lost theirs at the same time. They could want revenge…" She took another long gulp. "If they even remember."

"If they've lost their memories as I have, they can't be much danger to me," Lotan said. "I would rather stay with you, if possible."

"Let me get my arms around what the world looks like today," Cam said. "Once I have a chance to talk with the Council, we'll figure out what we're doing next."

Out of habit, she leaned toward him, ready to peck him on the lips, but she stopped herself, staring into his brown eyes. He seemed ready for something but confused at the same time. She opened and closed her mouth like a fish for a moment then covered her awkwardness by finishing the rest of her coffee.

"I'll be back when I can," she said, jumping up and walking to the bathroom.

After a quick shower and change of clothes, Cam headed out into the city, making a beeline for ICDM headquarters. The heavy military presence gave her pause for a moment, but someone called her name. Jack was jogging over, now sporting an ICDM jacket straight out of the past. He vouched for Cam with the guards and waved her through.

"Where'd you get this?" Cam asked, pinching the sleeve of his jacket.

"María said that if I was going to stick around, I might as well rejoin the force," Jack said with a wry smile. "Got one for you, too."

Cam nodded. "What else does María say?"

Jack gave her the brief rundown of his conversation with

María, and she shook her head.

"People are pissed, and rightfully so. They want all demons gone." Cam couldn't disagree with them.

"We're still trying to get a handle on how many demons are left," Jack said. "But it's not many. The noxes might've been completely eradicated."

"And what about our bridge between worlds?" Cam asked cautiously. "Any word from her?"

Jack showed Cam his new phone and texts from Anya. Cam wanted to believe there was something more behind them, but considering her behavior the day before, she wasn't holding out hope.

"If we start offing demons, can we be sure Anya won't retaliate?" Cam asked. "That the belus won't come to her and ask her to step in?"

Jack was silent for a long time. "I don't think she will, but…"

"But we can't be sure," Cam finished for him. "We know she can somehow bypass the athtar talismans, so that's great."

Jack nodded and looked over his shoulder, nodding to something behind her. "We're being summoned."

She turned to see a young ICDM agent waving at them frantically from the main tent, and they shared a look of exhaustion before heading in that direction.

"What's going on?" Cam asked, walking up to the display of screens where María was watching with a furrowed brow.

"There's been an attack," María said. "Demons have overrun

Berlin. It looks to be elokos."

"That's… Berlin is a lilin town," Jack said. "Where the hell would they have come from?"

María sniffed. "It *was* a lilin town, before the athtar disrupted everything. We need to send a team there quickly. The local ICDM office is overwhelmed." Her sharp gaze turned to Cam. "Do you still have the ability to move places quickly? Or has your athtar friend taken that ability?"

"You mean the athtar portal?" Cam shook her head. "No. Not anymore." She'd left it behind when Anya had disappeared, deciding that if Anya wanted to choose her magic over them, she could keep all of it.

But Jack nodded. "I do. But it won't work until we're further outside town."

"Make it happen," María said, nodding to the agent beside her. "Take a contingent and follow Agent Grenard."

Jack and the soldier left immediately, leaving Cam standing in the middle of the tent, stuck to the ground. She should've gone with him, but her soul was weary. She'd barely survived the attack less than forty-eight hours ago; she wasn't eager to walk into another one.

"Does your presence here indicate you're rejoining the agency?" María asked, turning back to the screen of the chaos in Berlin.

"I suppose," Cam said, not loving the icy tone in her voice. "You look like you could use the help."

"And your nox prince? I hear he's human once more."

Damn it, Jack. Cam had been hoping to keep that under wraps for a while. "Yes. He's… he's human now." She turned to María, her gaze suspicious. "I hope you aren't thinking of bringing charges against him or anything."

"I'm not," María said. "Others may feel differently. He's responsible—"

"Yaotl is responsible," Cam snapped. "And I'm fairly sure he and the rest of the noxes are at the bottom of what was once the noxlands."

"We have sources that say he survived," María said. "And I was hoping to ask your prince about it."

Cam almost laughed. "Tough luck, I guess. Lotan barely remembers what a nox is, let alone what happened in the hours before he became human. He's harmless."

María didn't respond right away, turning back to the screens and tapping her finger against the table. "Cam, it should not surprise you that the worldwide attacks yesterday awoke something in humanity. Countries are threatening to pull funding and staff. After all, ICDM's only charge is to protect the world from demons, and we allowed this to happen."

Cam bit her tongue instead of reminding María that she, Jack, *and* Anya had warned ICDM of this exact outcome.

"Most concerning, to them and to me, is that your athtar friend was seen in the middle of a city covered in talismans designed to prevent her appearance. Do you know how she did it?"

"No," Cam said.

María sighed. "Jack said she was unresponsive when he reached out to her. Perhaps you could try."

Unresponsive. That was certainly one way to phrase it. Perhaps Jack wasn't as ingratiated with ICDM as the jacket would indicate. "I'll do my best, but I'm not sure I'll get a better response."

Cam excused herself shortly after that, needing to get away from María and the thought that her weapons might be used against one of her friends—and the reality that it *might* be needed. So she'd hopped a ride with a unit of soldiers to the end of town where Jack had set up Anya's portal. It was huge now, the size of a whole house, to allow the soldiers and armored cars to drive through.

Surely, Anya knew something was going on. Would she show up to help?

By the time Cam arrived in Berlin, the fighting was in full swing. She unstrapped her macuahuitl from her back and stepped into the fray. The demons were young—none of them had the sort of power the demons in Geneva had displayed. It was a blessing, because the non-ICDM military were able to fight them without succumbing to their magic, and Cam's talisman-laden macuahuitl was more than enough to take them out permanently.

Cam swung her club, making a path for herself and the military so they could back up the first unit. More soldiers poured from the portal after Cam, a steady stream that would overwhelm the elokos before too long. It seemed…easy, almost. Too easy.

"Jack!" Cam called once she spotted him in the crowd. His knives cut through the elokos as easily as her club, mowing down demons as two soldiers flanked him with guns.

"Good of you to join me," Jack said with that typical cocky smile he wore in the middle of a fight. "Any idea where these jackasses came from?"

Cam shook her head. There was no one language; it was a true mix from across the world. How all they all managed to get together for this attack—especially since Yaotl was no longer pulling the strings—was a mystery.

A blade came for her head and she whacked it away. A mystery she'd solve once this city was under control.

"How many of them are there?" Cam asked.

"No idea. We found the first set and started fighting," Jack said. "There could be hundreds—maybe thousands. Maybe every eloko left on earth got pissed off and congregated here."

"But why here?" Cam said, digging her club into an advancing eloko and stunning him long enough for Jack to slice his head off. "And not Japan?"

"I have no answers, Cam," Jack said, panting. "I just…"

An intense energy was arriving from somewhere far away, and the sounds of fighting slowed. Cam actually exhaled in relief. Anya would put a quick end to this—and perhaps she and Jack would finally have a chance to talk about their argument the other day.

The belu athtar appeared on their left side, fearsome and terrifying in her power, especially compared to the pathetic elokos they'd been fighting.

And she looked pissed—at them. "I told you to stay in Geneva."

"Is that really all you have to say?" Jack barked back.

"What else do you want me to say?" Anya asked, her tone high—panicked. Why was she panicked? "You should have known I would take care of this. There was no need for you to leave Geneva."

"Are we so sure you would have?" Cam asked. "Because you haven't been very forthcoming in your intentions lately."

Anya licked her lips, staring at Cam as if she were considering her words very carefully. "I will protect this world. These elokos will be returned to their land. I'm not sure how I missed them the first time."

There was something unsettled about the way she kept looking past them, behind them, to the side of them. Almost as if she were waiting for something. Expecting something.

"Just, please," she said after a while. "Go back to Geneva. I will handle this."

"We'll leave as soon as this city is under control," Jack said.

"I'll get it under control," Anya said. "Just go. Please. Or I will do it for you."

"Anya, you can't just—"

Whatever Cam was going to say died on her lips as the world blipped. Every kappa in the city was gone—along with Anya.

"Again?" Jack said with a heavy shake of his head. "So what? She's just going to show up and move demons back to the Underworld?"

"I think she can," Cam said with pursed lips. "After all, she's the belu athtar. She can do whatever the fuck she wants."

CHAPTER FIVE

Lotan couldn't breathe.

He looked up to see a familiar face but couldn't find his name. The man was at once human and wolf—and Lotan recognized both for some reason. The man's large paw was on Lotan's throat.

"I wonder if I'm powerful enough to maintain my own connection," the man said. "Shall we test the theory?"

Lotan managed to find the strength to kick the man-monster off of him. Precious air came back to his lungs. "Are you so blinded by your ambition that you'd risk it all?"

"Merely studying new theories around belus," the man said. "Tabiko was quite helpful. She told us an athtar managed to survive after Bael's death. No living child required. I'm willing to gamble the same thing will happen when I destroy you."

That felt like a stone to the stomach, but Lotan had no idea why. There was something, some mystery he'd known intimately but now escaped his grasp. He wanted to ask the man-monster more, but...

"You're hesitating, boy," the man sneered. "Are you second-guessing your decision?"

Then, like a blinding light, his mind filled with the thought of Cam. She was standing firm in a room full of enemies, a fierceness in her gaze as she braved the magic and danger that Lotan knew but didn't understand. What he did know was this was the moment his heart had fallen for her, a feeling that would transcend even his own memory loss—and give him the strength to survive.

But just as he turned to the man-monster, the vision faded, and with a soft breath, Lotan opened his eyes to a much different room, with sunlight streaming onto his face. It took him a moment to realize he'd fallen asleep in the afternoon sun, reading one of the many books Jack's grandfather had around the apartment.

He put down the book and leaned forward, rubbing his face as he grasped at the dream and the context that still eluded him. It was all on the tip of his tongue, but he had no one to ask about it, not in this empty apartment. He rose from the chair and scoured the apartment for a paper and pen he could use to jot down his thoughts to ask Cam later.

As he was describing the dream, a name floated by his mind. *Yaotl.* The man-monster's name was Yaotl.

But that was all, just a name. Who the man was, why he'd

wanted Lotan dead, why Lotan had been so afraid—none of it made sense. He stared at the scant description on the paper and frowned as frustration bubbled in the bottom of his chest. How in the world was he going to be useful to anyone if he couldn't make sense of anything?

Now, that wasn't entirely fair. He could speak and read, and he could do basic tasks like taking a shower. But those things seemed more like instinct, and he wasn't sure how he knew how to do them. He just could.

His memory was shrouded in a thick, gray cloud, with shapes he could barely make out, but he knew they were there. Somewhere, in the deep recesses of his mind, he would find everything he needed to know. But for now, all he had were dreams that made no sense but left his pulse elevated.

He sighed and walked back to the window, retrieving the book and gently sliding it back onto the shelf. It hadn't been all that riveting anyway, but perhaps a different book might jog his memory.

His rumbling stomach interrupted his thoughts, and he ventured into the kitchen. Unfortunately, Jack's grandfather had left a sparse cupboard with mostly condiments and very little substantive food. Cam had told him to stay put, as had Jack, but he needed to eat.

Taking care to grab the set of keys hanging by the door, Lotan locked the door behind him and ventured downstairs and out onto the street.

For mid-afternoon, things seemed rather dead to Lotan. Not that he really remembered what a city was supposed to be like, but his gut was telling him something was off. He passed several small cafes, but they were all closed. Some were even boarded up.

Finally, he spotted an old woman sweeping her front step, and she glared at him for some reason. But Lotan wasn't deterred, and happily walked up to her, flashing her a smile.

"Pardon me, do you know where I can get a bite to eat?" he asked.

The woman spoke in words he didn't understand, and he took a step back, trying to parse it out. So perhaps his language skills weren't fully developed yet.

"I'm sorry, can you—"

But her swinging broom told him all he needed to know, and he dashed down the street out of the line of fire.

Lotan kept wandering, but his initial gut feeling that something just wasn't quite right in this city grew as he encountered a few more strangers. They didn't throw their broom at him, but their tight smiles and darting gazes left him uncomfortable—and he didn't approach them.

Finally, after an hour of wandering down mostly residential streets, he found something open and selling food. There was no one inside, save one old man behind the counter. Lotan walked right by him to peruse the aisles of packaged food and plucked a couple of things off the shelf he thought he remembered he liked. When he'd filled the small basket, he walked to the clerk, whose gaze was still glued to the television screen.

Lotan made a small noise, and the clerk turned, speaking words Lotan didn't understand. "I'm sorry," Lotan said with a shake of his head.

"Ah, American?" he asked in a thick accent.

"No, I'm..." Lotan furrowed his brow. What was he, anyway? Cam was American, so he'd go with that. "Yes, I'm American."

"ICDM?"

"Pardon?"

"Are you with the demon hunters?" he asked, taking the basket and ringing up the items Lotan had purchased.

"Er..." Lotan swallowed. "No. But my friends are."

"Picked a bad time to be a tourist," he said. "Many dead. Your friends?"

"They're...fine," Lotan said. "What do you mean?"

"The attack yesterday," the clerk said. "Were you asleep or something?"

Something tickled in the back of Lotan's mind, and he just nodded. "Right. Sorry."

The man looked at Lotan expectantly, and Lotan reached into his pocket, where he found a wallet stuffed with credit cards. The move was yet again instinctual, as Lotan didn't understand exactly what the man was asking for. But he pulled out one card and handed it over, watching the clerk swipe it.

"Be careful out there," the clerk said, giving him a firm nod. "Dangerous in the city. Especially for someone..." He shrugged.

"Just be careful."

Lotan nodded and walked out of the shop, carrying the bag of food until he found a suitable place to sit and eat. As he walked, he reached into his pocket again to pull out his wallet and stare at it. What kind of man was he that he'd have something like this? He inspected a small ID—one from Mexico —with the name *Levi Lobo* and an address. Was this where he used to live?

He closed his eyes and thought about home, but all that came to him was a vision of a jungle and the word *noxlands*.

Lotan turned a corner, and his stomach came to his throat. Dead bodies lined the street before him, many looking as if they'd been killed moments before. The stench of blood hit his nose, horribly familiar, and he stepped backward, covering his mouth.

Blood, death, Yaotl…

Yaotl.

It was as if a single part of a thousand-piece puzzle fell into place. Yaotl had caused this. He was a nox, like Lotan, a man who wasn't content with being second-in-command to Lotan. He'd roused all the demons into a fury and sent them to attack Geneva.

But not just Geneva—it was everywhere.

Lotan turned on his heel and walked back to the empty street, tossing the bag of food in the trash and leaning against a nearby brick wall to catch his breath. Mexico—Mexico City—it had been the site of his dream. Lotan had gone to face Yaotl one-on-one and had nearly lost his life in the process. But he'd…

What had he done?

The memory stopped abruptly, and Lotan swore under his breath. Just when it seemed everything was coming back, the fog would descend again, and he would find himself grasping at nothing. He straightened, wondering if the dead bodies in the street would jar any more memories loose.

But he blinked. A man had appeared in the street before him. He was not the same as the one who'd choked him in his dream—Yaotl—nor had he been in any other memory that had surfaced so far. But every fiber in his being told him to be on his guard—or, better yet, to run as far away as possible.

"Do you not remember me?" he asked with a smile that sent chills down Lotan's spine.

"I don't remember much these days," Lotan replied. "But somehow I think you already knew that."

The smile widened, and warning bells went off in Lotan's mind, but he remained still. Standing firm against this man was better than running away, he knew that as instinctively as he knew how to brush his teeth.

"Then I suppose you won't have an answer to my question," the man said with a sigh.

"I might. You never know."

"Very well, then." The man sauntered toward Lotan. "How did you do it?"

"Do what?"

The man smiled, but there was little kindness in it. "Revert to human."

Lotan wasn't quite sure how to respond. To tell the truth would be to admit he had no recollection, but would that give this man some kind of insight into his weakness? After a long consideration that didn't seem to faze the man, Lotan cleared his throat.

"You were right. I don't have an answer."

The man snorted. "It's just as well, I suppose. I have no interest in becoming like you. But you've made things somewhat difficult for me." His gaze lifted to the sky, as if something were amusing to him. "It is, perhaps, the way your kind always have been."

Lotan opened his mouth to inquire what this man was referring to, when he noticed a leaf on the sidewalk. It was caught in mid-air, floating as if time itself had slowed down around them. But it wasn't just the leaf, everything in sight was moving a fraction of normal speed, save this strange man.

"I don't understand," Lotan said, his brow furrowed. "What's going on?"

"You really recall nothing, don't you?" the man said, now within striking distance of Lotan. But up close, Lotan noticed there was something almost...ethereal about him. Like he wasn't even there.

Great. Was Lotan seeing ghosts now?

"Why...?" Lotan asked, unsure how to phrase his question.

"Why am I not whole?" the man said, cocking his head to the side. "I could explain it, but you wouldn't understand."

"Try me."

As if proving a point, the man swung his hand leisurely toward Lotan's chest. He flinched, but the hand went right through him, as if the man actually *were* a ghost.

"I'm unable to set foot in this city, thanks to the talismans that have permeated every inch of it," he said. "But rest assured, I have alternate means of doing what I want."

"And what…do you want?"

"For the moment, to see with my own eyes what had become of you," the man said. "I doubt you'll be consequential to my plans. It would be better to rid the world of you, but this is punishment enough, I suppose. Doomed to wither and die slowly over the next five decades."

Lotan opened his mouth, but as soon as he did, the man was gone, and the world had resumed its normal speed. The sound of leaves on the ground sent chills up his spine, a reminder of the absence of sound he hadn't noticed. He shook himself out of his trance and crossed the street to the apartment, hoping that whatever this man had been after, he wouldn't feel the urge to follow Lotan into his apartment.

CHAPTER SIX

Anya's Sight scanned the world, searching for more fires to put out. Berlin wasn't the only city overrun—just the only one that had managed to get out of hand before Anya could intervene. She'd been running nonstop for what felt like hours, arriving in a city as the elokos appeared from wherever Bael was grabbing them and tossing the demons back to the Underworld. Just as soon as she'd cleared one city of demons, another would pop up. Then another.

But once she'd cleared Berlin, the onslaught stopped. She'd expected Bael to show up, to gloat and do what he normally did. Perhaps even hurt Jack or Cam, as they'd been unprotected by the talismans in Berlin. That he hadn't… Anya could only guess what horrors he had in store for her.

"Sooner or later, my lady, you will have to tell them," Diogo said. "They may start blaming you for these massacres."

"Have you had any luck locating him?" Anya asked, instead of answering his question.

"None whatsoever," Diogo said. "I have gone back moments before the attacks began and Bael walks from some place I cannot follow."

She pinched the bridge of her nose. Bael had perhaps tens of thousands of years of knowledge of these powers on her. Was it idiocy to think she could even hold a candle to him?

Yes, came the strong voice in the back of her mind. She had no other choice. This was her mistake to fix.

"Perhaps you could—"

"No," Anya said with a firm shake of her head. "Me going back in time won't solve anything."

Diogo sighed. "I doubt you'll bring a second Bael back with you."

But she was adamant. Diogo had gone back thousands of times over the centuries and never run into Bael. That convinced Anya the only reason Bael was able to come back was because she was a belu. And her stepping back into the time river was just asking for trouble again. Diogo would have to handle it.

"The demons, they're all elokos?" Diogo asked. "And we are sure they aren't topside demons left behind?"

"I don't know for sure," Anya said. "But my hunch says he's gotten Biloko to swear fealty to him again. It's not as if he was eager to join forces with me."

"You could speak with him," Diogo said. "I'm sure he's a reasonable demon."

"Not unless I can offer something more than what Bael is giving him. And…to be honest, I don't think I have anything."

Diogo licked his lips and rested his hands on the kitchen counter. "My lady, I hate to point this out, believe me, I do. But you seem to have taken on a rather…defeatist attitude as of late. These don't seem like the words of a belu athtar."

They weren't, because she wasn't. She was just a cheap imitation of Bael, someone who'd stupidly lucked into his magic and managed to fuck everything up. If she'd been stronger, if she hadn't wanted to see Asherah one more time…

"No one who's ever known you for any amount of time would say that you're weak."

A pang opened in her chest, and she rested her hand on the glass. As much as she wanted to believe Jack would stand by her, would help her solve the problem, there was still that small risk he'd fly off the handle. That he would think she'd done this intentionally because she valued her power over her love for him. It would only be safe to tell him once Bael was gone.

Unfortunately, *she* was the only one who could make that happen. There was no time for moping or misery or feeling sorry for herself.

She straightened and turned back to Diogo, who seemed ready for anything. "I'm going to pay Biloko a visit to see what information I can glean from him. That may help us figure out where the demons are coming from."

"Good idea," Diogo said. "What would you have me do, my lady?"

"Keep an eye on things and let me know if any more cities catch fire," Anya said.

Anya wasn't looking forward to this conversation, but it was long overdue. The demons hadn't gotten their well-deserved earful from her after unleashing their monsters on the world, and now Biloko had struck again. If he got away with it, the others might follow suit.

She arrived in Elonsi, but something was wrong. The rolling savannah was gone, replaced by a never-ending desert of sand as far as the eye could see. There was nothing else—no hut, no elokos roving about. No other sign of life.

There should've been thousands of elokos here—at the very least, the hundreds she'd just kicked through the portal back here. She couldn't have messed that up; her portals were foolproof. But as she used her Sight to scan the lands, she found no one, save herself.

Her Sight expanded to scan the other worlds. In Liley, Freyja was still in her castle. Tabiko was rocking the baby in the castle in Kappanchi. The noxlands were still filled with mist and nothingness after Lotan had given up his powers. The Nullius remained shrouded in mystery for her. No other lands had been created in this world.

So where the fuck were all the elokos?

She couldn't even find Biloko, she realized with a jolt. There was nowhere else Biloko could have gone; he didn't like leaving his lands. And as she gazed at the desert, so different from the savannah that she'd grown accustomed to, realization dawned.

Bael had killed Biloko.

And since this world was reformed, unlike the noxlands, that meant he'd taken that magic and given it to someone else. Created a new belu eloko like he'd done thousands of years ago.

She had to press her hand to her chest as her stomach swooped out from beneath her. He must've extracted a loyalty pledge from whomever took the magic, and now they were doing his bidding.

After all, they knew, firsthand, that Bael could very easily find another to take the magic.

She turned to look at the world once more, the whereabouts of the elokos, this new belu, and Bael still a mystery—and that unnerved her most of all.

Anya returned to Ath-kur, taking a moment to scan her own lands for Bael—and just to be safe, traveling to different spots to ensure he wasn't hiding in plain sight. But even after checking every nook and cranny, he was nowhere to be found.

That meant he was in the human world somewhere. So why couldn't she find him?

"My lady." Diogo arrived by her side. "There has been another attack."

"Where?" Anya asked, already tired just thinking about it.

"Johannesburg. Shall I accompany you?"

"No," Anya said, her gaze darkening. "I don't know what kind of game Bael is playing, but I'm done playing it."

"I take it your discussion with Biloko wasn't very fruitful."

"Biloko's dead," Anya said, turning to face him. "You may want to pay a visit to the other belus and give them a heads-up that Bael could be coming for them."

The fighting in Johannesburg was well underway when Anya arrived—though it wasn't fighting as much as a slaughter. Bael had slowed time and unleashed the elokos on the unsuspecting humans. It was a massacre in slow motion. A woman was in mid-fall to the ground, her cell phone slowly flying from her hand as the life drained from her body where the eloko spear had run her through. In her mind, it was happening in seconds. She never would've known what happened.

Although Bael was nowhere to be found, this was his doing. This…this was a new level even for him.

Anya stood in the center of the chaos and closed her eyes, searching for the river of time that had slowed to a snail's pace. There was something already holding it, something she'd never encountered before. It looked like her magic, only it wasn't hers. She envisioned herself pushing up against it, forcing it off the river, but it wouldn't budge.

She closed her eyes and dug deeply, searching for that power she'd felt in Geneva—the one that had allowed her not to slow time, but to stop it completely. It was there, buried deep and just out of reach. She gritted her teeth and dove in deeper, reaching for it.

But it remained firmly out of her grasp.

"Ah, my love. I was wondering when you would show your

beautiful face."

Anya spun around, her fury mingling with her frustration. "This is too much, Bael. Stop your army."

"On the contrary," he said, looking out onto his handiwork with pride. "It's just enough."

Anya gritted her teeth and turned to the chaos once more, her focus back on speeding up time. At least if the humans could fight, they might be able to stop some of this. But Bael's hold on the magic was immovable.

"Bael," she said, her voice dropping. "Please. This isn't necessary."

"Oh, my love," he said, sliding his hands onto her shoulders and sending chills down her spine. "Since you asked so nicely."

Anya felt time move forward again, and immediately wished it hadn't. What had been a mostly silent killing was now punctuated by screams of fear, moans of agony as injured humans became aware of their pain, and the cheerful cries of elokos as they continued their bloodthirsty attack.

"Bael," Anya said, throwing his hands off of her. "*Enough.*"

With his grip on the time river loose, she was able to take it for herself, but could only slow time, not stop it. It was hard to concentrate with Bael watching her, and the well of power she was seeking had vanished completely.

"My, my," he said, approvingly. "You are quite powerful."

She felt him nudge at her grip, seeking a way to unclench her control over the time river. But just as she'd been unable to move him, he was unable to move her.

"Hm." Bael's amusement seemed a little less now, and she took that as victory. "Interesting."

"Why did you kill Biloko?" Anya asked

"Why?" Bael shrugged. "Why does anyone do anything?"

She balled her fists. His games were tiresome once; now they were infuriating. She hated that she still had to play them. Hated that he still made her feel powerless when she most assuredly was not. As she fumed, she felt his magic probe hers, seeking control of the river of time, and she tightened her grip—searching for that deep magic that had allowed her to stop time. Perhaps if she could overpower talismans, she could overpower Bael.

But the magic was nowhere to be found, lost in her own panic.

"Answer the question," she said, her frustration growing with each passing second. "Why did you kill Biloko?"

"Because it was what needed to happen," Bael said. "And now I have a belu eloko who will do as she's told."

"What you can't get by brute force, you'll get by bribery, hm?" Anya snorted. "You'll never change, will you?"

"Such an astute observation," Bael said, taking a step closer to her. "Did your human teach you that? What's his name? Jackson?"

It took everything in her to not lose focus, but she wouldn't. Not when every soul in the vicinity was at stake.

"I figured out who you are the day I realized you killed our daughter," Anya said. "The day I took Sharur to your neck and ended your reign of terror on this world."

Bael smiled, his probing increasing. But her control was rock solid, fueled by the surge of anger at his attempts to trick her. She would never fall for it again.

"You never answered my question," she said. "Why did you kill Biloko?"

He smiled. "I told you, my sweet Anat, that I have great plans for this world. And that starts with reminding the humans that they can cower behind their talismans all they want, but there are still areas of this world where they're vulnerable. And they can't hide from me forever."

"Then I will be there on every battlefield to make sure you fail."

He laughed, and the attempts to pry control from her ceased, but her grip didn't lessen. "You are something else, now, my love. I have to say, I'm a little excited to see where this goes between us. Are we destined to continue fighting each other forever? Or will one of us break, swear fealty to the other, and we can resume our torrid love affair?"

"It was never love," Anya said. "You needed someone to lord over, and you picked the first idiot you could get your hands on." She cracked a humorless grin. "So you can go ahead and break, because I've grown tired of your bullshit."

"So you say," Bael said, bowing slightly. "Until our next encounter."

And then he, and the elokos, were gone.

CHAPTER SEVEN

"Johannesburg?" Jack said, his voice groggy as he blinked into the darkness.

He'd been woken by his phone ringing, just as he'd laid his head down on the hard bench in Berlin. The voice on the other end was María's, he realized thirty seconds into the call, and she was telling him about an attack. Clearly, on the other side of the world.

"What do you want me to do about it?" he said, rubbing the sleep from his eyes.

"Get some coffee and take a team down there."

"Where the hell am I going to get a team?" Jack said.

"Fine, come to Geneva first and we'll have one ready for you."

Jack blinked at his phone as the line went dead and his mind sped up. Why María was bothering him and not the South

African ICDM was too much for him to process. He pushed himself to stand, cracking his neck and slipping his phone into his pocket as he ventured into the aftermath of the Berlin attack.

The German army had swooped in once Jack gave them the all-clear and set up hospital tents to tend to the wounded and dead. They'd been efficient about it, though Cam had hung around to help equip them with anti-eloko talismans in case they happened upon any straggling demons still inside the city, while Jack had found a spot to take a catnap.

Jack found Cam standing with a coffee in her hand, speaking with a German officer in hushed tones. She waved the officer off and jogged over to see him.

"Did you catch any sleep?" she asked.

"No, because María called," Jack replied, rubbing his neck, which was still sore. "There's been another attack in Johannesburg."

"Fuck me," Cam said with a sigh. "What the hell is going on?"

"I don't know. But Anya had better get her ass in gear if she's going to be the savior of the world," Jack said, swiping the coffee out of Cam's hand and taking a long sip.

"Did she seem…" Cam said, chewing her lip.

"Off to you?" Jack nodded. "But maybe she's just being weird after our fight."

"What do you think she's after by telling us to stay in Geneva?" Cam asked, taking her coffee back and shaking it. "Did you drink all of it?"

"Sorry," Jack said, but he didn't mean it. "María wants us to get back to Geneva, so we'd better get a move on back to the portal."

"I don't like using that thing," Cam said.

"You'd rather drive five hundred miles? This is more efficient."

"I just think it's weird," Cam said, but followed him anyway. "Anya's acting funny and we're using her magic. What's to say she won't just pull the plug on this portal?"

"She wouldn't," Jack said, and he was sure of it. Whatever was going on with Anya right now, she hadn't completely lost her way.

He hoped.

There was an ICDM SUV waiting for them when Jack and Cam stepped through the portal to Geneva, and Jack caught another catnap on the way into the city. Cam seemed too wired, unable to stop fidgeting or checking her phone when Jack woke up.

"What's wrong?"

"Just… I don't know. Something's wrong."

"Yeah, demons are attacking cities."

"But why?" Cam said. "And where are they coming from?"

Jack rubbed his eyes as the car came to a stop. "Maybe they were just hiding out. Maybe they had orders to attack after the initial onslaught. Or maybe they want revenge. Either way, we'll figure it out and put a stop to it."

But Cam didn't seem eased by his explanation. "Or someone out there is agitating them. I don't think it's coincidence that they're all elokos."

"Biloko is stuck in the Underworld."

"Unless someone decided otherwise."

Jack looked at her. "Are you saying Anya's responsible for this? She stopped the chaos in Berlin."

"Conveniently." Cam exhaled loudly. "I'm not blaming her. I'm just saying something is fishy and her behavior isn't helping."

Jack kept quiet, not wanting to argue with her, but also not wholly disagreeing. The pair walked in silence to the main tent where María and a couple of other ICDM agents were standing around.

"Cam, Jack, this is Agent Scavo from Rome," she said. "She's been tasked with monitoring these attacks around the world. We just caught wind of one in Johannesburg."

"Elokos?" Cam asked.

María and Agent Scavo wore the same grimace. "We aren't...exactly sure," Scavo said. "By all accounts, the massacre happened in the blink of an eye."

Jack heard what they said but he was having a hard time processing it. "So you're saying nobody saw it?"

"We're saying that one minute, the people were standing around, eating at cafes and walking down the street, and the next moment, everyone within a city block was dead." María cleared her throat. "Save one woman. We were able to get a statement from her."

"Did she offer anything else?" Jack said.

"Yes," Scavo said. "She said that there was a woman in the middle of the street for a brief moment. Middle Eastern, green eyes, long, curly black hair. But before she could do or say anything to her, the mystery woman disappeared."

Jack exhaled, looking at Cam, and knew his partner had already made up her mind. "There has to be a reasonable explanation for this."

"I think there is," María said. "The athtar Anat has declared war on humanity."

"After she just saved everyone last week?" Jack said. "That seems far-fetched."

"It's the theory we're working with," Scavo said. "Unless you want to venture to Johannesburg and find us a different one."

Looking at the faces staring back at him, Jack realized that if he didn't go, no one would, so he just sighed. "Fine."

Jack walked out of the tent, intent on finding a ride to the drop site again and heading to Johannesburg. He didn't really have any other theories, other than the strong one in his gut that Anya wasn't behind this. It just *made no sense*—especially after seeing her in Berlin. She hadn't looked any different, had been trying to help. If anything, she looked overwhelmed. Something —or someone—else was the source of this.

"Jack."

Cam had followed him, her gaze tired.

"What?" Jack said. "Are you coming to help?"

"What would be the point?" Cam asked, throwing her hands in the air. "There's only *one* demon in this world who can stop time. And clearly, the woman saw Anya. Can't miss those green eyes."

"There are two athtars, actually. Diogo can stop time as well." Though, even as Jack offered it as an alternative, he didn't believe it. Diogo hadn't shown much interest in anything other than his studies. "And maybe Anya was there to stop things but got there too late."

Cam sighed. "C'mon, Jack. I know you guys are in a weird place right now, but you can't deny that the facts are the facts. Even if it was Diogo… Anya has the power to stop him. She's his belu, remember?"

"The witness might've seen wrong." Jack turned to keep walking. "I have to exhaust every possibility before I give up on her. I owe her that much. Maybe someone else was doing it, and she just showed up to stop it."

"Then how did those humans just die?" Cam followed behind him, her voice rising an octave. "Just stabbed out of nowhere."

"Anya wouldn't—"

"Anya was a bloodthirsty monster for thousands of years," Cam said. "She's legend, in case you forgot while you were falling for her."

Jack glared at her. "I remember. But that wasn't her. Bael made her do it."

"Well, I don't see Bael around anymore, do you?" Cam sighed and put her hands on her hips, shaking her head slowly. "Though, this does seem like..."

"Like what?"

"Something he would do," Cam said. "Cause a ruckus, kill a bunch of humans, show up as the savior every time. Solve a problem he created like some big hero. Maybe Anya's taken a page out of his playbook."

Jack licked his lips. "So what, you're saying Anya is purposefully killing humans in one city while saving them in another just so we won't suspect her?"

"I mean..."

"In the first place, if she wanted to kill, she'd just kill," Jack said. "She doesn't need to manipulate us."

"She needs to manipulate you, Jack," Cam said. "She loves you, and she wouldn't be able to stand it if you hated her."

"Which is why I don't believe she's behind this."

"Jack, we may..." Cam paused, considering her words. "We may have to consider that perhaps it isn't her, but that magic she absorbed. Maybe it's made her go a little nuts. She was starting to act funny with the belus, and when she threatened Freyja in Paris... She looked real Bael-like."

"She was just showing off so Freyja would take her seriously," Jack said, waving his hand. "She and I talked about it. I told her how far to go."

"And now you aren't with her," Cam said. "So maybe now she's just doing whatever the hell she wants."

Jack swallowed. No matter how much some part of him agreed with Cam, there was a stronger part that couldn't accept it. Anya, who had so carefully washed his wounds, who'd held him as he mourned his grandfather, who had been so hesitant to open her heart to him, couldn't have done a one-eighty in such a short time.

"I'm going to South Africa," Jack said. "You can come or not. I don't care."

"Let me find us a ride," Cam said, after a moment. To his surprised expression, she shrugged. "I don't want to be right. She's my friend, too."

⁂

When Jack and Cam finally stepped through to Johannesburg, Jack was ready to find something that would prove him right. But the scene before them was another damning piece of evidence against the woman he loved.

It was as their one witness had described. Victims were strewn about in the square, some of them slumped in chairs and others on the ground. There were no signs of struggle, no sign that anyone had any clue that death was coming.

Cam flashed her newly reinstated ICDM badge to the policeman who'd come up to question where they'd come from, and she left to discuss the situation. Jack stuffed his hands in his pockets and walked around the scene, avoiding the photographers and investigators doing their work.

"What's the cause of death?" he asked, peering over one investigator who was examining a ghastly wound on one of the cafe patrons.

"Blade of some kind," he said, looking at Jack. "It's odd. I've never seen markings like this before. It's almost like the body was killed and placed in this position. Normally, they don't sit like this."

Jack nodded and moved on, continuing his perimeter, desperate for something that might calm the uneasiness in his stomach. But there was no mistaking it; the only way this massacre could've occurred was if someone had the ability to stop time. And the only two people who could've done that were Diogo and, more realistically, Anya.

He left the square, not venturing far, just out of the gore and stench of blood so he could collect his thoughts. Three streets over, he found a spot to sit and reflect, warring with himself as he still couldn't bring himself to admit that Anya had somehow gone off the deep end.

And yet.

"That's not what I want, Anya."

"But what about what I want? Doesn't that matter?"

She'd looked at him as if he'd struck her. He wished he'd been more careful with his words. That wasn't a discussion they should've been having when emotions were high. And now she seemed unwilling to spend more than a few moments in his presence.

Was he the reason for all this? Did Anya feel she had nothing left? She'd been that low once before, thanks to Jack's clumsy anger, and he'd promised himself he would never speak to her that way again.

"Here you are," Cam said, coming to join him. "Have you had enough?"

He nodded. "Maybe Anya is behind this."

"I don't have any evidence to the contrary," she said, and she sounded somewhat sad to admit it. "I just wish I knew why."

"Do you think it's my fault?" Jack asked. "Our last fight seemed a little…"

"She had no right to ask you to become a demon," Cam said with a firm shake of her head. "That's not who you are."

"Should I have at least considered it?" Jack asked.

"No." Cam turned to him. "The *only* reason I became athtar was to save you. I'd always thought it was temporary, because I'd had faith Anya would kill Bael and turn me human again. Being a demon isn't…"

"But if it's what she wants…"

"Anya doesn't need to be a demon. The world doesn't need her protecting it, and it would be better off if she got rid of the athtar magic," Cam said. "You said that yourself. She took this power to save us, the same way I took the magic to save you. Therefore…"

Jack nodded, slowly. "Maybe I should try to talk with her anyway. Maybe we can come to a better understanding."

But when Jack tried to open the portal to Ath-kur, the portal just fizzled and lay there. Jack tried again, more forceful with his commands, but it didn't budge. Anya had closed the bridge.

"Geneva," Cam said softly, pressing her hand on Jack's

shoulder. The portal flickered to life, revealing their drop site. "C'mon. Let's get back home and rest. We'll be able to think clearer in the morning."

CHAPTER EIGHT

Cam's concern for Jack grew as they sat in the backseat of the SUV, headed back to ICDM temporary headquarters. He didn't say much, staring out the window with that deep sort of reflection that put him out of reach. She hadn't seen him so low since Sara's death. This, though—this seemed a different kind of pain. That he'd asked if he *should've* become a demon… Perhaps Anya's manipulation was working better than Cam had thought.

When they arrived at headquarters, Cam held up her hand to prevent Jack from getting out. "You go back to the apartment. Have a beer and relax. I'll debrief María."

Jack nodded thankfully and sat back while Cam gave directions to the driver. When they were out of sight, she turned to walk through the square. Her mind was still running on adrenaline, but her body was starting to tire. It had been a very, *very* long day.

She pulled the flap back to find María where she now seemed permanently planted, in front of the row of television screens, speaking with various ICDM agents. Agent Scavo was gone, replaced by another agent who was at least a foot and a half taller than María.

"Cam, you're back," she said. "This is Agent Puszcz from Poland. He's gathering more agents from around the world to form a strike team. I was hoping you'd give him instructions on how to use the portal."

"As long as we can use it," Cam said with a shrug. "There's no telling if or when Anya will decide she no longer wants us to have that power." She looked at the agent and nodded. "Just tell the portal where you want it to go. If you have any problems, call me."

The agent nodded and left, and Cam yawned. "I haven't slept in almost two days. Can we speed this up?"

"Watch your tone, Camilla," María said. "I'm still a Councilwoman."

"And I'm not technically receiving a paycheck, so what do we want to do here?" Cam said, raising a brow. "Look, bottom line is that the current evidence supports your theory. I found nothing to say any other demon could've done something like that. Anya, and by extension, Diogo, are our prime suspects."

"Who is Diogo?" María asked. "I have heard his name before."

Cam explained in brief the not-really-spawn of Anya, and María nodded slowly. "So you're telling me that once a belu dies, there's a chance demons could retain their powers?"

"We're still not a hundred percent on that theory," Cam said. "Or why Bael chose Diogo to retain his. Maybe he just forgot about him. Maybe it's because Bael and Anya had a baby once, the thread was broken, like with Lotan's parents, and Diogo was able to hang on because of that. I don't know." Her head was starting to ache; she didn't want to discuss demonic spawning theory. "The point is, the only people who could have stopped time and killed those people were athtars, which puts our suspect list at two."

María nodded slowly. "We should have a large group arriving soon, then we can be better prepared to move." She cleared her throat. "I would like you to bring Lotan here. We need to know all we can from him."

"Good luck there," Cam said with a snort. "His memory isn't the best. He barely remembers who I am."

"Then we'll have to help prod him along," María said. "He's the only one who might be able to give us insight into the demonic world."

Cam narrowed her gaze, sensing something was afoot. "If this is a trap—"

"No trap, I promise."

"Promise on your sister's life," Cam said, her gaze deadly serious.

"I promise, on Juana's life," María said. "I'm only trying to understand the situation. Besides, if he is, as you say, a human, he poses no threat to us."

Cam nodded. "Is that all?"

"No, there is…one more assignment I'm giving you," María said. "I have summoned your team from Shanghai."

Something twitched in the back of Cam's mind. "For what purpose?"

"I don't think I have to tell you that it's become more imperative than ever that we continue our work on the talismans. We need to understand why Anya was able to overpower them when she stopped the massacre, and also…" She pursed her lips, as if she knew her next words would be taken poorly. "We need to consider the possibility that she is the enemy now."

Perhaps it was because the same thought had been sitting in the back of her mind since walking through that town square, or perhaps it was because she had nothing left, but Cam just nodded.

"Understood. Now I'm going to bed."

Cam didn't remember arriving back at Frank's apartment, or what she said to Lotan as she breezed past him to the bedroom. She didn't even remember falling asleep, and if she had any dreams, she didn't remember them. But she remembered María's new assignment—the words ringing in her ears when she opened her groggy eyes.

She fumbled for her phone to check the time—four in the afternoon. She'd slept for eighteen hours. She felt like a slime ball, and her breath was atrocious, so she padded into the bathroom to rinse off. There, she found her soaps already laid out on the mantel and a fresh towel and washcloth waiting. Whether that was Lotan or Jack, she didn't know. But she was grateful she had such thoughtful men in her life.

The shower was long, but she didn't feel quite clean. Not when she had this new information swinging around her mind. She couldn't tell Jack what she was doing. She didn't feel right about it herself; he would fly off the handle.

On the bed, someone had placed a fresh set of clothes, and Cam pulled them on, toweling her hair furiously before padding out into the kitchen. Her stomach rumbled, reminding her that she hadn't eaten in almost a whole day either.

Happily, there was an assortment of food on the counter—sandwiches and cans of soda. Cam didn't hesitate, stuffing half of one inside her mouth and cracking open a can.

"Courtesy of the food tent at ICDM," Jack said from the couch. "I stopped in to check on things and grabbed you what I could."

"Fank you," Cam said, her mouth full. She swallowed a large gulp and asked, "Any more attacks?"

"All is quiet at the moment," Jack said. "Which is somewhat odd in and of itself. It seems strange that they'd just stop after two cities."

They. "Who's they?"

"Whoever's behind this," Jack said.

Cam took another monstrous bite instead of arguing with him. Definitely shouldn't tell him about her new assignment.

While she chewed, she decided to change the subject.

"Where's Lotan?"

"He insisted on going to the store," Jack said. "More of his memory has returned, but it's still spotty. He says he remembered how to cook, so he's going to make us something."

Cam grimaced. "Great."

"María spoke with me today," Jack said, and Cam's blood went cold.

"She asked me to relocate to the outskirts of town so we'll be better able to react," Jack said. "I declined. It's better if I stay here. Thirty minutes won't do much."

Cam's stomach was already full, so she put the half-eaten sandwich down. "Did she say anything else?"

"She wanted me to bring Lotan to debrief her, but I told her I'd wait for you," Jack said. "I don't know if there's much he's going to be able to share."

"We'll check the box María wants us to," Cam said, sitting down on the couch with her soda.

"Yeah."

She waited for Jack to mention the new assignment, but perhaps María recognized that telling him about it was a bad idea. It would have been easier if she'd had the gumption to just spill the beans; they could've had the argument and gotten it out of the way. Instead, she was going to keep this to herself like a chicken.

Luckily, the door handle jiggled and Lotan walked in, carrying several paper bags of groceries. Cam's heart lightened when she saw him, and his eyes sparkled when he caught sight of her. Despite his memory loss, they still had that.

"Oh, excellent. I hope you're hungry. I have great plans for dinner."

Cam smiled. "I just had three sandwiches, but I'm sure I'll be hungry again soon. What…exactly are you hoping to make?"

"And have we checked the smoke alarms?" Jack added with a smirk.

"I don't recall why that's funny, but I do believe I can follow a recipe," Lotan said. "There was a cookbook on the bookshelf, and I found a recipe you might like. It was under comfort foods."

Jack peered into the open book on the counter and snorted. "'Some Like it Southern,' from my mother, of course. Frank probably never cooked a meal in his life."

"Maybe she just wanted him to look at photos of home," Cam said with a smile. "Are you sure that you don't want help, Lotan?"

"You two have done plenty," Lotan said. "Just sit and relax. And perhaps pour yourself a glass of wine."

Jack pulled a bottle from one of the bags and nodded appreciatively. "You heard the man."

Despite her reservations, Cam quickly relaxed as the scent of butter and aromatics filled the apartment, sipping on the excellent wine that Lotan had picked out. Jack seemed at the ready to step in if anything started burning, but Lotan had forgotten how to be a bad cook. When he handed them a plate of fish, potatoes, and green beans, the three sandwiches Cam had inhaled had long since been digested, so she sighed happily.

"Oh, Lotan," she said, her mouth full. "This is exquisite."

"So…was I some kind of bad cook before?" Lotan asked, topping off everyone's wine.

"You certainly have improved," Cam said. "But you also didn't used to have a cookbook. That probably helped." She twisted the stem of the wine glass. "Has any more of your memory returned?"

"Some," Lotan said, his gaze falling somewhat. "I remember Yaotl, and the things he said to me. I recall the events here in Geneva."

"Do you remember going to the noxlands?" Jack asked.

Lotan shook his head. "Things come in bits and pieces. But what I do remember is quite clear."

"Do you remember what you did to Yaotl?" Cam asked. María would surely be interested in that.

Lotan narrowed his eyes. "I remember… I remember feeling like he would no longer be a threat. That he would be powerless. But exactly what happened is still a mystery." His face lightened somewhat. "I do remember the day we met."

Cam couldn't help but smile. "Do tell."

"I remember you and Anya had barged into our lair, La Madriguera," Lotan said with a smile. "And I can't remember the specifics of why that was impressive, especially for you, but I remember watching you stand straight, fearlessly, demanding to be let past to save your friend." He looked at Jack. "This friend, in fact."

"Cam is very impressive," Jack said, hiding a bit of a smirk as he gathered the empty plates. "I'll do the dishes."

Cam realized too late that it would leave herself and Lotan alone at the small table, and Jack mostly out of earshot with the running water. She hadn't had a real conversation with Lotan since he'd lost his memory, and the small flickers of joy in her heart when she saw him were no match for the discomfort of the current moment.

"So," Lotan said, pouring the rest of the wine into her glass.

"So." Cam swiped the glass off the table.

"You look as if I'm about to eat you," Lotan said with a little laugh.

Cam fought the urge to grimace. She would've liked for him to do just that.

"We just haven't had a chance to talk yet," he continued, oblivious. "I figure I should take the opportunity while I have you stationary."

"Talk about what?"

A flash of hurt crossed his face. "Just talk. I don't remember much, but my gut tells me that you and I were very much in love before I lost my memory. I would hope that you still...feel the same way. With all the pieces coming back, it shouldn't be long before I'm back to normal. I hope."

That didn't sound very comforting, but she forced a smile onto her face. "Can I help?"

"I'm not sure how it happens, exactly," Lotan said. "A scene, a moment, the wind blowing the right way. The information is buried somewhere in my mind, I'm sure." His face softened. "Or perhaps, as you say, it's better if I don't remember. I must've been an abysmal chef."

"You were…eager," Cam said, clearing her throat. "You told me once it was because your father used to cook for your mother. It was how he showed love."

"I…" Lotan nodded slowly. "I remember that. There were hundreds of people around who would've done it, but she only wanted his food." His gaze met hers triumphantly. "You see? Coming back slowly."

"You have a few hundred years to remember," she said, rising. "I think all this food and wine has made me sleepy again. I'm going to head back to bed while I can."

"Cam."

She stopped.

"You never answered my question," Lotan said, looking at her. "Do you still feel the same way as before I lost my memory?"

Jack took that moment to shut off the water, and there was nothing but silence in the apartment again. Cam's pulse throbbed in her ears, and she scrambled for a truth that wouldn't hurt him. Mainly because she didn't know herself what to think.

"My feelings for you haven't changed because you lost your memory," she said softly, walking around the table to kiss him on the forehead. "But you should focus on getting it back, then we can talk about…everything else."

CHAPTER NINE

Lotan couldn't help but feel the distance between himself and Cam. What, exactly, he'd done was a complete mystery to him. She'd seemed sincere in her last words to him, at least. But something was holding her back. He stared at the ceiling, watching the shadows dance from the streetlight out front, and pondered until he fell asleep.

In the morning, Jack had taken care of finding breakfast and coffee. Lotan was growing rather fond of the other man, the best friend of the woman he loved.

"Were we friendly before?" Lotan asked.

"I'd say so," Jack said. "You got my seal of approval for dating my best friend."

"Oh, good." Lotan glanced at the bathroom, where Cam was in the shower. "Can I talk to you about something?"

"Shoot."

"I fear that Cam has fallen out of love with me," Lotan said. "I can feel it. She's pulled away."

"That's not it at all," Jack said with a shake of his head. "Look, you probably don't remember all of Cam's…unique personality traits. One of them is her fear of commitment."

"But she's so fearless."

Jack chuckled. "Look, here's the long and short of it: For the longest time, Cam was sure she'd never find anyone. And then she found you, and you are…" Jack gestured to Lotan's face and chest. "You are that. And it scared the absolute piss out of her because it meant she would have to examine her own feelings and take a leap of faith that maybe, just maybe, she's worthy of someone like you."

Lotan failed to see how someone like Cam could question her own worth that way. "But we'd clearly told each other how we felt—"

"Yes, but you were a *demon* when you did that," Jack said. "And in Cam's mind, you could never become human, ergo, there was always going to be something keeping you two apart. Now, of course, your memory is gone, which does throw a little wrench in things." He shrugged. "To be honest, I'm not sure Cam would be acting any different if you were your old self. But you'd just… I don't know, throw her over your shoulder and remind her why she's acting like an idiot."

Lotan didn't know if that was something he was able to do, not when she wouldn't spend more than five minutes in his presence. "I see."

"I didn't say it was logical, I just gave an explanation for it," Jack said. "But enough about that. We should probably talk about meeting with María today."

"Are you sure this is wise? I'm not sure I can offer much to ICDM—and I'm afraid I might say the wrong thing."

"Cam and I will be there," Jack said. "And you can't say the wrong thing if you don't remember anything. But you should have some background on who we're speaking with."

Jack explained María was Cam's great aunt, and one of the most powerful humans in the ICDM leadership. She'd taken over as the de facto leader on the ground as the one least injured, but there were others, too, who would be at this meeting.

"You might meet more than one Councilor today," Jack said. "And they will probably want to know more about how you gave up your powers."

"They'll be sorely disappointed," Lotan said. "I remember nothing."

"Cam and I will help fill in the blanks, from what we know," Jack said. "Don't worry. We'll be there to make sure everything goes smoothly."

"And then what?" Lotan asked, looking up. "I confess that sitting here in the apartment doesn't feel very helpful. If the world is truly as chaotic as you say, there must be something I can do."

Jack sat back. "That's going to be up to Cam. I don't know if you're ready to jump into a fight like we've been doing. The only time I've seen you fight has been as a giant dog."

"Dog?" Lotan furrowed his brow. The sensation of growing into something more than himself. The wind in his hair. Feeling Cam rest on his shoulders. Making crude jokes about her positioning. "Ah yes. I used to become a large dog, didn't I?"

"Yikes." Cam stood in the doorway, toweling off her hair. "Maybe Jack's right. You should stick close to the apartment after today."

Lotan just sighed. "Very well."

They took the same path Lotan had wandered the day before, when he'd come across the street of dead people. Perhaps he'd subconsciously known where to go. But he wasn't dwelling on it. Today, the bodies had been removed. Another sign that this city was slowly picking up the pieces after the attack.

When they arrived at the headquarters, Cam flashed her badge and Jack said good morning to the guards while Lotan just smiled and waited to be let through. The building beyond them was already under construction, with cranes and workers gathering behind the chain-link fence to clear the damaged material and search for survivors.

"Have they found any?" Lotan asked Jack, who shook his head.

"I doubt they will now."

They continued walking along the square until they reached a large tent with more guards out front. Inside, the ICDM leadership had set up various stations. A wall to monitor news reports from around the world, a table in the back to conduct business, and perhaps eat, and several whiteboards that had multiple theories listed. The word "Anat" was written several times.

"Is this him?" A somewhat familiar, older woman approached, wearing an ICDM jacket and dark pants. Lotan recognized Cam in some of her features, so this must be her great aunt.

"Pleasure to meet you," Lotan said.

"I'm sorry it had to come after you lost your memory," María replied. "Or has it come back?"

"Bits and pieces." Lotan looked at Cam with a frown. "So we never met before? I find it hard to believe that I wouldn't have met your family."

Cam cleared her throat and Lotan thought she began to blush. "Do we have a place to talk? Or are we going to be out in the open?"

María beckoned them to follow out the back of the tent into another set up nearby. This one had another set of guards, who seemed less enthused about letting them pass. Lotan offered them a cheery smile and earned nothing in return.

Inside, there were two or three people already seated, as well as a small laptop computer showing several others.

"D-dad?" Jack said, squinting at the small screen.

"Hey, Jackie. Sitting in for Shriver today while he's recovering from surgery."

"Jack's father George works for ICDM," Cam whispered to Lotan. "They live in Charleston—that's in the US."

"Where you're from," Lotan said. "I remember that about you."

She smiled, and for a moment, the wedge between them was gone. But when she turned, Cam was back to business.

"Shall we begin?" Cam said, taking a seat at the table. She motioned for Lotan to take the seat next to her, and he awkwardly pulled the folding chair out and sat down.

"Yes, I believe we're all here," María replied. "For those who can't see, Lotan, prince of the noxes, is here with Agents Macarro and Grenard."

"That's not my title anymore," Lotan replied a little bashfully. "At least, I don't think so."

Cam nudged him under the table. "As far as we know, when Lotan lost his powers, he took the powers of every nox in existence with him."

A disembodied voice spoke from the computer at the other end of the table. "And those who were responsible for the havoc in our cities?"

"I don't..." Lotan said, before something tickled in the back of his mind. "They're dead. All of them. I don't know the specifics. But I do know they're...they're dead now."

"And how can we trust that?" asked a female voice from the computer. "The word of a demon doesn't seem to be worth much."

"His is worth plenty," Cam said. "And we haven't found another nox around, have we?"

"They could all be in the Underworld," María said.

"The noxlands are gone," Jack said. "Completely obliterated when Lotan's magic was released from his body. That's what happens when a belu dies."

"Then the magic returns to the center of the Nullius," Lotan said, almost as if speaking from a dream. There was a large energetic field, it was the source of all demonic energy. Why or how he knew about that, he had no idea. "Where it will sit until another human finds it."

Cam looked at him, concern evident on her face. "You remember?"

"Sorry, that's all," Lotan said with an apologetic smile. "As I said, bits and pieces."

"What is the Nullius?" Jack's father jumped in now.

"It's the center of the demonic underworld," Cam said. "I ventured there twice—once as an ath..." She cleared her throat. "Once when I was with Anat, and again with Jack."

"Oh, that's right, you had become a demon then, hadn't you?" Lotan said. "Yes, I remember. You had taken Anat's power. She called you a polluelo."

Cam went stick straight and Jack cleared his throat nervously as silence descended around the room. Lotan became immediately aware he'd said the wrong thing.

"I don't think you remember that correctly," Jack said slowly.

"Perhaps not," Lotan said, grateful for the chance to backtrack. "But I do remember the athtars. They can stop time, right?"

Jack nodded. "Yes, they—"

"One was here in Geneva the other day."

This earned another round of stunned silence, but for once, Lotan didn't think he'd said the wrong thing. María leaned in across the table. "As in…after the massacre?"

"Yes," Lotan said. "I only knew he was athtar because the leaves had slowed."

"What did he say?" Cam asked.

"He merely wanted to know how I gave up my powers, asked me what I remembered," Lotan said. "He said I wouldn't be consequential to his plans, but…" Lotan trailed off as Cam's wide eyes landed on him. She looked unnerved.

"Lotan, why didn't you say anything?" Cam said. "Diogo's not supposed to be able to come to Geneva."

"Are we sure it was Diogo?" Jack asked.

"Who the hell else could it have been?" Cam said. "I don't think Anya's going around giving athtar powers to random people with world domination plans."

"Clearly, she's willing to spawn, since she made you a demon," María said. "A fact you hid from this council upon your initial debriefing."

"It wasn't germane," Cam said, a little too quickly.

"This explains how you thought it was a good idea to enter into a relationship with a demonic prince."

"I don't see how our relationship is a problem?" Lotan said, looking around the room. He wisely decided to shut up when Jack shook his head.

"We're getting off track here," Cam said. "Diogo showed up in Geneva, and that's not supposed to be possible. He wanted information from Lotan, and thank goodness he didn't get it."

"I still don't think it was Diogo," Jack said. "He's a bookworm. He sits in his little monastery in Lisbon, makes tea, and reads books all day long. He's not an evil man."

"Cam is right, we are getting off track," Jack's father said from the laptop. "We know athtars aren't susceptible to the talismans in certain cases, we just don't know what those cases are. And we should be focusing this meeting on what the nox knows and what he can do to help us."

"Gladly," Lotan said, leaning onto his elbows. "Please ask away."

"The Nullius," asked the female voice on the computer. "You said it was the center of the Underworld and the source of all demonic power?"

"Yes," Lotan said. "It's impossible for demons to venture onto that land unless..." He furrowed his brow. "I don't recall how Anya and I did it. But we did."

"You traveled through the time river," Jack said. To the rest of the room, he added, "Athtars can go backward in time to view events. Anya and Lotan went back to view past events, and apparently, while in the time river, they could venture into spaces where there were talismans."

"Perhaps that's how she was able to be here in Geneva," María said.

"She didn't just travel then. She stopped time completely."

Jack sat back, looking at María curiously. "But once it started again, the talismans were back in effect. Maybe you're onto something."

"So we just need to prevent her from stopping time," George said.

"Easier said than done," Cam said. "That was the problem with Bael, remember?"

"We didn't have talismans with Bael," María said.

"And clearly, the talismans aren't the cure-all we'd hoped," Cam said. María gave her a look that Lotan couldn't read, and she cleared her throat. "Are there any more questions for Lotan?"

"If I recall anything else, I promise I'll convey it immediately," Lotan said. "I'm eager to help in any way I can."

"Thank you," María said. "Agent Grenard, you may escort Lotan to the perimeter of the green zone, then report to Agent Sabrosky for next steps. Agent Macarro, please stay here to receive your next assignment."

Lotan looked at Cam, but she didn't seem surprised. She did, however, squeeze his hand under the table before he rose and walked out with Jack.

"That was…" Jack said, exhaling. "Man, you're going to have to be more careful about the secrets you spill."

"I'm sorry, I didn't know that was a secret," Lotan said.

"What did that athtar look like?" Jack asked, looking to the sky.

"He was very confident," Lotan said. "He felt familiar to me, but I can't exactly place him. Dark hair, bronze skin." He shrugged. "I'm sorry if I'm not more helpful."

"No, that's very helpful," Jack said as they reached the edge of the green zone. "Get back to the apartment and keep your phone on you. If you see any other athtars poking around, let me know."

"Are you going to meet with that director fellow?" Lotan asked.

"No," Jack said, his gaze darkening. "I have to find Anya and figure out what the fuck is going on."

CHAPTER TEN

Bael, master of the Underworld, Lord of the Mountain, emperor of all he surveyed, the original athtar demon, was a little impressed with this human.

This Jackson George Grenard.

The evidence was overwhelming that Anat had been the perpetrator of the attacks in the human cities. It bore all the hallmarks of an athtar attack, especially the most recent one. And yet, he steadfastly refused to admit what every other human around him had already accepted.

This would be heartwarming except that it flew in the face of Bael's very specific plans. For Anat to realize the error of her ways and come back, she would have to be forsaken by all three humans she called friends, as well as Diogo. There would have to be nowhere else for her to run, so she'd come back to him. And then, they could truly be the rulers of this world they were always destined to be.

It had become clear to Bael in the past few days that he'd been mistaken to believe Anat was destined to be his second. Her true role was to be his equal, his ruling partner in all things. With her powers and his, they could squash whatever human rebellions arose and bring order to the world. And he would finally have his true love by his side.

For she'd unlocked a power even Bael had been unable to master. She'd been able to stop time, so said the gaggle of humans. Stop time and be fully present in a town surrounded by athtar talismans. Even after thousands of years of trying, the most Bael could do was project a version of himself, as he'd done when speaking to the nox price.

At first, Bael hadn't believed that Anat could have a power that had eluded him. So he'd gone to see for himself, stepping back into the time river to the moment where Anat had saved the world from Yaotl's ill-advised plans. He'd been astounded when Anat, teary-eyed and at her most vulnerable, found the strength to put a halt to time completely—and somewhat annoyed to realize it was in the service of saving that human.

And then, she'd repeated the feat, this time to save the human's friend Camilla. But to Bael's eyes, she hadn't replicated it again—as much as she looked to be trying in Johannesburg. But that particular tussle had revealed something else, that he and Anat were absolutely evenly matched. The one with a grip on the time river was king of the castle, so Bael would have to make sure it was always him.

The elokos had done an adequate job in causing chaos, but the time was near for more demons to join the fray. The human demon hunters had already begun to suspect Anat, but Bael wanted more. It needed to be clear that a demon from the Underworld had made their way to the human one—evidence that not even Jackson George Grenard could deny.

And, if luck was on Bael's side, Anat's house of cards would continue to fall, and soon she would realize that the only person who'd ever loved her—truly loved her—was Bael.

Kappanchi was as disgusting and dirty as ever. Why Mizuchi had chosen to live in such squalor, Bael had never figured out. He said it reminded him of home, but with the world-building magic at his fingertips, a better home could've been imagined.

As Bael stepped into the village, he stopped short. Mizuchi was nowhere to be found. The turtle's mansion was in plain view, but the power wasn't there. There was *something* there, but it was infantile, growing.

Had that damned turtle made himself a child? Even after Bael had expressly forbidden it?

He balled his fist and walked further into the castle, finally turning a corner and coming across a recently-turned kappa.

She furrowed her brow. "Who are you?"

"I am Bael, King of the Mountain, Ruler of the Five Realms, and Lord of the Mountain," he said, advancing slowly on her. "And that you do not know my name is a slight that will not be overlooked. Where is your belu?"

"T-Tabiko isn't the belu," she said, her teeth chattering. "She's the Sewanin."

"I don't care about Mizuchi's whores," Bael said. "Where is the *belu*? Mizuchi himself. Where has that turtle slithered away to?"

"He's..." She swallowed. "My lord, he's dead."

Bael narrowed his gaze then straightened. "Dead? Then how are you here? How is any of this here?"

"T...the Sewanin would know. I don't know. I only just arrived last—"

The kappa's words died on the wind as Bael rid her body of her head. Using his Sight, he scanned the village, searching for a kappa who would know what was going on, and his magical gaze landed on Tabiko.

He was in her office in a moment, earning a cry of surprise from the kappa as her chair toppled over.

"You..." Bael could practically hear her heartbeat from across the room. "You're dead."

"Am I?" he said, waltzing toward her. "Because I seem to be alive and well."

"What sort of athtar witchery is this?" Tabiko said. "Or are you a lilin, glamoured to look like—"

A blood-curdling scream echoed from her lips as Bael took hold of her with his magic. It was a very specific sort of torture, one that took the victim's cells and slowed them down, stretching them out, pulling and pushing, extracting the maximum amount of pain a human or demon could feel at one time.

He released the hold, and Tabiko fell flat to the ground, her form trembling. "Now, we need to have a little chat, it seems."

"You..." Tabiko panted, her face wet with sweat. "You will get...nothing..."

Bael took hold of her again, righted the chair she'd turned over, and sat down. When he felt her consciousness slipping away, he released her.

"As I was saying."

"The kappas will hear me," Tabiko said.

"And what will they do? I can stop time. And it appears that your belu is nowhere to be found—"

"Because you *killed* him," Tabiko snapped. "Or does his death blend in with the billions of others you've massacred?"

"It certainly wouldn't rank high in terms of the kappa belus I've killed." Bael sat back. "But I would like to know why this world remains intact after the belu's death."

"The same reason the noxlands remained intact after Xo was killed," she whispered. "Mizuchi passed his line to another."

Bael clicked his tongue against the roof of his mouth. "That is impossible for a lesser demon."

"There are no lesser demons," Tabiko said. "There are just demons and humans. That's it. Th—"

Bael stopped her incessant noise with one stroke of his sword. With a snort, he walked out of the room and stepped out of himself, using his Sight to scan the grounds for this supposed second-to-Mizuchi. And when he found the wee babe in a side room, hidden away, he moved there.

The babe was asleep, so there was no one around. Bael peered down onto the small turtle spawn, an ugly thing that barely looked like a living, breathing animal. That it would one day grow into a belu kappa was hard to fathom. But Bael had ways of speeding things along. The last time he'd attempted this had been with Anat, but the magic was known to him.

Bael closed his eyes and felt the time river moving beneath him. The babe became like a boulder in the river, immovable to the rushing water. He created a bubble around the babe, then forced the river trapped inside to move faster, months and years turning to mere seconds.

The babe grew to a toddler, then a child, then a gangly teenager, then a fully-grown adult man, green, naked, and blissfully unaware of anything happening. His mind would be a blank slate, and Bael could do with it what he wanted.

"Hello," Bael said, removing the now-adult from time.

"Haye." The man's mouth moved oddly, as if he wasn't sure how to work the muscles or his vocal cords. He blinked, opening and closing his mouth. Bael half-expected him to stuff his whole fist inside his mouth, but he didn't.

"I'm your master now," Bael said.

"Mashtor."

Bael sighed. This experiment might be a failure if this man-baby wasn't even capable of managing his own people. It might be easier to just kill the thing and make a new one. But that wouldn't accomplish the very specific goal Bael had in mind.

"Master," the man-baby repeated. "Master."

"Yes," Bael said softly. "It means I'm in control and you will do whatever I say. Is that clear?"

It perhaps wasn't, but the man-baby nodded his head slowly.

"Good. Now the first order of business, you will force every kappa under your purview to swear fealty to me and only me. Can you do that?"

The man-baby blinked, and Bael sighed. Still, there could be more than one way to accomplish dominance over the kappas until this thing had more to say.

Bael and the kappa prince returned to Kappanchi, finding a group of kappas in a village a ways from Mizuchi's castle. It seemed they had all been dropped there—more than likely, by Anat—and were still trying to gain their bearings. But among them was a particular demon Bael wanted to use for the next step in his plan.

He appeared in the center of the kappas, the kappa prince in tow. Even though the prince was bumbling like an idiot, the power that radiated off him was clear, and got the attention of every kappa in attendance. Once they turned to the source, some of them recognized Bael, and he was pleased they feared him as much as they should.

"Kappas, as you can tell, this is your prince," Bael said.

A kappa pushed to the front of the crowd. "What did you do to him?"

"What did you do to Tabiko?" another cried.

"Tabiko is gone, and I'm your new Sewanin," Bael said,

earning another ripple of fear from the crowd. "Your prince will stay with me so I may mentor him in the finer arts of being a belu. He's clearly in need of," Bael sighed as the front of the man's pants grew wet, "help."

"Please, Lord Bael," cried a kappa who threw himself to his knees. "Don't hurt him. He's our only link to this land."

"I'm quite aware," Bael said softly. "Which is why I will be merciful. He's in my capable hands and therefore, you are all mine to command. If anyone would like to disagree..." He smiled. "They can join Tabiko."

Predictably, none of the demons said a word. The threat of losing their powers was a most potent motivator for a demon, and Bael should have wielded it more often. But one by one, the kappas knelt and murmured their fealty to Bael.

"Excellent," he said, looking to one of the more powerful kappas with her head bowed. "Doroteia, you will come with me."

"My lord?" she asked, gazing up at him with apprehension.

"Fear not," he replied. "I have a very special plan for you."

CHAPTER ELEVEN

Anya sat on the couch in Ath-kur, but her Sight was far away, running over the human world in search of massacres, fights, fires, *anything*. But over two days had passed, and there hadn't been a single attack. She'd even taken to checking the human news to make sure she hadn't missed anything that occurred in an athtar-talisman zone. But all seemed well for the moment—which meant it absolutely wasn't.

Why Bael hadn't struck again, Anya had no clue. She didn't think it was because she'd done anything different or proven anything. Which meant there was some larger game. His manipulation knew no bounds, and he didn't mind destroying an entire civilization just to prove a point.

She couldn't See Jack, which she hoped meant he was safe in Geneva. Finding him in Berlin had been like a knife in her stomach. Keeping the truth from him was even harder—

especially as he seemed to be trailing Bael's massacres. She'd felt him step through the portal to Johannesburg a few hours after she'd left, and she'd sent Diogo to keep an eye on things for her. If she saw Jack face-to-face, she might spill everything.

"My lady, you need to rest."

She turned, having felt Diogo arrive a moment before. "How was Johannesburg?"

"It doesn't look good," Diogo said. "The humans... Well, it's clear the attack was by an athtar."

She chewed her fingernail. "We need to find Bael's army and put a stop to this, then. Have you had any luck?"

"No, but I admit my time travel skills are much less potent than yours. I can only go back a few minutes at a time," Diogo said. "So unless..."

"We've gone over this," she snapped. "Try harder."

He sighed and approached her. "The next time there's an attack, let me know immediately, and I will do my best to locate the source. But to my eyes, Johannesburg is the latest. There haven't been any more, have there?"

"No, but that doesn't mean there won't be," Anya said. "Bael wouldn't be this merciful. He's planning something."

"He always is," Diogo said with a sigh. "But for the moment, you should rest. You'll be no good to any of us if you are exhausted. Even belu athtars need their sleep." He bowed his head. "I promise I will let you know the moment something catches fire."

Anya turned to the window once more then nodded. Just her

luck that Bael would strike the moment she laid her head on the pillow, but that would at least move things along. Sitting around and waiting was starting to grate on her.

She padded down the empty hallway toward the bedroom, pushing open the door to reveal the dark room. The sheets on the bed were still messed up, a reminder of the night she and Jack had shared together. Had she not slept since then? It was hard to remember.

She touched the bedsheets, and if she inhaled long enough, she could still catch the scent of Jack on them. Damn, but she missed him. Hated that all they had were single nights of bliss before the world tumbled into chaos again. Those stolen moments, though…

She'd never seen him so exhausted and desolate after the attack on Geneva and losing his grandfather, and it had stirred something deep inside her. She'd held him through his grief, healed his wounds and washed the blood from his body, wishing she could wipe the grief from his mind. She'd told herself to be strong for him, because he needed to be weak.

When he'd kissed her, every ounce of her strength had failed her. She fell fully into his arms, unafraid of the consequences that would come with handing the entirety of her heart to him. For the first time in her life, she had found a safe home.

But this time, it hadn't been Bael that came between them— it had been her own selfishness. Jack already had his doubts about her, and she could envision very easily what would happen if she told him the truth. He would say, if she'd just given up her magic, not traveled back in time and just *listened* to him, thousands of humans around the world would be alive. The world wouldn't be in disarray. He would never forgive her, and that safe home they'd built together would crumble.

Anya just needed to solve the problem, and when everything was solved, she would tell him everything.

But as the days passed, and there was no sign of Bael's army, she began to fear fixing the world was a bridge too far.

Anya must've fallen asleep, because the next thing she knew, Diogo was roughly shaking her awake. Bleary-eyed, she barely processed what he was saying, until she registered the words "kappa" and "drown."

"Kappas?" she croaked, sitting up.

"Come on."

She barely had a moment to wake up before she followed him to the human world. Diogo led her to South America, Brazil, the coast—but to the edge of the beach. It took her a moment to realize what she was looking at.

If not for the antennas and three or four skyscrapers peeking from the waters, Anya would've thought it a continuation of the ocean itself. The breath left her chest as she thought of the thousands—perhaps hundreds of thousands—of people who'd just been killed. It was a massacre just the same as Berlin and Johannesburg, just by drowning instead of by sword.

"Were you able to see where they came from?" Anya asked.

"By the time I arrived, the waves had been here for at least an hour," Diogo said. "My magic hit its limit."

"Waves?" Anya turned to him.

He nodded. "It looked to me like a tidal wave. I hope the humans will consider it as such."

"How do we know it was…" She squinted as a turtle-looking creature surfaced for a moment, carrying two bodies in its arms and swimming to shore. Newly transformed demons, perhaps. Then, they both disappeared—athtar magic.

"Follow them," Anya barked to Diogo.

He was gone and back in a moment, a bewildered look on his face. "I…have no idea where they went."

She turned to him. "What? It's simple—"

"It's not. There's no athtar trail for where they went—no path I could follow. Something reached out from nowhere and took them back to nowhere."

An incredulous laugh left her lips. "Diogo, that makes no sense. They have to have gone *somewhere*."

"Sure. Just somewhere I can't follow," he replied. "It is… possible that Bael knows more about the intricacies of athtar magic than I do. You'll remember he's thousands of years older than either of us."

Anya chewed her lip, barely able to process what she was seeing and hearing. "But we know this was kappas. That means he's gotten to Tabiko and the baby." She looked at Diogo with concern. "I want you to redouble your efforts to reach Freyja. Send a carrier pigeon if you have to. But she needs to know Bael is out there and needs to fortify her lands against him." She cracked a smile. "She should be able to handle that, if memory serves."

Diogo bowed and disappeared once more, leaving Anya alone on what used to be a cliffside, staring out onto the city that had been submerged before it had a chance to save itself. Was this Bael's new plan? He'd grown tired of bloodlust and wanted to drown instead? Death was death, after all.

Or was this some new phase in his plan, adding kappas to the mix? And had Tabiko and the baby fallen victim to his plans, or had they sworn fealty?

Only one way to find out.

Anya arrived in Kappanchi, ready for anything—but to her surprise (and immeasurable relief), it looked exactly the same. Perhaps Bael had found some other kappas to manipulate, ones she'd left topside.

Yet, as she searched the lands, her heart sank. Like Elonsi, there should've been thousands of kappas milling about. She should've been met by a pair of spears in her face when she set foot near Mizuchi's castle. But she easily opened the paper doors and walked inside.

"Hello?" Anya called, waiting for the response. When she heard nothing, she searched the rooms, both physically and with her Sight, until she came to the only thing in the place.

Tabiko's body.

Anya braced herself against the doorframe, pressing her hand to her chest. Tabiko had never really liked her, and the kappa had good reason not to, but Anya had respected her fierce loyalty to her belu and his spawn. There was no reason for her to die like this.

Kneeling next to the body, Anya searched the castle again with her Sight, finding the baby's hidden room and crib—empty. Bael must've taken the child, and used threats to force the kappas to follow his lead. It probably wasn't a hard bargain. They'd already proven themselves willing to take on the world—and unlike Biloko, the babe wouldn't have much to say about it.

Anya bowed her head in prayer over Tabiko's body. "At least you're with Ayumi. I'm sorry."

"Ayumi. I remember her."

Anya's eyes flew open, and her fury ignited like a wildfire. Bael had once again snuck up on her, and Anya hated it. "Why are you doing this?"

"Doing what? I haven't harmed the kappa child. In fact, I've given him the best tutors."

"Tutors?" Anya rose to face him. He was infuriatingly unconcerned, as if Tabiko had been nothing more than a passing thought. "He's a baby."

"Not anymore," Bael said with a knowing smile. "I'm sure you remember when I aged you from a scrawny child to..." He took a long, languishing look at her. "The woman you are today."

"And it's creepy as fuck," Anya spat.

Bael took a step back in surprise. "Spending time with the humans seems to have made you crude, my love. You should return to my side, and we can work these rough spots from your psyche once more."

Anya could barely believe he'd even said such a thing. "Why are you killing humans, Bael? What's your game?"

"They need to know their place," Bael replied. "As do you. Which is by my side."

An incredulous burst of laughter bubbled from Anya's lips. "You...are incredible."

"I know, my love. I know." He smiled. "But one day, you'll realize that everything I do is for you. And you'll appreciate it so much more."

He was gone in a moment, and soon after, Anya felt the distinct sensation of the world pushing at her. Like the kappas were expelling her from the world. To spare herself the embarrassment of being physically removed, she traveled back to Ath-kur, where she landed in her living room.

She exhaled slowly. Two demon races down, just the lilins to go. Bael seemed to be gathering his army. Would he find Lotan's power and add the noxes, too? Or would his next target be Freyja?

And would she, like Biloko and Tabiko, become yet another victim?

Anya sent a vibration through the connection with Diogo, and he was at her side in a moment. "Tell me you got in touch with Freyja."

He shook his head. "I have sent messages, but they've been unanswered. Liley, though, looks to be intact. So perhaps Bael hasn't made his way there yet."

"Yet being the operative word," Anya said. "But I think I know what he's up to. At least partially." She shook her head. "Some part of this is his hope to win me back to his side. I can only imagine it's because he realizes how evenly matched we are."

"You aren't...going to go back to him, are you?" Diogo asked, and she was somewhat offended at his tone. Then again, she'd done it a thousand times in the past.

"No. Never again," Anya said with a shake of her head. "But at least we know part of the why... Now we just need to figure out his next move."

"Are you ready to tell the humans?"

"No," Anya said. "Not until Bael is gone."

CHAPTER TWELVE

Jack tried six ways from Sunday to get the athtar portal to open into Ath-kur, and every time, he was denied. It was a little offensive, really, that Anya was able to just cut him off like this, and there was no way to get in touch with her. He'd even tried calling her phone, but it was going straight to voicemail, and all texts were coming back undeliverable.

But he was nothing if not determined. After all, if he gave up, *everyone* in the human world would blame her for these attacks.

He'd been rudely awakened by a knock from Cam, and a story about how all of a beach town in Brazil had been suddenly overcome by a large tidal wave—and the witnesses who'd survived said they saw turtle-monsters swimming in the waters. Jack tried to explain that it could've been leftover kappas, but Cam had clearly made up her mind.

"*No one else* who could've been behind Johannesburg," she said. "We have to face facts."

"Have you?"

She exhaled and closed her eyes, pain etched on her features. "Jack, until I have a better explanation, the one that makes the most sense is the one I'm going with. And you should, too."

But he couldn't. Not after all they'd been through, not after seeing her at her very worst and knowing that her go-to wasn't destruction, but self-implosion. If he knew her, and he did, if she was hurting from his rejection, she would be crying on a mountain, not sending demons into the human world to kill people. It was the exact opposite of everything she'd been for nearly two hundred years.

But with the portal a dead end, Jack decided on an alternative route. Namely, the only *other* person who could get him into Ath-kur. It was a stretch, for sure, but he had to try.

Lisbon was still covered in anti-athtar talismans, so he had to arrive outside the city limits and find his way inside. The town was somewhat familiar to him now, after spending time here with Cam and Anya, and yet it was completely different. The demons who'd invaded had made a mess of everything, and the town, with its limited resources, was still cleaning up. Geneva, at least, had enough space to remove the bodies, whereas some streets in Lisbon were still scattered with them . Jack felt for the traumatized people and made a mental note to ask María to spare some additional resources if she could find them.

Diogo's monastery was similarly destroyed, but not by the

demons. Per Anya, it had been destroyed in a Bael-led Demon Spring, and when Diogo had asked to live in the human world, he'd made a deal with the local kappa lord to cast a water-based illusion to make it look as if it had never been repaired to keep the humans out.

But Jack wasn't fooled. He walked up to the still-standing doors and banged on them.

"Diogo," he barked. "Open up. I know you can hear me."

Five minutes went by and no answer.

He knocked again. "I'm not kidding around. Open the damned door. I'll destroy them if I have to. Don't think I won't."

Yet again, no answer. So Jack decided to pull out the big guns.

"I'll tell ICDM where to find you if you don't open up in five—"

The door swung open, revealing a harried-looking Diogo. "You will do no such thing, you pesky human. What is it you want from me? And make it quick—the damned talismans in this city make me ill."

"I need to talk with Anya," Jack said. "Now."

"That's not advisable. She has explicitly given you instructions to stay in Geneva."

"And she's not the boss of me, is she?" Jack asked with a stupidly sweet smile. "This is insane. There's no reason she can't just have *a chat* with me. We need to talk about what happened in Johannesburg."

"What happened there was a tragedy," Diogo said. "As was Berlin—and Brazil. The belu athtar is working to handle the situation and does not need your input or help."

Diogo tried to close the door, but Jack stuck his foot in the way. "That's a bullshit answer, and you know it."

"I wish I could help you, but my loyalty is to the belu athtar." He honestly looked sad to be saying it. "All I can say is that you should trust that she has your best interests at heart."

"Would be nice if she could tell me that herself instead of hiding out." Jack sighed. "Look, can you at least deliver a message for me?"

Diogo pursed his lips, and Jack thought he was about to lecture on why he wasn't a messenger boy. "Fine. What?"

"Tell her…" Jack paused. "Tell her I'm sorry for what I said. That I want to talk to her about it and try to understand her side. But the silent treatment isn't helping anyone."

Diogo nodded. "I will convey it. Now *go home* to Geneva, where it's safe."

"Safe from what?" Jack asked, but the response was the door shutting in his face.

Jack left the monastery and strolled down the street, seething and trying to parse out what Diogo might've been talking about. It was clear something had spooked both of them—but why weren't they sharing it? If it was enough to make the belu athtar nervous, surely ICDM deserved to know so they could prepare for it.

Or was it so bad that not even ICDM could stem the tide?

Jack, at least, was starting to doubt that Anya was just plain mad at him, and he was now sure that she wasn't responsible for the attacks because she'd gone off the deep end. But the truth eluded him, no matter how much he poked at it.

He found himself down by the water, and the Belóm tower. Nearby, Solomao's restaurant still stood, but it had been boarded up since his death. Anya had been responsible for that, but Jack and Cam had been responsible for Edite. If they hadn't had that miscommunication, would there have been a reason for ICDM to start targeting demons at all? Perhaps not for a few years. But that was neither here nor there.

Jack leaned over the edge of the railing and gazed down into the murky depths. The water was high, nearly splashing over the side, and churned up, even though the skies were blue overhead. One wave splashed over the barricade, leaving a puddle where there had been dry land. Then another—and another.

Something tickled the back of Jack's mind. Demonic magic was nearby.

Kappas, to be exact.

He stepped back, looking up and down the street for the offending creature. But all he saw were tourists and leisurely daytime strollers.

The water was definitely rising, every wave now crawling over the edge of the barricade, making its way across the street. It was slow, but the water was powerful—it almost looked like the beginnings of a tidal wave. But with no earthquake nearby, this wasn't natural.

Then everything clicked.

"Get to higher ground!" Jack cried as another rolling wave crossed the street toward the unsuspecting diners at the cafe across the street. "Everyone, get to higher ground, *now*!"

But the tourists just stared at him, perplexed. The waiters rolled their eyes as if he was some crazy man. And it was then Jack realized that he was the only one who'd noticed the water— he was the only one who hadn't been taken by the kappa magic.

"Fuck me," Jack said, spinning as the water washed across the legs of the cafe patrons. They remained blissfully unaware, smiling and laughing even as the deadly water rose on their bodies. Even the waiters sloshed through it, oblivious as their aprons grew soggy and heavy.

Jack turned as another wave rolled toward him, this one nearly knocking him off his feet, as it was almost halfway up his legs. He turned and trudged back the way he'd come. That was higher ground, at least. Maybe there, he'd find the kappa responsible for all this. Maybe there…

But the water was rising fast, now up to his waist, and the current threatened to pull him back into the sea. He pulled his phone from his pocket and dialed Cam's number.

"What—"

"Lisbon's under attack," Jack said. "Kappas. They're flooding the city."

"Fuck. Where are you?"

Jack grabbed onto a nearby light pole as the current

threatened to pull him back again. "Trying to get to higher ground. Everyone in the city seems suckered. I have no idea where the kappa is, but it's got to be a bunch of them."

"Aren't they all in the Underworld?" Cam asked.

"I don't—" Jack grunted as he shimmied up the pole to escape the water that had splashed into his mouth. "Cam, I'm in some shit right now. Send the team." Then he cursed. "*Fuck me*, this city has talismans all over it."

"We'll be there as soon as we can," Cam said. "Stay—"

The phone fell out of his hand as a wave washed over his head. He coughed the water up and realized if he stayed here, he was going to be in trouble. The current was strong, but he wasn't a bad swimmer. He just needed to figure out which was the best way to find dry land. This damned city had seven hills—one of them would stay above water.

He hoped.

A table went floating by, and Jack took a leap to grab it. It sank a little but was buoyant enough for the moment. Jack kicked against the current, keeping his eyes peeled for dry land and finding nothing. Behind him, the street level had disappeared, and the water was rising above the second floor of the buildings. It was hard to remember what this place had looked like just fifteen minutes ago, but one rather unique building on the corner struck his memory. He'd walked downhill past it—he would head that way.

The water, however, kept rising. When he spotted dry land up ahead, it was submerged by the time he reached it. The kappas seemed content to drown the whole city—hills and all.

He took a breath, panic starting to rise in his chest. Forget all the civilians now assuredly losing their lives—Jack wasn't sure he could get out of this one. He could keep swimming, but his legs were already tired and there didn't seem to be an end in sight.

Diogo. The thought came to him like a light in the darkness. If he could reach the monastery again, maybe Diogo could help —or get Anya.

But the tide had overtaken most of the buildings, and Jack wasn't even sure what direction he was headed in now. The sun was blocked by a thick layer of clouds, so that was no help, either. It was as if he was lost in the middle of the ocean.

In the distance, he spotted the famous castle sitting atop the mountain in the Alfama district, though the water seemed nearly to the top of *that* hill as well. What kind of kappa had this amount of power? It had to be a coordinated effort. Who could've done such a thing? Tabiko didn't seem capable of this kind of horror.

Still, Jack headed toward the castle, as it was one of the highest points in the city. It seemed impossibly far, but he had no other choice.

"C'mon, Jack," he whispered to himself. "You can do it. Just keep swimming, isn't that what that fish—"

Something grabbed his ankle and yanked hard, pulling him underwater before he could catch a breath. As the light of the sky disappeared and Jack's lungs burned, he looked down to see what creature had grabbed him. It was a kappa—a very turtle-looking one, too. An Underworld kappa. It looked up at him with a gleaming smile.

"Transform and be saved, human."

Jack opened his mouth to argue, but all that left was an air bubble. He weakly kicked at the creature, but the grip was superhuman. He glanced up at the dimming light above, struggling to stay conscious and find a plan of escape as spots danced in his vision.

As the darkness closed around him, he thought he saw a splash overhead. A figure was swimming toward him, with long dark hair floating behind her. She had a gleaming sword in her hand, and with one hack, she freed Jack's leg from the kappa's grip. Then she wrapped both arms around Jack's chest and pulled him up.

They broke the surface, and Jack spat water, coughing as he gasped for air. But the water wasn't moving around him—nothing was. Time had completely stopped.

"A-Anya?" he croaked, looking behind him. "What are you doing here?"

"I told you to stay in Geneva," she said, paddling and kicking and making much better time than Jack had. "I told you it was dangerous out here."

Jack coughed again. "Why are you doing this?"

"Hush and let me concentrate. I think enough of the talismans have washed away now."

"Was that the point?"

Jack felt the world move under him, and his body landed in

a heap on dry land. He heaved a sigh of relief, taking deep, cleansing breaths and coughing up the rest of the water in his lungs.

"Anya, what—"

But she was gone.

CHAPTER THIRTEEN

Cam didn't care who was watching. When she finally laid eyes on Jack, she threw herself into his arms and hugged him so hard he swore she was trying to give him chest compressions.

"I'm fine, really," he said, gently rubbing her back. "Thanks to Anya."

"Yeah, it looks like a lot of shit is thanks to her," Cam said, stepping back with a scowl on her face. "Lisbon is..."

It had been horrible to watch on drone footage. The city was almost completely underwater, only the tips of the tallest buildings still visible. The body count would put the Lisbon head and shoulders above any other city—perhaps even worse than all the other attacks combined. But though the water was still churning, it had stopped rising.

Once Jack had his bearings, he'd been able to open a portal to the drop site in Geneva, and a horde of soldiers had come walking through, ready for action. But there was nothing to be done—not unless they wanted to don scuba gear.

"How many survivors?" Jack asked.

"None so far," Cam said. "The kappa magic was thick. I'm surprised you managed to evade it."

"I think panic took over," Jack said. "I felt the magic when it started."

"Or maybe you were intentionally not targeted," Cam said. "There was *a lot* of magic."

"I still almost drowned," Jack said. "If Anya—"

"Exactly," Cam said, turning to him. "Anya magically knew where you were, found you, and saved the day. How could she have done that if she hadn't known what was going on?"

"Luck," Jack said.

"Sorry to disrupt that theory," Cam said, motioning for him to follow her back through the portal. "We have video evidence of Doroteia in Lisbon shortly before everything went underwater."

"Doroteia?" Jack said, stopping short. "But she's…"

Cam clicked her tongue. "Supposed to be in the Underworld. Yep. How the hell did she get from down there to up here? Only one way."

"I mean—"

"Jack, *come on.*"

She hated the look of indecision on Jack's face. Yet again, he was putting aside all logical explanations in favor of Anya's sob story. Never mind that his gut had been right in the past, there wasn't anything Cam could see that could save the belu athtar now. Sooner or later, Jack would have to admit that the Anya they knew was gone.

"Did Anya say anything to you when she rescued you?" Cam asked.

"She asked me why I didn't stay in Geneva." He shook his head, brow furrowed. "She said she could transport me because enough of the talismans had washed away." He looked at Cam, horror in his gaze. "You don't think…"

"I think it's plausible that she flooded the city to wash away the talismans. I think it's reasonable to assume she'll do it again," Cam said. "And I think it's time we consider believing our own eyes. It would have been very easy for the kappas to just walk through Diogo's portal, even."

Jack crossed his arms over his chest. "But I was there, I—" His gaze lit up. "Maybe one of the other demons has figured out how to create a portal."

"Jack."

"No, It makes sense," Jack said. "One of the belus did it. Biloko or Freyja. I mean, if Lotan's mom could, then—"

Cam just watched him, wishing she could knock some sense into him. But he had that hero complex gleam in his eye, and she knew where that led. "And how are we going to prove that? Have you managed to get into Ath-kur yet?"

"No, but maybe I can go to one of the other lands," Jack said. "Maybe we try Freyja. She could offer us some—"

"Freyja is pissed at Anya, and by extension, *you*, so that idea is out the window," Cam said. She was starting to nurse a migraine and didn't think Jack was going to listen to reason no matter how many ways she tried to slice it. "Why don't you head back to the apartment and get some rest. I have some things to take care of at headquarters, then I'll join you. I think we've all had enough excitement for one day."

"Feels like you're sending me home as punishment," Jack said. "It's like you don't even care if she's actually guilty."

"That's bullshit, and you know it." Cam snapped, turning to him fully and poking him in the chest. "If you think my heart isn't breaking about all this, then you're wrong. The last thing I want is for Anya to be guilty. But you have to admit, she's not acting like an innocent person right now. And I have to go on what I know." She sighed, looking out onto the flooded city. "If she—"

The phone in her pocket buzzed and she snatched it, annoyed that her diatribe had been interrupted.

"Macarro."

"*Agent Macarro, the oddest thing. About twenty miles outside of Lisbon, there's a whole field full of drenched people. They say they don't remember how they got there.*"

Jack, who heard the voice on the other end, just smiled as he walked toward the portal. "Maybe you should open your eyes a little, Cam. See you back at the apartment."

Cam didn't stay long after Jack walked through the portal. ICDM had sent Agent Sabrosky to handle the cleanup and another agent from Madrid to deal with the field full of survivors outside the city. Despite Anya's assistance, there were hundreds of thousands still dead. It wasn't the win Jack was pretending it was, but it did sow a little doubt in Cam's mind about Anya's guilt. If only the bitch would show up and talk to them instead of giving cryptic answers, things would be a whole lot clearer.

When she arrived at the temporary ICDM headquarters, Cam braced herself for the onslaught of questions from María and the others on the Council. They would no doubt get a full report from Sabrosky and the others who were taking over the recovery mission. But they would want to know what Jack had seen—and would be very interested to hear about Anya's involvement.

She opened the flap to the tent and marched to the back room, where the Council was waiting. María beckoned her forward, but before Cam could speak, a voice piped up from the computer at the far end of the table.

"Jack's okay?" George asked, his concerned face filling the entire screen.

"He's a little waterlogged, but okay," Cam said with a weak smile. "I sent him back to the apartment."

George sat back, a relieved look on his face, and Cam considered what it must be like to have a child in the middle of all this. Her own mother was practically melting her phone on a regular basis.

"So?" María prompted. "What is your report?"

Cam cleared her throat. "It's as Jack said. The entire city is underwater. And I mean underwater. The people were entrapped by kappa magic and didn't have a chance to..." She trailed off. "Jack, for some reason, didn't get suckered, so he was able to save himself. He says a kappa grabbed him and tried to take him under but..." She took a breath. "Anya came to his rescue."

María snorted but motioned for Cam to continue.

"When he was being saved, she mentioned something about the talismans being washed away, which led me initially to believe that she was..." Cam couldn't finish that thought. "But after hearing that she'd moved as many humans as she could to higher ground, perhaps not. Doroteia's arrival provides yet another wrinkle—she's supposed to be in the Underworld."

"I think it makes perfect sense," María said. "She drowns the city, then saves a few to throw us off the trail. That's your working theory, isn't it, Cam?"

She nodded. "It's certainly a tactic. But even this seems... excessive for her."

"Not if you know her history," Councilwoman Chola, from Africa, said. "She earned a bloodthirsty reputation for a reason."

This seemed like a rehash of every conversation they'd had, and Cam was tired of it. Lotan had texted her to say he was making a beef roast and she wanted to help him with his memory recovery and not think about Anya setting the world on fire and putting it out.

"Your team has arrived from Shanghai," María said. "They're set up and ready for your direction. The Council wants you to get started right away."

Cam nodded, guilt tugging at her chest. "And just to be clear, the point of this mission is…?"

"We want you to build us a weapon that can be used against the athtar," María said. "We know she's capable of withstanding the talismans by stopping time, but that only seems to be in extreme circumstances. Find a way to neutralize those circumstances."

A task easier said than done. "And how will you know if we're successful? Are you going to shoot her the next time you see her?"

"If she continues to allow demons to terrorize humanity, we will have no choice," María said.

Cam nodded and rose slowly. "Then I'd best get at it."

Cam's team had been set up in yet another tent in the square, a stone's throw from the Council tent, but the distance felt interminable. She didn't like this mission, she didn't want to be a part of it, but at the same time…she didn't see how there was another option. She just couldn't tell Jack.

She walked through the open flap and put her hands on her hips, gazing at her team. They were mostly PhDs, specializing in demonic theory, with a couple of weapons experts thrown in for good measure. But all their book knowledge had been put to shame when Cam had handed them the five talismans last year.

"So," Cam began, "what do you have for me?"

They ran through the litany of new weaponry, updated guns and ballistics, which might prove useful if they were able to arm the military who were supporting ICDM. But nothing about Anya or the mystery of how she'd managed to evade the talisman magic.

"We've reviewed the video from the attack on Geneva, specifically the moment the athtar arrived," Arjun, one of the doctorates, said. "It's a blip. One minute, Grenard is there in the center of the mess, about to lose his head, and the next minute, all the demons are gone and he's making out with the athtar."

"I mean, that's how it goes," Cam said with a bit of a snort. Jack wouldn't be happy to hear that his romantic moment with Anya was being used in the name of scientific process. "And we've confirmed that the demons all left at the same time?"

They bobbed their heads. "Confirmed everywhere we had video timestamps. One second there then gone."

Cam sank into the empty chair, pulling the folder of photos to herself and racking her brain. "Anya said... It wasn't just slowing time. She'd *stopped* it completely. Somehow that seems different."

"Were you able to stop time when you were an athtar?"

Cam's gaze shot up to one mousy-eared young man, barely out of school, and luckily, he shrank under her gaze. "You must've misheard that. I was never an athtar."

She ignored the nervous shuffling around the room as she peered at the photos. There must've been something about stopping time that rendered the anti-athtar talisman magic useless. Anya and Lotan had been able to visit the Nullius, another source of anti-demonic magic, using the time river.

There was still so much they didn't know about that place, about how demonic and anti-demonic magic worked.

Cam stretched her shoulder, thinking of that winged monster who'd nearly killed her. That thing had been full of anti-demonic magic, too, and the only reason Cam hadn't turned into one of them was Lotan and Anya's quick thinking. Dousing her in demonic matter had effectively stopped the anti-demonic magic. Push and pull, yin and yang.

This line of thought seemed off track, but Cam followed it, chewing her lip and looking at the photos again. A sadness rose in her chest, thinking about Lotan, and how he would've jumped at the chance to tease out this mystery. But she buried those feelings for the moment, turning back to the matter at hand.

"What kind of talisman protections exist around Geneva?" Cam asked, feeling the curious gazes of her team. "Anti-athtar, obviously, but what of the others?"

"No others that we know of," Arjun said.

"Your first job is to pack this city as full of kappa, lilin, eloko, and nox talismans as athtar," Cam said. "Clearly, the demons are still agitated, and the last thing we need is them coming to Geneva." She picked up a small bullet, covered in three anti-lilin symbols. "I want you to stop making single-demon bullets—every bullet that ICDM makes from now on should have all five demonic symbols on it."

"Er..." Arjun began, looking to his left. "Five? We received a report that said the noxes were no longer in existence."

"They shouldn't be, but lots of things shouldn't be happening right now. Can't be too careful," Cam said, rising. "And in the meantime, come up with some kind of massive anti-athtar weapon. I mean something big—something that would take down a whale-sized athtar if such a thing existed. Go poke the military bros outside for their artillery. They tend to have a lot of toys on hand."

"And what will we do with this weapon?" Arjun asked.

"Hopefully, never use it," Cam said, walking to the door. "I expect an update when I come in tomorrow."

CHAPTER FOURTEEN

Lotan frowned and looked at his watch. Jack had arrived home and quickly devoured the dinner Lotan had made in five minutes, before professing he was tired and going off to bed. That was half an hour ago, and Cam had promised Lotan she'd be home shortly after Jack. What could be holding her up?

When she finally pushed open the door, there seemed a heavy weight on her shoulders now, and he forgot any chiding he'd saved up for her tardiness.

"Hey," Lotan said, crossing the room to meet her at the door. "Are you hungry?"

"Yes…but no." She shook her head. "Wouldn't say no to a glass of wine, though."

Lotan happily obliged, uncorking a new bottle and pouring her a heavy glass. She breathed in the scent and took a sip, a smile coming to her lips.

"Do you remember anything about picking wine, or are you getting help?" Cam asked with a sly look.

"Perhaps a little of both," Lotan said. "Come, let's sit on the couch."

He half-expected her to argue, but she sank onto the couch and took another long sip, looking at the glass with a smile. His hand itched to touch hers, perhaps out of habit, or even just run his fingers through her gorgeous hair.

She cast him a sideways glance, almost hesitant. "Have any more memory flashes today?"

"Some," Lotan said. "Nothing earth-shattering. A memory from my boyhood in the jungle. But I received a notification of a rather large bill for an airplane hangar." He paused. "Do I own a jet?"

"You do," Cam said with a little laugh. "Maybe. Not sure how all that works now that you're no longer prince."

"I assume it came out of this very sizable account," Lotan said, pulling out his phone. "I seem to be quite rich."

She just laughed, and it warmed him to hear it. Perhaps some of that hesitation Jack had mentioned was starting to thaw. Lotan's hand itched again, but he kept his distance. Something told him it was still too soon for them to cross that bridge.

Cam cleared her throat. "You said something about dinner? I think I'm hungry now."

Lotan rose to prepare her food and brought it out to the couch. She all but inhaled it, finishing so fast Lotan didn't bother to ask how it tasted, as he doubted she could tell him.

But she sat back, contented, and he refilled her wine glass.

"Do you feel like telling me what's got you so upset?" Lotan asked.

She sighed. "I've been given a task and I'm not quite sure how to go about it. Part of me..." She brought the glass to her lips then thought better of it. "You don't happen to remember anything about the Nullius, do you?"

"Nullius..." Lotan furrowed his brow. "A little, but it's mostly a blur."

"That's kind of the long and short of it," Cam said. "It's the center of the demonic underworld. You were certain that it would help you become human, and..." She nodded approvingly. "You were right, it turned out. But Jack and I went once, and we were attacked by these winged monsters we had no idea were there."

"And I found you in a castle," Lotan said, narrowing his gaze as the memory came back to him. "You almost died."

"I did," Cam said with a small smile. "You saved me."

"Anya did," Lotan said. "She's the one who traveled to the different worlds to get the soil. Freyja helped, too."

But just as soon as the memory started, it ended, fading into the usual hazy white that plagued his memories these days.

"Anyway," Cam said. "I'd like to go back there, but—"

"Why not?" Lotan asked. "We have a portal, don't we? Jack does, right?"

"Besides those monsters, the only thing I've seen there is sand. Last year, when we were trying to find a way to beat Bael, you and Anya took me to the Nullius so I could retrieve some to experiment on, but you said it wasn't useful."

"That's not what it was," Lotan said, furrowing his brow again. He looked down at his hands, a phantom pain skirting up his veins. "It was impossible for any of us to touch."

Cam sat up, her gaze full of curiosity. "Really? So it did retain its powers?"

He nodded. "Perhaps if we retrieved some, it might help you with this task?"

To his satisfaction, she grinned and lifted her wine glass to him. "Lotan, you are brilliant."

"Return to the Nullius?" Jack blanched the next morning when Lotan told him where they were going. "Are you... Do you not remember what that place is?"

"I do. Somewhat." He grinned. "Perhaps you want to accompany us?"

"I'd rather swallow a gallon of seawater again," Jack said with a frown as Cam walked out from the back bedroom, toweling her hair. "What kind of moronic plan are you concocting, Macarro?"

"What... Oh, fuck me, Lotan." Cam pulled the towel down angrily. "Why did you tell Jack?"

"Why not?"

She gestured to him. "Because he was going to overreact. You..." She pursed her lips. "The old Lotan would've known that."

"Good thing he's lost that memory," Jack said, smugly before rising. "Why the hell do you want to go back to that place, Cam? What possible reason could you have?"

Cam paused just long enough for Lotan to realize she was trying to come up with an excuse. Interesting.

"María put me back on anti-demonic weaponry," she said. "I thought the Nullius might offer clues as to why the talismans work the way they do."

Jack crossed his arms over his chest. "And for what purpose would you use this information?"

"I don't know, maybe do something about the demons who keep showing up and killing hundreds of thousands of humans," Cam barked at him.

"And this has nothing to do with Anya?"

"Have you been able to get in touch with her?" Cam asked.

"No," Jack said, and it was his turn to squirm a little. "But I left a message with Diogo. So I expect she'll get a message to me soon that she wants to talk."

"Okay, and in the meantime, we can't just keep counting on her showing up to save the day every time the world descends into chaos." Cam picked up her macuahuitl and strapped it to her back. "We have to be prepared. And the Nullius might give us answers on how to do that better. We won't be long, and we won't be venturing very far. I think we both know what happens when night falls."

Jack narrowed his gaze. "If you aren't back in an *hour*, I'm coming to pull you out."

Lotan had never actually used a portal, not that he could remember, anyway, and it was something of a mind-bending experience. One moment, he was on the streets of Geneva; the next, he was standing in the middle of a plain of white mist. It was hard to even see what was under his feet. But as he shuffled forward, he saw black roots, like a plant had withered and died in this place. Brown leaves crunched under his feet, and a large tree looked to have fallen nearby. Everything he could see, which wasn't much, was dead.

"As I understand it," Cam said, "a demon belu is the one responsible for building their world. Everything that's here comes from them. So when they die or, in your case, become human…" She gestured to the world. "It all goes away."

Lotan gazed at the world with something akin to sadness, like a distant part of him grieved what had become of this place. "Was this a jungle? The one from my memory?"

Cam nodded. "It was called the noxlands."

The noxlands, right. It had been lush and beautiful once, a land of plenty. As a boy, he'd run with wild abandon through the underbrush, getting hopelessly lost until someone found him. And as an adult, he'd walked these lands with friends, reminding himself of his parents and all the things he'd lost.

"Lotan?" Cam touched his cheek, and he realized he was crying. "It's okay."

"I must love you very much, to have given all this up," he whispered, but there was no remorse in it. Even though the exact details eluded him, his heart was absolutely sure the calculus had been the right one.

"Come on," Cam said, softly. "I think the Nullius is this way."

She walked through the mist, and Lotan wasn't sure she knew where she was going, until the mist cleared, revealing a white sandy desert, rolling dunes, and blue skies overhead. The dead, desolate land ended abruptly in a small stream, almost like some invisible force was pushing it, keeping it on one side.

Cam bravely stepped across the stream, casting her gaze to the sky, perhaps looking for those winged creatures. When none came, she turned back to Lotan and pulled a box of plastic bags from the satchel she'd brought along.

"Grab…something from there," she said, handing him a couple. "And let's hope your idea works."

Lotan reached down to the ground in the noxlands, grabbing a handful of dried leaves and colorless sand and dropping it into several bags.

"Lotan?" Cam said, glancing upward again. "I don't want to stay here longer than necessary."

Lotan followed her across the stream to the Nullius, the temperature shift immediate and drastic. Cam was already bent over, shoveling sand into the small bags with her hands.

"What would you like me to do?" Lotan asked.

Cam's gaze lifted again. "Keep your eyes peeled for those things."

"What will they look like?"

She cast him a wry smile. "You'll know them when you see them. Promise."

As they walked further into the desert, Cam dropped small stones from her pocket, leaving them a trail back to the noxlands. Lotan thought it quite clever, as after they crested one dune, the noxlands disappeared behind them and it was virtually impossible to remember where they were.

"Almost done," Cam said, putting another plastic bag back inside the satchel. "I—"

A loud screech echoed from overhead, sending Cam's entire body stick straight. In the distance, a black winged dot swooped from the sky, and it was fast approaching them.

"Time to go," Cam said, turning on her heel and running back the way they'd come. Lotan waited until she was past him to start, making sure his body was between the monster and Cam. But one look to the rear told him the creature would probably make it to them before they could cross to the noxlands.

"Cam," Lotan said. "Give me one of the noxlands bags."

"Lotan, we should—"

But the creature shrieked again and Lotan barked at her, a little harshly, to hand over the bag. She dug inside the satchel and tossed him two bags of the colorless sand and leaves.

Lotan turned to face the creature fully, readying himself with a handful of material.

"Lotan, what are you doing?" Cam barked. "Let's *go!*"

"You go, I'll buy you some time," he said. "I'll be right

behind you."

Cam's gaze widened and Lotan turned just as a large, black clawed hand swiped at him. He managed to evade it, and quickly tossed the handful of material at the creature as it rose for another attack. Almost instantly, the creature let out a blood-curdling cry of pain, careening in the air as it struggled against the dirt before falling to the ground.

"Okay, great, now let's get back!" Cam said, her voice high and terrified.

"Wait." Lotan approached the creature, another handful of noxland material in his hand. "Something's happening to it."

There were splotches where the leaves had landed, but they weren't red. They almost looked like dark human skin amongst the black leather. And the marks on the creature's hands seemed to be transforming them from claws to human-like hands.

Lotan took a breath and tossed the rest of the dirt on the creature, earning another shriek of pain. But the monstrous face slowly faded into one that looked more human.

"Grab his leg, Cam," Lotan said, bending down to take one of the monster's still-clawed feet. It fought weakly, but Lotan was able to drag him forward.

"What are you doing?" Cam asked, still a healthy distance away.

"You wanted samples," Lotan said, dragging him along the dune.

She frowned, tilting her head down at it. "Looks like it's dying."

Lotan managed to pull the creature across the small creek separating the worlds, and the cries of pain increased, like the thing was being killed by the very process of becoming human. But Lotan kept dragging it until it was fully in the other world then set to tossing more noxland matter on top of it.

"Lotan, stop!" Cam said, grabbing his hand and pulling him aside. "It's..."

He looked down, and his heart sank. The thing was now mostly human, but also...dead. Dark eyes stared up at the sky, frozen in time with a grotesquely open jaw. And yet...

"I remember him," Lotan said, kneeling. From where, he had no idea.

"Was he a nox?" Cam asked.

"Yes...no." Lotan shook his head and rose. "I don't know what I was thinking, bringing him across. There was no need to kill him."

"He would've killed us." Cam nudged the body. "Do we take him back to ICDM with us?"

"Might as well," Lotan said with a heavy sigh. "Perhaps he can give us some more answers then."

CHAPTER FIFTEEN

Anya was agitated now, angry that even with all the powers in the world, she still couldn't predict what Bael would do next. Lisbon had been completely underwater by the time she'd noticed, and she'd only been able to save a few—and Jack.

When he'd disappeared under the water, her heart had stopped—and somehow she'd broken through whatever mental block she had about stopping time. As grateful as she was that he was safe, she was also growing annoyed with *him,* too. He needed to do as she said and *stay in Geneva.*

She paused, looking at a rather rough storm off the coast of Thailand, but it seemed natural, so she moved on, scanning the coastlines around the world.

It couldn't have been coincidental that Lisbon was attacked while Jack was there, or that he'd been one of the only humans to avoid the kappa's spell. Then again, if Bael's goal was to kill

Jack, why bother with keeping his wits about him?

The shimmering connection between her and Diogo lit up, and he materialized in front of her, bowing his head in respect.

"My Lady, I've come with a report."

"How bad is it?" Anya asked, her voice quietly echoing in the room.

"The city is still underwater, so it's… They still don't know how many have perished," Diogo said. "Safe to assume it's most of the city."

Anya sank back into the couch, closing her eyes. "Unless the kappas took them all as their demon spawn."

"Yes, we can hope that's the case," Diogo said.

It was the better scenario. Kappas had flooded Geneva a few hundred years before, during a particularly gruesome Demon Spring. There had been no one left in the city then, and she feared the same for Lisbon—a much more densely populated town. At least if they'd been transformed, they'd still be alive.

"Why is he doing this?" Anya asked, more to herself than to Diogo. "And why hasn't he shown himself to the humans yet?"

"In the chaos, I forgot to mention," Diogo said, clearing his throat. "Your Jackson came to visit me."

Anya nodded. That explained his presence in Lisbon, at least. "And?"

"He wanted me to pass on a message. He said to tell you that he was sorry. For what, he didn't explain. And that…" He paused, perhaps remembering the phrase. "That the silent treatment wasn't helping anyone."

Anya blinked; Jack thought she was giving him the silent treatment? She supposed it made sense. She hadn't exactly been very forthcoming about what was happening. Better for him to think her mad at him than the alternative.

"Can you take over keeping an eye on things? I've been scanning the coasts and large lakes, just in case."

"Of course," Diogo said, bowing. "Will you be going to speak with Jack?"

"No," Anya said. "If Bael is drowning whole cities, then I'm going to need some help. The only belu who might is Freyja."

"She hasn't answered any of my messages," Diogo said.

"Then I will fling myself at her feet and beg her to forgive me," Anya said, her gaze serious. "Because if I can't get through to her, she will die."

Anya stood on the edge of Liley and Ath-kur and inched a toe across the border. Very swiftly, the lilin magic shoved her foot back over the line.

"Freyja," Anya called, hoping her voice would travel. "This is ridiculous. We need to talk."

A three-eyed crow landed on the tree nearby and squawked angrily at Anya.

"Tell her it's important."

The crow cawed and ruffled its feathers.

Anya tried another toe, and to her relief, the magic pushing her back didn't come. Anya took a breath and transported herself to the front steps of Freyja's castle, nervously adjusting her shirt and readying herself for whatever she needed to do to talk with Freyja.

She raised a hand to rap on the door, but it swung open quickly.

Freyja's beautiful face was a mask of fury. "What."

"We need to talk. It's a matter of life and death—"

"Is it about your betrayal in Paris?"

Anya exhaled loudly. "I'm so sorry I embarrassed you and questioned your authority in front of the humans." She bowed her head. "It won't happen again."

"Hm." She opened the door wider but didn't invite Anya to come in. "You come here and think your sweet words will sway me? Who am I, Bael?"

Anya jumped, looking behind Freyja and expecting to see the lord of the mountain behind her. But the castle was empty.

"You're on edge," Freyja said, narrowing her eyes.

"Bael is back," Anya said. "Has he come to see you yet?"

"That's impossible." She didn't sound convinced, though. "How?"

"I don't know, exactly, but somehow I managed to bring the Bael from just before his death to this time," Anya said. "It was an accident."

Freyja's lips pursed, and she finally beckoned Anya inside. She gratefully followed, being sure to keep her head down and show deference. Freyja still held a huge amount of animosity toward her, and the wrong thing could get Anya kicked out of these lands.

"So? Why come to me? I can't do anything to fix this," Freyja said.

"No, but..." Anya licked her lips. "I think Bael has killed Biloko and found himself a new belu eloko."

She snorted. "That's not how this works. God chooses the belu."

Anya looked up at Freyja, realizing for the first time that the belu lilin didn't know her own origins. *Really* didn't know.

"Who told you that?" Anya asked.

She started then adjusted her robe. "It doesn't matter who did—"

"It does if it was a liar," Anya replied. "Bael... He's done a lot more than even I knew. You were hand-picked to be the next lilin belu after Bael killed the previous one. How many times he's done that in the past, I have no idea. But I know that it's—"

Freyja's disbelief didn't seem to be budging. "You are clearly speaking nonsense."

"I promise you, I'm not." Anya decided to switch tactics. "The point is you need to keep your guard up. If he shows up, send him away immediately. You can't trust that he won't kill you and find someone who'll be more loyal."

"Oh, that's not fair."

"Freyja—" Anya's magic pulsed out around her, hoping to slow things down. But it was too late. A scream left Anya's mouth as Bael's blade moved through Freyja's neck in one swift movement. The belu lilin's look of surprise was permanently etched onto her face as her head slid to the ground.

Anya's whole body went numb. "You…"

"What?" Bael said, standing over the body and putting his sword away. "You warned her."

Anya advanced on him, snarling as she pulled her own weapon. He held up his hands, laughing at her as if she were merely a plaything as the world around them crumbled in slow motion. But once his back hit the wall, he apparently realized she might actually kill him and transported himself behind her.

"What the *fuck* do you think you're doing?" Anya said, whirling around on him.

"My love, I understand you're mad, but you'll forget about her soon," Bael said, his dismissive tone sending Anya's fury even higher. "Especially when you realize what I have in store for us in the future."

She barked an incredulous laugh. "There is no *us*, Bael. There is you and your murder spree, and I want *no* part of it. You…" She took a step back. "You've killed so many innocents. Biloko. *Tabiko*. Now Freyja. Why?"

"I told you," Bael said, sidestepping her as a piece of the roof fell slowly in the spot where he'd been standing. "There are so many plans afoot for us. You've been angry with me before and you've gotten over it. This will be no different. After all…" He paused with a smile that bode nothing good. "We are immortal. Unlike others."

"Stay away from Jack," Anya barked then regretted it. Bael would certainly use this against her.

His back was to her, walking to the space where a ball of lilin magic was gathering over Freyja's body. "*Speaking* of your very capable human, I have a burning question for you. It concerns Lisbon. And…well, Geneva as well, I suppose. All of the cities where you managed to save all the humans."

She shifted uncomfortably. "I don't know what you're talking about."

"How did you do it?" Bael asked as he gathered the magic in his hand, carefully, as if it were a time bomb.

"Do what?" Anya stammered.

"Stop time. Get through the talismans in Lisbon?" Bael asked. "I can't seem to figure out how."

"The talismans were washed away in Lisbon," Anya said. "But I'm sure you knew that."

He shook his head. "Not enough. Not enough for me to have done anything. Believe me, I tried. You, on the other hand…" He exhaled. "You stopped time *completely*. I want to know how."

Anya opened her mouth, for the first time realizing that Bael was asking her because *he couldn't do it himself.* In his thousands of years on this earth, he'd never managed to stop time the way she had. And that he was asking her about it meant it bothered him. Meant she could potentially hurt him—*kill him*—when time was stopped.

The problem was, she didn't quite understand when and why it happened herself.

"I guess it's mine to know and yours to guess," she replied, lifting her chin.

He turned to her, his eyes flashing with danger, and her first instinct was to cower in fear, to let apologies bubble from her lips. But then she remembered he couldn't physically hurt her anymore. Emotionally, though…that was another story.

He left the lilin magic suspended in the air and walked over to her, his fury plain on his face.

"Is that how you want to play this game, my love?"

"I'm not your love," Anya said, her voice barely above a whisper. "And the only game I want to play is the one where you tell me what you're planning."

"I'll tell you if you tell me, Anat," Bael said in a sing-song voice, but the danger was clear in his gaze.

"My name is Anya," she replied, feeling her strength grow.

"That's the name the human gave you."

"The name I took for myself the day I decided I didn't want you anymore," she replied. "That feeling hasn't changed, Bael. But if you *ever* loved me like you say you do, you'll stop this senseless massacre. You will allow me to send you back to the time you came from and let things return to normal."

"Don't you understand?" Bael said with a smile. "With this lilin magic, I have three demon belus under my control once more. They will do what I ask, or I will replace them with someone who will." He shook his head. "You know, my mistake has been to let them live in their own lands. Now I've got a much better solution."

"Then where do you keep them?" she asked, betting that his ego and need to show off would overpower his common sense.

But she was disappointed. "What is it that you said to me? That's for me to know, and you to guess?" He took a step backward. "Dearest *Anya*, you are very new to this game, and I have been playing it for more years than you could even imagine."

He leaned in and pressed his lips to her cheek, and it took everything in her not to slap him away.

"As far as what I'm planning, you have only seen the beginning. Until we meet again, my love."

His words died on the wind as he disappeared, taking the magic with him.

Time sped forward, and the crumbling of the castle continued in earnest, but Anya didn't move to leave. She plodded over to Freyja's body and knelt beside it, bowing her head in silent prayer, asking forgiveness. That she'd brought this evil on the world, that she hadn't been able to protect her oldest friend from Bael.

Her sadness turned to rage. This wasn't her fault. This was Bael—it always was. And the sooner she dealt with him, the sooner this reign of terror would end.

CHAPTER SIXTEEN

"Hey, Jackie, it's Mom. I just wanted to let you know that we've scheduled Frank's funeral for tomorrow afternoon. Please come home if you can. We miss you. Please let Cam know, too."

Jack listened to the voicemail with a frown. He'd just gone to pick up his second new phone in as many weeks, and this was the only notification there.

He still hadn't quite gotten around to accepting that his grandfather was gone; it felt more like Frank was just out of town, and Jack was crashing at his apartment until he returned. It was also odd to think that in some parts of the world, there were still things like funerals going on. For Jack, it had been one crisis after another, but for those blissfully out of the demonic fighting activity, there was time to plan funerals.

Jack didn't want to go, but he knew he had to. He wasn't looking forward to facing his parents, their questions about what was going on with Anya—especially George, who was privy to all the details. The scene would be oddly reminiscent of Sara's funeral, too.

He rolled out of bed and walked into the living room, but Cam and Lotan had already left. They'd returned from the Underworld late last night, telling Jack they'd had to make a pit stop at the ICDM headquarters tent with the samples they'd collected. Cam wouldn't specify what kind of samples they'd taken, but Jack was hoping Lotan's penchant for speaking freely would spill the truth.

He guessed they were back at headquarters, so he showered and shaved, and mentally calculated when he'd have to leave to get to Charleston, six hours behind Geneva. He would have most of the day to waste—assuming no more demonic attacks.

Shrugging on his ICDM jacket, he left the apartment and walked the fifteen minutes to ICDM headquarters. To his eyes, the demolition had been mostly completed on the former building, but he was sure there was plenty more to do. The work had been nonstop all day and night. ICDM was ready to heal this blemish on their security and forget the shame of how they'd failed to protect themselves.

Jack walked to the headquarters tent. Neither Cam nor Lotan were there, but one of the aides said she was in the tent out the back flap. Jack followed their directions, walking out the back to another, smaller tent. Like the headquarters tent, there were two armed guards in front. But unlike the headquarters tent, they moved to block Jack's entry.

"I'm sorry, but you aren't authorized," the guard said.

Jack frowned. What could Cam be doing that she wasn't telling him about? "Can you tell Agent Macarro that I'm here to see her?"

"I'm not your messenger boy."

Jack cleared his throat. "Considering I almost drowned yesterday and lost my phone, you might do me this favor. Please."

The guard rolled his eyes but ducked inside the tent for a moment before returning. He said nothing to Jack nor would he make eye contact. Jack just snorted and turned to give them some distance. After a moment, Cam appeared, and Jack waved her over.

"Hey," Cam said. "Sorry about that. What's up?"

"What are you doing in there?" Jack asked. "And why am I not allowed inside?"

"Because it's ICDM bullshit," Cam said with a wave of her hand. "Need to know only."

"Then I need to know."

"Trust me, you don't. It's boring as hell in there."

Jack wasn't convinced. "So why is Lotan in there?"

"Because he went with me to the Nullius, and he has valuable insight to provide," Cam said, lowering her voice. "What's up your butt today?"

He sighed. "Mom called. Frank's funeral is in a couple hours."

She softened, her hand landing on his arm, but she said

nothing.

"Will you go with me?" Jack asked.

"Of course," she replied with a friendly smile. "You know I wouldn't miss it. You might want to let María know, too. I know she would want to be there."

Jack would've rather kept it family only, but Frank wasn't just his. He'd been a member of the Council for fifteen years and an aide for most of his career.

"I think I might head over there now," Jack said. "If you want to come."

Cam shook her head, sadly. "I have to finish up the report here. But we'll be there as soon as we can. Promise."

Jack pointed the portal at the drop site to his parents' house in Charleston and stepped through, marveling at the environmental change. The air was muggy and wet in the early hours of the morning, but the light in the kitchen was already on. His mother probably hadn't slept at all.

He maneuvered around to the kitchen, knocking over the pig and grabbing the key. But before he could use it, the door opened, revealing his mom's smiling face.

"I thought I heard you," she said, pulling him into the sort of hug that told him she'd been more worried about him than she'd let on. Jack closed his eyes and leaned into it, holding her nearly as tightly.

"It's good to see you," he said.

"C'mon, I'll put on a pot of grits for you," she said, resting her hand on his lower back and guiding him inside. "Coffee?"

"Sounds great."

Jack sat at the kitchen table while his mother fussed and fretted, grabbing a stock pot more often used for a low country boil.

"Mom, I'm not starving," Jack said with a small laugh.

"You aren't the only one I'm cooking for, son," Karen said, shaking her wooden spoon at him. "Ana and Marco are upstairs, and Marco's been up at the crack of dawn lately."

Jack straightened, a smile coming to his face. "Cam's parents are here?"

"Of course. They flew in yesterday afternoon." She smiled, but it was a little sad. "We also have others from the US Council. After all, we have the bedrooms for it." She glanced at him. "I assume you'll be going home this evening? I already gave away your bed."

Jack nodded. "Things have settled for the moment, but who knows when the demons will strike again?"

She tipped the salt cellar into the large stockpot, her lips pursed in thought. "And you have to be there when they do?"

"It's my job, Mom," Jack said.

She turned to him, her gaze full of concern. "It doesn't have to be. Your father tells me they're gathering more ICDM agents from all over the world to form a strike team. You can just…sit the next couple out."

"But if I do, Anya won't show up," Jack said, a little offhandedly, but it was somewhat true. She seemed to appear just in the nick of time.

"Your father…has opinions about her, Jackie," Karen said, walking to the table to sit down. "I wouldn't mention her unless you want to hear them." She reached across the table. "I know you care for her."

"I don't know what to think, Mom. She says one thing, she does another, then she does another. It's like I'm getting ten percent of the story, and we're all left to fill in the blanks. Cam and ICDM are defaulting to the worst possible solution, and I'm just…" He sat back in the chair. "I'm just trying to find the truth."

Karen bit her lip, squeezing his hand. "You will get there, Jackie. But if you ask me, that gut of yours has never steered you wrong before. You know what's right. You always have."

"Thanks, Mom," Jack said.

Jack borrowed an extra black suit from his father's collection, finding the fit a little large, but it would do in a pinch. He hadn't really looked at himself in a mirror in a long time, and the similarities between himself and his father were starting to become more pronounced.

He glanced at the clock; the ceremony would begin at two, but visitation would begin around ten, accounting for the hundreds of people who were expected to attend. Jack rode with Karen to the ICDM Charleston office, where the funeral would be taking place in the atrium. Jack was grateful the beautiful glass building hadn't been destroyed by the demons, though

Karen told him brusquely that they'd tried.

"We were lucky here," she said. "They didn't hit us as hard as other places."

"What protections are here?"

"Enough, Jackie," Karen said, reaching across to pat his hand. "Today, you don't have to worry about any of that. Just be the grieving grandson. You owe yourself that much." She glanced at him. "Don't do what you did with Sara."

"Bottle up my emotions and deal with them in unhealthy ways?" Jack asked with a wry smile. "Don't worry, Mom."

"I always worry."

The back of her car was already laden with flowers, so Jack helped her carry those inside to waiting aides, all dressed in black. Some had red-rimmed eyes and gripped his arm as they offered their condolences to Jack, while others seemed sad enough but had probably never met the man.

"He was just the most amazing boss," the woman Jack recognized as one of his long-time aides said, dabbing the corners of her eyes with her already blotted handkerchief. "He thought the world of you, too. Had your photo on his desk, you know."

Jack smiled and glanced into the large conference room that had been cleared out. "Is he in there?"

She nodded, patting his arm. "If you want a moment alone, now would be the time. Things will get a bit more hectic when everyone arrives."

Jack didn't particularly want a moment alone, but Frank's

aide practically guided him to the doors and shoved him inside. There, he was faced with a brightly lit room, wall-to-wall with flowers that gave off a sickly-sweet aroma. Frank's awards and photos of him with presidents and dignitaries were interspersed, showcasing the life of a man who'd lived it well. Jack's gaze lingered on the photo of Frank and Jack's grandmother on their wedding day. They both looked unbelievably young and happy.

In the center of the honors and tributes was the man himself, lying in a casket with the top half open, and an American flag draped over half of it. The ICDM flag and US Division flags stood on either side.

Jack walked up to the casket, looking at the peaceful face of his grandfather and barely recognizing him. Frank was always full of expression and life. Seeing him like this was almost an affront to the life he'd lived, and irrational anger rose in Jack's chest at the indignity of it all.

A prickle of energy lifted the hair on the back of his neck and the conversations around him disappeared, as did the sound of the air conditioner. He didn't have to turn to know who'd arrived at his side, whose hand had slipped into his, and whose cheek rested on his shoulder.

"I'm sorry," Anya whispered. "He was a good man. I always liked him."

Jack exhaled. He could've torn his hand away, to have demanded that she fuck off after what she'd done. But there was sincere hurt in her gaze, and despite his confusion, he'd missed her presence. She was the only one he'd wanted by his side today and he didn't want her to go just yet.

"Thank you," Jack whispered. "Thank you for coming."

"I knew..." She released a shaky breath. "I didn't want you to be alone."

"How are you doing this?" Jack asked. "There's anti-athtar talismans everywhere."

"You needed me," Anya said with a shrug. "And I came."

Something inside broke free and tears slid down his cheeks. It wasn't just grief; it was relief. Anya could move heaven and earth if she wanted to—and she only wanted to for him. Whether it was in Geneva, when he was outgunned, or standing at the casket of his beloved grandfather, she would always be there for him. And damn it all if he didn't feel the same.

"I miss you," he whispered. "Come home to me."

She bit her lip and tightened her hold on his hand. "Soon. I hope." She sighed softly. "I miss you, too, Jack. More than you know."

He turned to her, surprised to see her eyes glassy with unshed tears. "Then tell me the truth. What's going on?"

She opened her mouth, as if ready to tell him everything, but her gaze turned to the side, and she quickly wiped her eyes. A moment later, Diogo appeared, his gaze full of concern as he bowed.

"A thousand apologies for the interruption—"

"Out with it," Anya barked, her voice still thick.

"I'm afraid it's Paris." He straightened, looking at Jack nervously. "And it's as we feared, I'm sorry to say."

"Fuck," Anya swore, releasing Jack and looking to him. "I'm so sorry. I have to go."

"Anya, wait." Jack grabbed her hand again. "Please, give me something to tell ICDM. They suspect *you're* the one causing all these problems."

She blanched as if she'd never heard anything so ridiculous in her life. "I'm the one *stopping* this, Jack."

"Then who—"

But she was gone, and the din of conversation returned as time restarted. Jack was left with more questions than answers, and the smallest bit of vindication that Anya seemed surprised to hear she was being suspected of killing the very humans she was saving.

"Jackie?" His mom was calling from the other end of the room. "The guests are starting to arrive. Can you come help me and your father greet them?"

He nodded and looked at Frank, wishing for one more grandfatherly chat, for guidance. But Frank just lay there, a grotesque shell of the man he'd been, and Jack was once again alone.

CHAPTER SEVENTEEN

Cam smoothed the black dress she'd picked up and tapped her foot as she rode with María in an ICDM SUV to the drop site. There, they'd pick up the portal to Charleston, where there would be a convoy to take them to ICDM headquarters. The visitation had already begun, but considering the number of people arriving, it would take a while to even get inside. Cam had intentionally delayed her arrival, hoping to blend in with the crowd as much as possible.

"Stop fidgeting," María said beside her. "What can you have to be nervous about?"

María knew damn well why Cam was fidgeting. Although she'd told Lotan he didn't have to go, he *insisted* on joining them, even managing to find a suit that made him look like a male model.

It wasn't just bringing him that was making Cam nervous, it

was who else would be at the funeral. Namely, her parents, who she'd successfully kept from meeting her mysterious boyfriend for the past year. And now all those carefully executed excuses were for naught. This was happening and Cam just hoped the sadness of the day would overpower any awkwardness.

The car arrived at the portal site and María stepped out, gazing at the portal with a judgmental stare.

"You've never taken one of these before, have you?" Cam asked.

María gave her a once-over then strode toward the portal and stepped through without hesitating. Cam sighed as Lotan stood next to her. She half-expected him to take her hand, but he remained distant.

"Shall we?" he asked.

Cam didn't really want to, but with Lotan in tow, she stepped through the portal, landing in Charleston in the middle of the afternoon.

This time, she opted for a different car than María, sitting in the back of a smaller car driven by one of the ICDM agents— perhaps his personal vehicle.

"Agent Macarro," she introduced herself. "And..."

"Levi Lobo," he said then added, quieter, "It's the name on all my bank accounts."

Also the name he'd introduced himself with all those months ago, Cam thought with a small laugh. She settled in next to Lotan, waiting for him to rest his hand on her knee, the way he'd done a thousand times before. She found herself craving not just his touch, but the familiarity with which he'd place his hands on her body.

ICDM loomed in the distance, and Lotan craned his neck. "Looks like a beautiful building."

"It is," Cam said, though her pulse quickened as the car pulled into the security checkpoint queue. "Look, so I should probably tell you that my parents are going to be here. And you haven't exactly…met them yet."

Lotan frowned. "Why not?"

Because I never thought it would come up. "We just couldn't make it work out. Schedules and all that."

"You're a terrible liar," he said, though he wore a smile. "Don't worry. I'll be my usual charming self."

And that was the concern—he *wasn't* himself. But she couldn't do anything about it as the car pulled into the roundabout, and Lotan opened the door, sliding out and taking her with him. She adjusted her skirt once more, looking at the building she'd been so fond of her entire life. Beyond the glass front, there was a large crowd of black-clad mourners milling around, eating hors d'oeuvres and drinking from small plastic cups.

Once inside, she recognized a fair number of people, but she kept her head down, hoping none of them recognized the man leading her through the crowd—and that she could avoid seeing her parents.

"There you two are," Jack said, but there was something in his voice that set Cam on edge.

"What's wrong?" Cam asked.

He glanced at his parents. "Not here. We need to talk somewhere private."

"Cam!" Karen turned to her and her eyes lit up. "Oh, sweetheart, it is so nice to see you. And who is this handsome man?" George must not have told his wife about Lotan.

"Levi," Lotan said, flashing her a dazzling smile. "You must be Jack's mother—though I find that hard to believe. You barely look older than thirty."

Karen tittered, and Jack scowled as her cheeks reddened. "Cam, you certainly have found yourself a charmer, haven't you?"

"He's super charming," Jack said, nudging his father as Karen turned to greet another guest. "Dad, Cam's here."

George Grenard turned and as much as his smile widened when he saw Cam, his face darkened when he saw Lotan. He, clearly, knew who he was. And didn't quite approve.

"Cam, I'm glad you could make it," he said, before looking at Lotan. "And you've brought…him, I see."

George's disapproval felt something like her own father's, and she shifted from one foot to the other under his gaze. Finally, Jack elbowed him slightly and gave him a swift shake of the head, and George nodded again.

"Please, eat something and mingle. Your parents are somewhere around here, too. I know they're eager to see…you."

"Thanks," Cam said, wishing she could slide away from George by slipping through the cracks in the tile floor.

"Dad, I need to talk with Cam about something," Jack said. "I'll be right back."

He didn't give George a chance to respond, taking Cam's other hand and walking her away from the receiving line.

"That sucked," Cam said.

"He's in a mood," Jack replied. "Sorry about him, Lotan."

"I didn't notice a thing," Lotan said with a cheery grin.

Before they could find a corner, another voice called Cam, and she closed her eyes, bracing herself. But when she turned around to face her parents, the overwhelming feeling was one of relief. Ana was thin and willowy like Sara had been, and Marco was stockier, with short black hair that had been in the same style for as long as Cam could remember. Now, however, there were flecks of gray in it, and crow's feet around his eyes that she hadn't noticed when she'd been home for Christmas.

"Hey, Mama, Papa," Cam said, dropping both Jack and Lotan's hands to walk into her mother's open arms.

"Mija," Ana said, enveloping Cam into the sort of hug that only came from a mother. She kissed Cam's forehead and whispered, "I'm so glad to see you."

"Me, too," Cam said. "I'm sorry I haven't called."

"You've been busy," Marco said as Ana released Cam and she fell into her father's arms. His were strong and warm, and Cam breathed in his cologne deeply, the sensation almost bringing tears of joy to her eyes. It was easy to forget why she'd been so willing to keep her distance.

Marco's chest rumbled under Cam's cheek. "And this must

be your Lotan, hm?"

Oh yeah, that was why.

"Levi," Cam said. "I don't necessarily want everyone to know."

"Oh, honey, everyone knows," Ana said, waving her off as she approached Jack and Lotan. "At least, everyone who counts. Jack, mi querido hijo, it's so wonderful to see you." She took his hand and kissed it gently. "I'm so sorry about your grandfather. He was a special man, and he loved you very, *very* much."

"Thank you," Jack said. "I'm glad you could be here. I hope you and my mom have had a chance to catch up."

"It's been wonderful staying there," Ana said, dropping his hand in favor of facing Lotan. "And now. As for you."

She turned to size up Lotan, and for the first time, Lotan looked nervous. Then again, Cam recognized her mother's scrutinizing stare.

"Come here, mijo," Ana said. "Let me look at the man who's stolen my daughter's heart."

Cam exhaled nervously as Lotan approached her mother, and her mother made a good show of inspecting him from head to toe.

"Why are you so nervous, mija?" Marco asked, sliding a strong hand over her shoulder and squeezing. "It's not as if he's some sort of former demon prince who you hid from us while carrying on a secret relationship that could've effectively ended the career you worked so hard to build."

"I didn't hide him," Cam muttered, her face beginning to

burn. "And, as for that career..."

Marco turned to her, expectation clear on his face.

"Maybe it's not what I want anymore," Cam finished lamely.

Marco made a noise that conveyed nothing of his opinion, but Ana turned and nodded to Cam with something like approval.

"He's not bad to look at," Ana said with an appraising smile. "Mama was right."

"As much as I hate to break this up," Jack said, taking the opportunity in the awkward silence. "I really need to have a quick chat with Cam alone."

And before either of them could argue, Jack dragged Cam away.

"That went somehow as horribly as I thought and also better," Cam said, following Jack into a quiet corner. "How is that possible?"

"Cam, Anya showed up," Jack said, turning to face her and stopping all thoughts about Lotan and her parents.

"What? Where?"

"Here, five minutes ago," Jack said.

"That's—"

"But," Jack said, waving her off, "Diogo showed up and we were interrupted. I don't know exactly what he was talking about. He said 'it's as we feared' and 'Paris' and that seemed to really unnerve her before she disappeared."

"What does that even mean? What does Anya have to fear?"

She shook her head. "Did you tell ICDM?"

"Tell them what?" Jack said, looking a little defensive.

"Tell them she showed up and is doing...something," Cam said. "Seems like that's something they'd want to know, considering she's their prime suspect. Maybe they should be on high alert with cities around the world."

"They already are," Jack said. "I'm not going to report on every single sighting."

"And why not?"

"Because..." Jack sighed. "Look, I think..." But he didn't seem to be able to find his words. "She told me she had nothing to do with any of this."

"And you believed her?"

"She looked downright indignant when I told her ICDM suspected her," Jack replied.

"Well, guilt speaks," Cam said.

"She's not guilty, Cam. She's... Whatever's going on, I don't know if she knows. Or if she does, she's trying to put a stop to it."

Cam sighed. Always the same song and dance with him. "What else did she say?" She nudged him. "What aren't you telling me?"

"She came because she didn't want me to be alone today," Jack said. "Because she knew I was hurting. I can't imagine she'd feel that way if she'd gone off the deep end."

"Bael professed his love to Anya all the time," Cam said. "Didn't mean it was real."

"This was real, Cam," Jack said. "Because I think I've figured out why she's able to overpower the talismans." He looked at her, his gaze steely. "And this isn't something you can share, do you understand?"

"Jack—"

"I'm serious. Promise me."

She exhaled loudly. "Fine. I won't share it unless you die or are kidnapped or something like that."

"I think..." Jack stared off into the distance. "I think it has something to do with me. When I'm in danger or, like today—with her wanting to be here for me. She's somehow able to find the power to overcome this anti-demon magic."

Cam furrowed her brow. "That does make sense. We noted that she was able to actually *stop* time, versus just slow it, in Geneva."

"I can't imagine she'd have that kind of willpower unless..." He smiled. "Unless she really loved me."

This wasn't the direction Cam wanted Jack's mind to go, but she couldn't deny it was useful intel. At the same time, she worried—Jack used to be the cautious one, and she'd been the one goading him to open himself to Anya. Now the situation was reversed, and Cam didn't know if Jack would be able to be objective.

Their conversation was cut short by the announcement that the funeral was about to begin. Jack ran his hand over his face and sighed loudly.

"I guess I should get back there," Jack said. "I'm not looking forward to this."

"Well, good news, partner," she threaded her arm through his, "you aren't going in there alone."

CHAPTER EIGHTEEN

"So."

Lotan was sure that in the life he barely remembered, he'd faced down enemies who wanted him dead. He was sure that in those moments, he'd been brave and fearless, wielding weapons like a champion. But faced with his love's judgmental parents and their appraising stares, he found himself quite without that courage that he was sure he possessed.

"I would love to tell you whatever you want to know," Lotan said, before adding, "Within my current ability, of course."

"George told me you'd lost your memories," Marco said. "So how is it you know how to speak?"

Lotan opened and closed his mouth; he hadn't considered that question yet. "English was the language first spoken to me when I awoke, so perhaps that has something to do with it. I understand I'm something of an anomaly in demonic reversions, seeing as I was never human to begin with."

"What do you remember?" Ana asked.

"I remember my parents," Lotan said. "I remember certain events shortly before my memory lapse. The attack on Geneva, for example." He didn't feel like dwelling on that. "I know I like to cook, but context tells me I wasn't very good at it. And, of course, I remember Cam."

"Do you think you'll get your full memory back?" Ana asked. "And if you do, what then?"

"I don't know," Lotan said. "I hope I regain enough of it to be of use to this world in some way. I don't feel as if I've been very helpful to Cam and Jack."

"You saved her life on many occasions," Ana replied. "Perhaps it's fine for you to take a backseat and let her do the saving for once."

Lotan smiled. "I feel that's not in my nature. Where Cam goes, especially if it's into danger, I want to go with her."

"And, what, exactly, are your plans for Cam?" Marco asked.

Lotan furrowed his brow. "In what way?"

"My husband is asking if you plan to marry her," Ana asked, elbowing him. "Without much tact, I'm afraid."

"I would very much like to marry her," Lotan said with a smile. "Though I confess I don't exactly remember what that means. But I do recall that it was in my plans."

Ana just laughed and crossed the space to hug him. Like Cam, she only came up to his shoulder. "You are absolutely wonderful, Lotan."

An aide announced to the mingling crowd that the funeral ceremony would begin shortly. Ana, still holding onto Lotan's arm, led him into the large room with an open casket at the front. Cam was already seated in the second row, so Lotan and her parents joined her on either side. She gave him a grim thumbs up, and he returned it with a cheery smile.

"Is everything okay with Jack?" he whispered.

"Yes and no," Cam replied, glancing at her parents. "How did everything go with them?"

"They're wonderful. Terrifying, but wonderful." He nudged her. "I see where you get it." He leaned in closer. "What does it mean to marry someone?"

Cam whispered under her breath and glanced at the ceiling. "I'll explain later."

A woman came to the podium to make some quick announcements, and to ask everyone to take their seats. A few moments after the crowd settled, the doors opened, Jack and his parents walked in, and those gathered rose. Jack held his hands behind his back as he followed his mother and father, who were nodding and thanking those they recognized on the way up.

They sat in the pew directly in front of Lotan and Cam, and Jack turned to smile at them before taking his seat on the outside of the row.

Karen's shoulders shook when the casket was closed, and Jack looped an arm around her, pulling her close to him.

Cam slid her arm through Lotan's and held his hand as the

ceremony began. There were a few prayers, during which Lotan followed Cam's lead and bowed his head. These were followed by some discussion of Frank's lengthy career and accomplishments, an anecdote about his first stint as the Councilman that earned a few titters from the audience, and some more somber stories, especially about Jack's grandmother. And Lotan remembered...

"Mama and Papa are...dead?" The words made little sense in his own mind. "What does that mean?"

"It means, boy, that they are..." Yaotl's eyes were sad, the first time Lotan had seen such an emotion on his mentor's face. "They will not be coming home."

Lotan didn't understand what was going on, only that the two woven bags that the noxes carried were supposedly his parents. Yaotl had wanted him to witness their bodies, but Oce and others had been vehemently opposed to it. Lotan had sat in the corner while they screamed at one another, unable to speak for himself because he didn't understand it.

The noxes had placed the bags on two daises in front of the castle to allow all the noxes to pay their respects. All day and night, a nox stood guard over their bodies, many in tears as they mourned their beloved belus. One night, though, the guard stepped away to relieve himself, and Lotan took his chance.

He snuck up to the daises, willing to prove to himself that these bodies were not his parents. This was some kind of game Yaotl and the others were playing on him. It was impossible for a person to have been so alive and then suddenly not.

Barely breathing, he approached the bag on the left and untied the top. His heart seized as his mother's hair spilled out then—

"Lotan?" Cam asked, her fingertips wiping away the tear. "Are you all right?"

"Yes," Lotan said, smiling down at her. "Just remembering."

She nudged him softly. "Remembering what?"

"The day we said goodbye to my parents," he said, looking ahead at the casket. "It was nothing like this, and yet..." He swallowed. "The feelings are the same."

Her small, warm hand slid into his and it was as familiar as coming home. He closed his fingers around hers, bringing the knuckles to his lips and earning a soft sigh from her. They hadn't as much as bumped elbows recently, but this—this was natural. So natural he wondered why he hadn't been doing it all along.

The officiant at the front of the room then asked if the Grenard family would like to come up and say a few words. But instead of Jack's father, Jack rose, patting his mother on the shoulder and whispering something to them. They nodded solemnly as a hushed murmur descended on the room.

"I didn't think Jack would want to speak," Cam replied with a frown. "I hope he's up for this."

Jack approached the podium and cleared his throat, looking out at the crowd. For a moment, Lotan worried Cam might be right, that he wasn't ready, but a calm, sad smile spread over his lips.

"Those of you who've known me a while, which I think includes most of you," Jack chuckled wryly, "know that when I was younger, I was very eager to let everyone know who my grandfather was. But what started as youthful coattail-riding eventually became something much deeper.

"My grandfather was the sort of person I think all of us aspire to be," Jack said. "No matter what mess I got myself into, he was there to help me navigate my way back. And now that he's gone…" His eyes grew distant. "Now that he's gone, I'm not quite sure I'm ready to steer the ship back on my own. But that's the thing about life. Sometimes we have to follow our own gut and do what we know is right, even if everyone thinks it's wrong."

Cam snorted. "Well, now he's just being ridiculous."

"Frank taught me that, and I think that's why we all loved him so much. It wasn't about politics or what would get him promoted—it was about helping the most people, making the world a better place. I—"

Jack's gaze narrowed as the doors in the back opened. Lotan and Cam turned as an ICDM agent hurried into the event, his head downturned but his pace telling.

"Shit," Cam muttered, looking at Jack and nodding. "I think we're going to find out what Anya left for." She stood then shifted past her confused parents to meet the agent.

Jack cleared his throat. "A-Anyway, on behalf of my parents, I wanted to thank everyone for coming today. Frank would've been very displeased to see such a fuss made over him, but I know, deep in his heart, he appreciated every one of you." He nodded. "Thank you."

"What's going on?" Marco asked Lotan.

"Your guess is as good as mine," he replied, rising. "But I will go find out."

—⁂—

Lotan followed Jack and Cam out the back, finding them in conversation with the aide who'd interrupted.

"What's going on?" Lotan asked.

"Attack in Paris," Cam said, casting a look at Jack. "Lilins. So now all three demon races are active in the human world again."

"We don't know these were Underworld demons," Jack replied.

"Doroteia was, and she nearly drowned you in Lisbon. You have to start looking at this objectively," Cam barked.

"We don't have time to argue," Jack said. "I already sent a message to the headquarters team in Geneva, so I hope they're on it, but they've got something of a skeleton crew with most of ICDM here."

Cam chewed her lip. "You don't think…it was intentional, do you?"

"What do you mean?"

"Striking during the funeral?" Cam asked. "When they knew we'd be distracted?"

"If it was, it had nothing to do with Anya," Jack said. "And on that point, you can't budge me. She's not a great liar, Cam— and I trust my gut on this."

His eyes were on fire, and even she had to admit that Anya's past track record with hiding the truth wasn't great. But that didn't change the facts—and the athtar demon now knew she was the prime suspect.

"If she's innocent, I welcome her to clear her name," Cam said. "But until then—"

"Are you coming with me to Paris or not?" Jack asked, annoyed.

"Of course," Cam said.

"I'm coming with you," Lotan said.

"No way," Cam snapped. "You stay here where it's safe. Just hang out with my parents at Jack's house until we get back."

"If you're going where it isn't safe, I'm going where it isn't safe," Lotan replied.

"Absolutely not." She leaned in toward him, and Lotan thought she might sock him. "You barely even remember how to hold a sword. I don't want you caught up in this. I can take care of myself, but I can't take care of us both. Now *stay here.*"

And with that, she and Jack dashed out the door, leaving Lotan by himself.

CHAPTER NINETEEN

Bael, master of the Underworld, Lord of the Mountain, emperor of all he surveyed, the original athtar demon, was inching closer to the final act in his plan. A narrative was forming in the minds of humanity about Anat and her participation in the most devastating attacks on humanity in modern history. And soon, her entire house of cards would fall —and she would be his once more. Everything was going according to plan.

Everything, of course, except for that pesky human Jackson Grenard. He was steadfastly resistant to Bael's mounting evidence, convinced *he* knew Anat in ways only Bael did. Anat, predictably, would not tell her human the absolute truth, but the small seeds of doubt weren't enough to break his will.

Still, he'd been helpful. Bael had managed to infiltrate that little display of mourning and listen to his conversations with his friend. The human seemed to think Anat's attention toward him was tied with her ability to outmaneuver the talismans. It was outlandish, really, that he thought any human could hold her attention when she'd spent millennia in the sunlight of Bael's affections.

And yet, there *was* a connection. Bael had gone to watch her stop time, and at each instance, that obnoxious human had been the one in danger—usually along with one of his friends.

It would be simpler to dispose of him, but Bael didn't want to risk Anat's ire just yet. He hadn't yet understood what it meant for his own powers when she stopped time. Only one of them could maintain control over the time river to slow it, but Bael had a suspicion that if she managed to stop it completely, she could wrench control from him.

So Bael kept his distance. Soon, the evidence of Anat's betrayal of humanity would be overwhelming, and the humans would have to take action. Once Bael's final act began, Anat wouldn't be able to *look* at the human, let alone stop the flow of time for him.

For now, Bael would sit back and watch the show in Paris.

CHAPTER TWENTY

Anya watched helplessly as Paris was overrun by thousands of lilins. Freyja had had no child to carry on her magic, so every lilin in the world would've lost theirs at the moment of her death. But Bael had worked quickly, it seemed, and in complete secrecy.

When Anya walked into the city, Bael's magic already had a tight grip on the time river, rendering Anya's magic useless. But it wasn't as if he was trying to hide this attack; time had only slowed a nanosecond.

Anya's sword hung limply in her hand, unsure what to do first. The lilin magic was thick on the air and the humans affected by it were a grotesque mix of terrified and orgasmic. It was hard to know which of the crowd was generating the magic and which were simply suckered by it. Not only that, but most of those pumping out magic had to be neophytes themselves, only a week or two transformed and still high on the new demon thrill. Killing them wasn't necessarily the best option, either. She doubted any of them had any say in their transformation.

My love, you are very new to this game, and I have been playing it for more years than you could even imagine.

Understatement of the century.

Pulling her other sword off her back, she walked up to the first group of lilins, advancing on a small huddle of humans who were simultaneously terrified and horny.

"Back off," Anya said. "The belu athtar commands it."

"We don't take orders from the lesser athtar," a tall woman said, her eyes fluttering with the high of having recently spawned. "You will soon be dead, and this world will belong to us."

Anya snorted. "The only lesser being is you, lilin. Now do as I say, or—"

But they turned their backs on her and their focus back to the humans, who hadn't taken the hint and run. Before Anya could react, the lilins had grabbed their victims and pressed their mouths against them.

"Fuck me," Anya said, turning to the rest of the chaos. But it all seemed to be the same. Bael had seemingly directed the lilins to spawn first, and if the humans weren't cooperating, then to pump them full of magic until they did. That made it harder for Anya to start hacking. It was literally thousands against one, and though Anya was somewhat indefatigable, soon, even she would find herself overwhelmed.

A shot rang out behind her, and she turned as a convoy of human tanks rolled into the city. But as the tanks drew closer, and the accompanying soldiers hopped out, Anya's heart sank. These soldiers didn't even have anti-demonic weapons, just regular human guns—they weren't ICDM, just the regular human military. Their bullets struck the lilins but didn't slow them any. And before too long, the human soldiers were surrounded—and began stripping their clothes off.

"Shit," Anya said, sticking her swords back in their holsters and dashing toward them. But before she could get very far, a wall of demons blocked her path, pumping their miasma at Anya and advancing.

Anya pulled her swords again and licked her lips. "Stand down, lilins. I don't want to kill you, but I will."

The lilins hissed at her, sending more flowery scent in Anya's direction and tickling her nose. Anya wouldn't get suckered by it, but it was slightly obnoxious—and the wall of lilins was thick. By now three soldiers had been transformed, and the others were starting to sway.

"Fine," Anya said, twirling her sword in her hand and running toward the lilins, praying for forgiveness as she went. She hacked and sliced but stopped short as a lilin wearing a soldier's uniform reached for her.

"What's wrong? Don't want to kill a poor, pitiful soldier?" she asked, her eyes still white with newly transformed power.

"Goddamnit," she whispered, stepping back and rushing away, looking for the demon who'd transformed the soldier, but that demon was long gone. The human-turned-lilin launched herself onto Anya's back, pressing the gun to Anya's temple.

"Let's see how you like it, athtar."

"That won't work on me," Anya growled, elbowing the human-turned-lilin roughly but unable to break her grip.

Another shot rang out from somewhere nearby, and the lilin screamed as she slid from Anya's back. Blood poured out of a wound in her chest, and she gasped as her skin turned ashen then heaved her last breath. She was dead.

More shots, more screams. Anya spun around, searching for the source and finding more chaos. The lilins were retreating, but there were so many of them, they were easy pickings. Finally, enough had left that Anya could see the shooters—ICDM had finally arrived and brought anti-lilin talismans.

"Anya!"

She spun, hearing Jack's voice in the distance. He and Cam, still dressed in their funeral garb, ran toward her. They'd at least stopped long enough to grab their weapons.

Despite herself, she smiled. "I told you to stay in Charleston. What about the funeral?"

"Overcome by events," Jack said. "These events, actually."

Cam leveled a glare at her. "How did the lilins get here, Anya?"

"One or two lilins infiltrated the city and started spawning, I would guess," Anya said, the best lie she could come up with on the fly. "Most of these demons are newly transformed—we can't kill them."

"One or two…made all this?" Cam said, dubiously. "In a matter of minutes?"

Anya was saved by answering from an incoming lilin with an axe. She threw her sword at its neck and it stumbled backward, dead. Jack pulled the weapon from its throat and walked back to Anya, handing it to her.

"I know this looks bad, but I promise you, I'm handling it," she said.

"Anya, I'm not…" He shook his head. "I want to believe you—I do believe you. But I need something. You have to give me some kind of answer to take back to ICDM."

"Because all we have right now is you standing in the middle of a bunch of lilins and not killing any of them," Cam said.

"I told you, they're all newly transformed," Anya said.

"Then stop time," Cam said, slamming her macuahuitl into an advancing lilin and allowing Jack to sever his head. "Jack said you did it in Charleston, so do it now."

Anya turned away from them, looking out onto the battlefield and wishing it were just that simple. Bael's grip had somehow *tightened* on the city, and she could do nothing to loosen it. But with ICDM firing their bullets into the crowd, at least the tide looked to be turning in favor of the humans.

"Where did these weapons come from?" Anya said.

"Don't change the subject," Cam replied. "If you really want to help us—if you want to save all these demons, stop time, move them out of here, then come to Geneva and discuss what the *hell* is going on with the Council."

Anya opened and closed her mouth. "I can't do that. Not yet. Soon—"

"You've been saying that for weeks now, and meanwhile, people are dying," Jack said. "If it's not you doing this, tell us who is and we can help you."

"You can't help, Jack," Anya said, looking to him with sorrow in her gaze. "The safest thing for the two of you is—"

"Stop telling me to go back to Geneva, especially if you aren't going to be honest with me," Jack said.

Anya was tired of lying to him, of fearing what would happen if he knew about Bael. Clearly, he wasn't going to listen until she gave him something—and perhaps he was right, her secrecy was suspicious. And her own attempts to cow Bael weren't going very well.

"Jack, it's—"

Something sliced through her leg—a bullet.

"*Fuck!*" Anya screamed, falling to her knees as pain radiated up from her thigh. She trembled as it spread across every inch of her body, taking her breath away. She fell forward onto her hands then weakly pushed herself onto her back, gasping for air.

"Anya!" Jack's voice was far away.

She blinked, staring at the sky and the gray clouds overhead. Her mouth tasted like metal, like blood, and her whole being was slowly losing feeling. In the distance, Jack screamed her name, but he might as well have been on Mars. She was dying.

Let it go. The voice was back, and Anya knew exactly what it meant. She could let go of this magic and become human once more—perhaps the same way Lotan had. But then the world would be at Bael's mercy.

But if she stayed a demon, she would surely die from this wound. Her fingers twitched on the ground as spots danced in her vision.

"I can't," she whispered, tears slipping down her cheeks. "I have to stay. I have to fix this."

"Fix what?" Jack had reached her. "Anya, fix what?" He pulled his knife from his pocket. "I'll get this thing out of you."

But when his knife touched her, she screamed, more pain radiating through her.

"Goddamnit," Jack said, throwing his blade to the side. "I'm sorry, I forgot Cam etched talismans on it."

His brown eyes were full of concern. Her breath came in short spurts, barely enough to raise her chest.

"I'll fix this," Jack whispered. "I promise. Just stay with me, Anya." He rose from her side and dashed away, crying out for help. But no one would help her. Not when the chaos was still going on. Not when the city was overrun.

The only one who might be able to help her was…

She pushed a weak call through the connection. Moments later, the thread lit up with concern and the prickle of energy came closer.

"I'm here, my lady." Diogo's face filled her vision. "I will take you somewhere safe."

The world was a blur, but the calming presence of Ath-kur

returned some magic to her body. The agony remained, though, as did the slow drip-drip-drip of her life force from her body.

Anya had been hit once by one of these talisman bullets, but it hadn't hurt this badly—at least that she could remember. Her whole body was on fire and at the same time, her teeth wouldn't stop chattering. The blood dripping down her leg didn't seem too bad, but the talisman bullet...something was different about it. It wasn't just anti-athtar. Whatever was inside her was killing her completely.

"You have to remove the bullet," Anya said, her breath coming in ragged gasps. "That will stop this."

"I can't..." Diogo shook his head. "I can't get near it."

"Then find someone who can."

She fell back into darkness.

CHAPTER TWENTY-ONE

Jack ran back to the spot where Anya had been, but all that was left was a pool of blood. He exhaled, rubbing his forehead, torn between going to find the portal and knowing that unless Anya had changed her mind, it would be fruitless.

"Where did she go?" Jack asked.

"Diogo arrived, took her away," Cam said. "And meanwhile..."

He turned around, finally recognizing that the city was quiet. There was no one in the streets, save the soldiers and ICDM agents, and the dead lilins. The attackers had vanished.

"Jack, this doesn't look good for Anya," Cam said softly.

"She was fighting the demons, Cam," Jack replied.

"Was she?" Cam asked. "Besides that, when she disappeared, they did, too. That can't be coincidental."

"I'm sure it wasn't, but it doesn't mean *she* was responsible for it. I—"

"Human." Diogo was back. "Come with me."

Jack didn't even have a chance to argue, because the next thing he knew, he was standing in the replica of his house in Ath-kur. His head spun for a moment before his gaze landed on Anya on the table. She was even grayer than before, her lips a pale blue as she stared at the ceiling.

He pressed his head to her chest, hearing a faint pulse. "Shit, why isn't she healing?"

"You tell me, human," Diogo barked. "Fix her."

Jack looked down at the bullet wound and licked his lips. "Find me a knife."

Diogo didn't even seem to move as he disappeared and reappeared with a surgical knife in his hand. With shaking hands, Jack looked at Anya and hoped this wouldn't hurt her too much. Then he stuck the knife inside the gushing wound, searching until the metal met the bullet lodged in her muscles.

Anya didn't even react.

He dug around the bullet, jiggling it and moving the scalpel around until he managed to hook it. With effort, he pulled the metal ball to the surface of her skin then used his fingers to pull it out.

Anya sat up, taking in a huge gulp of air. It was like watching a demonic transformation in real time—her skin flushed with energy, her eyes sparked to life, her lips turned a deep brown once more. The wound on her leg healed almost instantly, the only reminder of it the fresh blood still staining her pants.

She pressed her hand to her chest and steadied her breathing before looking up and staring into Jack's eyes. For a moment, there was fear, but then her eyes filled with tears.

"Jack?"

"I'm here." He pulled her into his embrace and held her as she breathed into his chest. "You're okay now."

"What happened?" she whispered. "I was…hit. What the hell was I hit with?" She pushed him away. "ICDM hit me with something."

"I don't know what it was," Jack said. "I swear to you."

"Where is it?" Anya asked, swinging her legs around to sit up on the table.

"It's…" Jack's gaze widened. "What the hell is going on?"

The bullet had fallen to the floor, and it had effectively drained the color from everything within a six-inch radius. Jack knelt, almost afraid of it, but he'd already touched it without any adverse effects, so he picked it up.

Immediately, the color returned to the spot on the floor.

"I think it has markings on it," Jack replied, bringing it closer to his nose to inspect it. "I think that's an eloko…maybe a lilin."

"Perhaps all five symbols," Diogo said from the other side of the room. "It could be the reason it was so potent—and why it was able to overpower the lady's belu magic in this world."

Jack shook his head. "I don't understand why this is different. We wore talismans around our wrists for years. It was nothing like this."

"Individual talismans versus a single object, perhaps?" Diogo asked.

"I don't care what that thing is. Get it *away* from me," Anya spat, and the disgust was clear on her face. "It feels like…like…"

Jack looked up at her, confused. "Like what?"

"Like the Nullius," she said softly. "Like if I get any closer, I will die. Fuck, I had that thing inside me and I *was* dying."

Jack sucked in a breath. "Cam and Lotan—they went to the Nullius for samples. I wonder if they put something from the Nullius inside. Even a grain of sand would be enough, maybe."

Anya stared at the bullet, her gaze full of hurt. "They're making weapons to hurt me?"

"I don't know if they knew it would hurt you, Anya—"

"The Nullius has the same effect on me as it does any other demon," she replied, her voice rising. "There are anti-athtar symbols on that bullet. Clearly, they're after me, too."

Jack sighed. "I don't agree, but I can't say I blame them. You haven't exactly been forthcoming lately." He took her hand in his. "But if you tell me what's going on—who is bringing these demons to the human world…"

"What would it matter?" Anya said, her voice growing soft. "You don't believe me, even though I've been spending every *waking* moment watching over this world and keeping the chaos at bay—"

He stared at her. "I'm the only one who *does* believe you, Anya. But I'm starting to wonder if maybe everyone else is right. Thousands of humans are dead."

"I can't be everywhere at once," Anya snapped. "I'm doing my best."

Jack stared at her as she wouldn't meet his gaze and his heart broke for her—for them. The solution was so simple, and she just refused to see it.

"Your best would've been to give up these Goddamned powers the way Lotan did."

"It's not that simple—"

He closed his eyes and tilted his head upward. "Anya, you can't... Even when you had that bullet inside of you, you said..." He softened, wishing he'd heard otherwise. "You told me you wanted to stay a demon. You still want this magic more than anything else. More than... More than me, even."

Her chest rose and fell as she heaved, and the pain on her face was palpable. Tears leaked down her face, and Jack was sure that Anya would finally break. But the next thing he knew, he was back at his mother's kitchen door in Charleston.

"Fucking hell."

Jack didn't want to go in at the moment, but there was good booze inside and he really wanted a drink. He was almost immediately bombarded by mourners who wanted to pass on their condolences.

It felt like years, but the funeral had ended perhaps an hour ago. It had continued while he and Cam had fought off lilin demons. While Anya had nearly bled to death and *still* clung to this power. His ears rang with the words he'd said, but for once, her teary-eyed pleas didn't affect him. She was master of her universe, and she was opting to make things difficult. And *still* refused to tell him anything.

But his attempts for solitude were thwarted by the crowd at his mother's house. He would excuse himself just to be caught by someone else. The whole house was packed, and at this rate, he'd be lucky to make it to his father's study in the next year.

"Jack?" Karen said, her brow furrowed. "Jack, what in the world? Why are you covered in blood? What's going on?"

"It's handled," Jack said. "I need a drink."

He jogged up the stairs, grateful no one had ventured up there, and walked down the hall until he reached his father's study. It was more study than library, and it was where George kept his good liquor for meeting with dignitaries.

It was quiet inside, and Jack helped himself to the best bottle he could find before easing down into the chair and covering his eyes with his hands.

That woman—demon, athtar, whatever—was *infuriating*. One minute, he was breathlessly hoping she wasn't dead, the next, he wanted to strangle her for refusing to see reason. He'd seen it in her eyes before she was shot; she had been about ready to tell him everything. But she'd chosen to send him back to the human world instead of having a damned conversation. She could be absolutely childish when she wanted to be.

And yet, in the depths of his heart, he still couldn't let her go. He was too loyal for his own good, he supposed.

"Jack?" Lotan poked his head in. "Karen said you might be in here."

Jack grunted in acknowledgement and took another sip.

"Is everything all right? Where's Cam?"

"Probably back in Paris, cleaning up," Jack said, examining the glass. "She's fine."

"Then whose blood is all over your shirt?"

"Anya's." He took another sip. "What did you put in those bullets?"

Lotan frowned. "What bullets?"

"The ones that nearly killed a belu athtar," Jack said. "Was it something from the Nullius? What the hell did you guys bring back from there, anyway?"

"A few bags of sand, and…" He licked his lips as he helped himself to the liquor. "A creature. One of those winged monsters who attacked you and Cam the last time you were in the Nullius. At least, that's what she told me."

Jack lowered his drink. "How the hell'd you manage that?"

"It was susceptible to the matter from the noxlands, and when it was wounded, we dragged it across the border," Lotan explained. "Then back to ICDM. They've been studying it, I assume, but I don't know what they've found."

"Cam didn't mention any of that," Jack said with a long breath. "Nor that she was making anti-athtar weapons."

Lotan hesitated before he sat down, taking a sip and nodding appreciatively. "I don't know what they're doing, exactly. She hasn't exactly been forthcoming with me either."

"Well, cheers to that," Jack said, offering his glass. Lotan clinked it, and they both sipped.

"Is Anya all right?" Lotan asked.

"Physically, yes," Jack said. "But she still won't tell me what's going on—and now she's even further away because she realized that ICDM isn't as friendly as they used to be." He sighed and sank lower into the fine leather chair. "And here I am, wanting to go back to Ath-kur for round two. What the hell is wrong with me?"

"I believe you're in love," Lotan replied. "As difficult as that is right now."

Jack shifted, glancing at him. "How was it with Cam's parents? They seemed to like you all right."

"They've been putting me through my paces," Lotan said. "They want to know every intimate detail about our relationship, and I confess… I still don't have much I remember."

"Have any more memories come back?" Jack asked.

"Some. Not enough to really be of much use. Now they're talking about suiting me up and teaching me how to use a weapon. I fear it might be a ruse to beat me up."

Jack snorted. "The Macarros certainly have their quirks. I remember when I was dating Sara—"

"Who's Sara?"

Jack started, for just a moment, before relaxing. "She is…*was*

Cam's little sister. I started dating her when I was in school and it wasn't that well-received." He chuckled. "Marco took me shooting in the country, and I thought I would end up with bullet holes."

"Did you?"

"No, especially when I told him how serious I was about her," Jack said. "The Macarros are fiercely protective of their family. But once you become that family, there's nothing they won't do for you. You see that with Cam. She's given up everything to bring my ass back from the brink more times than I can count. And with you—"

He sighed, and his face fell. "Jack, I'm worried my full memory may never come back. It's been a few weeks now and all I have are scraps." He looked up. "Am I doomed to be gathering pieces for the rest of my life?"

"Maybe instead of trying to remember the past," Jack began, rising with his glass in his hand, "you should create a new future with Cam. It'll probably be better than anything you had before anyway. After all, you were willing to give up immortality to be with her. I think that's saying something."

CHAPTER TWENTY-TWO

"From preliminary reports, it appears Anya was severely affected by the new weapon," Agent Roma said. "Can you confirm, Agent Macarro?"

Cam rubbed her hands together, wishing she were anywhere but here. Since all the lilin demons had disappeared with Anya, there had been nothing more for her to do in Paris, so she'd returned to Geneva for an emergency Council meeting. Most of the Councilmembers were still in Charleston, and several were huddled in what looked like George's office, including María.

Beside her, Agent Roma was giving a long description of what had happened, and every bit of it was damning for Anya.

"Agent Macarro?" Roma pressed. "Can you confirm what

you saw with regards to the athtar Anya?"

Cam licked her lips. "Confirmed. When she was shot, she was… She was dying."

She glanced at the screen, expecting to see something like concern from George, but he wore the same look of triumph as the others gathered. The Council had clearly made up their minds about Anya—and who could blame them?

"We also noted an immediate reaction to the demons that were hit in the city," Roma said, pointing to the video of the lilins being slaughtered that was being simulcast to the others. "We are now in possession of a potent weapon, Councilmembers. I think this will turn the tide."

Cam couldn't look at the faces on the screen; she could barely look at herself in the mirror. When she'd brought the bags of sand back from the Nullius, she'd hoped they would find microscopic inscriptions of the talismans on them, or something that would explain their power. Arjun, in his infinite wisdom, had suggested they incorporate the sand into some bullets, just to see what it would do. They had a set of bullets inscribed with talismans, another set that had talismans and Nullius sand, and one with only the sand.

Anya, of course, had been hit with one of the talisman/sand combos. With Cam's help, ICDM had unwittingly built a belu-killing weapon.

"I say we take the fight to the demons," Councilman Zhao said via the laptop. "We have the ability to move troops into the Underworld. We should infiltrate, find the demon belus, and kill them."

"If you'd like to sacrifice those troops, sure," Cam said, looking up from the blank sheet of paper where she was supposed to be taking notes for herself. "Once the belu dies, the world disintegrates. Unless they've got a child, like Mot and Xo had Lotan, everyone in the world will most likely perish. It's not…" She snorted. "It's not fun."

"It's an option we can offer," María said. "Giving our soldiers full knowledge of the outcome."

"A suicide mission?"

"If it means we can eradicate demonkind, yes."

Cam sat back, knowing when it was better to keep her mouth shut than argue futilely. If only she could go back in time…

But she couldn't put this genie back in the bottle.

The meeting adjourned, and Cam walked out into the dark evening. It was well after midnight here in Geneva, but she wasn't the least bit tired. Not when she had so much to think about—so much to regret. She wasn't looking forward to—

"Hey, partner."

She looked up to find Jack standing in the center of the square, his arms crossed over his chest and a large bloodstain on his shirt. His gaze was fiery, and she braced herself for the onslaught.

"Look, I know you're mad—"

"I'm not mad," Jack said, though his tone said otherwise. "I'm just curious why you're building a weapon that can kill

Anya—and why you chose to withhold that information from me."

"I didn't know they'd use…" She couldn't even get out the lie. "I'm sorry, Jack."

"Are you?"

"Is she…all right?"

"Cam, that thing almost killed her," Jack said, dropping his arms. "I mean *almost killed her*. She's not supposed to turn gray, Cam. And that bullet, it… It stripped the magic from Ath-kur."

"You went to Ath-kur?" Cam asked.

"Because Diogo couldn't go near her to extract the bullet," Jack barked. "Don't try to change the subject."

"I'm not changing the subject," Cam replied. "Did she tell you why all these demons keep showing up and killing people?"

"Because, as she said, they were all neophytes," Jack said, though his tone was much less forceful than it had been. "She was trying to find a bloodless solution."

"She has one. She can freakin' stop time. Why didn't she? What could she possibly have been waiting for?" She licked her lips, wishing Jack could see things the way she did.

"I don't know." Jack lost his bluster completely as his shoulders sagged. "Maybe I'm holding onto something that isn't there. When she was dying, she was saying she needed to stay a demon. She would've rather kept that magic than lived." He looked off into the distance. "And she didn't really like me pointing that out to her."

"Seems to be something of a sore subject," Cam said. "Do

you think…maybe the athtar magic has gotten in her brain and started changing her?"

"I honestly don't know," Jack said. "There's something she's afraid to tell me—it's the same damn shit as when we were back in Seattle. Whether that's the athtar magic or something else…" He exhaled loudly. "I need another drink."

"Smells like you already had one," Cam said. "Have a quick top-off in Ath-kur?"

He snorted. "She dropped me off back home in Charleston. So I grabbed a drink with Lotan before heading back here."

"Did you bring Lotan back with you?"

"He's staying in Charleston to get some one-on-one time with your parents," Jack replied with a smirk.

"Oh shit, Jack, why didn't you bring him?" Cam groaned. "That's the last thing I want."

"The last thing *I* wanted was for you to lie to me about what you're developing," Jack shot back. "So turnabout is fair play. You are, of course, welcome to go back and get him, but I daresay he's the most interesting thing that's come to Charleston in years."

Cam scowled. "Fine. I guess it's safer for him there than here. At least my folks can keep an eye on him."

"That's the spirit," Jack said. "So about that drink…?"

"It's two in the morning. Everything is closed."

"Then we'll just have to scrounge Frank's apartment until we find something."

Cam was about to respond, but was interrupted by the

sound of running footsteps. She sighed and looked over her shoulder—there was an agent running toward her and Jack.

"Agent Macarro, we need you in the weapons tent. Emergency."

Her heart dropped. "What's wrong?" The agent looked at Jack, and she nodded. "You can tell him."

"The evidence from the Nullius, the weapons—they're gone."

"Where are they?" Cam said, standing in the middle of the tent. The five plastic bags of Nullius sand she and Lotan had gathered should've been sitting in various evidence boxes in a locker. But the locker was wide open and the bags had been removed from the boxes.

"We don't have any cameras up here yet," the guard said. "And we didn't let anyone in or out who wasn't authorized."

"I need a headcount of the workers here," Cam said. She wanted to go home and go to bed, not deal with yet another crisis. "Find out who doesn't report into work tomorrow."

"Why would someone have taken it?" Arjun asked.

"Because it's a deadly weapon," Cam said, looking at Jack whose gaze had darkened considerably. "Clearly, it was enough to injure the belu athtar and every lilin."

"But no demon could've set foot inside this tent, unless..." Arjun began.

"Anya stopped time, walked inside the tent, and took it for herself?" Cam suggested. "I mean, I wouldn't put it past her.

Self-preservation and all that."

Jack shook his head. "This doesn't sound like her. She would hide away in Ath-kur, but she wouldn't have taken away a weapon that would help in the fight."

"Didn't you *just* say that she would've rather kept her magic than lived?" Cam asked, turning on him with a glare.

"Her holding onto her magic is a whole separate subject than her stealing weapons from ICDM." Jack put his hands on his hips. "This wasn't her. I know that in my bones."

Cam ran her hand over her face, unable to stand Jack's continued defense of someone who was so plainly guilty. "I'm going home. I'll deal with this in the morning. I'm sure María is going to want me to go back to the Nullius to get more, and I just can't think about that tonight."

She walked out of the tent, ignoring the questions from the others, but didn't get two steps before yet another agent came running up to her.

"Agent Macarro, we have a problem."

"Another one?" Cam sighed heavily. "Tell me in the morning."

"It can't." He took a hesitant step forward. "The portal is gone."

"Portal?" Jack had followed her outside. "The athtar portal?"

"It was at the drop site then… It just closed. It's gone."

Cam turned to Jack, her patience gone. "What say you now, partner? Her portal, her magic—now gone. To my eyes, it looks like she's declaring herself no longer an ally to ICDM."

"Alternatively, ICDM declared themselves an enemy when they *shot* her," Jack snapped back. "I can't say I blame her for picking up her ball and going home after that. Maybe if ICDM apologizes, she might give it back."

"You still think she's in there, don't you?" Cam asked. "The athtar magic is warping her brain, Jack. Without you there, she's sliding down a slippery slope toward Bael-town. If we aren't careful, we'll have another dictator amongst us."

"And you don't think ICDM just hastened that outcome?" Jack asked, his voice raising. "Meanwhile, because of ICDM's action, whatever is actually behind this will continue to wreak havoc on humanity, and we've lost our ability to mobilize quickly."

"Why does it sound like you're blaming me for what ICDM did?" Cam barked.

"Because you're the one who went to the Nullius," Jack said. "If you hadn't done that, none of this would be happening."

Cam tossed her hands in the air and kept walking. She wanted to go to bed and forget any of this had happened for a few blissful hours. She just hoped Frank *did* have a bottle of something strong in his apartment, since she was now stuck in Geneva for the foreseeable future.

Her steps lessened as she realized something else. Reaching into her pocket, she pulled out her phone and dialed Lotan's number.

"Hey, there you are." His voice was like velvet. "Are you all right? Jack said—"

"I'm fine," Cam said, though she really wasn't. The tears came as she left the perimeter of ICDM headquarters. For the moment, it didn't matter that Lotan was still a veritable stranger, she missed him. "I just really want to see you."

"I'll head to the portal—"

"That's the thing," Cam said, wiping her tears. "It's closed. Anya… She clearly doesn't want us using it anymore."

"I see."

"I just… I really wanted you to know that I miss you," Cam whispered, her throat thick with emotion and unshed tears.

"I wish I could be there," he replied. "But I promise, I'm all right. Your parents are taking good care of me. As soon as I can figure out a way back to you, I'll be there."

And he probably would, but it wouldn't be enough. She didn't just miss him, she missed *him*. The man who had stormed into her heart and fearlessly offered his love, even as she was keeping her distance. The one whose patient and strong hands had worn down the fear she held in her heart to make space for himself. That sexy man who found her brain just as attractive as her body—but knew when the time was right to kiss and when it was right to just hold her until the storm passed.

In her self-pity, she began to accept that she'd never get the love of her life back. It was such a dumb thing for her to be weepy over, especially after spending so long trying to keep her distance. But tonight, with what felt like the entire world falling down around her, all she wanted was to fall asleep in *her* Lotan's warm embrace.

CHAPTER TWENTY-THREE

If Cam wanted him there, Lotan would move heaven and earth to get back to her.

He'd never heard her sound so…unsettled before. Although they'd slowly been moving toward romance, her tone was something more than that. She felt wholly alone, and he was the only one she craved. The thought made him want to sprout wings and fly to her.

But maybe wings of his own weren't required—he did supposedly own a private jet.

He'd been on the front porch, trying to avoid the chaos inside the Grenard house. The black-clad mourners wearing pearls and expensive cufflinks had been replaced by a swarm of

ICDM windbreaker-wearing agents, first buzzing about the attack in Paris, followed by a new conversation about missing weapons and the missing Nullius sand Lotan and Cam had retrieved, followed by a fresh hum about the missing portal. Lotan had overheard María complaining about how they were going to get back to Geneva when Cam had called.

Now, nothing else mattered except getting to her in a timely manner. Fumbling with his phone, he sifted through emails and contacts until he found information about the plane he owned—who managed it, and more importantly, the phone number to call to retrieve the plane itself.

As he punched in the number and pressed the device to his ear, he prayed he didn't have to answer any odd questions.

One ring and a cheery female voice answered. "Good evening, Mr. Lobo. Would you like us to ready your plane?"

"Yes, please," Lotan said, guessing they must've had his number on file or something. "But I'm in Charleston. Can you come here?"

"Of course." She typed into her computer. "And where would you like to travel to today?"

"Geneva? As soon as possible, please."

"We will prepare your plane now." She paused as she typed on the keyboard. "We should be there roughly three hours after we complete preparations. Expect us at..." She typed again. "Five AM local time."

Lotan thanked her and hung up the phone and stared at his phone, grinning to himself that he'd solved his own problem.

Sure, flying wasn't as quick as stepping through a portal, but at least he could be the master of his own destiny.

"Lotan?" Karen opened the back door and looked down. "Oh, here you are, sweetheart. Are you all right?"

"Perfectly fine," he said, rising. "Just stepped out to take a call from Cam."

"And how is she?" Karen asked, leaning against the doorframe. "I take it she made it back to Geneva before…before the portal closed?"

Lotan nodded and looked at his phone once more.

"Why don't you come inside for a bit?" Karen said with a smile. "I'm going to put on a pot of tea, and I'd love to chat a little."

Karen walked Lotan through the chaotic house, excusing her way around the different agents and waiting until they passed her in the narrow hall before they finally made it to the expansive kitchen. It was quite a sight, with copper pans hanging from the ceiling and two large multi-burner stoves against the wall.

"Do you often feed a crowd?" Lotan asked.

"Oh, this? No." She tittered. "We have a smaller apartment on the back of the house where we usually spend our time. We use this mostly for entertaining and…well, this."

She ventured to the two large refrigerators and plucked the food from the funeral out and placed it on the large island, along with some silverware and plates, telling Lotan to help himself.

He picked at the deli meat and cheese, and Karen went to one of the ovens with a full kettle.

"Have they found the portal?"

"No," Karen said. "Nor the missing equipment. They still don't even know how it could have walked away." She forced a tight smile onto her face. "Not to worry, I'm sure George and the others will figure this out. Perhaps it's just been misplaced."

"It doesn't sound like that's possible," Lotan said. "Cam was fairly broken up about it on the phone."

"Perhaps not just because of that," Karen said. "I understand that they've developed a weapon that can hurt demons—Anya included." She brought the cup to her lips. "After all that girl's been doing for this world, I think that's…well, I don't think that was very fair."

"So you like Anya?"

"She has my Jackie's heart, how can I not love her?" Karen asked with a sad smile. "I confess, I've never met her, but I want to, one day."

Lotan wondered what it must be like for Karen and Ana, mothers who had to sit back and watch their children walk off into danger. He was, perhaps, fortunate that his own mother…

The flash of her hair falling out of the bag chilled him to the bone, and he hastily took a sip of the tea.

"I have some news I need to share with those upstairs," Lotan said. "If you think they'd let me inside?"

"Mm…" Karen shook her head. "But I have a little trick I'd use when George was stuck in a meeting and I needed to talk with him. I'm sure I have everything in the pantry."

"What is it?" Lotan asked.

"Cookies. No one can resist. C'mon, I'll show you how to make them."

Under Karen's careful tutelage, Lotan measured and stirred the dry and wet ingredients, more than he thought was necessary for the two of them, especially when she brought out four large cookie sheets. But as soon as the cookies were out and cooled, she piled them onto a plate and handed them to him.

"Take these upstairs," she said with a knowing smile.

Lotan nodded, taking the plate and walking out of the kitchen. Although there were others in groups whose heads popped up at the scent of the baked goods, Lotan marched up the stairs and down the hall. He rapped on the door before poking his head inside.

"Karen asked me to drop these off."

"Come in, come in," George said, beckoning him. Lotan opened the door wider to reveal a room filled with computers, cameras, and in-progress video calls. Three televisions had been stacked up in one corner, each displaying a different news station with one anxious staffer waiting to see what news story would break next.

"Have you been able to locate the portal?" Lotan asked George.

"Not yet," he said with a sigh. "You wouldn't happen to know where we could find one, do you?"

"No, but—"

"Well," George stuffed two cookies in his mouth and turned away from Lotan, "thanks anyway."

He returned to the gaggle, not dismissing Lotan, but not exactly asking him to stay either. But he had a purpose, so he was eager to engage where he could. So he attempted to fade into the background, waiting for the opportune moment.

"We need to establish better security," George said, leaning over the table. "Sign in for everyone going in and out."

"That'll be hard, considering it's a tent," replied one of the aides sitting around the table. "It might be wise to move operations here to Geneva."

"I don't like the message that would send," María said. "ICDM's headquarters has been in the same place for hundreds of years. We aren't about to move it because of pressure."

"But perhaps a more secure environment is necessary," George said, looking at the staffer behind him. "Where are we in securing alternate office locations?"

"Still in work," she replied, stepping forward eagerly. "There are a lot more damaged buildings in the city than not. Especially if we want to stay within the athtar perimeter."

"I think the first thing is for us to return to headquarters," María said. "Has anyone been able to secure plane tickets yet?"

"Yes, ma'am, but they don't leave until tomorrow evening."

Lotan sensed his chance. "I have a plane that will be here in a few hours."

Six heads turned to him. "You have a plane?" George asked.

"I do. It's quite a nice one, from what I understand," he said.

"I can't promise I can take all of you. I don't exactly remember how big it is, but I will be returning to Geneva as soon as it's here. Five in the morning was the time I was given."

María glanced at the clock; it was nearing one. "That's better than this evening. Thank you."

Things moved quickly, and nobody slept, not even Karen, who brewed a large pot of coffee for everyone in the house and baked another batch of cookies. Even after offering his plane, Lotan was somewhat sidelined, with most of the conversations going over his head. But at least he felt confident that he'd been able to provide something of value—and he would be on his way to Cam soon enough.

Most of the ICDM staff ordered cars to drive them, but Karen insisted on driving George and Lotan. Lotan sat in the backseat with nothing but his phone to keep him company, as the two in the front were locked in an intense conversation.

"Karen, I have to go."

"Do you?"

"I'm needed."

"You were handling it well from Charleston. What happens when the demons attack Geneva again?"

"They attacked Charleston—"

"It's different."

"I promise to keep an eye on him," Lotan spoke up from the backseat. "We all will. Jack won't let anything happen to him."

Karen offered him a smile from the rearview mirror, but it

was gone as soon as she looked back at her husband. "When you get there, don't be hard on Jack. He's dealing with a lot."

"He needs to wise up and see the situation for what it is. It's like when he dropped everything to help her and got himself taken to the underworld and tortured."

"Bael isn't around anymore."

Bael—why did that name sound familiar? The feeling that Lotan had missed something important settled on his chest, but he couldn't figure out what it was. The dots were like stars in the sky, too far apart to connect, but somehow related.

That question sat on Lotan's chest until they arrived at the airport. A large, beautiful jet was parked with the ladder down as they were waved onto the tarmac.

"Is that it?" Karen asked.

"Let's hope so," Lotan said with a smile.

The pilots seemed to recognize Lotan, bowing and speaking in Spanish to him. He made a show of smiling. Even though he didn't quite remember how to speak the language, some of what they said made sense. And they were at least in the right place.

The ICDM Council members followed him up the stairs one by one, followed by a smattering of their aides. Lotan couldn't take the entire support staff, so they would be flying separately on a commercial flight.

Lotan settled into a seat and looked out the window.

George was still on the tarmac, clearly getting an earful from his wife. Their conversation was heated, but in the end, Karen embraced him and they shared a chaste kiss and a few more words spoken more lovingly. Then he grabbed his overnight bag and jogged to the plane.

Movement in front of him drew Lotan's attention and he was surprised to see María take the seat across from him. She smoothed the lines on her pants, paying close attention to them in much the same way Cam did when she was nervously fidgeting. It brought a smile to Lotan's face. He would soon be reunited with his love.

"I hope you don't mind me joining you for the flight," she asked with a smile. "I do apologize that we haven't had much time to meet and discuss."

"Discuss?"

"Cam," María said. "Ana tells me you made quite the impression on her and Marco."

"I'm glad to hear that," Lotan said. "I'm sorry I didn't get more time with them."

"They were needed back in El Paso." She sat back. "But perhaps once the world settles, you and Cam can pay them a visit." She glanced around the plane. "It's a blessing that you had this plane on its way already."

"Cam called. She sounded like she needed me," Lotan said. "I thought it prudent to get back to her as quickly as possible."

María took a breath. "George tells me that you once had a portal in Mexico City. How did you come by this portal?"

Lotan stared out the window as the plane's engines roared to life. "I don't recall. It's something I've always had, I think." He gestured to his head. "My apologies—"

"Your memory isn't what it used to be," María said with a knowing nod. "But if you could try—we are desperate. That athtar portal was our only lifeline to the Underworld, and to the Nullius sand. With both gone, we are at the demons' mercy once more."

"I do...I think I remember there is another portal," Lotan said, tapping his finger to his chin. "A man named Diogo had one."

"I have heard his name before," María said. "He's the one who took Anya back to Ath-kur—and who came back for Jack, isn't he? He's athtar?"

"I believe so. The one who helped Anya obtain her powers."

"Please," María said, crossing one leg over the other and leaning forward. "Tell me more."

CHAPTER TWENTY-FOUR

Anya had slept for three days to recover from her bullet wound. She woke up for short moments, reaching out for Jack in the space beside her, and when he wasn't there, falling back into dreamless sleep. But finally, when her strength had returned somewhat, she pushed herself up and out of bed, in search of something to eat.

Her thigh ached, and the wound hadn't healed all the way yet—another sign that it wasn't purely an anti-athtar weapon. So after grabbing a bag of cheese puffs, she plopped down in the center of the living room and stuffed her face, staring out into the empty forest.

She'd felt Cam and Lotan step through her portal into the

noxlands, but she'd thought it was to try and jog his memory. She hadn't cared before when ICDM had used it, thinking that they were in an alliance against the onslaught of demonic attacks.

Now, she wasn't sure what to think.

She would still help; at least, she wanted to. But knowing what they were capable of now, knowing that they could *kill* her if the right people weren't around... She was a little hesitant to leave Ath-kur.

Her argument with Jack echoed in her mind on repeat. He didn't know *why* she needed this magic, but something in his gaze had frozen her to the spot. There was still that underlying fear...and she couldn't forget what he'd said to her on that beach in Lisbon months ago.

"You're still enamored with Bael and his magic, and you always will be. I will never be enough for you."

"You look despondent, my love. Trouble in paradise?"

Anya closed her eyes, hating that Bael had come in her moment of weakness. "How do you do that?"

"Do what?" He walked around to sit in the chair across from her.

"Appear in these lands when I very clearly don't want you here? Hide your presence from me?"

He smiled. "Do you really want me to share all my secrets?"

"Yes."

"Well, I confess, I don't know the answer to the first," Bael said, leaning back and smiling down at her. "You and I are in uncharted realms. There have never been two belu athtars in existence at the same time, so I'm not sure how this magic works. My educated assumption is that because we share the same magic, I'm able to venture into this land." He smiled. "Unless, of course, you're lying and really want me here."

She looked up at him and used her magic to expel him from the land. But he didn't move.

"No, I very much want you gone," she said, stuffing her hand into the bag. "In more ways than one."

"Why are you so mean when I've brought you a gift?" He rose from the chair and crossed the room to stand before her. Something slipped from his palm. It took her a moment to recognize it.

Jack's portal.

"Why do you have this?" Anya asked.

"A clever trick, beloved, to make such a thing," Bael said, nudging it with his toe. "But perhaps a folly to give it to the humans. They clearly aren't worthy of having such a thing."

"Put it back where you found it," she said, looking up at him. "They need it to clean up your messes."

"They need it to make weapons against you," Bael replied. "Or would you have them go to No Man's Land once more and retrieve more sand to hurt you?"

"It is not up to you to determine what they do and do not deserve anymore," Anya snapped, the hair on the back of her neck rising.

"And what of this weapon they've developed? Do they

deserve that?" Bael asked. "The one that nearly killed you? It was built by these so-called friends of yours, after all."

She looked away, unable to come up with a response that wasn't agreement but not wanting to give him the satisfaction.

"I hope it will please you that I've taken care of those weapons," Bael replied. "Every piece from the Nullius has been removed from their possession."

Something stirred deep inside her—fear. Had Bael figured out how to stop time? "How?"

He looked somewhat ruffled, and Anya exhaled silently. "Since I'm not welcome inside the city, I bribed one of the human scientists. Sometimes the less graceful methods are the best. I had him gather every bit of sand and dump it in the lake —and do the same with the bullets they've developed. There is nothing left for them to hurt you with."

"You mean hurt *us* with," Anya replied, narrowing her gaze. "Don't pretend your grand gesture was anything more than self-preservation."

"Why do you think so little of me, beloved?"

"Experience," Anya snapped. "Now get out, before I—"

Something came up from the bottom of her soul, something painful, like the moment she'd seen Asherah's bloody body in her bed. Like her very soul had been torn asunder. Like...

"What is it, my love?" Bael asked, his gaze full of concern.

"I have... I have... I have to go," Anya whispered, grasping at her chest as she frantically searched for that golden connection. But the thread had gone dark. There was nothing on the other end.

"Does it feel like a piece of your heart has shattered?" Bael asked, coming to stand behind her. "Like someone has taken something precious from you?"

She turned to him. "What did you do?"

"I did nothing," Bael said, reaching to brush the tear off her cheek. "But I know that look well. It's how I felt when you killed Ekur in Geneva. Someone has taken an athtar from you."

Her blood ran cold. "Diogo."

The world slipped beneath her, and she knew what she was seeing before she arrived. Diogo on the floor, blood pooling from the wound on his chest, his gaze unseeing. His tea steamed on the table, along with a book. He was preparing for another afternoon as he'd spent thousands of them. And monsters had come in and taken it away.

For what?

"Holy shit…"

Anya's fury spiked and she glared over her shoulder at the three black-clad ICDM agents, their guns still smoking from the bullet they'd fired.

"If you know what is good for you," Anya whispered, her voice low and dangerous, "*get out of my sight.*"

But one of them raised their gun. "We have orders."

The shot rang out, but the sound ceased as the storm in Anya's mind unlocked that deep well of power and the river of time stopped completely. The bullet hung in mid-air, the fired gun in mid-recoil, the face of the ICDM agent set in stone. Anya could easily slaughter him. He might deserve it, too. Except, as he'd said, he was just following orders.

With time stopped, she slipped to Geneva, to the center of ICDM headquarters. There, a mix of agents and soldiers milled in the square where she'd saved all of them. The headquarters building had been cleared of rubble and was now under construction. A set of tents sat to the back.

Anya took her time walking toward them, her footsteps the only sound in this deadly, silent world. She'd grown so furious she was numb, her body somewhat moving of its own accord. She had no weapon on her, but perhaps she didn't need one.

She passed the two still guards out front and stepped inside. The Council was gathered around a group of television sets, all of them tuned in to a picture of Anya standing in Lisbon. She shook the time river, creating a small bubble around the tent, and the humans began to breathe again.

"What's going on?" María asked. "Why has it frozen?"

"Did she kill them?"

"I did not."

She felt a little sadistic glee as five heads turned in shock to stare at her. Anya thought for a moment Jack was amongst them, but the human was much older. His father George had made the trip, it seemed. Somehow that made the betrayal worse.

"How are you here?" María asked. "There are—"

"Your talismans are no match for me," Anya said, her voice low and emotionless. "You knew this when I saved all of you from the demonic attack that leveled your headquarters building. Which begs the question…"

A man to María's left spoke up. "You've been unleashing more of them on this world, haven't you?"

She had to laugh. Perhaps Bael had a point. It didn't matter how much she sacrificed for them; they would never be worthy of her help. They'd taken the gifts she'd given them and tried to kill her then taken an innocent life.

"Why did you kill Diogo?" Anya asked. "What has he done to hurt you?"

"He's an athtar, therefore, he's dangerous," María said.

"You are brave to speak to me," Anya said with a smirk. "I still remember how you screamed when I tortured you. But perhaps I should've rid the world of your miserable leadership then. You are not worthy."

She looked down as a sword appeared in her hand. But not just any blade. *Sharur.* The weapon she'd wielded for three thousand years at Bael's side. The one she'd used to kill the belu noxes. She could practically feel his lips on her cheek as the sword's weight fell into her hand.

Bael would have her use this, would have her reclaim her bloodthirsty ways. She'd been a terror by his side for thousands of years. The ruthless noxslayer who would destroy the world to sate her bloodlust. She could take control of humanity and rule with an iron fist.

But that wasn't who she was, no matter how much her soul hurt from the loss of Diogo. She couldn't take her revenge. She'd done that once before, only to find out that those she'd slaughtered had been innocent of the crimes against her.

Bael might not have pulled the trigger, but she could see his manipulation all over this situation. And they'd all played their parts perfectly. But unlike the humans, Anya wouldn't be Bael's puppet anymore.

The sword dropped from her hand. "You have betrayed me at the deepest level," she whispered. "You're on your own."

Once her feet landed in Ath-kur, she released her hold on the time river and fell to her knees, emotion coming over her. She wanted release, she wanted revenge, she wanted something to end the pain that threatened to overwhelm her.

It was as if Asherah had died all over again. The two losses blended in her heart, pummeling her with an ache she felt inside her bones. It had taken years for Anya to even get out of bed after her child had been snatched from her. Perhaps another hundred-year nap was in the plans for her.

After all, what else did she have?

Jack… Her heart found new ways to hurt thinking of him. Whether he knew or not, he was affiliated with those monsters. Perhaps he'd tried to stop it, and perhaps, in his own way, he'd tried to warn her of their treachery. But she would never see him again, not until she could stand without wanting to fall to her knees again. And by then, his mortal bones would be dust.

A warm hand landed on her neck, massaging it in a familiar way. "There, there, my love. I'm here."

She allowed herself to believe, just for a moment, just for a reprieve from the pain. She closed her eyes and let him pull her head into his lap as he stroked her hair.

"It's a pain you feel deeply," Bael continued, his rhythmic strokes soothing. "And it will never go away. But you can take solace in me being here, as I always have been, to support you."

She lifted her head, staring at him curiously. "Where did you find Sharur?"

"It's not the same blade," he said, wiping her cheek. "I don't know what happened to the original. But I found a craftsman with the same skills and set him to work. I'd hoped—prayed—that one day you would wield it for me once again."

For me. The spell was quicker to break this time, and for that she was grateful.

"Go," Anya said, straightening as she moved away from him. "Your comfort is not wanted here."

"But, my love, who will comfort you if not me?" He snorted. "Your human? He's the one who—"

"Don't you dare speak to me as if I'm some weakling in need of constant care and feeding," Anya seethed. "I'm the Goddamned belu athtar, the strongest creature in the world. I'm the Lady of the Mountain. I need no one, and I want no help from a liar such as yourself."

"But—"

Anya had heard enough, and, finding the last of her strength, she shoved him from Ath-kur to *somewhere else*. Liley, Elonsi, the noxlands even. Just away from her.

Then, content in her solitude, she peeled herself off the floor and dragged herself to the bedroom, bolstered by the strength of her own words, before collapsing and crying herself to sleep.

CHAPTER TWENTY-FIVE

"You have betrayed me at the deepest level. You're on your own."

Jack stared at the security camera footage that had somehow managed to capture Anya's arrival in Geneva even though the timestamp didn't change. She was distraught, her face blotchy and her cheeks streaked with tears. But she'd resisted the urge to swing the sword Jack hadn't seen in almost a year. She'd simply told them goodbye.

Not exactly the actions of a mass murderer.

"Those idiots dodged a bullet," Cam muttered. "Why didn't she kill them all?"

Jack couldn't find the maturity to turn and look at her.

They'd been walking on eggshells since their fight the night before, and Jack felt like a coil ready to spring whenever she opened her mouth.

So he kept his tongue to himself, instead watching Anya's expression on the grainy footage. She'd been moments away from taking that next step, but something had changed her mind. Even if this athtar magic had somehow taken root in her mind, she still had enough control over herself.

She wasn't completely lost yet.

"Reverse the footage," Jack said. "To the point where the sword appeared."

The tech pressed the button and let it run until the sword disappeared from her hand. Then, pressing play, Jack leaned in close to the monitor. The sword wasn't there, then it was.

"What are you looking for?" Cam asked.

Jack still didn't turn. "She's not supposed to be able to do that," he said. "Just materialize things out of thin air. I don't think."

"She probably stopped time and went to get it."

"Pause it," Jack said, pointing at the screen. "Look at her face. She doesn't look like she knows what's going on."

"Jack—"

"Again," Jack said, leaning in so close that the image was mostly pixels. There was no discernible difference between the frames, but he *knew*. That sword wasn't even supposed to be in existence anymore.

"I know you're trying to find something, and it's a good

thing she didn't kill the entire ICDM Council, but we have to face facts."

"She hated that sword," Jack said, ignoring the rising anger at her tone. "Bael gave it to her."

"She used it to kill him, too," Cam said, lightly.

"And then she threw it away."

"It fell when the world collapsed. Maybe she found it again."

Jack felt it—the final crack in his patience. But instead of exploding at Cam like he wanted to, he merely turned on his heel then marched toward the front of the tent.

But Cam had followed him. "Where are you going?"

"To talk to someone who can help me," Jack barked. "Which isn't you."

Whatever kappa magic Diogo had been using to disguise his monastery was powerful stuff, Jack mused. It had withstood the flood that had left a stink of salt water in the city. Jack hadn't wanted to return to Lisbon, not when he could still taste salt water when he coughed, but this was the first place to start.

It hadn't taken much convincing for Lotan to volunteer his now-very-useful private jet. He'd been hesitant to leave Cam behind, but Jack had insisted. He couldn't deal with any more negativity from her. So what if the entirety of humanity had given up on Anya? He wouldn't. Not until she brought her blade to his neck herself. That would be the only way he'd be convinced she was lost.

The plane was slower than portal travel, but eventually, he

and Lotan were standing in the monastery that was swarming with ICDM agents taking photos of the scene.

He stared at the bloodstain on the ground where Diogo had been shot down. They'd come in covered in anti-athtar and kappa talismans (the latter to break through the magic surrounding his monastery) and killed him with one of the bullets inscribed with all five symbols. There was body cam footage of his death, which had been immediate. It had to have been, otherwise, Anya would've saved him.

Her red, teary-eyed face after he'd extracted the bullet from her leg was seared into his memory, a constant reminder of how he'd failed her. He should have been less accusatory in the brief moment she'd let him inside Ath-kur, should have watched his tone and his words better. Had he just taken a breath instead of speaking from anger, he might've gotten her to open up—and all this could've been avoided.

Or maybe if María hadn't been so trigger-happy.

"Agent Grenard," the ICDM scene investigator came up to him, "can I help you with something? We need to finish our sweep."

Next to the bloodstain on the floor, there was an unopened book and a cold cup of tea that had been steeping so long the water was pitch black. Diogo had probably just sat down to enjoy it. Jack had never asked him if he'd had a chance to read every book in his expansive library.

"Did you locate the portal?" Jack asked, glancing at him.

"It's gone."

"Well, that makes sense," Jack said. "Considering the one who made it was gunned down here."

"Easy, Jack," Lotan said, reading one of Diogo's books in the corner. "This man didn't kill him."

The agent scampered away under Jack's glare as Lotan came to stand beside him.

"If you want someone to blame, you may blame me," Lotan said.

"I fail to see how any of this is your fault."

"María asked me about Diogo, and I told her what I knew," Lotan said, solemnly. "I feel as though I should've been more discreet with her, but I thought her an ally. I'm... I'm very sorry."

Jack snorted. "They knew who he was before you spoke with her. But she's not an ally. She's manipulative, and she's left Cam to die on more than one occasion. I wouldn't trust anyone on the Council at this point."

"Even your father?"

Jack gritted his teeth. He hadn't been able to speak to George since Anya had nearly killed him. Nor his mother, who'd called so many times that Jack had just shut off his phone. The only person he wanted to speak with wasn't taking his calls anyway.

"I'm not going back with you," Jack said. "I don't... I never really liked what ICDM was doing, but I thought I'd help out to honor my grandfather. But these people...they just don't get it. They killed demons around the world and brought the backlash on themselves. And now, killing Diogo? They've effectively burned the bridge to the *one* demon who could've saved them from whoever *is* behind this." Jack shook his head. "I can't be part of this anymore."

Lotan watched him, and Jack half-expected him to argue, but he just nodded. "Then at least let me give you my plane—"

"No," Jack said. "I don't want anyone—even you—to know where I am. I just need to disappear for a while."

"Cam will be heartbroken," Lotan said. "At least give her some hint—"

"When she comes to her senses," Jack said with a glare, "I'll talk to her. Until then, she can continue fighting for the wrong side."

The city of Lisbon was almost completely empty, and it took Jack a few hours of walking until he found civilization again. The outskirts of the city, where the kappa water magic hadn't risen, was dry, but the residents were skittish, waiting for the next attack. Jack felt bad for them, but he was on a mission.

He walked into a small shop that was open.

"I need a ride," Jack said, opening his phone. "To here."

The man shook his head and said something in Portuguese. Jack heard 'kappa' amongst the quick words and got the gist when the man pointed toward the door. Jack nodded and held up his hands in surrender, turning to walk out the door.

"You looking for a ride?"

Jack turned around at the voice, spoken in unbroken

English. The woman was perched against the wall, almost waiting for him. It was too much of a coincidence, but Jack didn't really care at this point.

"I am," Jack replied. "Need a ride to the northern part of the city. How much?"

She shook her head. "On the house."

Jack wasn't one to look a gift horse in the mouth, but he was still glad he'd come to Lisbon with his knives as he climbed into the car with this perfect stranger. She drove based on the GPS coordinates without much conversation for the first fifteen minutes, but eventually spoke up.

"So what's the rush?"

"I'd like to visit somewhere then head to the airport," Jack said. "Like I said, I'd be happy to pay you."

"Times are tough around here. Everyone is gone."

"A demonic drowning of the city will do that to you," Jack said.

"So why the stop?" she asked, looking at him. "It's not exactly on the way."

"If it's too much, I can find someone else—"

"No, no," she said. "Just curious."

They drove in silence until they reached their destination: a house on the coast.

"I'll be back in a few minutes," Jack said, slamming the door behind him. He jumped over the gate and walked down the dirt path to the mansion. This had been the place where they'd hoped to meet Diogo, but they were instead ambushed because

Anya had trusted the wrong person. Jack had lost his cool and said hurtful things—all of which he would come to regret. It was becoming a pattern, and he wanted to break it for good.

He bypassed the house, still in disarray from the nox fight, for the cliffside. After Jack had left Anya in the house, she'd taken matters into her own hands and ventured to this rocky outcropping. Her intention had been to end her life, but Diogo had intervened and taken her to Ath-kur instead.

Jack stood on the rocky edge, looking out onto the Atlantic Ocean and trying to imagine what she must've felt like. Abandoned and alone, much like she probably felt now. But unlike back then, today, Jack was determined to prove her wrong.

"Anya, if you can…" His voice died on the heavy wind that blew in from the open ocean. "Anya, if you can hear me, or if you go back in time to this moment, I just want you to know that I'm not giving up on you. No matter what you might be afraid of, or what you're scared of, I'm on your side."

He waited, hoping, just a little, that she might make an appearance.

"I didn't know what they'd do to Diogo until after it happened. If I had, I would've done everything in my power to stop it," he continued. "I'm… God, Anya, I'm so sorry. This has all spiraled out of control."

He looked down at the rocks then sharply back up, not wanting to think about what might've happened that night had she decided to take that step.

"I know you're hurting, and you don't want to see me, but please know I'm here for you. I want to help you." He released a laugh. "I don't really know how I can, but if it would make you feel less alone…"

He paused once more, hoping with all his heart to hear her voice. But it was just the sound of waves on the shore.

"You don't have to explain yourself," Jack said. "You don't have to tell me anything you don't want to. But I'm not going to stop until I find a way to get to you. So maybe you could make it easy on me and show me how to find you."

Despite his most ardent hopes, no one appeared on that cliffside, and his heart broke a little. But he was nothing if not determined. He turned and walked back to the waiting car, where the girl was playing on her phone. She sat up when he opened the car door and sat down.

"Where to now?"

"The airport," Jack said, giving the cliffside one final look. "I have a plane to catch."

CHAPTER TWENTY-SIX

It was rare for Cam to be on the other end of a fight between her and Jack. Usually, she was the one throwing tantrums, refusing texts, and stubbornly insisting that she was right. Being on this side was hard, and she felt bad for every time she'd put Jack in this position.

Lotan had promised he'd try to talk some sense into Jack on the way to Lisbon, but Cam wasn't optimistic. The only way Jack would speak with her again was if she did a complete reversal and accepted that Anya was innocent of everything.

Cam sat in the back of the tent, listening to the Council debate and discuss their security measures, frantic for a solution now that Anya could get past their most ardent defenses. They'd combed the weapons development tent for a grain of Nullius sand, but found none. Cam's team had been meticulous about keeping it all together, giving whoever had taken it easy pickings.

But in Cam's mind, the missing weaponry was the least of their problems. As Jack had so clearly pointed out, they were now dependent on the speed of human travel. No longer could a platoon of talisman-laden ICDM agents move to places around the world at a moment's notice. Cam didn't think the demons would stop attacking just because ICDM couldn't get to them. If anything, the shit was about to hit the fan.

When the Council conversation lulled, Cam cleared her throat and sat up. "Can I put a new item on the agenda to discuss? What are we doing to prepare our ICDM agents around the world?"

"What?" María asked.

"Have we given them directions on talismans?" Cam asked, looking around. "Have we told them to draw on their bullets, mark their skin? I think we should be preparing them. Since, you know, we can't be there to help when the demons attack again."

"We have given them some instruction," María said. "But our focus—"

"The sand is gone, and it's not coming back," Cam said, exhaustion overpowering her filter. "So we need to focus on the tools we do have. And unless the demons decide to strike up an attack in our backyard, we're going to very quickly move from an active suppression force to one that merely monitors the situation."

George glanced at her and nodded. "She does have a point. Is there any pattern to the attacks? Can we possibly predict where they might begin?" He directed the question to the aide behind him.

"They're as random as Demon Spring," the aide admitted. "Elokos showing up in kappa strongholds, lilins in former nox cities. Kappas in the middle of the desert."

"So we need to focus on a whole-world defense," Cam said.

"We don't have the resources for that," María said. "We're already getting complaints from governments about the number of casualties. Portugal is threatening to pull out of ICDM altogether."

"Now's not the time for that," Cam said. "If anything, they should be joining with ICDM to help protect the world."

"That's not their job," George said, heavily. "That's our job. And they expect us to figure it out."

Cam was growing frustrated with humanity, but most of all, these defeatist Councilmembers who seemed to want to shoot down every idea she had. No wonder Jack wanted to fuck off for a while.

The tent flap flew open, and another aide ran inside, and the bottom fell out of Cam's stomach. Running aides didn't bode very well these days.

"We have reports of attacks in ten cities," she said, her face ashen. "New York, Riyadh, Karachi, Bogotá, Salvador, Incheon, Buenos Aires, Lagos, Montreal, and Budapest."

The Councilmembers looked at one another and two of

them hung their heads. "We can't do anything from here."

"Yes, we can," Cam said. "Send them instructions to build anti-demon talismans."

The staffer shook her head. "Initial counts from the news report put the demons in the tens of thousands. There's... It's not going to be enough."

Tens of thousands. Cam sank down into the chair, a buzzing in her ear. There wouldn't be a single human left in those cities within a few hours.

And as easy as it would be to blame Anya, to say that the athtar magic had addled her brain and driven her nuts, this was...beyond even what Cam considered to be something she'd do. But what other explanation was there? She didn't have Jack's blind faith in Anya, but damn, she wished she did.

That would make this reality much easier to stomach.

Cam didn't stop shaking, even when she arrived back in the apartment. It was all so ridiculous she actually laughed about it, before the tears came. So many humans, so many casualties. Cam's only hope was that, like Paris, the demons would be more interested in conversion than murdering. It certainly seemed they were expanding their ranks.

She sank into the couch, burying her head in her hands. She couldn't help but think about Freyja and Tabiko. How could they condone such a thing? Freyja was clearly angry with Anya, but to allow her demons to wreak havoc on humanity seemed way out of character for her.

Cam wanted to go to the Underworld herself and shake the demonic belus, including one very confusing athtar, but she was stuck. And she absolutely hated it.

The lock on the door turned, and Cam rose, hoping that it might be Jack. But her heart sank when Lotan walked in alone.

"I'm not that bad to look at, am I?" he asked with a little laugh.

Cam didn't care if he'd lost his memory; she needed human contact. So she crossed the room in seconds and fell into his arms, breathing him in. Burying her head in his chest. And for the briefest of moments, she was at peace, grateful that in this chaotic world, she still had the feel of his heart under her ear.

"Jack will come around, I promise," he whispered, running his hands up and down her back. "But he's gone to find Anya."

"He won't find her," Cam said. "Unless she wants to be found."

"Then I suppose he will just search forever." Lotan walked Cam to the couch. "That man is nothing if not determined."

"Did he…" She didn't know if she wanted to ask. "Did he say anything about me?"

Lotan cleared his throat, perhaps measuring his words. "He remains convinced of Anya's innocence."

She sank into the couch. "I need a drink."

"Then let me oblige." Lotan rose and walked to the cabinet then frowned. "Bad news. We are out of alcohol."

"Perfect," Cam said with a watery laugh. "Just fucking perfect. I have to deal with this sober."

"But I'm here," Lotan said, walking back to the couch to join her. "Surely, that counts for something."

He flashed her his winning smile, and she sighed, resting her head on the couch. "I never did get to ask what you thought of my parents."

"Because you left me in Charleston?"

She winced. "Yes?"

"I don't love that you think I'm useless, but you've had a hard day, so we'll discuss that when things aren't so dire," Lotan said with a knowing look.

Cam expected his wandering hands to find her hips and take his revenge, but they stayed where they were. And just as quickly as a small fire had begun in her core, it went out.

"What is it?" Lotan asked.

"Nothing," Cam said with a half-smile. She didn't want to have to explain the way things used to be, to expect Lotan to be the same person. But damn, what she wouldn't give for him to just *know* what to do.

"No," Lotan said, taking her hand. "What is it?"

"Nothing."

"It's not nothing, because you've been keeping your distance from me," Lotan said. "And I can't help but feel there's something you aren't telling me."

She licked her lips, unsure what to tell him. There was a chance he would never recover, and she hadn't wanted to think about what that meant for the two of them.

"Cam."

"I miss you," she whispered, tears falling down her cheeks. "The old you."

"What specifically do you miss?" Lotan asked.

"Just…your presence," Cam said. "The way you'd somehow keep me on my toes and make me feel safe at the same time. Waking up next to you and crawling into your arms. Knowing that whatever was bugging me, I could come to you and you'd help me figure it out."

"You can still come to me—"

She closed her eyes. "I'm so sorry. I shouldn't be telling you this. It's not your fault that you don't remember." She covered her face with her hands. "You gave up everything to be with me, and I'm just being—"

"You know, Jack had some good advice," Lotan replied, removing her hands to hold them, sending chills down her spine. "He told me I should stop trying to recreate the past and that you and I should build a new future with what we have today."

Cam looked up at him. "Jack said that?"

"And he's right, I may never get everything back," Lotan replied, tugging her closer. "But I knew the moment I woke up that I loved you with everything I have. It's etched deep in my bones, something neither magic nor time nor anything else could erase." He brought her knuckles to his lips and kissed them softly. "I believe that's why they call it soulmates. My soul calls to yours because they're meant for one another. It doesn't need a reason."

Cam stared into his eyes, terrified of the emotion she saw

there. And yet, she began to question why—why was she always running from him? Why, when he was the only one she wanted to see at the end of the day? Why, when she found herself wanting to talk to him first instead of Jack for the first time in her life? Why couldn't she just accept that everything he said was true?

Because you're a damned coward.

No, she wasn't; she was a Macarro. She'd faced down demons and monsters and the worst the world had to offer without blinking. And here she was, wringing her hands because this man had confessed his undying love to her. It was ridiculous —and it needed to stop.

"I...I love you," Cam whispered, as a tear fell down her cheek.

"Well, I should hope so," Lotan replied, with a knowing smile.

She couldn't help it; she broke down into sobs and he pulled her close, kissing her for the first time. It was different, but only at first. His wandering hands seemed to remember her body, and as he deepened his kiss, she sighed and allowed herself to fall into it.

"You know," Lotan said, "I think my memory might be coming back. This all seems *very* familiar to me."

It *was* familiar—the touch of his tongue against hers, the weight of his body as he pushed her onto the couch, the scent of his skin. She opened her eyes, searching his for that spark of light that she'd grown accustomed to seeing when they locked gazes.

And there it was, shining just for her. The man she'd been looking for had been here all along, and she'd just been too cowardly to let herself accept it.

"What?" Lotan asked.

She slid her hand behind his head and pulled him back down, taking from him what she'd been missing. He slipped his hands under her shirt, finding her skin, and to her absolute delight, he began exploring down her stomach, finding the button of her jeans then—

She giggled and gasped as he kissed her neck. "Lotan…"

Oh, but he surely remembered what she liked, and she arched her back. His fingertips dipped inside of her, toying and teasing and gently massaging as warmth spread throughout her body. She'd allowed herself to become his domain once, and clearly, he was reclaiming his territory.

She gasped and moaned his name, and he covered her mouth with his, whispering her name on his lips. "I missed hearing you beg for me," he said with a devilish grin.

And oh, he'd made her beg. In his arms, she'd put down her guards and put away the weight of the world. She submitted to him, she realized just what she'd been missing. Lotan was her private island, her sanctuary. The place where she could fall apart and be dependent on someone else for a change.

"Come for me," he whispered against her skin.

She obliged shortly thereafter, not caring that it was late and the neighbors probably heard. Lotan had a way of making her forget every rule she'd ever tried to abide by.

She opened her eyes as she came back down to earth, her heart pounding and her breath deep. He was smiling, proud of himself, but more importantly, waiting for the go-ahead to continue. Wordlessly, she found the buckle of his belt, quickly releasing him from his pants. He helped her shrug off hers before they settled back on the couch, and he carefully slipped inside her.

He exhaled a long breath, a ragged smile on his lips. He rested his hands on her hips and moved slowly at first. She rocked her hips with him, finding their usual rhythm and falling back into it as easily as breathing. She clenched with each thrust, earning moans and grunts from him.

He stopped abruptly, turning her over and positioning her on her hands and knees before finding his way inside her again. Each thrust sent shoots of pleasure up her spine. She held on to the couch cushion, her knees buckling. If not for Lotan's strong grip on her hips, keeping her in place, she would've fallen over.

With a final thrust, he, too, cried out, falling on top of her and bracing himself with his hands. His heart pounded against her back, his breath coming in gasps. But he placed a gentle kiss on the back of her neck before rolling over and pulling her with him.

There they remained, enjoying the aftermath and the closeness.

"Yes," he said, after a long moment. "Very familiar."

She giggled and closed her eyes, resting her cheek on his broad, sweaty chest. Perhaps he wouldn't get all his memories back. Perhaps he wouldn't be exactly the same person he'd been as the nox prince. But he was still her sanctuary. And she would never forget it again.

CHAPTER TWENTY-SEVEN

Lotan couldn't sleep, enraptured by the sight of Cam's soundly sleeping face, her cheek pressed into his shoulder. She was exquisitely peaceful, something he hadn't seen since awakening for the first time. Here in his arms, this strong, capable woman could be vulnerable and know what it was to find respite from the world. That he alone could lift the heavy burden from her shoulders, even for a moment, was a power he wouldn't ever take for granted.

She made a noise, looking up at him sleepily, confused, then rolled onto her other side, curling into a ball and dragging the covers with her. He smiled, propping his head up on his arm and watching her for a moment longer before deciding to let her rest.

He slipped out from the covers and dressed himself, then ventured into the kitchen in search of food. When he found none, and his stomach protested going back to bed, he quietly left the apartment for the all-night shop around the corner.

It was close to midnight, and there didn't seem to be a soul out on the street except for him. But the store was open, and the same grizzled, old clerk was there.

Lotan smiled at him. "Evening."

The man grunted and turned back to the television.

Lotan frowned; they were usually somewhat chatty, since Lotan had started to frequent this place often. He grabbed a basket and a few items, mostly snacks and chips in case Cam woke up, as well as some bread and eggs to make breakfast in the morning. He walked up to the clerk, finding the television off for once.

"Nothing good on?" Lotan asked.

"Too much," he said heavily, ringing up Lotan's things. "First it was here, now it's all around the world." He looked up at Lotan. "You said your friends were ICDM?"

"I did," Lotan said.

"They're nothing but useless money-suckers," the clerk replied, bagging Lotan's things with a scowl. "They didn't protect Geneva, and they aren't protecting these other cities. Why do they exist at all?"

"It seems as though they're doing their best," Lotan said, hoping he wasn't going to get thrown out for saying the wrong thing. "This is, as I understand it, unprecedented."

"Then they should've prepared for it," he said, his dark eyes growing fiery. "It's not as if this wasn't always an inevitability."

Lotan just nodded. "Soon, they'll find a solution and will have this taken care of."

"And in the meantime, how many people will die?" The clerk sat back down in his chair and stared off into the distance, saying nothing more.

"Take care," Lotan said, grabbing his bag and taking a few steps backward before briskly walking out of the store.

Lotan hurried back to the apartment, full of uncertainty. Cam had said the humans were growing weary, but to hear someone like the clerk, who'd previously been very complimentary of ICDM, become so jaded was disconcerting. ICDM might've had their hands full, but they were the only ones qualified to deal with this problem, weren't they?

But something else unnerved Lotan. It wasn't just the anger; it was the hopelessness he'd seen in the clerk's eyes. He, like the rest of the world, had grown weary of the constant danger and surprise attacks. If Jack was right, and there was someone else behind this, was that part of their plan?

And if so, *why did this plan sound so damn familiar?*

He opened the door to the apartment as quietly as he could and put the groceries away. Though he probably should've returned to bed, he made a beeline for the living room and flipped on the television, turning the volume down so he didn't wake Cam in the other room.

He flipped through the channels until he found the news station the clerk had been watching, showing the scene as it was there. Smoldering buildings, helpless victims, dead bodies everywhere. Demons running amok. The presenters spoke in French, which was starting to come back to Lotan, though he was a long way from speaking it. Even they seemed at a loss for words at the chaos, except they all seemed to be questioning the same thing—where was the woman who kept showing up to save them? And more importantly, where was ICDM?

"Where'd you go?" Cam said, appearing behind him, wearing nothing but a t-shirt and underwear.

"Did I wake you?"

"No," Cam said, coming to sit next to him. She pulled her bare knees to her chest and held her legs with a sad sigh, and he put his arm around her. Instead of pulling away, she leaned into him, closing her eyes. "This is some shit, isn't it?"

"And there's nothing we can do?" Lotan asked.

She shook her head. "Lotan, I don't know what to think. I wish there were someone else I could pin this on. We just found out that ten cities are under attack. Demons just appearing out of nowhere, slaughtering, converting—like ten Demon Springs at once."

"Demon Spring?" Lotan shook his head.

"It's when Bael used to cause a schism between the worlds," Cam said. "He'd pick a random city, send his horde of demons to destroy it for two or three weeks, then they'd all go back down to the Underworld."

"Bael." Lotan blinked, rubbing his chin. "Why is that name familiar?"

"He was Anya's ex—the original athtar demon," Cam said. "But he's dead. Anya killed him."

"I see."

"Anyway, without Anya or her portal, all we can do is sit back and watch the carnage," Cam said. "Well, they'll sit back and watch it. I couldn't stomach being in that tent much longer." She shook her head. "I don't… I'm not sure I can be part of this anymore, Lotan. Ten thousand demons against a few hundred ICDM agents isn't a fair fight."

"Then maybe Jack's attempts aren't in vain," Lotan said. "If he can get through to Anya…?"

"Anya has this thing called the Sight, where she can see things around the world. If she's looking, there's no way she's missed this. So either she hasn't been looking, or she has, and she doesn't care." Cam licked her lips. "She looked pretty finished with humanity in that video."

That same thought came back, that this all seemed so coordinated, so *familiar*. It was on the tip of his tongue. "What if it's not Anya, like Jack thinks?"

"That's the thing," Cam said. "There's no way it could be anyone else. ICDM thought it could've been Diogo, but he's…" She shook her head. "And so that it's still happening points to one person."

"Explain it to me," Lotan said, hoping hearing it in more detail might jog his memory.

Cam released her legs and dropped her feet to the floor. "You see the way the demons just show up? That they appear seemingly out of nowhere? Only an athtar can do that." She gestured toward the screen. "Especially now, where they're in multiple places at the same time."

"They could have a portal," Lotan said.

"There aren't any more."

"Jack said the noxes had a portal, right?" Lotan said. "Perhaps one of these demons made one."

"The nox portal was static," Cam explained. "It was in Mexico City and led to the noxlands. Only Anya could make one that jumped around like the one we had. Even Diogo's just stayed put in Lisbon."

"And there's no one else it could be?"

Cam rested her hand on his thigh. "Lotan, I know you want her to be innocent. Fuck, I want her to be, too. But unless some other athtar sprung out of nowhere—"

Finally, something clicked in Lotan's head. "Bael."

Cam blinked. "What about him?"

"He could do this."

"He could, but, as I said, he's dead."

But now it was all making sense to Lotan. He'd *seen* Bael in Geneva. That was why it had been so odd to him—so unsettling. Bael was supposed to be dead, but he was standing in the middle of the street. He'd spoken to Lotan.

He was alive.

"He's not," Lotan said, leaning forward. "I saw him. Here.

Right outside this apartment."

"That's impossible," Cam said, sitting up. "Maybe you misremembered something from your past."

"No. That man I told you about—the athtar who slowed time—that was *Bael.* I thought it so odd at the time, but now I remember. I remember..." He could scarcely breathe as his thoughts tumbled faster than he could process them. "I remember him and watching him die. I remember running for our lives. But he's *alive.* Somehow."

Cam was staring at him and he half-expected her to say he was insane, that she didn't believe him. But she exhaled slowly.

"Assuming that's true, which I'm not saying it is, because I don't even know *how* it could be, but...it would explain... *everything.*" She ran her hand through her hair. "The demons, how Anya's trying to fix this and won't tell us who's behind it. It would be very much like her to hide this from us."

"Would it?"

"I mean, would you want to tell your friends that your ex who terrorized humanity for three thousand years was back?" Cam asked before sinking back into the couch.

"No, I suppose not," Lotan said. "But she would've at least told Jack."

"Unless she was trying to keep her distance," Cam closed her eyes and sat back, cursing softly to herself. "She kept telling us to stay in Geneva. Because *Bael wouldn't be able to reach us.* Did he seem—"

"Ethereal? Like he wasn't really here?" Lotan nodded.

"Another oddity."

Cam jumped to her feet and started pacing, chewing her thumb so much Lotan was sure she'd cleave it off. "Fuck me, this is making so much sense. Bael is back, somehow—some way. He's bringing these demons to attack, and Anya..." She stopped and looked at him, her eyes wide. "We have to find Jack. We have to tell him what's going on. If Bael is back, Jack has a target on his back. And if Anya's turned a blind eye to humanity, nobody will be around to save him."

CHAPTER TWENTY-EIGHT

Bael, master of the Underworld, Lord of the Mountain, emperor of all he surveyed, the original athtar demon, was starting to grow annoyed with that human. Jackson George Grenard. Aged twenty-eight. A blink in Bael's lifetime. But his hold on Bael's beloved Anat was unshakeable—as was, apparently, hers on him.

The lilin assigned to get information out of him had been unsuccessful. She'd described a man willing to walk for hours to reach a desolate beachside cliff before getting a ride to the airport. Bael had stepped back to the moment when the human had stood on the edge, declaring his love to the wind and promising he wouldn't give up until they were reunited. It was all so sickening and threatened to throw Bael's carefully laid plans into disarray.

Now this Jackson George Grenard had arrived in Mexico City, presumably to poke around the old nox den in search of a portal. But as with Lisbon, he would come up empty. Still, this human was persistent and that could spell trouble.

Bael's only saving grace was that Anat had not left Ath-kur in days. She was confined to the little house she'd built for herself, refusing to allow him entry. She would never know the lengths this human would go to in order to reach her. And if Bael played this right, perhaps she'd never see his fingerprints on the human's death.

It had taken him some time in the river to locate the moment when the nox prince had given up his powers. It was all so heroic and idiotic, but the boy had always had an odd streak about him.

Bael had hoped that the ewû, the winged creature formed from humans who'd ventured into the Nullius, would take the prince for another of its legion of mindless guardians of the Abbunatu—the central location for all demonic power in the Underworld. But Anat and her humans had been faster, and they'd saved the reverted human.

But for Bael, the rehû, the magic that had been given to Lotan when his mother gave birth to him, was the more intriguing thing to follow. It floated back toward the Abbunatu, completely ignored by the other ewû circling the area. All the winged creatures wanted was human flesh to create more of themselves.

Bael walked down the craggy rock into the cave where the Abbunatu could be found. It had certainly grown more powerful over the millennia, thanks solely to Bael. It was Bael who had found out that the nox Xo had transformed her husband from human to demon, that this power could be *passed* from belu to human. His first experiment, Anat, had been a resounding success—until recently, of course.

And when he'd allowed the belus into the world, telling them how to grow their powers, what had once been a tiny ball of energy had turned into this, a sprawling, massive creature that took up nearly the entire cave where the ewû had imprisoned it at the dawn of time.

The rehû magic from the nox prince floated toward its final resting place, connecting with the white outer shell of demonic power and being absorbed almost immediately. It shimmered and shook as it took back every ounce of power the noxes had accumulated over the millennia then expanded another two feet.

Bael smiled as a ball of magic came from the center, now a kūbu, a baby magical source that would feed a new belu and race of noxes. It was that magic Bael now followed to the human world.

It often took a kūbu several days to find a final resting spot, so Bael was patient. After all, his monsters were distracting the humans, and without Anat's assistance, they could no sooner stem the tide of demons than stop the flow of a waterfall. And if he knew Anat, and he did, even if she did cast her gaze on the world, she wouldn't want to help them. Not after what they'd done to poor Diogo.

Bael arrived in the human world, walking behind the small ball of black magic as it sizzled and popped. He'd always thought the kūbu remained in the Underworld after the death of a belu. But the nox who'd held the magic before Xo had killed himself, that kūbu had traveled to the human world. And so, apparently, had the kūbu Lotan had given up.

It took its time, meandering through the world until it finally settled in a small cave in the middle of the Mongolian desert. Once it had settled, Bael returned to his body out of the time river then transported himself to that spot in the present, where the small ball of magic was there, waiting for an unsuspecting human to stumble across it.

Bael gathered the magic in his hand, knowing the perfect human to take this magic as the new nox belu —one who would not only already have an intimate knowledge of what it meant to be a nox, but who would also very nicely solve his Jackson Grenard problem.

CHAPTER TWENTY-NINE

Anya wasn't sure how many days it had been since Diogo's death. She'd given him a burial worthy of the most fearsome warriors, placing several of his beloved books next to him to keep him company in death. It had been a solitary exercise, but she couldn't think of one person she wanted there with her.

In her angrier moments, she considered destroying the house she'd built for herself and building anew but couldn't bring herself to do it. After all, moping around was something she'd done a lot of in this house in Seattle, so it made sense to hide away in the Ath-kur replica. She even had a steady stock of cheese puffs to keep her company.

Bael hadn't come back to visit, and she was pleased she'd

managed to expel him for good. In a couple decades, perhaps, she might start to care what nightmare he was unleashing on the humans, but at this point, she couldn't help but feel like they deserved it.

But in her weaker moments, she missed Jack. They'd come so close, and she might've invited him into her sanctum, but then he would bring his heroism, his need to protect the humans, the real world. He would never be content to sit around and watch the world go by—and he'd made it clear he did not want to join her in demonic immortality. And as much as she wanted to convince him otherwise, even in her darkest moments, she knew it wouldn't be fair.

So she sat in her misery, staring out the window as the demonic sun rose and fell, creating more junk food to eat, and even managing a hike up the mountain to sit and look out across her solitary domain.

There, she mourned Freyja, Tabiko—even old Biloko. Figures in her long memory who'd been always there, antagonists and friends alike. Bael was single-handedly changing the fabric of the things that had been steady in her long life, but if she stayed here in this bubble, he couldn't change everything.

Her stomach grumbled. She couldn't subsist on cheese puffs alone—as much as she wanted to.

She leaned back on the rocks and thought about all the places she could go and what delicacies she could enjoy. The world was at her fingertips, and she could pick anything the humans had come up with to sate her appetite.

But all she wanted was a burger from the hole-in-the-wall place at the base of their mountain near Seattle.

Jack had introduced her to it, and she'd practically inhaled the meal, barely tasting it. But she'd gone back the next day then three more times in the next month. And now, the salty fries and juicy sauce on the burger were all she wanted.

The sun was shining, and the air was crisp, but the small neighborhood market center was desolate. No cars were in the grocery store parking lot—odd for a (she checked) Saturday afternoon. And the burger place was closed, as was every other store in the shopping center, save the grocery store.

Anya walked in, catching the attention of the manager, who seemed to be the only one actually working. She opted for some nice cheese and sausage and a few bottles of wine that would last her for the evening. But the manager's gaze was on her as if she were about to shoplift.

She offered him a smile and walked up to the check-out counter, placing the basket on top.

"Slow day?" she said.

He grunted and began ringing up her things.

"Where…is everyone?" she asked. "Seems odd for this place to be so deserted on a Saturday."

He gave her a sideways look. "Have you been living under a rock?"

"More or less," Anya said. "So…?"

He turned around and clicked on the television behind him,

showcasing a scene straight out of the worst Demon Springs Anya had ever seen. It was in Lagos, but as the video rolled through the different scenes, there were more. At least fifteen if the chyron at the bottom was to be believed.

Elokos scampered down the street, taking what they wanted from the empty stores. There didn't seem to be a live human in sight—they'd either been transformed or killed.

"Shit," Anya breathed. "How long has this been going on?"

"A week? Two weeks? It's all blurring together. ICDM's been completely useless about it, too. I don't know what they're doing in Geneva, but they've basically left us all to fend for ourselves."

Anya licked her lips. *She'd* left the humans to fend for themselves—and she'd been gleeful about it. But Bael had taken things to a new level—he was destroying *everything*.

"Do they know who's responsible for this?" Anya asked. "Someone like Bael, perhaps?"

"He's dead."

Shit. So Bael hadn't revealed himself yet. "Demons don't—"

"Look, lady, if you want my opinion, I think these demons have figured out that they can destroy all of us because we ain't got anything to defend ourselves with."

At least, not against numbers like that.

"Maybe Bael wasn't the worst thing," the manager said. "At least we had peace for four years. Was a nice compromise."

Something clicked in Anya's mind. "Thank you. Stay safe."

She hurried out the front door and dashed around to an alley where she'd be out of sight of the manager. This was starting to make sense—and it was so quintessentially *Bael.*

He wasn't raising an army to destroy everything; he was raising an army to beat the humans into submission and then show up as a savior. They would turn against ICDM, turn against each other, become hopeless, then he would appear and the chaos would end. It would, of course, end because he'd started it, but he would never let the humans know that. They would fall to their knees and thank him for his mercy.

It was all so sickeningly familiar—the pattern she, herself, had lived for three thousand years.

But this time, Bael's intended victims would have a fighter in their corner, someone to shine the light of truth over the lies and help them realize that the savior was really the monster. The way Jack had helped her see the light all those months ago.

Anya returned to Ath-kur, determination set in her bones. If she was going to unmask Bael, she needed to find out where his hordes were coming from. Thus far, she'd been too scared to step back into the time river, lest she bring back another version of Bael. But without even Diogo's limited power, she had no choice —it was the only way to know what was really going on.

She stood in the center of her living room and pressed her hand over her pounding heart as she reached for the river of time. It was familiar, even after all these weeks. And with a final reminder that she was in command of her own destiny, and she had nothing to fear from Bael, she adjusted her sails and headed backward to the initial moments of the attack in Budapest.

Anya walked along the streets, watching the destruction undo itself in slow motion. Elokos moved backward, and she followed their path until she saw it—the portal where they were entering the city.

Anya took a long breath and pressed forward until she reached it, stepping around an eloko jumping out of the portal to climb inside.

Her breath caught in her throat. This place was nothing like she'd ever seen before. It was as expansive and populated as a city, with makeshift houses dotting the landscape. Demons of every stripe mingled, gathering weapons and preparing for the onslaught. It was a place that should've taken a hundred years to put together, but Bael had managed it in a couple of weeks.

She gazed up ahead to where Bael's castle stood above the rest. It was identical to the one they'd shared in Ath-kur before his death, and it sent chills of fear down her spine. This almost seemed like a new Underworld.

"Do you like it?"

Anya swallowed and turned to Bael.

"I confess, I didn't think I'd see you out and about so soon, my love," he replied, coming to stand next to her. "I thought you too afraid of the time river to venture into it again."

"The endless massacre in the human world forced my hand," Anya said. "What is this place, Bael?"

"A reminder of the depths of my power, dear Anat," Bael said. "I told you that I'm all things, that I can make the world whatever I want. And now you see what I meant." He lifted his chin toward the castle. "The old demonic underworld no longer holds any space for us. We can build anew in our home. I have made it exactly the way you remember it, and your chair is waiting."

"Will you stop the slaughter of humans?" Anya asked.

"Soon, there will be no more humans to slaughter," Bael said. "And then, yes."

"That's not what I meant." She turned to him. "But you knew that."

"Just like I know this silly affection for the humans isn't what's truly in your heart," Bael said. "You have killed more humans than—"

"I know exactly how many humans I've killed, Bael," Anya said, stepping toward him with fire in her veins. "I know this because when I thought I was cursed, I felt I had to atone for every single one of them. But you never thought to ask, or care when I cried myself to sleep after Demon Spring. You saw who you wanted to see as your Lady of the Mountain, and I'm sorry to tell you that I'm *not* that person."

She wanted him to get angry, but he just smiled, like she was a dog who'd taken his socks out of the closet.

"You will see, in time, that everything I've done is for you. But for now, you need to go."

His magic pushed against her, and she lost her footing, flailing back to the present time, where she collapsed onto her knees in the middle of her living room. But there was no time to mope or wait around. The humans had no idea what was coming, and she had to find the one human who might still believe her.

CHAPTER THIRTY

Jack awoke slowly in a strange room, taking a moment to remember where he was—a hotel in downtown Mexico City. Juana would've been happy to host him, but he didn't trust the Macarro grapevine not to spill the beans and didn't care to let María or Cam or anyone else know where he was. So he'd paid for a couple of nights when he arrived and promptly gone to bed wearing his clothes.

He rolled onto his back and stared at the ceiling. His mind spun from jet lag and latent anger. Anya's face on the pixelated screen haunted his dreams, the pain in her voice like a dagger in his chest. And it wasn't just Diogo she was mourning; she could see anger at *him* reflected in her gaze. He'd let her down by allowing ICDM to betray her. She would see it that way, at least.

Dragging himself out of bed, Jack made himself a cup of coffee in the machine and opened the blinds, looking out onto the city. There'd been a handful of people on the plane, the airport practically desolate. When they'd approached the city, the scars of the demonic attack could be seen from above. Large swaths of the city had been leveled. Now, here in the business part of town, there were few signs of life on the sidewalks below. Some men in suits and a few women on their phones. Nothing like it should've been.

After showering and dressing, Jack put his knives on his hips and a handful of talisman coins in his pocket. He didn't expect to need any of them, but he couldn't be too careful.

The hotel lobby was similarly empty, except for the small room serving breakfast. The television was on, blasting some images from the demonic attack. Jack almost walked by, until he realized that these cities were new—and happening now.

He grabbed an apple and stood a distance from the television. Jet lag and a lack of practice left him a little lost at the Spanish, but soon he managed to get the gist. Twenty cities under assault at once—a rolling onslaught.

ICDM nowhere to be seen.

Jack took a big bite of his apple and turned on his heel, walking out of the lobby. If he stayed longer, he might throw something at the television.

He had something of an idea where to start, having spent several weeks skulking around the nox neighborhood with Cam, looking for Lotan. It was hard to find a rideshare in the city (a common issue, it seemed, when the world was under siege), so he had to hoof it, taking most of the day to cross the city.

Deep in the bowels of his phone's memory banks, he found some of the addresses he and Cam had tried, and stopped by each one. They were all boarded up, the owners gone or dead.

Jack walked for what felt like hours, up and down the streets, back and forth the cross streets. He didn't come across another soul—human or otherwise—and was starting to think this was a fool's errand.

But when he turned the corner onto a small side street, he stopped short as recognition dawned. He'd been here before, the day he'd shown up armed to the teeth with anti-nox weaponry to rescue Cam from Yaotl's clutches and it had gone disastrously. It was only thanks to Anya's newfound athtar powers that he was saved. At the time, there had been no hope he could see, and yet Anya had pulled through for him.

Would the same happen now? More importantly, had he ever thanked Anya—really thanked her—for saving them that day? Probably not, as he'd been too focused on what her becoming athtar meant for their relationship. Selfish, selfish man.

He wrenched his gaze away and spotted something interesting a few paces away. A doorway with two black dog statues out front. They both had a crack going down the center, and as Jack reached out to touch them, they crumbled under his hand. There was something about them, like the air, that told him they'd once been filled with nox magic.

The threshold was dark, and he could see nothing beyond it,

but he stepped through anyway, keeping his hands on his knives. Almost immediately, he reached a set of stairs bathed in darkness. He descended slowly, making sure of his footing and keeping his ears open. He'd witnessed Lotan's magic disappearing into the Nullius, but one couldn't be too careful where noxes were concerned. One or two of them could be skulking about still.

He came to the bottom of the stairs and into a large room scarcely lit. Using his cellphone light, he illuminated the sides and the tall columns lining the room. Clawmarks had marred the stone floor, remnants of the wolf monsters walking around, but nothing else jumped out at him.

That was, until he stepped onto something wooden that echoed. He shone his light downward, revealing a trapdoor— perhaps a place to hide a portal?

The door was heavy, but with some effort, he managed to pull it up and over, revealing another set of stairs that plunged even deeper into the abyss. He shone his phone light down the staircase then carefully found his footing on every step, keeping his hand on the cool rock to his left.

He reached the bottom of the staircase and found another antechamber, again with claw marks on the floor. But as he shone his light around the room, there was nothing else—not even another hidden door.

"Shit."

He walked over to the wall at the far end of the room to get a closer look at the markings there. It was hard to make heads or tails of it, but the image of the portal carved into the stone was unmistakable. He was in the right place—the portal just no longer existed. Another dead end.

Deterred, but not defeated, Jack climbed both staircases until the bright light of the afternoon shone on him once more. He cast his gaze down one street then the other one, wracking his brain for his next move. Diogo's portal gone, the nox portal gone. Could there have been another *somewhere* in the world?

Stuffing his hands in his pockets, he walked the sidewalk, thinking of all manner of insane possibilities. He had nothing else to do, after all, except spend his time looking for ways to get to Anya. Perhaps one day, she might get curious about his attempts and come to find him. But that could take years. He might even be dead by the time she lifted her head.

He nearly tripped over his feet when the hairs on the back of his neck stood up. Athtar magic. A grin formed on his face as he turned, but then his heart sank. It wasn't Anya—it was a portal. And something *powerful* was about to come out of it.

Sensing it might be smart to find a hiding spot, he dashed into a nearby alley and pressed himself against the wall, scarcely breathing, lest the demon hear him.

"Ah, it is good to be home."

"Yaotl?" Jack put his hand over his mouth, hoping the demon hadn't heard. With a pounding heart, Jack peeled himself off the wall and turned the corner just enough that he could see the street.

Yaotl—and it *was* him—stood in the center of the street. His suit was impeccable, black on black, as always. But there was something different about him, something new and powerful. More concerning was the sense of overwhelming dread Jack felt as the nox's magic reached him.

How the actual *hell* did that magic still exist?

Behind him, out of an athtar portal, more noxes arrived—none of whom Jack recognized. They lacked Yaotl's power, and they seemed willing to follow every word.

"Secure the area," he said. "My lord promises me the humans are distracted at the moment, so we can reclaim our property without them bothering us."

"What if they do?"

"Then they will join our ranks or die," Yaotl said with a look.

"Yes, belu nox."

Jack's heart stopped in his chest. *Belu nox?* Had Yaotl somehow found Lotan's magic and taken it for himself, the same way Anya had?

But that was impossible. Lotan had sworn Yaotl had been taken care of. So how was he standing here, a belu nox, alive and well?

"Dammit, Lotan," Jack breathed. It was a pity the former nox prince didn't remember shit—he might have some explaining to do otherwise.

Yaotl walked down the street toward Jack, but his attention was elsewhere—on the same doors Jack had just come out of. He strolled down the dark stairwell, barking orders to the noxes who came behind him to find some oil and light the torches.

And what a parade followed. The portal widened, allowing ten noxes at a time to jump through the portal, hooting with excitement. Some ran up to buildings, wrenching the boards off the windows and heading inside. Others followed Yaotl down to the depths of La Madriguera.

The nox magic became so thick Jack had to reach into his pocket to grab his talisman. He needed to get out of here before any of them noticed him. He was a sitting duck, and they would soon notice a human in their midst. Yaotl, most assuredly, would have no mercy for him.

He peeled himself off the wall and slid toward the other end of the alley, but the noxes had managed to fill the street on the other side as well. Jack slinked back to the center of the alley, crouching to hide himself as best he could. If he could wait until darkness, he might have a shot at getting out of here.

In the meantime, he decided to swallow his pride and turn on his cellphone service. A notification loudly pinged, and he scrambled to turn his phone on silent, casting a wary gaze down the alley to make sure no one had heard him. When the coast was clear, he silently sent a text to Cam.

In Mexico City - Yaotl is back. He's the belu now. Emergency need for ICDM in the nox neighborhood.

He exhaled as he sent it, not sure what the local ICDM—hobbled by Yaotl's initial attack—could do. But at least they could alert the humans.

His phone buzzed and he looked down, hopeful—then his

heart sank.

Message undeliverable. Will try again later.

Swearing silently to himself, he pocketed his phone and settled in to wait until the onslaught of demonic abnormalities disappeared. Or until they found him—whichever came first.

CHAPTER THIRTY-ONE

Cam certainly didn't want to be flying to Mexico City, even if it was the nicest plane she'd been on. The last time she'd flown on Lotan's jet, she'd been a prisoner. This time, she was offered champagne and wine by a very nice attendant, and they had a three-course dinner as they flew over the Atlantic.

But it was still not as fast as stepping through a portal. And when the world was on fire, time was of the essence.

"I can't make the jet move any faster," Lotan said with a kind smile. "As much as I wish I could."

Cam exhaled through her nose. He was making sense, but she didn't want to listen. They really had no idea where Jack was, so Cam was making an educated guess based on...not much at all. Jack had gone to Lisbon in search of Diogo's portal, and the only other one in existence had been in Mexico City, at the bottom of La Madriguera.

He hadn't checked in with Juana, but that probably just meant he was staying at a hotel and trying to lie low. After all, he'd been explicitly clear that he didn't want Cam's help.

"What can I do for you?" Lotan asked, kneeling in front of her. "What can I do to make this time pass faster?"

She looked up into his eyes and half-smiled. At least he wasn't suggesting they go to the back and get handsy with each other again. "I'm afraid this isn't something you can fix. You're doing plenty, though. Don't worry."

"Perhaps we can talk about something else," Lotan said. "Something to distract you?"

Cam sat back. "Do you remember anything else about Bael?"

"Nothing I haven't told you already."

"Tell it to me again," Cam said. "Just in case."

Lotan sighed. "He was standing outside the apartment in Geneva. He'd slowed time, or so I guess. He wanted to know how I'd lost my magic, and I told him I couldn't recall. He then showed me that he couldn't touch me, thanks to the talismans. His hand went right through me."

"Was there anything else? Anything about his plan?"

"No. I think... I think he just wanted to see me as a human," Lotan said. "He said that becoming mortal and dying slowly was 'punishment enough,' if memory serves."

"So he was just coming to gloat," Cam said. "Sounds like

Bael."

"I disagree with him," Lotan said. "I'm quite content with my life, especially if it means I get to spend it with you."

In her distraction, all she could manage was another half-hearted grin. She toyed with her phone, turning the airplane mode on and off. There wasn't a signal up here, but she still thought she might try. The plane's Wi-Fi was spotty, so she wasn't getting much through that either.

Then her phone vibrated, nearly falling out of her hands. A series of texts from Jack came in and her heart sank into her stomach.

"Lotan."

"What?"

She showed him the phone and his brow furrowed.

"I remember Yaotl," he said. "And I remember taking his magic from him. He was human, of that I'm sure. Jack must be mistaken."

"Jack wouldn't make a mistake like this," Cam said, jiggling her foot as she looked out the window. They were still a few hours away from Mexico City. "The thing about magic is that it doesn't ever disappear completely—at least, if you and Anya are to be believed. It sits and waits for someone to claim it and start all over again. So your nox magic, once you gave it up, would've landed somewhere in the human world."

"Yes, but what are the odds that this particular former nox was the one to find it?" Lotan said.

"Perhaps..." Cam chewed her lip. "Anya said she heard Bael

calling to her and that led her to the magic. She thought maybe Bael wanted her to have it. Maybe Yaotl heard the call?"

Lotan abruptly stood. "I may not remember much, but I know I would *never* have wanted Yaotl to have it."

"You…did," Cam said with a little bit of a wince. "When you were still trying to figure out how it all worked, you thought you might bestow the magic on Yaotl, if he proved a good steward of the noxes."

"And then he led an attack on humanity around the world," Lotan said. "Clearly, my mind had changed."

"But obviously you didn't kill him," Cam said. "Maybe… maybe after you gave up your magic, he was so powerful he kept his."

"No…" Lotan blinked slowly, as if the memory were coming back to him. "Before I gave up my magic, I turned him into a human." He put his hand to his chest, grasping his shirt and furrowing his brow. "The only thing he craved was power, and so I left him powerless."

"Then how did he get it back?"

"I don't know," Lotan said, dropping his hand. "But that doesn't matter right now. Jack's in trouble. Once he's safe, we'll figure out how all this happened."

Cam nodded and looked down at her phone.

Hang tight, Jack. We'll be there as soon as we can.

Lotan arranged for a car to meet them on the tarmac and before long, they were zooming through Mexico City. Although it was rush hour, the streets were empty, which made the trip that much faster. Cam's text to Jack had finally gone through, and his *I'm safe and hidden, but need extraction* response finally allowed her to exhale somewhat. He'd provided them a cross street in the middle of the nox neighborhood and said that there were a few thousand noxes roaming around keeping him pinned down.

Cam had put a call in to her cousin Silvia to find out the story on the ground. Like most places, ICDM was functioning on a skeleton crew after Yaotl's attack, and even more agents had quit once the random demon fighting had started. This was the first they'd heard of demons in the old nox neighborhood, and they couldn't promise they could do much about it.

"So we're kind of on our own," Cam explained to Lotan when she'd hung up. "If it's as bad as Jack says, we may have to wait until dark to get him out."

"Should be soon, based on the sun," Lotan said, glancing at the sky before turning his attention to the streets. "This all looks so familiar."

Cam worried at her bottom lip. "Maybe it's not the smartest idea for you to come with me."

"Why not?" Lotan turned to her quickly with a furrowed brow.

"If Yaotl is really there, we don't know what state his memory is in... Lotan, he might try to kill you."

"Might try to kill you, too," Lotan said.

"What I mean is that Yaotl is vindictive. He might just..."

Cam didn't know how to explain it. "He might want revenge on you for kicking his ass last month."

Was it really just last month that all this had happened? Time was simultaneously moving too slowly and too fast.

"I'm not letting you go in there alone," Lotan said, a flash of his old, protective self coming across his face. "Besides, you won't be able to carry all the weaponry we brought."

It was one bag, but it was filled to the brim with as many anti-demonic talisman launchers and bullets as Cam could grab before leaving ICDM headquarters. After the mystery man had stolen their Nullius-sand filled ones, her staff had reverted to creating bullets with all five symbols on them. There weren't a lot, and certainly not enough to take on the thousands of noxes Jack had told them would be waiting in Mexico City, but it was something.

"I just...I just need you to be extra careful," Cam said. "And don't trust *anyone* you don't recognize."

The car driver dropped them off a few blocks from the nox neighborhood, and Lotan tipped him heavily and warned him to get out as quickly as he could. Cam shivered as nox magic reached her skin. If she hadn't believed Jack before, that was the only evidence she needed that the noxes had reemerged.

"We need to prepare." She pulled a pen from her pocket. "Turn around."

Lotan did as instructed, and she drew several anti-nox talismans on his skin. Then, she drew the symbols on her arms and stomach. She hoped they wouldn't find more demons in their midst, but Jack had only mentioned noxes.

"I still don't think this is a good idea," Cam said. "Protected and armed is great, but these noxes are dangerous. And you're human now—"

"So are you." Lotan looped one gun around his shoulder, and put another, smaller pistol in his waistband. "I suggest you save your breath so we can find Jack and get out of here before we attract any unwanted attention."

Lotan took the lead, guiding her through the darkening streets with a confidence that was so familiar. If Cam hadn't known better, she would've thought Lotan was back to his old self. But he wasn't, and she hadn't yet seen him with a weapon. Come to think of it, she hadn't seen him with a weapon as a demon, either—he hadn't really needed one as a house-sized dog monster with razor-sharp teeth. It would be better if they just got in and out without any fighting.

It didn't take them long to find their first nox, sitting on the stoop under a small apartment building, smoking a cigarette. Cam had almost missed him, but Lotan had yanked her to a hiding spot.

"Thanks," Cam said. "He looks freshly turned, but I don't want to take any chances."

"What do we do about him?" Lotan asked.

She glanced behind her. "We'll duck through this alley and go around. Hopefully, there aren't that many on the other street."

"I think I know a shortcut," Lotan said, taking her hand and giving her a grin that warmed her from head to toe.

They weaved in and out of the streets, aided by the darkening sky and the fact that their presence was hidden by the nox talismans on their skin. Cam's heart beat in her throat, but so far, all they had found were noxes who'd been freshly turned.

"Are we getting close?" Lotan asked. "These streets are familiar to me."

Cam didn't answer, motioning to a pair of noxes coming down the street, so they hid once more. When the coast was clear, they kept moving until they reached the cross streets where Jack had said he'd be hiding. But it was empty.

"He's supposed to be here," Cam whispered, walking into the alley. "Jack?"

Jack's head popped up, relief on his face. He put his finger to his lips and nodded at her to join him. "Thank God you're here."

"Thank God we were already on our way here," Cam whispered back as they knelt next to him in his small hiding spot. "Where did these noxes come from? Is there a portal in La Madriguera?"

"No, there was nothing down there," Jack said, looking over his shoulder. "It was some kind of portal in the middle of the street."

"Athtar?"

Jack clenched his jaw and nodded. "Don't even start—"

"It's not Anya." Cam shook her head fiercely. "Jack, it's...it's

Bael."

He turned to her slowly, his eyebrows almost disappearing into his hairline. "Come again?"

"Bael is back. We don't know how or why or any details. But Lotan saw him in Geneva," Cam said, glancing at Lotan on the other side of Jack. "And it makes sense—it's the explanation that makes so much sense, I can't believe we didn't think of it before."

"Except that we all saw his head separate from his body," Jack said.

"Like I said, no idea how he's back in the world, but he's definitely back," Cam said. "I'm sure Anya will be able to fill us in on the details."

"Assuming she'll ever speak to us again," Jack said. "There's no portal here, there's no portal in Lisbon. There's no way to get to her." He sighed. "And I'm out of ideas, Cam."

"We'll think of something," Cam said. "Just—"

"Well, well, well. What do we have here?" Cam's heart slipped into her stomach as she turned toward the sound of the voice. "Our former prince has returned to us."

CHAPTER THIRTY-TWO

Yaotl.

Lotan rose slowly, taking him in and allowing every conflicting emotion to run through him. Fear, familiarity, love, hatred. Memories of his childhood, of Yaotl's betrayal, of the good and bad times, it all blended in a murky watercolor that was somehow still understandable. If there had been any question in his mind why he'd been unable to kill Yaotl, this certainly answered it.

The nox had come alone, but that would be enough. Lotan knew that in his bones.

"I must admit, I didn't expect to see you here," Yaotl said. "I would've thought you and your bride would've been far from here, enjoying the fruits of your betrayal and living out a simple human life."

Lotan straightened and edged closer to Cam, who had her macuahuitl in her grip. "Hard to do that when it appears my mother's magic has been stolen."

"Oh? So your memories have returned?" Yaotl asked, his smile widening. "From the descriptions I was getting, I expected a simpleton who barely remembered his own name. Yet you stand before me, speaking as if you still have any say over this gift."

"Lotan, we need to get out of here," Cam murmured under her breath. "He's powerful."

"He's a fraud," Lotan said. "Who gave you that magic? Bael? What did you get in exchange?"

"The only thing I've ever wanted," Yaotl replied. "My pack."

"It was never yours," Lotan said, the words coming from somewhere deep inside him. His anger was ingrained, a knowing that awoke as his pulse quickened. "You never deserved it. And any nox that did, you made sure they didn't live long enough to receive it."

Yaotl walked closer. "There were hundreds of noxes who deserved this gift. You massacred them the day you chose your own selfish desires over the good of the pack."

"Selfish?" Lotan had to laugh. "The ones who followed your lead and slaughtered humans without mercy were the only ones who met their fates that day. There was no redemption for them." He shook his head. "I should've killed you when I had the chance."

"But you're too soft," Yaotl replied. "I clearly taught you nothing."

It was a fluid movement from man to monster, one Lotan was instantly familiar with. Instinctively, he dug within himself to answer, but there was nothing there, as much as the phantom magic wanted to. Today, he was just a man and his only defense would be the symbols drawn on his body—and the launchers he and Cam had brought.

"We need to go," Cam said, tugging Lotan's hand. "We can't fight against an original demon ourselves."

"Go where?" Jack said. "There are noxes everywhere."

"I'll take my chances against a bevy of new noxes," Cam said.

"I'm not running," Lotan said. "There's nowhere I can run where he won't find me. Might as well end this here and now."

Cam grabbed his hand and forced him to face her. "That means *you* end here and now, and we're not doing that."

"You should listen to your bride," Yaotl said, his voice echoing off the buildings. "You are not the demon you used to be. I could tear you in two without breaking a sweat."

"Get Jack out of here," Lotan said. "Find safety. But I'm not running from this fight."

Yaotl lunged, practically unhinging his large jaw as he drew closer. Lotan pushed Cam out of the way and rolled to safety moments before the teeth smashed down where they'd just been

Before Lotan could even lift his head, something large and black picked him off the ground and tossed him in the air. He landed hard against the brick wall, Cam's screams echoing in his mind. His head swam in a very unfamiliar way, and his body ached from the impact. Slowly, he leaned on his hands so he could find his feet again, but he looked up to see another large paw swinging at him. He couldn't move in time, and the rough pad flung him into the street. He rolled, his skin ripping wherever it made contact with the asphalt, until he came to a stop.

Yaotl's laughter echoed in his dazed head, and Lotan blinked as spots danced.

"Get up, boy. You are a prince, not a weakling."

He could vividly see himself as a young boy in the noxlands, learning to hold a sword and fight. The Yaotl then had been the same as now—merciless, angry, taking perverse joy in attacking an opponent much weaker. And yet, Lotan had felt something else in his hatred. There had been a desire for Lotan to obey, something that no amount of beating had ever brought forth. He would fight until he could no longer. Only this time, there would be no relief. Yaotl had no reason to keep him alive now.

But instead of more pain, a cry of anger came from the monster.

Cam stood with a talisman launcher, her eyes blazing and furious as she faced down the nox belu without a shred of fear.

"Did that hurt?" she asked, cocking the gun again. "I have more where that came from."

Yaotl turned to her, his wolfish teeth bared. "You are no longer amusing to me, human."

"Really?" Jack said, standing on the other side with another launcher. "Because I find her hilarious. You must need an attitude adjustment."

Lotan's voice cracked as he spoke. "Go! Run!"

"We don't leave people behind," Cam said. "And I think if we pump this guy full of enough talismans, he might just cry uncle after a while."

But Yaotl didn't look concerned, shaking off the talismans as they fell from his body with a small *clink*. "Your human defenses are of no consequence to me. I'm the belu nox, and that means I was touched by God himself."

"That doesn't mean anything anymore, haven't you heard?" Cam said, firing off another one. "You're just a dude who absorbed some magic. Nothing special about you whatsoever."

"I beg to differ."

A howl echoed through the night, and Lotan's blood ran cold. Shadows moved from all around, the alleys, the rooftops. The nox magic thickened, sending a chill down his spine. They were already outmatched with Yaotl alone; if he'd called every nox to him, they would be dead in seconds.

"You see, this is the sort of power you never could harness, boy," Yaotl said, transforming into his human form and smiling. "The ability to control and empower your pack to their greatest calling."

"I managed to control you, in the end," Lotan said, coming to his feet and wiping a trickle of blood from his forehead. "And take your magic."

"And I thank you for demonstrating that," Yaotl said. "Because now, I have ultimate control over every nox I've sired. I have eyes and ears in every corner of this world, allowing me to grow my power and dominance."

"Bael won't let you," Jack said, casting a wary look at the noxes on the roof above. "There's only one king in his world, and he's it."

"I have pledged my unending fealty to Lord Bael," Yaotl said, his voice taking on a new tone—caution. "And whatever he commands, I will obey."

"Is Daddy listening?" Cam said with a chuckle. "Gotta make sure you don't get too—what did you used to call it, Jack?"

"Too big for your britches," Jack replied. He turned quickly and fired the talisman launcher at a shadow that lunged from the rooftop. The shadow screamed and fell to the ground, motionless.

"Your fight is not with them," Lotan said, limping toward Yaotl. "It's with me. Let them go and you can have me."

"Fat chance," Cam said.

"You heard the lady," Yaotl said.

The onslaught was instantaneous, a river of noxes pouring into the street and filling the empty space in seconds. Lotan made to run toward Cam, but he was blocked by a trio of noxes, who smiled menacingly.

"Leave him to me," Yaotl said, parting the chaos with only his voice. "But give the boy a sword. I'd hate to fight someone more defenseless than he is already."

A sword landed in front of Lotan, and he picked it up, finding the weight familiar and hoping that muscle memory was stronger than his actual one. The pain in his limbs faded as his pulse quickened, and he steadied himself, this sight familiar.

Yaotl pushed him into the wall, their blades locked. Lotan knew the nox belu could crush him if he wanted to, so why wasn't he? What could he possibly be waiting for?

"Are you tired already, boy?" Yaotl asked.

Lotan dug deep, but he wasn't strong enough. Not by a long shot. This fight was a hopeless, one-sided endeavor. He was alive because Yaotl wanted him so.

"That's the thing about humans," Yaotl said, grabbing his chin. "They can fight all they want, but in the end, we will always win."

Lotan felt the magic seep from Yaotl, absorbing into his skin and through his bloodstream straight to his heart. It seized in fear, and his vision clouded. He was no longer in the alley, but the place was familiar. The dais, the two woven bags atop the stairs, the two nox guards with tears in their eyes, the fear that echoed in his chest.

Unbidden, his feet moved toward the bags, and some part of him knew what would happen next.

"So," Yaotl said, observing from behind him. "This is what you see."

"Stop," Lotan whispered.

But Yaotl was gone, there were just the two bags on the dais, and Lotan's young fingers untying the knot on the bag, the dread that filled him with knowing what he was about to see, a vision that had haunted him for years afterward.

The knot fell apart, and black hair spilled out. But it wasn't his mother's long, curly hair.

It was Cam's.

Lotan cried out, fighting against his own body to keep himself from looking further, but nothing was in his control. His Cam was dead, and he'd failed her.

"There is a choice," Yaotl said. "You can accept this gift from me and protect her."

A tempting offer. Lotan could almost make himself believe that if he took the magic, he would regain his former strength and stand tall against Yaotl. But the voice in his mind, the one that sounded like Cam, reminded him that he wouldn't be the prince, he would be Yaotl's spawn—his control effectively shot.

"No," Lotan whispered, finding a ray of hope somewhere in the bottom of his heart. "I refuse."

By sheer strength of will, perhaps helped by the talismans on his body, the nox magic was pushed from his mind.

As the last remnants of the fear magic slid from his consciousness, it was as if a veil had lifted from his mind. A thousand memories came rushing back to him, small moments and big ones, contexts around the flashes he'd been seeing all along. It was almost too much to process, so he didn't fight it— just let it wash over him like a river.

And when he took a deep, calming breath, he knew himself. He was Lotan, son of Xo and Mot, prince of the noxes. He was the man who'd chosen to give up his power, his extended life, his entire being to be with Cam Macarro.

He turned his gaze to her, fear etched on her face as she watched him, and he smiled. Even if this was the end of his journey, he was grateful he'd made the choices he'd made, if it meant knowing what it was to be in love with this magnificent woman.

"Well, boy? Will you submit to the belu nox?"

"I'm not your boy," Lotan said. "And you aren't a belu nox. No matter how powerful you think you are, you are still beholden to another, more powerful creature." He cracked a smile. "Same as it always was."

Lotan stood upright, refusing to bow, even in his final moments. He would welcome this death like a champion, like the prince he was, even if his throne had crumbled and turned to dust.

But Yaotl's sword was held aloft and didn't move—his body had gone completely still.

"Nice speech. Does that mean you'll kill him this time?"

CHAPTER THIRTY-THREE

Anya stood in the center of the alley, her grip on the time river absolute. Bael hadn't thought to protect his new nox belu, leaving him and every nox in the vicinity vulnerable to Anya. Perhaps that was his plan all along, or perhaps he thought Anya wouldn't cast her Sight on this world.

But she had, and the moment she'd Seen the nox in Mexico City, she'd arrived here in search of answers. She hadn't been surprised to see Yaotl as the nox belu, except that she hadn't known he was alive at all (and she'd have to have a conversation with Lotan about finishing what he started). But she had no choice but to step in when when her Sight had shown her the events in the alley.

She held her breath, gazing at the three of them and suddenly reconsidering her desire to tell them everything—especially Jack, who was staring at her with wide eyes, the talisman launcher hanging limply in his hand.

"Are you guys all right?" Anya said, her voice echoing in the street.

"I think so," Lotan said, pushing himself upright. "Might need some of that super healing."

She took a step back, surprised. "You…remember that?"

"Everything," Lotan said, trying to take a step forward, but his knees buckled. Cam was by his side in a moment, easing him to his knees and cupping his face. "I'm fine, my love. I promise."

"Don't do stupid shit like that again," she said. "I *told* you he was vengeful."

"Perhaps I should thank him," Lotan replied, taking Cam's hand and kissing it. "Because now I remember every single detail of why I love you."

She stared at him for a moment then grabbed his face and kissed him roughly. Anya turned away to give them privacy, but that meant she came face-to-face with Jack.

His face was smudged with dirt and blood, some of it his, and his hair stuck up from sweat. But his eyes, those brown orbs that held so much emotion, were now full of surprise. "You…came…"

"Of course," Anya replied with a nervous laugh.

He was grateful to see her now; why should she overturn the apple cart?

Because he deserves to know.

"Look, there's something I need to tell you—"

"Bael is back?" Jack offered.

She looked up, shocked. "How did you…?"

"I saw him," Lotan said, as Cam helped him to his feet. "In Geneva, weeks ago. It wasn't until yesterday that I recognized him. And for that, I'm sorry."

"We all are," Cam said, her eyes full of remorse. "God, Anya —I'm so sorry we ever doubted you."

Anya's lips parted. This was certainly not going the way she'd planned. She'd expected to be the one apologizing, not the other way around. But this was just the beginning. Once they found out *she* was responsible, they would be singing a different tune.

"Well," she cleared her throat and pulled her sword from its sheath, "I think we need to deal with this nox situation first, then we can…we can talk about Bael."

Lotan straightened, grimacing, and gently pushed Cam away. "I'll do it."

"Are you sure?" Anya asked.

"I thought turning him human was the correct punishment at the time," Lotan said. "But now I see… I see that I was wrong."

Anya stood aside as Lotan approached the monster who'd been moments away from killing him. With a little effort, she released the nox belu from the time river just long enough for him to recognize what was happening.

Then it was over. Yaotl lay in two pieces on the ground, and the only sound was Lotan's heavy breathing.

The magic floated up from his body, perhaps only visible to Anya, as neither Lotan nor the other two seemed to notice.

But killing Yaotl wouldn't change much in the grand scheme of things. Bael would find the magic again. He would find another willing participant. Endless.

"You don't look happy," Jack said.

"It's a temporary fix," Anya said. "Bael will capture this magic and give it to another human—that's what he did with Yaotl." She paused. "And Freyja. Biloko."

"Tabiko?" Cam asked.

She nodded solemnly. "I think he's just got the baby and is making it do what he wants. But I'm not sure. I haven't been able to find where he's storing his demon army. Diogo was..." She swallowed her burgeoning anger. "Anyway. I'm sorry I didn't tell you before."

"Why didn't you?"

"Because she doesn't want you to know that she's the one who brought me back."

Anya tensed, her hand going to her sword as she slowly turned. Bael had yet again masked his power in a show of his greater skill. He wore a look of amusement as he took in the scene, and Anya didn't like how his gaze lingered on Jack before finally settling on Yaotl.

"Such a pity," Bael said, nudging the body with his foot. "Yaotl was so eager to prove his worth as the rightful belu of the noxes after they'd been rudderless for so many years. And killed by a mere human. Oh, well."

"He was never the rightful belu," Lotan said. "My mother never liked him."

Bael's sharp eyes drew upward. "So your memory has returned, has it?"

"Enough to know when you're bullshitting me," Lotan said. "I haven't missed you, Bael."

Bael turned on his heel, his gaze back on Jack, and sending the hair on the back of Anya's neck up. "So all is forgiven, hm? Don't forget they killed your spawn, my dear love."

"You killed my daughter," Anya spat back.

Bael didn't react, his focus still on Jack. "Do you not care, human, that your *Anya* is the one who brought me back to this time? Perhaps in her subconscious, she knew that she needed her equal back with her. You were clearly lacking."

Anya braced herself for Jack's horrified gasp, for his accusations, the words, the very same she'd been dreading all this time, that had kept her silent even when all logic said to speak up.

Instead, Jack just stared at Bael, that beautiful, cocky smile dancing on his lips. "Tell me, does it get exhausting being so delusional? Anya couldn't have been clearer how she feels about you. You probably should've just stayed dead."

Bael smiled. "Then why did she seek me out?"

"I didn't," Anya said, bolstered by Jack's smile, and that he hadn't believed Bael. "You brought yourself here."

"And you believe her?" Bael asked.

Jack turned to Anya, confidence in his gaze that melted whatever fear still lingered in her heart. "Why would I not? I love her." He turned back to Bael. "You might not understand that, considering you've never loved anything but yourself."

Bael's upper lip curled, followed by a flash of anger in his eyes that set off warning bells in her mind.

"You know, I think I agree with Jack," Cam said, picking up the talisman launcher. "I think you shoulda stayed dead. Shall we help you out?"

"As mouthy as ever, aren't you?" Bael replied. "Surprising you can show your face, considering you developed the weapon that nearly killed Anat."

"That's all right, I'll just use it on you next time," Cam said with a grin, aiming the gun. "I know it'll work. Do you want to try it?"

"Your pathetic talismans can't harm me," Bael replied, impatience in his tone. Anya's heart pounded, knowing that his wrath would be unmerciful. She needed to defuse this situation before—

No, I don't.

She was the Goddamned belu athtar, after all. Bael couldn't hurt her, and she had control over the time river. There was nothing he could do now. Nothing she couldn't stop.

"I think it's time for you to go," Anya said, looking at him with a steely expression as she pulled her sword.

"Do you think you can tell me what to do?" Bael asked. "Do you think yourself so high and mighty now that you have the power *I* gave you?"

The ghost of a shiver fell over her chest. That used to be a red flag—a sign that Bael's anger was about to erupt. A past version of herself would've dropped to her knees, begged for forgiveness, anything to keep the monster at bay. But today, she stood before him and did not cower.

"I gave it to myself," Anya said.

"You know so little, my lady," Bael replied, his voice low and dangerous. "You don't know the stakes you're playing with nor the breadth of what this athtar magic can do."

"Yet, you still can't figure out how to stop time completely," Anya said with a smirk.

His eyes flashed again and she knew the ice was thin, but for once, she was fearlessly stomping on it.

"I would not speak so carelessly, not when your humans are right here," Bael said, pulling his sword from the sheath at his hip. "You cannot protect them from me forever."

"Can't I?" Anya said, her heart pounding in her chest.

But instead of attacking them, Bael simply disappeared. And somehow…that was worse.

Anya closed her eyes and tilted her head up, exhaling loudly and letting her sword dangle from her hands. Despite her fierce words, her body trembled with adrenaline, her knees weak as she stood completely still. This fear was ingrained deep in her bones. Yet with practice, it seemed, she was getting better at defeating it.

"Anya?"

She opened her eyes to the trio behind her. Safe, for now. But what horrors would Bael concoct? And would she be able to stop them?

"Are you all right?" Jack said, walking toward her slowly. "That was…"

"Amazing?" Cam offered.

"Intense," Jack finished. "I didn't think you had that in you."

"I don't think I do," she admitted softly, looking at her still-trembling hands. "Jack, you have to know that I didn't bring him back intentionally." He'd said as much in front of Bael, but she needed to hear it from him, just one more time, before she'd believe him.

He tilted his head to the side. "I said I did, but…" He licked his lips. "How…exactly is this possible?"

"I don't know how," Anya said. "But I found him in the time river—not in the past, but…*in* the river, like me. I believe him to be the Bael from the weeks we were on the run in Europe, because he knew you, Jack. And the only way I can explain it is that he…well, I guess he just hitched a ride to the present."

"But that makes very little sense," Lotan said. "When we were in the river, we weren't really *there*."

"And why would he be in the time river at all?" Cam asked.

"He used to spy on me," Anya said. "I couldn't sense him when he was viewing me in the past. He was in the time river watching us in Europe, at that fondue restaurant."

"So if you brought *that* Bael back, how do I remember being in the Underworld?" Jack asked. "I wish I could forget that."

"I don't know that either," Anya said. "Bael said something about it being different timelines and it being my future—to be honest, it didn't make a lot of sense to me. But he's definitely here—in the flesh. There have never been two belu athtars in the world at the same time, so I don't think either of us know quite what to expect. All I know is that he's here and he's got all the powers of an athtar belu—the exact same as me. Neither of us is stronger than the other, which is why…why I've had a hard time dealing with him."

"So, why didn't you just come to us?" Jack asked, stepping even closer to her. "We could've helped you."

"Because…" The exhaustion of the day had worn down her defenses, and she couldn't find it within herself to lie. "Because I was afraid of what you'd say when you found out. That you'd… you'd blame me and I…" She licked her lips. "I only went back into the time river because I wanted… I wanted to see Asherah one more time. Before I gave up this magic for good."

Surprise dawned on his face, and he didn't say a word.

"But then Bael was back, and things just…" She weakly gestured to the world. "I wanted to fix my mistake, and I couldn't."

The corners of Jack's lips turned upward. "And so instead of just talking to me about it, you've been suffering in silence all this time?"

"Yes, because I just wanted to…" She frowned as he

struggled to contain his laughter. "Why is that so funny?"

He slid his hands across her cheeks and pulled her in for a kiss, his lips firm and warm against hers. "Because you are absolutely infuriating, and I love you just the same. Now let's get the hell out of here and go home so we can hash all this out."

CHAPTER THIRTY-FOUR

She was so predictably predictable it was downright hilarious, but all Jack cared about was that she was with him. They'd defeated Bael once before, and they'd do it again. And after that day happened, Anya would give up her magic and they could get back to trying to build a normal life together. He really couldn't see a downside.

"Except, you know, Bael," Cam muttered, pouring herself a large glass of wine in the kitchen as Anya healed Lotan in the living room. "You heard her. They're evenly matched in power. Not sure how that's going to help us."

"Anya was weaker than he was and still managed to kill him," Jack said. "And she can stop time. He can't. That should help us."

Cam sighed and leaned against the kitchen counter and brought the glass to her lips. "I just don't think we should celebrate yet."

But Jack couldn't help but feel like everything in the world had been righted. Especially when Anya looked up from a fully healed Lotan and smiled at him.

"Bring me some of that, will you?" she said, nodding to the bottle.

"Just bring the bottle," Lotan said, rotating his arm and testing. "I think we could all use some."

The four of them settled in the living room, and for a moment, no one spoke. Jack draped his arm around Anya's shoulder, and she nudged closer to him, but her brow remained furrowed. Cam was next to Lotan, sipping her wine a little too quickly as he rested his hand on her knee.

"So I guess we should start with the first bit of good news," Jack said, breaking the silence. "Lotan, you're all better?"

He nodded, looking at his hands. "I'm not sure what it was, perhaps the taste of nox magic knocked something loose in my mind. But I'm back to normal." He paused, clearing his throat. "I mean, relatively."

Anya snorted and settled in a little closer to Jack. "Bael will find someone else to take the magic. So we can't assume we won't see noxes again."

"And you said he killed the other belus?" Cam said.

Anya nodded solemnly. "I think... I think he's much older

than even I realized. He knows things about this world, about this magic that seem..." She brought her glass to her lips but didn't drink. "I think he cleans house every few thousand years."

"That certainly checks out with what we saw in the time river," Lotan said. "With that..." He sat up. "That's where I'd seen that winged beast before—the one who attacked us, Cam. He was the nox we'd seen in the time river. The one who'd given up his magic before my mother took hers."

"So he was…what?" Cam said. "Half-demon?"

"He was human," Anya said.

"So those winged things were once human?" Jack grimaced, recalling how disfigured they'd become. "But we're getting off topic. So we know Bael can just lop off belu heads and reassign the magic to someone who'll swear fealty to him."

"Not only that, but he's built..." Anya leaned forward, cupping the wine glass with both hands. "He's constructed an entirely new Underworld. I don't know how he did it. But it's how he's been able to build this giant army outside my Sight."

"How did you find it?" Cam asked.

"Up until…recently…I haven't wanted to go back into the time river," Anya said, her gaze falling. "But I couldn't let my fear rule me anymore. I had to know for sure. But Bael's the only one who can open the door, and even when I visit in the time river, I'm just..." She shrugged. "I don't know this magic like he does, apparently. If he's able to project himself."

"But you can stop time," Jack reminded her. "And he can't?"

"I wasn't sure, at first, but now..." She brought the glass to her lips and took a long sip. "He wouldn't have looked that pissed if he could do it."

Silence descended again, and Jack rested his hand on the small of Anya's back. That she'd gone through all this by herself made him mad, and even more so to know that the only thing prolonging her suffering was her own stubbornness.

No. It wasn't stubbornness. It was fear. She'd been afraid of *Jack* and what he'd say. That he wouldn't believe her, and he'd shut her out. He moved his hand up and down her back, hoping that perhaps now she might realize that was never the case.

"So, I guess the next question is... What do we do now?" Lotan asked, breaking the silence again. "What does Bael want?"

"I have several theories," Anya said, finally leaning back to settle against Jack again. "My initial working theory was that he was trying to isolate me so I'd come back to him. After all, if we're exactly the same, there's a chance I could kill him. So he resorted to his old tricks to make me feel..." She exhaled.

"Seems like a lot of death just to get you back," Cam said.

"Agreed, which is why I think it was just part of a larger scheme," Anya said.

"From my observations," Lotan began, "it seems as if we understand the strategy, but not the target. It's not you he's trying to convince to submit to him—it's the world. The one that he'd existed in was without talismans, and this one is chock-full of them. My guess is he's trying to scare humanity into submission."

"And then do what?" Jack said.

"Turn things back the way they were," Cam offered. "ICDM is falling out of favor around the world. So Bael... Bael might just go directly to the governments themselves. The same way he killed the belus and found others who'd swear fealty to him. If he can't get the old guard to listen, he'll just make himself a new one."

"It's not just that," Jack said slowly. "Anya's the sole cause of these problems, so everyone thinks. Once humanity is good and beaten down—"

"He'll show up like he wasn't the cause of all of it," Anya said, looking at him with a soft nod. "It is his favorite trick."

"How do we stop that?" Lotan asked.

"We need to get to ICDM and tell them the truth," Cam said.

"They won't believe us," Jack said.

"Then we bring Anya to them, or somehow draw Bael out of his hidey hole so that they lay eyes on him themselves," Cam said. "Best case—we do both."

Jack rubbed his chin. He didn't have a lot of faith in ICDM right now, and he didn't want to bring Anya anywhere near Geneva, not when they were so trigger-happy. "What about Bael? He's going to continue terrorizing humanity in the meantime."

"I don't know what we can do about that," Anya said. "At least, I don't know anything I haven't tried yet. He's picking places at random, and I'm always late to the party. When I get there, he's got control over the time river, so I can't slow things down at all. It's me and my sword and that's it."

Cam snorted. "So that's what you meant when you said you couldn't do anything in Paris?"

Anya's gaze landed on her. "Yeah. But if I could somehow get control of the river, I'd be able to help."

"Could you stop time?" Lotan asked. "You're able to when there's talismans around. I wonder if the same principle applies with Bael?"

"I'm not...exactly sure how I do it," Anya said, looking at the glass in her hands, now empty. "It only happens sporadically."

"Practice makes perfect," Cam said, putting her glass on the table. "Listen, this is all very exciting, but I'm exhausted. Can we pick this up in the morning? I don't think I can absorb anything else today."

Jack didn't even ask, following Anya back to the replica of his bedroom in Seattle and waiting for her to send him away. But as she opened the door, she glanced behind at him, a smile teasing the corners of her mouth. He stepped inside with her, still keeping his distance and waiting for her to tell him to leave. But she sat down on the bed and looked up at him, expectantly.

He crossed the room in seconds, pushing her onto her back and climbing on top of her. His lips found hers, no longer waiting for an invitation. He touched every inch of her he could find, her hips, her breasts, her stomach, greedily seeking her bare skin, warm under his fingertips. He lifted his head, gazing down at her red-tinged lips and dizzy eyes, and grinned.

"Hey," he said.

"Hi," she replied softly. "I missed you."

He lowered himself again, this time kissing her softly as he worked the button of her pants and slid them off, along with her underwear. He trailed kisses across her face, down her neck, her exposed collarbone, then lifted her shirt to kiss her stomach as his hand found the already wet folds between her legs.

"Jack…"

He looked up, expecting her to ask him to stop, but she wore a dreamy smile on her face, so he continued his journey, kissing slowly and teasing her until he reached his destination. He pressed a single kiss there, then another, then slid his tongue, tasting her. She released a moan, but her hooded gaze remained on him. He moved his tongue slowly at first, sliding in and out, listening to her whimpers and moans as he figured what she wanted, before increasing his speed.

He looked up once again, and her eyes had closed, her head tilted back as she'd given in to him fully, allowing him to take her powerful body and do whatever he wanted. And the only thing he wanted was for her to be happy.

His work was methodological, and based on the way her legs had begun to squirm and the sound of her increased panting, she was appreciative of his work. His pants had become uncomfortable, the urge to rip them off and finish her off that way was strong, but he kept at it, until…

"*God!*" She sat up, her cheeks flushed, her breath labored.

She caught his gaze, a lazy smile on her face. "Jack, that was…"

He climbed up to meet her lips, and she pulled him back down onto the bed, fumbling with his pants and releasing him while he stripped the rest of his clothes and helped her with hers. He took in her body, the pert breasts, her slim frame, the line of muscles down her leg. She was absolutely beautiful—and all his.

She cupped the back of his head, kissing him, while the other guided his taut manhood toward her. He slid inside her, grunting his appreciation for her, before using his knees to widen the gap between her legs and settling his hips there. She wrapped her legs around him as he moved, her nails digging into his back as he moved. Back and forth, slow and beautiful, taking his time, listening to every sound she made. He threaded his fingers through hers and kissed her, his own release close at hand.

She tightened around him, an invitation that he readily accepted, and he exhaled against his lips, earning a smile from her. He stayed there a moment, gazing upon her face and the softness of her expression as his pulse came down to normal.

"That was…" he began.

"You said it." She kissed his shoulder and he pushed himself to lie beside her.

"Can't believe we keep finding reasons not to do that." Her face darkened and he realized he'd said the wrong thing. "Anya, I —"

She didn't meet his gaze. "How many more chances am I going to get?"

"As many as you need," Jack replied. "As long as you'll

forgive me when I screw up, too."

She tilted her head upward, and the smile blossomed on her face once more. "Maybe we're both lucky we don't hold grudges."

"Never," he replied, kissing her forehead. "Just don't close your door to me anymore. I couldn't stand it when I couldn't get to you. I hated feeling so…helpless."

She rested her hand on his chest. "I'm sorry. I was just…"

"I know." He toyed with a lock of her hair. "It's a shame you didn't hear my big speech in Lisbon," Jack said. "It was so much more heartfelt and poetic than anything I can come up with right now."

"I'll take this," she rested her hands on his chest, "over heartfelt words any day."

"But they were good words. Doubtful I'll be able to recreate them."

She shifted next to him, and he sensed he might've said the wrong thing again. "I don't want to go in there unnecessarily. The last thing I want is to repeat my mistake." She pursed her lips, and he sensed there was more she wanted to say but was afraid to.

"Was it…okay?" Jack asked, looking down at her. "Seeing Asherah?"

She sighed and that soft smile came back to her lips. "It was wonderful. She was…" She rolled onto her back and stared at the ceiling. "Even after all Bael's done, there's a part of me that doesn't regret going back to see her. I know I should—"

"No, you shouldn't," Jack said, propping himself up on his elbow.

She tilted her head toward him. "Are you just trying to tell me what I want to hear?"

"Maybe," he said. "But I also don't blame you for wanting to see her one last time. You couldn't have expected any of this to happen."

"Now I just have to fix it," Anya said, and the real world's problems crept back onto her face. "I don't even know where to begin now."

"What about what Lotan was saying?" Jack asked. "You can try stopping time? You might be able to overpower him."

"Just one problem," she said with a snort. "I don't know how to do it predictably."

"Don't you?" Jack said, pleased he'd figured it out before she had.

She furrowed her brow. "You do?"

"The only constant seems to be that someone you care about is in danger," he said. "Which explains why you can stop time and Bael can't."

She opened her mouth to argue, but no words came out.

"Do you remember what I said right before I left Seattle?" Jack said. "How I told you you had a beautiful heart with a huge capacity for love?" He rested his hand over her beating heart. "That heart can do amazing things."

"Jack…"

He leaned in to kiss her then stopped abruptly.

"Wait a minute," Jack said, releasing her for a moment as a new thought popped into his mind. "So you said Bael used to spy on us using the time river? And he was watching us in Europe?"

"Yeah."

"Do you think…" Jack blanched. "Do you think he saw us fucking in New Orleans?"

She snorted. "I don't think he stayed around for the whole thing, but I'm sure that's how he…knew things had changed between us. I'm sure he felt it over the connection, too."

He cracked a grin. "Do you think he was watching us just now?"

"I couldn't answer that," she said, feeling a little chill. "He's not allowed to set foot in this world anymore, but I don't know if that applies to the time river." She furrowed her brow. "Why?"

"Because I think I'd like to piss him off a little more."

He closed the distance between them, kissing her roughly and completely, and pushing her onto her back for round two.

CHAPTER THIRTY-FIVE

Cam stirred, blinking in the darkness and forgetting where she was. The night before had been a blur; she didn't even remember getting into bed or taking her clothes off. But considering the fingertips dancing along the edge of her hip, she had a hunch who had been so kind as to relieve her of her clothes.

"Morning," he said softly. "I think."

She rolled over, snuggling close to him and resting her hands on his chest. Sure, she'd accepted that she might never get Lotan back, but now that she *actually* had him—the real him, with his mischievous smile, his familiar hands, the way he knew just where to hold her—she definitely preferred this version.

"That's a smile I haven't seen from you in some time," Lotan whispered. "Was I really so terrible? I should've let myself get knocked around sooner."

"You know you weren't," she said with a snort. "And don't be mean. You almost died yesterday."

"We all did," Lotan said before shaking his head. "But I must admit, it's the first time I've come to terms with my own mortality. I don't want to keep flirting with death, if that's what you're angling. Without my demonic powers, I'm much better off staying out of the way and letting the real fighters do their thing."

His gaze slid away from her, looking far off. Cam's pulse skipped. "Do you…do you regret it?"

"What? Becoming human?" He smiled. "I admit, I'd hoped we'd conquered the major demonic evils of this world and that my own magic was no longer necessary. But…" He leaned in to kiss her gently. "Even in this current quagmire, I'd still give it up a thousand times over if it meant I could spend the rest of my mortal life with you."

But even as she wanted to coo, to kiss him, to build up a fire and let him show her exactly how much he remembered, even the mention of what waited for them outside the bedroom door was enough to squash any fire that might've been building. Lotan was back, but so was Bael, and if Anya was to be believed, she was struggling to contain him.

"What are we going to do?" Cam asked.

"Our first step should be to set up a conversation with

ICDM."

"Really?" Cam sat up. "After all they've done?"

"They were operating under the same set of facts as you were," Lotan said. "Perhaps with some enlightenment, they might adjust. Not only that, but we could cut Bael off at the pass. If his goal is to appear as a savior, it might thwart his plans if they know he's behind everything."

"And you think they'll believe us?" Cam asked.

"I don't know," Lotan said with a small shrug. "But we owe it to Anya to try. If they do, they could provide us with forces that could stand against Bael, if it comes to that. Coupled with Anya's powers, it might be enough to stem the tide."

Cam sank further into the pillow, grateful for Lotan's calming planning and wishing she shared his optimism. "I wish I could talk to Frank. He always seemed amenable to our crazy schemes."

"You'll have to settle for María, I guess," Lotan said.

"Great."

Cam couldn't linger in bed, as much as Lotan wanted her to. There was too much on her mind, and she needed to get up and resolve something or she'd never be able to relax. She walked into the kitchen, intent on making herself some coffee to gear herself up to speak with Anya about ICDM, but Anya was already there.

The athtar belu looked good and properly fucked, with mussed hair and lips that were still a little swollen, not to mention the sparkle in her eyes. Cam was glad someone was getting some action—and yet again questioned why she wasn't in bed with Lotan getting some herself.

Anya turned, looking like a deer caught in headlights, and Cam hated that they had this chasm between them now—and that it was all Cam's fault. Well, not *all* her fault, but mostly. Fifty-fifty.

"Are you looking for Jack?" Anya asked, hesitation in her voice.

"No," Cam said, looking back at the bedroom. "I don't know who I'm looking for. Or what. I'm just…" She rubbed her hands over her face, wishing she'd had more time to prepare for this one-on-one session. "I don't know."

Anya was silent for a while, and Cam felt the need to fill the silence with more babbling.

"I'm sorry that ICDM shot you," she said. "I should've just… I didn't…"

"Don't worry about it," Anya said, turning to the coffee maker.

"You have to know I'm going to worry about it," Cam said, taking another step forward. "I should've just *listened* to Jack and not let ICDM get in the way of what I knew to be right. You and I have been through hell together, and I feel like…"

"It's okay," Anya said, flipping the switch and turning on the machine. "I know how it must've looked."

"But Jack never doubted you," Cam said. "And I should've been a better friend. I'm sorry about that. I hope you can forgive me."

She laughed, looking down at her hands. "And here I thought I'd be the one groveling. All is forgiven, Cam. You're here now, and you're safe, and that's all I care about."

"Then look me in the eye," Cam said. "I don't want your forgiveness because you're scared of me."

To Cam's surprise, Anya turned to her fully. She really did look...different. Not unlike herself, but somehow more at peace. It honestly brought a lump to Cam's throat to see how far she'd come from the morose, beaten-down woman she'd been.

"There, are you happy?" Anya asked. "And don't be ridiculous. I'll always be a little scared of you. Even when you were my polluelo."

The word brought a smile to Cam's face. "I mean, I take that as a badge of honor."

Anya snorted and turned to the coffee maker, retrieving some cups.

"Look, I wanted to ask, if it's okay..." Cam swallowed. "Lotan thinks it's a good idea to tell ICDM what's going on."

"Got all his opinions back, too, does he?" she asked wryly.

"You don't have to go, obviously, but—"

"I think it's smart," Anya said. "But only if you think they'll believe it."

"Honestly..." Cam leaned against the counter. "I don't know. It'll be easier once Bael reveals himself to them." She was almost afraid to ask, but she couldn't not know. "Have there been any more attacks?"

"No," Anya said, her eyes growing dark as she scanned the world. "And there won't be for a little while. He has something of a pattern. A big show of aggression, then a few days respite, and just when you've gone crazy from waiting, he'll strike again. That he showed himself to you yesterday..." She chewed her lip. "I'm not sure how that plays into his game, but I'm sure it does."

"Do you think us knowing will make things better or worse?" Cam hadn't even considered what he might do if ICDM knew the truth.

"I don't see how things can get worse," Anya said, pouring the coffee into three cups.

"Don't say that," Jack called, walking out of the back bedroom wearing his boxers and nothing else. "That's just asking for more trouble."

Anya's entire face lit up at the sight of him, and Cam's heart grew three sizes. There was nothing insincere about the way they looked at each other. Finally, after so many stops and starts and missed connections, Jack and Anya had managed to find their way to peace—even in the middle of chaos.

"Go put on some pants," Cam barked at him. "We have strategizing to do."

Lotan joined them shortly after that, and the four of them gathered in the living room to continue catching each other up. Cam told Anya everything that had happened from ICDM's perspective, and all the reasons they suspected the only athtar they knew to be in existence for the massacres. Anya listened intently, getting in a few choice comments about Bael, especially as Cam told her about when the Nullius sand was stolen.

"Bribery? Like money," Cam said, shaking her head. "And here I thought he was above such lowly tricks."

"He wanted that weapon out of ICDM hands," Anya said, taking a long sip of her coffee. "But I don't think it was for my benefit. If that weapon could kill me, it could presumably kill him as well."

"If we could get him to stand still long enough to do it," Jack said. "Do you think he'd make himself that vulnerable?"

"That was my thought, exactly," Lotan said.

"It's hard to say. He's careful, but he underestimates his risk when his ego gets in the way," Anya said. "So we can probably safely assume that he'll know our next step is letting ICDM know what's going on. Either that's what he wants us to do, or he thinks it's inconsequential to his plans."

"And then what?" Jack asked. "We still don't have any idea how we're going to deal with him."

Lotan cleared his throat. "We know that the Nullius bullet did significant damage to Anya, and logic says it would do the same to Bael."

"We'd just have to get him in a place where we can shoot him," Cam said.

"Easier said than done," Jack replied. "He seems to have been a step ahead of us this whole time."

"Agreed," Anya said. "I can't predict when or where he'll show up. And I can't reach him when he's in the new world he's created." She sighed. "Meanwhile, thousands of humans are being killed whether he's there or not."

"Is there any pattern to where he shows up?" Jack asked.

"He likes to come when he thinks I'm…" She licked her lips. "Weak, I guess. But now that you and I are together, it's harder to predict." She sank back into the couch. "Three thousand years and I still have no idea what's going on in his head."

"Then we should be ready for him at a moment's notice," Lotan said. "And that starts with ICDM and creating more Nullius weapons to quickly dispose of Bael's army when it arrives."

"No," Anya said with a swift shake of her head. "Most of those demons were human a week ago. Victims themselves. It's not fair to kill them."

"We may not have a choice," Cam said heavily. "Which is probably the calculation Bael is making."

"But again," Lotan said with a patient smile, "if we had an army of ICDM agents with weaponry that could kill Bael, we could train our firepower on him."

"Bael knows the weapon could hurt him," Anya said. "He won't show anywhere it's being used. It's too much of a risk."

Cam was starting to understand Anya's frustration. Bael seemed to be holding all the cards. "As much as I hate to admit it, the more people we have on our side, the better. At least if ICDM knows Anya is our ally, they won't train their guns on her."

"*If* you think you can convince them without any evidence,"

Jack said.

"I have no idea," Cam said. "They know I have no reason to lie. And my hope is, by now, they may be willing to listen to anyone who says they'll help."

"That's what I'm afraid of," Anya muttered darkly.

CHAPTER THIRTY-SIX

Lotan decided to accompany Cam, more for moral support than because he thought he'd be helpful. He certainly had a better understanding of the intricacies of their situation, but he had no track record with the Council, not like Cam did. If anyone could convince them of the truth, it would be her. But if anyone could give her the confidence to speak her mind, it was him.

"Are you sure you don't want to come, too?" Cam asked Jack. "Three voices are better than two."

"They'll just think I'm under her spell or something," he said, catching Anya's eye. "She's bewitched me like a lilin." Anya ducked her head. "Besides that, the last time I was in that tent, my professionalism wasn't on display." She created a new portal and set it to the outskirts of Geneva where they'd be coming and going. "Good luck."

"Thanks." Cam looked behind her at Lotan. "Ready?"

"After you, my love."

Together, Lotan and Cam stepped through to the portal back to Geneva. With his memories returned, he was able to recall recent conversations with less confusion and more... embarrassment. He couldn't believe it had taken him so long to put the pieces together about Bael—how many more lives could've been saved had he just been a little quicker?

Beyond that, he was still adjusting to this new body. He looked no different than he had as a nox, yet he felt different. It was only thanks to Anya that he wasn't dead. A feeling he wasn't very happy to become acquainted with.

"You look distracted," Cam asked, tugging on their joined hands. "What's wrong?"

"At the moment? Absolutely nothing. Besides the obvious." He cleared his throat. "What's your strategy for speaking with your aunt?"

"Figured I'd just come out with it and hope for the best."

Lotan nodded, and they descended into silence once more. Something Anya had said tickled in Lotan's mind, a nagging worry that they were playing into Bael's hands. He never did anything without purpose, and his appearance in Mexico City had seemed solely to prove his realness to Cam, Jack, and Lotan. Or, more likely, to Jack.

But that hadn't been necessary, because they'd already been convinced. Lotan had remembered. So what other reason could there be?

The walk was long, and Lotan's human legs were aching by the time they reached the tent city. They were waved through, and Cam made a beeline for the headquarters tent. Lotan followed behind, a little slower, remembering the carnage and death that had happened just weeks ago. How many more overrun cities would there be before the end?

"Yes, we do need to talk," María said, by way of greeting Cam once they were inside the tent. "Because we have it on good authority that noxes were briefly seen in Mexico City. Care to comment on that, Lotan?"

"I believe we told you it was a possibility," Lotan replied.

The Councilwoman furrowed her brow, but Cam waved him off. "We have more important things to talk about. Namely, Bael is back."

A dribble of laughter came from María's lips. "Bael? Did you hit your head, dear niece?"

"It's true," Lotan replied, taking a step forward.

"Pardon me if I don't believe someone who can't remember what he had for breakfast," María said. "The athtar wants us to believe she's capable of bringing people back from the dead?"

Cam nodded. "It may defy logic, but—"

"It doesn't just defy logic, it's absolutely ridiculous," María said. "You told us Bael was beheaded."

"He was."

"So who put his head back on?"

"This version of Bael was never beheaded," Lotan said. He did his best to explain the athtar's ability to move time, stop time, and view past events. Cam helped where she could, but based on María's expression, they could talk until they were blue in the face, and she wouldn't believe them.

"It doesn't actually matter," María said, pulling her glasses from her face. "Whether it's Anat or Bael or some new evil we've never seen before, ICDM's ability to do anything about it is limited. Our charter is in danger of being revoked."

"Now's not the time to be dissolving ICDM," Cam said, sharing a look of concern with Lotan. "Not when we have to band together to defeat this common enemy."

"It's not up to me," she said. "Several of the partner countries have sent letters indicating they're pulling out of the ICDM cooperative—including the United States. Without their participation, we don't have the funds to continue our mission."

Cam shifted her weight. "Surely there's something we can do. Some way we can convince them to hang on a little longer."

She pulled her glasses from her face. "Perhaps. There was a lot of talk about how we managed to lose the one piece of weaponry that seemed effective against the athtar. If you could use your...connections...to construct more weapons, we might have a chance of convincing them."

Cam swallowed, considering her words. "I'll do it, but I want your word—on your sister's life—that you won't use this weapon on Anya ever again."

"I can't do that," María said. "But I can promise I'll listen to her if she wants to plead her case."

Lotan nudged Cam with his foot. "I think that's as good as

we're going to get. At least, until Bael decides to reveal himself to humanity."

"I don't think it'll make that much of a difference," María said.

"The most feared creature in existence back from the dead?" Lotan asked. "I think that'll turn a few heads. Give us a few days to retrieve and construct your weapons. In the meantime, let your colleagues know what we've told you."

"I don't want to give ICDM another weapon to kill Anya with," Cam said as soon as they passed the perimeter.

Lotan didn't either, not when they couldn't be trusted. But he also saw opportunity. If ICDM was truly losing favor with world governments, they would be desperate to do what they could to restore it. Desperation made for a more willing ally.

"Not to mention," Cam continued, turning to look at Lotan, "Anya said Bael won't show up where the bullets are. So are we just shooting ourselves in the foot?"

"It's possible," Lotan said. "But until Bael appears again, we're playing by the rules we know about. I would rather be ready if he happens to grace us with his presence than…"

Lotan's brow furrowed. Cam seemed to have slowed down considerably.

"Plotting to kill me, whelp?"

Lotan spun around at the sound of Bael's voice behind him. He stood five feet away, the ethereal version that told Lotan he wasn't really there, but merely projecting himself in the time river. Although the athtar could do nothing to harm Lotan or Cam, his appearance was always cause for concern.

"How is it that you're here?" Lotan asked. "And not?"

"I couldn't imagine a nox would understand." Bael sniffed. "It's too complex for your brain."

"You just don't want me telling Anya."

Bael rolled his shoulders. "*Anya*. The titles I bestowed upon her over the years seem to be forgotten in favor of such a simplistic, *human* name. I gave her immortal life, a place by my side, and she opts for that man, that *Jackson*."

Lotan could've explained it, but he didn't think Bael would understand if he did. That he was still agitated about Anya's lack of fealty was a good sign, and perhaps a weakness they could exploit. One thing was for sure: Bael wouldn't hesitate to kill Jack if he thought it would bring Anya back to him.

"It is just as well, I suppose," Bael continued, agitation melting from his face. "All things must end in time. I'd hoped we might rule together forever, but even in my most optimistic dreams, I knew that one day she would betray me. It's why I did what I did."

"And that is?"

"Retain Diogo," Bael said. "Goad him into finding her. I knew she would bring me back."

Lotan couldn't help but snort. "Bael, you may be old as the dirt itself, but even you can't control everything like that." He took a step forward, leaving Cam and trusting that Bael could do nothing to her in this city. "If you want my opinion, it was that central repository of magic—"

"You mean the Abbunatu?" Bael asked. "You are aware of its existence?"

Lotan nodded. "It seems to be pulling all the strings—including yours. The way Anya tells it, seeing you in the time river was merely a fluke."

"And you believe her over me?"

The question hung in the air long enough for Lotan to doubt himself. Even with his memory restored, the intricacies of time travel seemed too much to grasp. How this Bael could coexist with Lotan's experience of fighting in the Great Demon War was beyond Lotan's understanding. It was possible, of course, that this version somehow ended up back in the past. But then why would Bael have made the mistakes he'd made?

"Your silence is damning," Bael said.

"I'm merely considering the question," Lotan replied. "But as it stands, I still tend to believe her over you. After all, only one of you has a proven track record of lying about almost everything." He smiled. "Including who killed your own daughter."

Bael's eyes flashed, and he adjusted the cuffs on his shirtsleeves. "Very well. I suppose it's time to accept that my Anat is lost to me forever. I cannot change her heart, as much as it pains me to admit it."

"And as much as you've certainly been trying," Lotan said.

"I wouldn't speak so carelessly, whelp. There are events in motion that not even Anat in her great power can stop. I'd hoped we could rule this world together, but if she no longer wishes it, I suppose there's only one thing for me to do."

Bael's gaze slid to Cam for a moment and Lotan jerked toward her, earning a laugh from Bael.

"Your human is of no interest to me," he said. "And neither is Jackson Grenard. Once I've killed Anat, there must be someone left to mourn her." He sighed. "Because it won't be me."

Lotan opened his mouth to speak, but time snapped back to normal.

"Lotan..." Cam said. "What just happened?"

"We have to get back to Anya," he said, turning back to her. "I think the game is changing."

CHAPTER THIRTY-SEVEN

Bael, Master of the Underworld, Lord of the Mountain, emperor of all he surveyed, the original athtar demon, knew that the first thing the humans would do was to scurry to their little demonic management agency and tell them that the greatest demon had returned from the dead. He'd had a feeling the human Camilla Macarro would consider rebuilding the Nullius weapon, but it didn't matter. Bael had constructed himself an army to do his bidding, and his presence was no longer necessary.

More importantly, that agency was faltering, much as everything else had in Bael's absence. And he was nothing if not a benevolent king. He would throw them a bone, allowing them to regain their standing amongst their fellow vermin, and in return, they would be an ally to him and him alone.

He'd set the next phase of his plan in motion several days ago, when he realized that Macarro and that whelp had figured out he was alive. He'd contacted the young scientist who'd been so persuadable to deliver a letter to the Council, requesting a meeting "with the belu athtar." Only ten members had accepted his invitation, but that would be enough. It wouldn't take long for word to spread.

He'd arranged for them to meet him in a small restaurant outside Geneva, far enough away from the talismans that Bael wasn't bothered by them. The staff had been turned into lilins, thanks to the new lilin belu Bael had found, and were eager to do what they could to please their athtar lord. A large, round table was already set for eleven, and several bottles of wine were waiting.

Bael sat at the head of the table, snapping his fingers to beckon the lilin waiter to pour him a glass of wine. He swirled, sniffed, and tasted the vintage, decided it was up to his standards then sat back, waiting.

Ten minutes later, the front doors opened, and ten members of the Council walked into the room—cautious, at first, just before the terror fell across their faces. It was one thing, Bael supposed, to be told something. Another to see it with their own eyes.

"How can this be?"

"What is this magic?"

"Evening," Bael said, gesturing to the table. "I'm so pleased you could join me. Please, have a seat and we'll share a glass of wine in friendship."

"So it's true then," María said, not moving. "You've come back from the dead."

"I'm very much alive," Bael said. "The hows and the whys aren't quite important at this point, don't you think? Not when I can offer you so much more."

But it seemed García had grown something of a backbone. "You are not the belu athtar we expected to meet with."

"Were you expecting Anat, then?" He chuckled. "She's merely a placeholder. She can't possibly know the true power of a belu athtar, and she's been woefully inadequate wielding it. As evidenced by the oceans of blood spilled over the past few weeks." He tutted. "You will recall thousands and thousands of years of peace under my watch."

"With the exception of Demon Spring," María replied coolly. "When you released your demons on humanity. We do not have such short memories."

"A small price to pay," Bael said, shaking his head. "One fortnight every four years, versus a nonstop slaughter. I hardly call that a sacrifice."

"Tell that to the humans killed," María said.

Bael licked his lips, already tired of listening to this woman speak. "Do the rest of you feel the same way? Am I such a monster that you would prefer the current status to the peace I can provide?"

"How?" Councilman Zhao asked.

"I'm so very glad you asked," Bael said. "I, alone, have control over the other belus that Anat cannot begin to possess. She's... Well, she's unprepared to be the sort of monarch that's needed in these troubling times. And now things have gotten out of control, and she's just..." He smiled. "Pathetic."

"If you are both the belu athtar, how can you possess more power than she does?" Zhao asked.

"It's quite simple. The previous owners of the belu magic did not comply, so I killed them and gave their magic to ones who would."

As predicted, the room became quite silent as the humans considered the implications of Bael's words.

"It's a lie," María said. "There's no way a belu could kill another belu."

"I can manipulate time, you idiot woman," Bael barked. "It's quite simple to kill anyone. I only let the others live as long as they did because they posed no threat to me."

"You forget that Anat is still out there," María said. "And two of our best agents."

"And a former nox prince, oh yes, I know," Bael said. "But as you've seen, they haven't been able to lift a finger against me. So I don't believe they will be of any consequence. Anat will soon be a memory, and your agents..." He smiled. "They can live if they swear fealty to me. I am kind."

He rose, pressing his hands on the table.

"So, dear Councilors, are you ready to join me and finally

have peace in our world once more?"

They stared at one another, murmuring and seeming to compare opinions. Bael waited patiently, knowing humans needed time to think these things through. Finally, María stepped forward, her shoulders back and chin high.

"The answer is no," she said.

"So you choose chaos?" Bael asked.

"The only one sending chaos into this world is you, Bael," María said. "And we choose not to subject ourselves to—"

Bael slowed time, more for his own need for silence, and crossed the room. María's lips were moving in slow motion. Bael pulled a knife from his belt and took his time sliding it across the delicate human throat. Her eyes bulged, the pain reaching her puny human brain. Bael released his grip on the time river and the woman collapsed on the ground, gasping for air.

"Anyone else feel the same?" Bael asked, twirling the small knife in his hand. When he heard no responses, he cast a haughty look over his shoulder. "I promise you that I can find alternate Councilors to take your place quite easily. The same way I found new belus after I killed the previous owners of the magic."

One by one the Council stepped forward to sign their names. Bael smiled, enjoying the way their hands trembled before him. This was better than Anat's affection. This was ultimate submission.

CHAPTER THIRTY-EIGHT

It was something else to wake up next to Jackson Grenard. Anya turned over, lulled by the soft sound of his breathing. He was such a beautiful man, with perfect lines on his cheeks and lips that begged to be kissed. Here in their bed, there was peace —real peace. Not the kind that was dependent on her acting a certain way or his mood that day. But a solid foundation that bolstered her for a world that was anything but peaceful.

He slid his hand across her hip and pulled her closer, pressing a sleepy kiss to her lips before settling back down on the pillow. She nestled her nose against his, the intimacy terrifying and thrilling at once. After all they'd been through, this man still trusted her implicitly, still wanted her as close as possible. She could even feel his heartbeat beneath her hand on his chest. A delicate, human heart that was all hers.

She closed her eyes and vowed to enjoy this moment, this peaceful joy that came with loving Jack, with knowing he loved her, and that he would treat her heart as delicately as the one in his chest.

He danced his fingertips across her hip, and she cracked open one eye to look into his. He leaned in to kiss her, but this time, he seemed wide awake, wearing that little smirk that told her he was up to no good, along with his hardness pressed against her leg. She giggled as he kissed her lip, then her neck, his wandering hands reaching every inch of her they could find.

"I love you," he whispered into her skin.

And she let him take control, let him own her body and use it however he wanted. Because now, it was her choice, and she chose him. Over and over again.

Anya lifted her head from Jack's chest, the sensation of her portal rippling rousing her from a light snooze. "Cam's on her way back."

He grunted. "Wanna take bets on whether it's good news or bad?"

"Not particularly," Anya said, turning her head toward him and pushing herself up to kiss him. "C'mon."

She found her clothes strewn about the floor and caught Jack watching her a few times. He was...well, *happy*, for lack of a better word. She hadn't ever seen him look so light—at least, not when she was concerned. That his joy was from her and her alone…

She hid a giggle as she left him in the bedroom, but as soon as she reached the living room and saw the looks on Cam and Lotan's faces, her good mood evaporated.

"Do you want the bad news first or the worst news first?" Cam asked.

"Neither?" Jack said from behind Anya. "God, Cam, we gave you one job."

She didn't even chuckle. "So the bad news is that ICDM seems to be losing their funding. María said that governments around the world are considering pulling their support."

"What does that matter?" Anya asked.

"If there's no funding, ICDM goes away," Jack explained. "What's my father doing about it?"

"George wasn't there," Cam said. "Hopefully, that means he's in Washington, talking with the feds about why pulling their support right now is a stupid idea. But humanity's growing tired of these attacks. I don't think the US will be the last to throw in the towel."

"What do they plan to do instead?" Anya asked. "ICDM, at least, has training to deal with demons."

"If I were to guess?" Jack said. "The military would confiscate everything they could from ICDM, bundle it in with their own weapons. Then it would be a free-for-all in every country. ICDM had its faults, but at least it was a unified front when it came to humanity versus demonkind. Negotiating with a hundred and sixty individual countries would be a nightmare."

"More importantly," Anya said, "if Bael shows up and promises a return to normalcy, then humanity will fall to bended knee without question. He'll be seen as a savior. And once that happens…" She looked at Cam. "You told María that Bael is back, right? Did she believe you?"

"Yes and no," Cam said. "She said that *if* we could get her another Nullius sand weapon, she might be able to bring that to the world leaders to prove ICDM still has the ability to do their job."

"Absolutely not," Jack barked.

"I think it's worth looking at," Lotan said, when Cam gave him a sideways look. "María did say that if we brought it to her, it wouldn't be used on Anya."

"She said maybe," Cam said with a grimace. "But I also don't know if we have a choice."

"Why?" Jack asked.

"The worse news is that Bael had a chitchat with Lotan," Cam said. "And…"

"And it seems as though his goal is to kill Anya," Lotan said, looking at her.

Jack scoffed. "He says that a lot—"

"No, he doesn't."

Anya sank down on the couch, exhaling. Bael had always made her *think* he would kill her, but he had much more fun torturing her than killing her. After all, she had been his favorite plaything.

Now, though…

"What exactly did he say?" Jack said.

"He said there were events in motion that she couldn't stop, and that if she no longer wishes to rule the world with him…" Lotan licked his lips. "There was only one thing left to do. And that he wouldn't hurt you or Cam because…as he says, someone needs to mourn her."

Anya fought the ingrained urge to flee to Bael's side, promise him that she loved him above all others, and grovel for his forgiveness. He wasn't more powerful than she was. She repeated that in her mind until her pulse slowed.

"Anya?" Jack asked.

"It changes our strategy," she said. "We can't assume he won't try to kill me—and we also can't assume what he's doing is designed to win or scare me back." She met Jack's gaze, full of fear and trepidation, and smiled calmly at him. "I'm fine."

"So we have Bael who is now willing to kill Anya and we have ICDM potentially about to fall apart," Cam said. "But we may be able to save ICDM if we build them another belu-killing weapon. Which they may very well use on Anya."

"Is ICDM the only agency who can build the weapons?" Lotan asked. "Could we do it here?"

"No," Jack said. "The bullet I pulled out of Anya's leg practically drained the ground of magic. It should be built somewhere in the human world—far from here."

Anya chewed her lips, considering her options. They wouldn't get very far against Bael's army by themselves. Bael also might sense ICDM's desperation and try to swoop in to save them. It was better to fight one enemy than two.

"We rebuild the weapon," she said, after a long pause. To Jack's furrowed brow, she waved her hand. "I don't trust them, either, but they're the only ones equipped to help us. And we need all the help we can get."

That meant, of course, that Jack, Cam, and Lotan would be venturing into the Nullius—which Anya wasn't very comfortable with.

"You'll come right back out, right?" Anya asked Jack as he strapped his knives on his hips. "You won't dawdle."

"Promise," Jack said with a grin.

"Fear not, Mother Athtar," Lotan said. "Although I do wonder what secrets the Nullius might offer. Maybe I can better explore them now that I'm human."

"The only secrets are those winged monsters who infect you with anti-demonic magic," Cam said, glaring at him. "We won't dawdle."

Anya nodded, opening a portal to the farthest edge of Athkur she could manage then following the others as they stepped through. The Nullius was palpable, as usual, and didn't help her already unsettled stomach.

Jack walked over to her, a kind smile on his face. "You should get back. We'll be careful—in and out before you know it." He leaned in to capture her lips in another kiss. "Round three later?"

She smiled, threading her fingers through his belt loops and pulling him closer. "Don't make promises you can't keep."

"I don't," he said.

"Oi!" Cam barked. "Quit making out and hurry up. We need to do this quickly."

"How the tables have turned," Jack said, capturing her lips once more. "I'm coming, I'm coming."

"I'll say," Anya said, releasing him and feeling cold as he cast her an appreciative look over his shoulder.

Cam scowled at them both, hiking her backpack higher as Lotan just laughed and turned toward the tree line. Jack adjusted his knives and backpack and started to follow them.

"Jack?" Anya said, stopping him.

"Hm?"

"I just..." She licked her lips. "Be careful."

He beamed. "I will. Love you, too."

She couldn't help the grin that spread across her face as he turned and disappeared through the woods. Anya crossed her arms over her chest and exhaled, already impatient for them to return. Depending on how much sand they were bringing back, she might not be able to stomach being around them, but just knowing they were back would ease most of her anxiety.

"So this is what you'll do."

Anya spun, pushing against the sound of the voice with her magic, but finding nothing. The Bael that stood before her was ethereal, perhaps the projection of himself that Lotan had spoken about.

"Leave me," she snapped. "I don't wish to hear your voice."

"No, I hear you've been hearing another man's," Bael said. "Does he make you tremble like I used to? Does he know all your intimate pleasures?"

"More than you," Anya said, leveling a glare at him. "And he doesn't use them to hurt me, either."

Bael smiled, coming to stand beside her. "I'm surprised you let your little human venture into such a dangerous place. Do you not know the secrets of the Nullius?"

"I know enough."

"Then you know of the ewû?" Bael asked. "The guardians of the Nullius?"

She glanced at him. "Ewû? The winged beasts?"

"Oh, they won't enjoy hearing you call them that," Bael said. "Freyja, especially."

She turned on him, furious. "Freyja is dead."

"You know, there was a much simpler way for your nox prince to lose his magic," Bael said. "You could have beheaded him."

She narrowed her eyes, waiting for the second part. "And?"

"My dear Anat, have you not discovered the ability to move time in small pockets? It's a marvelous tool to repair what has been broken, to pump life back into a dead body…" He cast her a long look that made her skin crawl. "To grow a child into a woman."

"What are you saying?" Anya said. "That you… You killed Freyja and then somehow brought her back to life?"

"She was mostly dead, of course. The brain does not function long after losing its connection, and the heart will stop beating. But nothing a little magic can't resolve."

Anya's heart dared to hope, but this was Bael—nothing was ever easy with him. "What did you do to her?"

"The same thing I did to every belu who crossed me in the past," Bael said. "I brought their human husks to this land and I let the magic transform them into something useful. Guardians to ensure no one else found the Abbunatu."

"The..." She swallowed. "The center of demonic power?"

"Demons were repelled by the inherent magic, of course, but humans..." Bael smiled and gazed out into the desert. "They needed an extra deterrent. I'm just so pleased I thought ahead to prepare for someone to betray me."

"Jack and Cam have fought them before," Anya said, but her heartbeat was racing. "They can defeat them now."

"Can they?" Bael asked. "When I send every ewû to rip them limb from limb?"

Anya turned to the Nullius and took a step toward it, the magic in her veins warning her not to venture further. If she did, she would die or become human—and she couldn't do either yet. Not when Bael still needed that smug smile wiped from his face.

"What will you do, my love? Risk your magic to save your friends?" Bael asked, his breathless lips near her cheek. "Or let them succumb to the magic? At least then, you can all live forever."

She spun on her heel, but he was gone, leaving nothing but her rising panic in his wake.

CHAPTER THIRTY-NINE

Jack crossed the small river separating Ath-kur from the Nullius and immediately felt a difference on his skin. Unlike when he and Cam had taken an SUV here the first time, he was much more leery about the dangers this land possessed. The sooner they got in and out, the better.

"Where are you going?" Jack called to Cam, who was pressing on. "There's sand right here."

"The further in we go, the more potent it is," Cam said. "If we're killing a belu athtar, I want the most potent shit we can get our hands on."

Jack frowned, gazing at the sky, then turned to Lotan, who was staring off into the distance. "What?"

"Just remembering the moment I gave up my power," he said, his words barely audible over the desert wind.

"Hope you aren't having second thoughts." He made sure Cam was well out of earshot, before adding, "Say, when exactly are you going to ask Cam to marry you?"

Lotan turned to Jack, a wide grin on his face. "Should I ask permission first?"

"Not from me," Jack said. "But you know, tick-tock."

Cam called for them to keep up, and Jack dropped a rock to mark their path as he and Lotan started up the dune Cam had disappeared over.

"I promise you, it's in the forefront of my mind," Lotan said. "I was somewhat hoping for the exact right moment with the right lighting, the right mood—and you know, without the former king of the demons murdering thousands of humans every few days."

"That might take a while," Jack said. "Might as well just pop the question and get it over with."

"Do you think she'd prefer that?"

Cam called for them again.

"I think she's a woman of action," Jack said, starting at a bit of a jog to catch up to her—and his pulse skipped when she cried out again, this time in fear.

"Did you hear that?" Lotan said.

"I hope I didn't," Jack said, looking to the sky. "Because—"

Another loud shriek, but this one clearly the shriek of one of those winged monsters. Jack wouldn't forget the sound any time soon.

"Shit, I told you," Jack said, pulling his knives. "Cam, hurry up! We have to get out of here!"

But when no answer came from over the dune, Lotan and Jack shared a look of fear and high-tailed it up the dune. Once they'd crested it, they found out why. Cam was surrounded by four winged monsters, their skin smoking in the sunlight.

"Now would be a good time to use some of that Ath-kur dirt, guys," Cam said, holding her hands out as they jawed at her.

"I don't understand," Lotan said. "How are they standing there in the sunlight? It's killing them."

Jack grunted. "They clearly don't care. C'mon!"

He slid down the dune, landing awkwardly before popping back upright and pulling his knives. But Lotan was faster, passing Jack and pulling the bag of dirt they'd brought from Ath-kur. He tossed a handful at the closest monster, and it let out a bone-chilling scream. Cam was then able to knock it out of the sky with her macuahuitl. Lotan tossed another handful of dirt at it and it shuddered, then stopped moving.

The other three monsters who'd been waiting nearby drew closer, shrieking so loud it made Jack's ears ring.

"Oi!" Jack called, inching closer to one of them. "Can't let Cam have all the fun."

The closest monster turned away from Cam and Lotan, flashing razor-sharp teeth at Jack and releasing a loud squawk. It unfurled its large wings, rising up into the air and flapping over to hover above Jack. The skin almost seemed to be sizzling in the sunlight, and the monster was clearly in pain. Yet it remained ready to attack, either oblivious or driven by something external.

"That's it, come a little closer," Jack said, twirling his knives. The monster dove, and Jack jumped out of the way, swinging his knife and catching nothing but air. He tried again, but the monster was faster in the air than he was on the ground—and more than once, the sharp nails almost brushed his skin.

"Got any more of that sand for me?" Jack asked.

"In a minute," Cam barked back, as she and Lotan were trying to deal with their own monsters. "These things won't sit still."

A shadow moved behind Jack. He turned around just in time to see the clawed hand come within a hair's breadth of his nose, but it was stopped in mid-air. The hot, desert wind had also stopped blowing—and the presence of athtar magic lifted the hair on his neck.

"Anya?" Jack found her standing in the middle of the desert, her face red with exertion. "You did it."

"B-barely." She exhaled, lowering her arms slowly and catching Jack's gaze for a lingering look before turning to Cam and Lotan, still mid-swing against the others. "Kill those things already."

Jack and Cam did as she was told, and within seconds, all four monsters lay dead on the ground. Lotan knelt down to pour a few handfuls of sand into his now-empty bags.

"Are you all right?" Jack asked, putting his knives away.

"Can you use your magic to get us out of here?"

"No," she said, with a bit of a pant. She pointed toward the sky, where more of the black monsters were still flapping their wings. "I can only hold this small area."

"So there *are* limits to this power."

Jack's knives came back into his hands as Bael appeared next to Anya. He stepped onto the desert sand, taking in a deep breath as he tilted his head toward the sky. Anya remained silent, watching him with a wary gaze, as if he were a bomb about to explode.

Cam held her ground as Bael approached her—or rather, the winged monster she'd slain. Bael knelt down next to the creature and lovingly brushed the hair off of its grotesque face.

"Such a shame you killed them," Bael said. "They would have been loyal guardians."

"You're the one who sent them out in the sunlight," Jack said. "They were already dying."

"But not before they took you with them," Bael said, his dark eyes landing on Jack as he rose once more. "And unfortunately, they failed at doing even that."

"Who are they?" Lotan asked.

Jack looked at him. "Monsters."

"No," Lotan said, raising his sword and pointing it at Bael. "One of them spoke to me, when I was here last. It was the nox who had the magic before my mother." He looked down at the creatures on the ground. "Who were they?"

The smile that grew on Bael's face sent chills down Jack's

spine. It was the same one he'd worn parading Sara around his castle, and when he'd taken it upon himself to torture Jack with visions of her death. Bael was completely in control and about to share some horrible revelation.

"The ewû were human, once," Bael said, nodding to the first one Cam and Lotan had killed. "This one, in particular." He looked up at Cam, and his smile widened. "You don't recognize your great-aunt, Camilla?"

Cam took a step back, shock plain on her face as she shook her head. "You… What did you do to her?"

"I didn't do anything," Bael said. "In fact, I brought her back to life."

"After you killed her, I'm sure," Anya said, taking a few steps forward. "So you've been to see ICDM, then? Revealed yourself?"

"Who gives a shit about that?" Cam said, her voice rising as she pointed her club at Bael. "What did you do to María?"

Bael rose, the tip of Cam's club following him, and that smug grin never left his face. "The ewû are the result of a human arriving here and venturing into the Nullius. This magic is not for them, and thus, over a period of years, it changes them."

"Or you speed up the process," Anya said with a frown. "Who are the rest?"

"Freyja," Bael said, pointing at the one about to kill Jack. To the one near Lotan's, "Biloko. And that one was the little spawn of Mizuchi. In the end, it was easier to kill him and start over after all."

"Enough of this," Anya said, walking forward and holding her sword aloft. "You will do no more damage here. So either get going or let me kill you, because I'm tired of hearing you talk."

Bael stared at the tip of her sword, amused. "Oh, but, Anat, this was merely the beginning."

Anya turned, her body going straight as the sky darkened above them. More of those monsters—ewûs—filled the horizon. Far too many for them to attempt to fight off by themselves.

"How long can you hold onto the river, Anat?" Bael asked. "Long enough to get your friends to safety?"

Then he was gone.

"Fuck," Anya said, breathing heavily. "I can't... I'm losing my grip."

"That asshole," Cam said. "How far are we from the border?"

"I have no idea," Anya said. "My Sight doesn't work here."

"I see the trail," Jack said. "So we can't be too far. Maybe half an hour—less if we hurry."

Anya swallowed. "I don't know if I can last half an hour in the Nullius."

"The magic gets sucked out of you quickly," Lotan said, inching backward as the demons descended down the dune toward them. "But we'd better make a decision soon."

"Anya, can you try to move us?" Jack said. "Just as far as you can."

She winced, and a trickle of sweat fell down her cheek. "I can try. But I don't know if we'll get past the ewû."

"We don't have a lot of time to debate this," Cam said,

holding her macuahuitl ready as the ewû came closer.

"Don't worry," Jack said. "I'll make sure you get to safety. Promise."

She stared into his eyes, a little fear in the depths of her emerald eyes. But something in his own gaze must've persuaded her, because she nodded. "Come here. It's easier if we're all together."

Cam put her hand on Jack's shoulder, and Lotan rested his on Anya's back. She inhaled and exhaled and the earth shifted beneath them. But Anya's breath left her lips and her eyes shot open for a moment before rolling back into the back of her head. Jack caught her as time resumed.

They hadn't gotten very far, just over the first dune, and unfortunately the ewûs were faster.

"*Run!*" Jack barked, shifting Anya onto his back with Lotan's help. It was hard to run over the sand, but adrenaline and fear goaded him on. Shadows danced in front of him as the ewû crossed in front of the sun. Lotan, with the longest legs, reached the top of the dune first, helping Cam up the last few steps before they slid down the other side.

"There!" Jack said, as he crested the dune. "I see the trail."

Cam screamed as the sand exploded inches from where her foot landed. She turned behind her and the color drained from her face.

"Jack..."

He turned and to his shock, thirty demons were standing with guns pointed at them.

No, not demons. *Humans.* ICDM agents.

"Fuck me," Jack swore, backing up.

The shots came every few seconds and were too close for comfort. Jack's mind ran rampant with theories as he scaled the dune, kicking the stones he'd left in his wake behind him. More shots came, but the humans were still human, and Jack and the others had a hundred-foot head start.

"There!" Cam said, as the woods of Ath-kur rose in the distance.

Jack adjusted Anya on his back and doubled his speed, hoping that once they crossed the border, they'd be in the clear. He sailed over the small river between the lands and kept running through the misty woods.

"They're still coming!" Cam cried, a few steps behind him.

"Anya needs to expel them," Lotan said, holding up the rear. "She has to wake up."

"Anya," Jack said. "Anya, wake up." But she was still fast asleep. "I need to find a safe place to put her down."

"I don't know if that's possible," Cam said.

"We'll hold them off," Lotan said, slowing his gait.

"Babe, they have guns. We have a sword and a club," Cam said. "We won't do much."

"Anya," Jack said, stopping short and gently pulling Anya off his back to lay her on the ground. She'd regained some of her color, but not enough for his liking. He patted her cheek gently. "Anya, come on. You have to wake up."

She moaned and shook her head. "No…"

A bullet landed in the tree just above their heads. Cam exhaled and turned toward the approaching crowd. "I hope Anya can heal bullet holes."

"As long as they don't hit you in the head," Lotan said, inching in front of her as the humans broke apart to surround them.

"Anya." Jack cupped her face. "Just for a moment. Just to expel some humans from the land so they don't kill us."

She cracked open an eye. "Fine."

"By order of the ICDM Council, surrender your—"

One by one, the humans around them stepped backward, as if someone was pushing them back. They dropped their weapons along the way, crying out as they toppled off their feet and were dragged out by some invisible force. They didn't stop until they were past the river.

Some got up and tried to march back in, but the barrier at the river stopped them.

Jack exhaled in relief, looking down at Anya, who'd fallen back asleep, nestled against his shoulder with a pleased smile on her face. He leaned down to kiss her on the forehead, saying a prayer of thanks they'd gotten out of that one all right.

"God."

He looked up and his heart dropped to his stomach. The ewû were now circling the humans, and without weapons, they were defenseless. One dropped down and took a large bite out of an ICDM agent's arm, his screams echoing into Ath-kur.

"We have to..." Cam whispered, putting her hand over her

lips. "Bael just left them to…"

"C'mon," Jack said, hoisting Anya onto his back. "We can't help them now."

CHAPTER FORTY

Cam took a long sip of the wine, grateful that it was here, but wishing it was something stronger. Her body was electrified from the day, her skin still warm from the sun. Her heart broken from what she'd learned.

She had no reason to doubt Bael about María, not when he was so smug about it. To think her stoic, strong great-aunt who'd calmly led the Mexican and Central American divisions for almost two decades could be turned into…into a mindless monster. And to know that she'd been the one to…

No. She wouldn't pin this on herself. It was Bael. It always seemed to come back to him.

Lotan had theorized that Bael had used the famed athtar healing powers to resuscitate mostly dead people, but that was as much as Cam could hear before she confessed a need for air and solitude. Lotan had, at least, brought her this bottle of wine and a glass and kissed her forehead, saying nothing else and retreating inside to strategize with Jack. They both seemed to know Cam needed space to grieve the loss of her great-aunt.

Cam let a tear fall down her cheek, wondering what her grandmother would think once she found out. Juana and María hadn't always been of the same mind about things, but they'd loved each other fiercely. Juana would be devastated. As would Cam's parents—the whole family. ICDM, if it still existed, would feel her absence acutely, as it had Frank's.

Unbidden, the day's events replayed in her mind. Bael showing up as he did, as if he'd planned everything to a T and they'd been unwilling players in his theatrics. Anya had said he was unpredictable now, but this seemed a new level of cruelty. Perhaps he wanted her dead, but he wanted all of them to suffer as much as possible first.

Cam wiped her cheek, topping herself off with the rest of the bottle and wishing she felt more drunk. ICDM had sent agents —willingly or otherwise—to help Bael. To kill them. Even if María was gone, that was a step farther than ICDM had ever gone. Perhaps they were desperate to hold onto their kingdom. Or Bael had frightened them into submission.

She closed her eyes, pressure building in her chest. What options remained to them now, if ICDM was truly under Bael's control again? And what other horrors did Bael have up his sleeve?

"You okay?" Jack walked out onto the front porch and sat down next to her.

"I think I asked to be alone."

"You've had enough alone time," Jack said, reaching for the bottle and frowning. "Damn, didn't you leave any for me?"

"How's Anya?"

"She promises she'll be right as rain in the morning," Jack said, looking up at the dark sky. "Color's better, at least."

They fell into an awkward silence, and Cam sniffed back her tears. "Do you think ICDM knew what would happen to their agents when Bael took them?"

"I'm sure Bael will spin a horrible tale about how we murdered them in cold blood."

Cam looked down at her half-empty glass. "We did. We could've helped them."

"We couldn't have, Cam," Jack said. "They clearly had orders to kill us. ICDM seems to have thrown in their loyalty with Bael."

"Whoever is left," Cam said, finishing off her wine. "I don't even know who that would be. Frank's gone, María's gone. The others seem spineless at best. They were more concerned with keeping their funding than…"

"My dad," Jack said. "Bael didn't say anything about him."

"It's only a matter of time, Jack," Cam said. "Bael is going to emotionally rip us limb from limb, then he'll kill us."

"Is this hopelessness I hear?" Jack asked.

"I can't see any reason to hope," Cam said.

"Lotan grabbed the Nullius sand," Jack said. "We have some guns the agents dropped. So we can build a weapon to defeat

Bael."

"We just have to be able to catch him," Cam said. "Anya didn't seem to think she could do that."

"It's just going to be a surprise, then, like we did during the Great Demon War," Jack said. "No more talking, just slice his head off. Preferably when Anya's got control of the time river, so he can't slow it."

Cam rubbed her face. "We need help, Jack. We can't do this alone. We had… We had an entire army gathered against him last time to distract him. Now there's just us four."

"Where do you suggest we get one?"

She wasn't sure, but her gut said that she should go back to ICDM. She needed to know for sure what had happened, and why they seem to have lost their good senses. And she needed to let them know what Bael had done to María.

"Cam?" Jack prompted. "What are you thinking?"

"I'm going to Geneva," Cam said, putting her empty glass down and rising. The wine finally caught up with her, and she swayed on her feet. "Tomorrow."

She expected Jack to argue. "I'll go with you. For backup, if you need it. No telling what sort of welcome we'll get."

"As will I," Lotan said from the door, another bottle of wine in hand that he looked at longingly. "But I guess we won't get to enjoy this."

Cam shrugged. "I could have another glass. If you two will join me."

⬧

The pounding headache Cam had the next morning was almost a harbinger of the bad day they were about to have. Anya seemed completely back to normal as she listened to the plan, a frown on her face.

"At the very least, Lotan and I can steal some more weapons, if we need them," Jack said. "Besides that...I need to know if my dad's all right."

The crease between her brows finally loosened. "Be careful. Bael might not be able to physically get inside Geneva, but that doesn't mean he can't hurt you." She glanced at Cam. "Clearly, he's got reach."

"We'll be in and out as quickly as we can," Cam said. "C'mon, boys."

Anya opened a portal to the south of the city, as close as she could get, and Lotan stepped through first, followed by Cam. Jack remained behind, and Cam turned to give them some privacy as he brought Anya in for a long kiss and soft conversation. It was nice, at least, that things were going well for them, even with Bael floating around.

Lotan's fingers snaked through hers and he squeezed them. "Are you up for this today?"

"No," Cam said as Jack joined them in Geneva and the portal shrank to pocket-sized. "Which means it's the best time to do it."

Jack exhaled, looking at the city beyond. "I guess we have to walk, huh?"

"Does the body good," Cam said. "Or something."

By the time they reached the tent city, Cam's headache had dissipated, and she was left with stoic resignation. She had very little confidence—much less than the last time she'd been here—that the Council would be willing to give them anything. But she had to tell them the truth, at least.

The tent city seemed much less guarded than before—which Cam took as a bad sign. ICDM might have extracted a promise for protection from Bael, which meant they no longer feared a demonic attack. Or, perhaps equally concerning, the military that had been providing additional security could have pulled it with the collapse of support around the world.

"We'll hope for the latter," Jack said. "The good news is that we shouldn't have as much trouble smuggling more weapons out of here."

"You two head toward the tent," Cam said. "If you run into the scientists, tell them you're there on my orders. And if that doesn't work—"

"I won't hurt them," Jack said. "Badly."

"Once you've got what you need, get out of there," Cam said. "Don't wait for me."

Lotan made a face like he disagreed with the direction, but squeezed her hand and kissed it. "Be quick."

"I will."

She turned on her heel and walked away, but no one was paying attention to them. The guards that were there seemed barely interested in what they were doing, and the two at the front of the Council tent waved her in without asking questions.

They must not have known the winds had changed. But that was the last time she'd probably get that sort of welcome.

The Council was similarly thinned out, with fewer aides about. In fact, it looked like someone had packed away half the things and taken them somewhere else. Boxes of files sat on the tables next to unplugged monitors. They were…

"Going somewhere?" Cam asked no one in particular. The agents who heard her just averted their gazes and continued their work.

Cam continued until she found Sabrosky, sitting in a backroom and typing on a laptop.

"Macarro," he said. "What can I do for you?"

"I'd like to know why ICDM gave Bael twenty agents," Cam asked. "And why those agents tried to kill us."

Sabrosky looked up, confused. "How…?"

"He took those agents to the Underworld," Cam said. "They're…dead. As is María."

"We know," he said, sitting down. "We had no choice."

"There's always a choice."

"If it's between sacrificing twenty agents or another hundred thousand innocent human lives, there isn't," he said, looking up at her. "We've been given our marching orders, and what happens if we fail to follow them. I'm sorry, Cam."

"María wouldn't stand for this," Cam said.

"María is gone," Sabrosky said. "As is Frank. And the rest of us would be, had we not agreed to Bael's terms."

"He's not invincible."

"There's a reason humanity was under his thumb for thousands of years," he said. "We can have all the talismans in the world, but against him…we're powerless. He's demanded we move our offices out of Geneva to a place more accessible to him, and if we don't…"

"What? He'll kill all of Australia?" Cam said, but she was only half-kidding.

"We're trying to do what's best for the world, while we still have the power to do so," he said. "Right now, our Council has the unfortunate task of telling the world leaders what we've learned, and get their decision about still funding us. I do not think Bael cares much what the outcome is. He'll ensure any country who steps out of line understands the consequences."

There was something defeated about his tone, reminding Cam of the times when Anya would swear there was no escaping Bael. When she'd resigned herself to death and given up hope that anything would change.

"Mark my words," Cam said. "We will defeat him again. Somehow, some way. And if we have to do it by our-damned-selves this time, we will." She took a step back. "But if you could offer us something to help, that would be great."

"I have a family," he said, as if that were an answer. "And there's been so much loss already. I don't know if I could stomach any more."

CHAPTER FORTY-ONE

"So how are you planning to ask her to marry you?" Jack asked, almost as soon as Cam was out of earshot.

Lotan stopped short. "What?"

"Cam. How are you going to ask her to marry you?" Jack kept walking, nodding and smiling at an agent walking by.

"You like to have these conversations at the wrong time," Lotan grumbled. "Maybe we should discuss this when we aren't trying to sneak around."

"But then we'll be back with Cam, and she'll get suspicious if we go off somewhere," Jack said. "Trust me, I know her. Tell me you've thought about it, at least."

"Of course I have, but as I said, I was waiting until things weren't so...dire."

"And I told *you*, time is of the essence these days," Jack said. "Can't be sure we'll all survive this, after all. Remember, you're human."

Lotan opened his mouth to argue, but Jack had a point.

"So I suggest you find a moment and just do it. That way, you'll have no regrets," Jack said, nodding toward the place where Cam used to work. "There's the weapons tent."

"How shall we broach it?"

"Lie until that doesn't work then use force," Jack said, adjusting his jacket as he walked toward the tent. The guards outside were gone, which seemed odd to Lotan. But once they got inside, he saw why.

"It's...empty." Jack's brows rose. "Why is it empty?"

"Because ICDM is destroying all the weaponry," Cam said, walking through the flap and joining them inside. "Bael has regained control of them and demanded they cease production of all talisman work. Not to mention..." She glanced at the tent city. "They have to move offices to somewhere he can more easily keep track of them."

Jack exhaled, but Lotan didn't take his eyes off Cam. "And what of the Council?"

"They're scared shitless," Cam said, meeting his gaze. "They're off in their various countries, telling their leadership what they've found out."

"Fuck," Jack said. "So that's it, then? ICDM won't help us? What the hell are we supposed to do?"

Lotan walked up to the empty table and rested his hands on the plastic. "We gathered a few weapons from the agents who'd broached Ath-kur."

"A few. Against an army," Jack said.

"We only need one shot," Cam said. "Bael's the real enemy. The rest of them…"

"And he won't let us get within five feet of him with this weapon," Jack countered. "Even when Anya has the time river stopped, he can come and go as he pleases. So we'd have to surprise him, which doesn't seem possible these days."

Lotan drummed his fingers on the table, thinking to himself. Bael was a slippery foe, to be sure, but he wasn't the *only* target. The Abbunatu, as Bael called it, was still the source of Bael's power. And right now, it was unprotected in the Nullius. If Anya could stop time, they could venture to that cave, use the talisman bullet on the Abbunatu, and…presumably end all demonic energy in the world.

"Lotan?" Cam's voice pulled him back. "What are you plotting over there?"

"Nothing," he replied with a smile. Because just as quickly as the perfect plan came together, the reality of the aftermath became clear. Once the Abbunatu had vanished from this world, so would Anya's magic—and her ability to escape the Underworld.

"Lotan?" Cam pressed. "Anything you want to share with the class?"

"Not at this time, no," Lotan replied. "I think we should, at least, create a weapon that could kill Bael on the off chance he shows up to gloat. At least then we'll be prepared. And as for ICDM..." He looked around. "I don't think there's anything more for us here. Our only hope is that some countries may stand and fight against him. But for now, we should return to Ath-kur."

Anya looked visibly relieved when Lotan, Cam, and Jack stepped through the portal and back into her protective custody. Jack and Cam told her about the current situation while Lotan remained quiet. He couldn't get the Abbunatu out of his mind, or the perfectly deadly solution that would come from it. How quickly would it perish? How soon would it sever connections with its spawn? Was it possible Anya could kill it and escape?

He glanced over at her, knowing she would probably volunteer to go today if it meant this would end. But one look at Jack, watching her with what appeared to be true happiness, and Lotan decided it was better to look for alternatives.

"The good news is Bael seems to have stopped attacking humanity for the moment," Anya said.

"As long as ICDM plays along with him," Cam added.

"Which leaves his other goal still unfulfilled," Jack said. "Getting rid of Anya."

"As long as you stay in Ath-kur, he can't hurt you, right?" Cam said. "And he's not going to go back on his word."

"It's not..." Anya said. "I can't just hide here forever."

"And you won't," Jack said. "What we need is to find a way

to draw Bael out, distract him, then destroy him—same way we did before."

"He'll expect that, precisely *because* we did it to him before," Cam said.

"What if you do it under the auspices of asking him to forgive you?" Jack asked Anya. "You could feign like you've seen the errors of your ways, allow him into Ath-kur, then once he's in our sight…" He made a bullet sound.

She licked her lips. "I don't know. If he thinks… If he assumes my heart has completely turned away, he'll know something is up if I suddenly decide otherwise."

"Then we frame it as a truce," Lotan said. "Bael can have humanity, but as long as you and your humans are safe, you'll retreat and let him do what he wants. If, as you say, you two are exactly evenly matched, it may just be believable."

"Then what?" Anya asked.

"We nail him with an anti-athtar talisman bullet," Jack said.

"He'd see that coming."

Jack shook his head. "Not if we use a portal and appear right behind him. And when he's incapacitated, you can lop his head off."

"It would have to be very precise," Cam said. "The incoming bullet, you stopping time, all of it would have to happen at the same time. If memory serves, the reaction is instantaneous."

"We will have to practice," Lotan said.

"And make said bullet," Cam added. "Where is the Nullius sand we brought back?"

"Over there," Anya said, pointing toward the front of the house.

Lotan rose to follow Jack and Cam. Near the front door, there was a hole, almost as if something acidic had eaten through the wood. But on the ground, lying in a patch of colorless sand that seemed closer to the Nullius itself than Ath-kur, were the backpacks Lotan and Cam had hastily shrugged off when they'd brought Anya back from the Nullius.

"It's the same as that bullet," Jack said, looking at Anya, who was keeping her distance. "Clearly, this stuff is potent."

Lotan jumped down to the patch of sand and picked up the bags, sliding them over his shoulders. "I'll take these somewhere else and get to work."

"I'll join you," Cam said, taking one bag from him. "Don't worry, Anya. You just focus on what you're going to say to Bael."

"If you go behind the house, away from the mountain, about thirty minutes, you'll find a space that might be conducive to working," she said. "You can't miss it."

"What is it?" Cam asked.

"The site of the Great Demon War," Anya said. "Complete with anti-athtar talismans still embedded in the ground. It's a little unsettled there, so be careful you don't stray too close to any of the holes."

Much like the Nullius sand had transformed the small area where it had been set, there seemed to be a large swath of land where the trees and rocks and mountains were nonexistent. As they drew closer, Lotan noticed bodies lying on the ground in the nothingness, and cracks and holes in the desert. It looked the same as from his memory, when he'd scoured the empty land for survivors after Bael's death.

"Is this…?" Cam whispered, looking at Lotan.

He nodded. "This will be the perfect place to make our weapons. Anya already can't set foot here—and my guess is, Bael can't either."

"Could do without the dead bodies," Cam muttered, glancing at a dead kappa cut in half on the ground as they walked. "Is this far enough? I don't think I want to walk across the entire battlefield."

"Should be," Lotan said, turning to her as he offloaded the guns onto the white sand beneath them and she set down the two backpacks. "What do we do first, my love?"

She picked up one of the guns, opened the barrel, and tipped it over. Five bullets fell onto the sand. Lotan took another and did the same, and together they emptied every one of the six guns they'd managed to recover, finding a total of twenty bullets inside.

"Hopefully, we only need one," Lotan said, gathering the small metal pieces and handing them to Cam.

She used the tips of her fingers to twist the bullet until the top came off. It was hollow inside, but empty.

"Good," Cam said, with a bit of an exhale. "I was worried they'd stopped hollowing them out."

"How much sand do we put in?" Lotan asked.

"The one that hit Anya had a grain," Cam said. "But since this is Bael, let's stuff as much in as we can."

Carefully, Lotan took a pinch of sand and dropped it into the bullet, finding his fingers nearly too large for the effort. Cam worked much faster, her tiny fingers nimble.

"Time is of the essence these days. Can't be sure we'll all survive this, after all. Remember, you're human now."

Jack's warning was clear in his mind, but Lotan couldn't bring himself to ask her just yet. Not in this desolate land, surrounded by dead bodies and misty air. Not when they had much more important things to focus on. Cam might chastise him for losing focus and never give him an answer.

"What?" Cam said, glancing at him.

"Nothing."

"You've been awfully quiet lately," Cam said. "You've got that 'I'm about to do something stupid' face on."

"I have no such face."

She put down the bullet. "Lotan. Talk to me. What are you thinking?"

"I'm thinking how very happy I am that we are back to our normal selves," he replied, deftly changing the subject. "And how much I'm looking forward to—"

Something whistled in the distance, and an arrow landed ten feet from where they were sitting.

"The hell is that?" Cam asked.

Lotan loaded one of the weapons and handed it to her.

"Maybe we'll end this earlier than we thought. C'mon."

They walked toward the boundary between Ath-kur and Liley. But as they drew closer, the mist that had been shrouding Liley lifted. Lotan threw out a hand to stop Cam from walking further, although they were still a way from the border itself.

On the other side, thousands of demons had amassed, ready to venture onto Anya's land.

"Holy…" Cam breathed then blinked. "What are they waiting for?"

"They can't cross the border unless Anya gives them the green light," Lotan said. "Thankfully."

"Does Bael think she'll do that?" Cam asked, looking up at him. "What *possible* reason could he have to bring all these demons here just to basically sit around and wait?"

Lotan honestly couldn't say. Back during the Great Demon War, Bael had left the borders open and used threats to dare them to cross it. Was he hoping Anya would be similarly minded and open the borders in a dare? Or was he merely waiting for some plot to unfold that none of them had considered?

"We should get back," Lotan said, after a moment.

"Should we take the weapons back with us? I don't know if it's safe to leave them out here like this," Cam asked. "Especially with those monsters sitting in wait."

"We should bring them, but not too close to the house," Lotan said. "The last thing we need is for Anya to be ill before she faces whatever this is."

CHAPTER FORTY-TWO

"I am the belu athtar."

Anya stared at Jack, who was attempting to playact as Bael, but the only thing he was succeeding in doing was making her smile. Since Cam and Lotan had gone to make talisman bullets, that left them to practice the other half of the plan, where Anya would distract Bael long enough for one of them to sneak up and shoot him with the bullet. But clearly, Jack was having too much fun.

"I am the master of all things," Jack said, puffing out his chest. "I am Bael, lord of the universe. King of the five realms. Whatever else he says. You are peons."

She snorted. "Stop it and be serious."

"What? I'm not smug enough?" Jack said. "I could go off on a ten-minute monologue about how I'm the most impressive specimen ever to set foot on the world, if that would help?"

"It wouldn't," she said, biting her lip to keep from laughing.

"Fine." Jack cleared his throat and lifted his chin. "I'm serious now."

But the look on his face just made her break out into laughter, the kind she hadn't experienced in ages. That deep, belly-shaking laugh that filled her with warmth and joy and affection for the man who'd caused it. She straightened, swallowing hard and trying to shake off the lingering giggles, almost succumbing to them when she caught sight of Jack's so-called "serious" face again.

"This isn't going very well," Jack said. "Maybe I should've gone with Cam. Lotan might've been a better guinea pig."

"I don't know if anyone could improve on this," Anya said. "So let's just pretend like you've given a long monologue and we'll go from there."

"Fine," Jack said. "So I've monologued, and you will at some point—"

"Stop time. Open the portal," Anya began.

"Then bang," Jack said, clutching his heart. "Oh, I'm dead. For real this time."

"Then I'll do the rest," Anya said, mimicking a slicing motion toward his neck. "As long as he doesn't know it's coming, or slow time..." She chewed her lip, doubt rising in the back of her mind. "Which he can do if he's got control of the river when we get there."

"But you can overpower that by stopping time," Jack said. "Right?"

Anya wasn't sure. She'd stopped time around talismans, stopped time in the Nullius, but against Bael? So far, that hadn't happened.

"C'mon," Jack said. "Let's practice that again. Or else I will start monologuing for real, and nobody wants that."

She nodded and reached into the time river, finding the familiar hold as she bent it to her will, slowing it. But as usual, she couldn't find that extra level that allowed her to stop it completely. She dug deeper into her memory banks, grasping at those scenes where Jack had been a hair's breadth from death.

She looked at the barely breathing man before her, his face almost frozen in that half-smirk he'd been wearing all day, and reminded herself to be grateful that he was all hers. For the moment, anyway. If she couldn't get her shit together, she might lose him forever.

Anya stared into his eyes, imagining what it would be to have Bael hurt him. She leaned into that fear, that pain, the horror of losing him, as she reached in deep to the time river. But as hard as she tried, she couldn't do it. Imagined danger didn't hold a candle to the real thing.

"Well?" Jack asked when she unfroze him.

"Couldn't do it," Anya said with a half-shrug. "Standing here, like this, it's not going to work."

"Then I'll just have to put myself in danger," he said,

walking toward her. "Just throw myself at Bael's mercy and see what you do."

"Not funny," Anya said, though she wore a smile as he rested his hands on her hips.

"It wasn't meant to be funny," Jack said. "If me almost dying is what it takes to save the world..."

"But what if I'm not quick enough?" she replied, looking up at him. "What if—"

He captured her lips in a kiss that seemed an invitation for something more. She probably should've stopped him, should've become serious once more and attempted to stop time. For their plan to work, it all had to function in perfect unison. But it was hard to pull away when Jack had snaked his hand up to unhook her bra.

The door slammed open. "Quit making out," Cam barked as Anya and Jack broke apart. "We've got problems."

"Maybe," Lotan said, holding up his hand. "Anya, have you checked the border with Liley recently?"

She frowned as her Sight lifted out of the house and toward the boundary. "Not recently, I—"

Her breath caught when she saw them, the horde of demons amassed on the border with Liley, waiting for their marching orders—or the ability to cross. There weren't just lilins in the bunch, either. All four demonic races, side-by-side. Anya's Sight did a U-turn and headed to the other border, the one with Elonsi.

"What?" Jack asked.

"We've got a demon army waiting for us on the border with Liley," Cam said.

"And Elonsi," Anya said, after checking the other border. "All under Bael's banner."

"But they can't do anything, can they?" Jack said. "You've still got control over the land."

Anya nodded, but concern grew in her chest. What was Bael playing at? He wouldn't just stick his army there for no reason, would he? He was sending a message—or wanted to speak with her.

"I need to go," Anya said. "Once I show up at the border, he will appear."

"Unless that's what he wants," Jack said.

"We're going with you," Cam said. "At least as backup."

"You can't back me up against him," Anya said. "And—"

"He can't hurt us, as long as we all stay on our side," Jack said. "Don't let him force you into making an error."

Anya gazed into his eyes then nodded slowly. "Fine."

Anya opted for the Elonsi border, as the Liley border was still covered in anti-athtar talismans. As she'd Seen, there were demons as far as the eye could see, standing at the ready with weapons as basic as spears and swords—and a few with talisman launchers. Presumably anti-athtar ones. Anya was surprised that Bael had allowed such a thing in his ranks.

"Now what?" Jack asked.

"It won't be long," Anya said.

"Are we sure he'll show?" Cam asked.

"He will," Lotan said.

As predicted, a hush descended over the demons on the other side. At the back of the group, they parted, another show of force by Bael. He was nothing if not a showman.

"I was hoping you'd come," Bael said. "Is this not impressive?"

"If memory serves, we had a similarly-sized army to defeat you before," Lotan barked. "Perhaps ours was a little bigger."

"But yours was already made," Bael said. "I, on the other hand, have built this army from the belu up."

Lotan nodded to a wolf creature in the distance. "I see you found a new caretaker of my mother's magic."

Bael stopped just short of the border, his black, shiny shoes immaculate. "It was what had to be done, considering. But don't think you can find your way to them. I have them safely secured away where even your precious Anat can't reach them."

"And where they can't use their belu powers to expel you," Lotan replied.

Bael's attention turned to him. "You know so much, then?"

"I know my parents refused to let you set foot in their lands," he said. "My guess is these new belus don't have that power if they don't live in the Underworld."

Anya's brow furrowed; she hadn't even considered that before. If that were true, the belus were under Bael's total and complete control.

"So what's all this?" Cam said. "Are you just here to show us how many friends you have?"

"Merely to demonstrate my might," Bael said. "This stalemate has gone on long enough, Anat. It's time to face me and find out who really deserves to be the belu athtar."

"Clearly, she's winning," Jack said. "Since you're over there."

"What you don't understand, Jackson, is that I know Anat better than you do," Bael said, his gaze turning hard. "I've known her for thousands of years, understand every quirk in her soft little mind."

Soft. Anya braced herself—Bael was about to lower the boom.

"The true belu athtar isn't afraid to sacrifice those weaker to show power," Bael said, his fierce gaze turning to Anya. "And for that reason, I will be moving my army to the human world to demonstrate just how different things will be from now on."

"You just… ICDM…" Cam swallowed. "You got them to agree to your terms?"

"I am all-powerful, you mouthy little vermin," Bael snapped, glaring at her. "The humans will agree to whatever terms I give them. After all," he smiled, looking at Anya once more, "they only believe there's one demon in this world capable of such a thing. And once ICDM is gone, there will be no one to fight. Only submission."

"We will fight," Jack said. "Anya will fight."

Bael's gaze once more landed on her, and she felt his unspoken challenge. He would barter the entire world to destroy her. And he wouldn't stop until every human was dead or demon. "I believe I'll start in Charleston. Then, perhaps, Mexico City. El Paso seems like a nice place to decimate a population."

Of course. Jack's parents, Cam's abuela and her parents. Bael was going for the jugular, as only his twisted mind could do. He would tempt the humans away from her by endangering everyone they loved.

Anya felt the gazes of her friends on the back of her neck, but she remained silent. Better to keep her mouth shut and let Bael reveal his plans fully. Then they would find a way to stop them.

He smiled. "Of course, all those plans will end if Anat steps aside and allows the true original athtar to reclaim his throne."

"You're not an original demon," Lotan said. "There's no such thing."

"Isn't there?" Bael said. "You're such an expert, having lived all of five hundred years, boy. I have seen demons rise and fall."

"Killing them, too," Lotan said. "I saw what you did to the nox who preceded my mother."

"And the one before him, the one before her—there've been so many," Bael said. "Each of them outlived their usefulness and I had to seek out another to take their place. This current crop has been the shortest, and most disappointing." He turned to Anya. "You know what I speak of, Anat. That magic inside you was given to me by God himself."

"You've said that before," Jack drawled. "But isn't there a giant blob or something that is actually the source of your power?"

"Indeed," Lotan said. "This whole touched-by-God thing seems a little far-fetched."

"Believe what you will, *humans*, but I will reclaim my throne," Bael replied. "You have until tomorrow to make your decision. I will see you in, " his gaze landed on Jack, "Charleston, I suppose. At noon."

CHAPTER FORTY-THREE

"We'll just have to move up our plans, then," Jack said, breaking the silence of the living room. "Anya, you're going to have to get really good at stopping time."

She didn't respond, her mind working on the problem but apparently not coming up with anything. Jack didn't like her silence, and he hoped she wasn't thinking of doing anything drastic.

"Maybe we move Cam and Jack's parents out of harm's way," Lotan said. "He seemed to only opt for Charleston because of Jack."

"We can't leave hundreds of thousands of humans to Bael's whims and just save a handful," Cam replied. "Even if they are our parents."

"But what can we do against that army? What can they do?" Lotan asked. "Especially if ICDM has begun dismantling their weapons under Bael's order."

"We need to warn them, at least," Jack said. "Maybe they can evacuate the city—"

"That will tip Bael off," Anya said. "Although he probably expects we'll do something like that. Perhaps he's planning for it, and he'll have something waiting for us that's worse."

"Can't imagine anything worse," Cam muttered. "But Jack's right. Charleston first, then Mexico City, if we need to. If Bael's going to send his army in tomorrow, they deserve some kind of preparation." She looked at Jack. "Who's even in charge now that Frank…?"

"No idea," Jack said. "But my dad would know. He seems to have stepped in temporarily. We'll go to Charleston and raise the alarm."

"We'll go to Mexico City and let them know then come join you," Cam said, looking at Lotan. "Hopefully, they'll be a little more welcoming than last time. I guess we'll all meet at your mom's house, Jack?"

"Then what?" Anya said, rising. "We are still four against thousands. You three—sorry to say—are human and won't be much help. And if Bael takes control of the time river—"

"Then you can take it from him by stopping it, and we continue with our plan," Jack said. "Nothing's changed except now we have a place to do it."

"Bael might not even show," Anya said. "He likes having others do his dirty work."

"He'll show," Cam said. "This is very clearly a personal vendetta against you, so he'll be there to monologue."

"And when he does, we'll be ready," Jack said. "As will you."

But Lotan cleared his throat. "I don't want to mention it, except that we may be facing certain annihilation tomorrow. So I would like to offer an alternative as a very last-ditch effort to end this. And when I mean last-ditch—"

"Out with it," Anya snapped.

"We have the Nullius sand bullet, we have a weapon, and we have a way to reach the Abbunatu," Lotan said. "The bullets are lethal to belus, so it stands to reason—"

"They would be lethal to the Abbunatu," Anya replied softly.

Jack's anger spiked. "Abso-fucking-lutely not. Besides that, there's Nullius sand all around the Abba-whatever. Clearly it's not bothered by it."

"Maybe not," Lotan replied. "It was always strange to me that there was a desert of anti-demonic energy around the supposed center of all magic. Why?"

"Because it was keeping it contained," Cam suggested. "But I'm with Jack. If we kill that demonic core, what happens to the person doing the shooting?"

"They'd...be stuck," Lotan said. "I don't know how quickly the magic would dissipate from Anya, but—"

"It would be a one-way trip," Jack said, looking at Anya. "This is ludicrous, right?"

But her gaze was distant, and he feared she was actually considering it. She wasn't above self-sacrifice, and the guilt she felt for bringing Bael back in the first place was weighing on her.

"We'll find some other alternative," Jack said when she didn't answer. "Maybe we'll find something in Charleston that can help us."

But based on the grim looks around the living room, he seemed to be the only one with optimism.

Jack walked up the sidewalk to his childhood home. It was early morning already, the sky tinged with pink. Anya trailed behind him, a nervous look on her face as they walked along the tall fence that bordered the home.

"Do you remember when you broke into the house to steal Cam's laptop?" she asked, looking at a tree that leaned over the yard on the other side. "You climbed that tree, didn't you?"

Jack smiled. "She was so mad."

"Seems she got over it." Anya took a step then frowned, backing up. "I can't go any further."

"What? Why?"

"Talismans," Anya said, backing up another step until she no longer wore the frown. "I suppose that's good. Means Bael can't get here."

"He can send his minions, though," Jack replied. "You stay here, and I'll go inside. I won't be long."

Jack walked to the front gate, but it was closed, so he backtracked and climbed the very same tree. He landed softly on the grass in the backyard and smiled when he saw the kitchen light on. His mom was an early bird, but even he hadn't been sure how early she'd be awake.

His footsteps softly echoed on the gravel path and he raised his hand to rap on the door. A moment later, the latches unlocked, and he came face to face with his surprised mother.

"Jackie?" She opened the door further, revealing her fluffy robe and a nightgown. "What are you doing here so early?"

"Is Dad here?" Jack asked.

"He's upstairs," she said. "What's wrong?"

Jack didn't want to lie to his mother, and she'd find out soon enough, but he didn't want to worry her so early in the morning. "I just need to talk with him about something."

"Come in, baby," she said, opening the door further. "Do you want some coffee? Breakfast?"

"That would be nice," Jack said. "Also…Anya's hanging around outside. You could remove some of the anti-athtar talismans so she can come in."

Karen's face lit up. "Is she really? Oh goodness, we can't have her out there. Let me move what I can. I know your father hid them all over the place."

She tied her robe around herself and walked outside, bending over to pick up talismans carved into pebbles in the gravel. Jack watched her for a moment, unsure it was smart to remove their protections.

"Make sure you put those back," he said after a moment. "Once we're gone."

She straightened and pursed her lips. "Of course, Jackie. Now get."

Jack left her in the yard and walked through the kitchen, almost lured by the scent of coffee, but forging on through the front of the house, quiet and empty, climbing the stairs to the back where he'd find his father's study. Inside, the light was on, so Jack cracked open the door. "Dad?"

"Jackie?" George said, rising. He looked like he was wearing yesterday's clothes. "What are you doing here?"

"We need to talk," Jack said. "About Bael."

Jack told his father what Bael had said, and how he was targeting Charleston in the morning. His father listened to everything and didn't look the least bit surprised by the news. Jack hoped that meant George would have some good news.

"We've been waiting for something like this," George said. "The US Division has refused to sign the treaty, so they're going to target our headquarters and beat us into submission."

Jack leaned forward. "What?"

"After..." He swallowed, glancing at his computer. "After what happened to María, there was no way the Mexican Division would sign on, and the other countries under her purview followed suit in a sign of solidarity. The US Division has opted out as well."

Jack couldn't help but be a little proud of his father and the organization he'd once worked for. "So all might not be lost, then?"

"I don't know what we can do," George said. "We've barely

begun our preparations, but what we have, we'll use to defend the city." He glanced behind Jack. "Is your athtar friend here?"

"She is," Jack said. "And ready to help defend us."

"Well, that'll be something," George replied. "Maybe they can fight each other to the death and leave humanity out of it."

"I wish it were that simple," Jack replied. "But at least if we have you guys behind us, we'll have a chance."

Karen seemed to have taken care of the talismans and found Anya in the minutes Jack was upstairs, because they were sitting at the kitchen table with mugs of coffee. Anya's gaze landed on Jack when he walked in, and she offered a half-smile before glancing at George.

"Jackie, she's absolutely wonderful," Karen said, sitting up. "Sit and have coffee. I'll put on some breakfast."

"Actually," Anya said, rising. "Jack, can I talk with you for a moment?"

Jack followed Anya outside, his brows knitted together as he waited for her to speak. She leaned on the railing, gripping it lightly, but also with the sort of fear that set him on edge. It was a look that said she was about to do something selfless and stupid.

"How was my mom?"

"Sweet," Anya said with a soft smile. "Welcoming. Told me I should've come for Christmas last year." She snorted. "Maybe if I had, we wouldn't have gotten so far off track."

Jack came to stand next to her. "We figured it out."

"Jack, look..." She turned to him. "There's a good chance today doesn't go the way we want."

"Just as good a chance it does—"

"Don't." She turned, her green eyes shimmering. "Bael has everything in his favor, and even if we manage to kill him...his minions will continue what he started. This may not end well—and millions will die."

Jack shook his head. "What are you telling me?"

"I'm saying that if this doesn't work... If Bael manages to evade our grip, or it looks like things aren't going well..." She exhaled and took his hands. "I'm going to the Nullius to destroy it."

"It?" Jack blinked. "That Abbacadabra thing Lotan was talking about?"

She nodded. "I don't know what will happen when I do. If these talisman bullets will actually kill it. But if it does—when it does—I probably..." She swallowed. "I won't be coming back."

"You've said that before," Jack said.

"I don't see how I can escape this time," Anya said. "Once that thing is dead, I'll be human again. I don't know if it'll be instant, but maybe. I won't have a way to get out of the Underworld if I don't have my athtar magic—no way to stop time to give myself a chance to escape."

She felt Jack's gaze on her, and to her surprise, he just smiled. "Then I guess I'll just have to figure out a way to save you."

"Jack—" Tears had gathered in her eyes. "People have died.

It needs to end."

"And it will, when you kill Bael."

She cupped his face, her thumb gently stroking his cheek. "Why are you always so naively optimistic?"

He took her hand and kissed it gently. "Because I know you, Anya. And I know your heart. You'll come back to me, like you did before. Like you've done every time since. I have faith that things will work out."

She bowed her head as tears fell down her cheeks. "And what if it doesn't?"

He tilted her head up to look at him, wishing he had some words of comfort, but coming up short. The truth was he was holding on to his optimism because he wasn't sure he could handle it if the alternative happened. They'd gone through hell and back repeatedly to find this brief moment of heaven. It seemed cruel that fate might separate them now—almost personal.

But as he stared into her tearful eyes, brushing away tears that fell down her perfect cheeks, it was hard to succumb to that darkness again. They would find a way. Jack would find a way.

"One thing to know about Grenard Christmases," Jack said, his voice thick. "You will eat way more than you ever thought possible and feel more at home than you've ever felt before. I think you'll have a blast this year."

She smiled and rested her head under his chin. "I hope so."

CHAPTER FORTY-FOUR

"Do you remember the night before the Great Demon War?" Lotan asked, a smug smile on his face.

"I do," Cam said, turning away from him purposefully. "We have things to do, Lotan. We can't screw around."

"Spoilsport."

"Do you have the weapons?" Cam asked.

He opened the black duffle bag to show the three guns with six Nullius bullets each. "Let's hope we don't need them."

"We aren't going to get that lucky."

She opened the portal Anya had left for them, the already warm air from the very early morning in Mexico City hitting her skin. She stepped through, gazing up at the familiar stars and house before her.

"This doesn't look like ICDM," Lotan said with a frown as they stood in front of La Hacienda. "Shouldn't we be getting to them?"

"In a minute," Cam said, walking up to the dark house and rapping on the door. "I want some intel first." When no one answered, Cam opened the door and poked her head inside. "Abuela?"

"Aquí, Camilla."

That voice wasn't her grandmother's, but it was still familiar. Cam frowned at Lotan and opened the door wider, walking toward the sound of the voice. In the living room were ICDM agents from El División—and her parents.

"Mom?" Cam blinked. "Dad? What are you doing here?"

"It's all hands on deck," Juana said, coming to stand next to them. "The El Paso Division gave your parents permission to come down to help us fend off the demons, should they show up."

"How..." Cam began, shaking her head. "How did you know that the demons were coming? Bael only threatened us yesterday."

"Bael?" Marco said, lifting his head. "You've seen him?"

"More than that," Lotan replied. "He's planning on bringing his army to Charleston tomorrow—then he's bringing them here. We were coming to warn you, but it seems..."

"After Tía's death, the Mexican Division unanimously decided not to sign that cursed treaty," Silvia, Cam's cousin, said from the corner. "The other countries under her purview have declined as well."

"We figured it was only a matter of time before Bael marched on our cities," Ana said. "But it seems we aren't his first target. The US also declined to sign it."

A little pride swelled in her breast. Her familial country and birth country, joining forces to defeat evil.

"What do we have?" Cam asked, walking toward an empty spot next to her mom on the couch. "In terms of forces?"

"A few thousand. The Mexican military has given us some support," Ana said as Cam sat down. "We've been working on overdrive to create talismans—"

"Just athtar?" Cam asked, holding her breath.

"All of them," Marco said on the other side of Ana. "We aren't fully prepared, but we can send soldiers to Charleston to support. It will take some time, though."

"We have a quicker way," Lotan said with a smile to Cam. "But will it be enough? Bael has hundreds of thousands of demons."

"That many…" Ana whispered, putting her hand over her mouth as silence descended in the room. Cam let the weight of what they were up against fall over her. If they only had a few thousand…

"Do you think he'll set his forces on Charleston?" Marco asked. "Or will it be a dual-pronged attack?"

"This is personal for Bael," Lotan said. "He's furious with Anya, and he wants to inflict as much pain on Jack as possible.

He will send his army to Charleston first and destroy the city and everyone in it."

"What is his goal?" Juana asked, standing in the doorway of the living room. "Will he kill Anya?"

"He'll try," Cam said. "But we have a few tricks up our sleeve, too."

"Why can't Anya just stop time?" Marco asked.

Lotan explained the concept of the time river, and how Anya wouldn't be able to control it while Bael had his fingers in it. Cam looked at her hands, sending a silent prayer that their plan would work. Bael would have to show his face, and there was no guarantee he'd be so stupid. Especially after what had happened the last time he'd shown up in the middle of a battle.

"So our only hope is that he shows, and that he's distracted long enough that you, Cam, and Jack are able to kill him?" Silvia said with a frown. "And then what?"

"Then, hopefully, Anya will remove all demons to the Underworld," Cam said.

"She can't," Ana said. "Many of those now-demons were innocent humans, coerced against their will. Bael's been rounding up humans all over the world and transforming them. We have twenty binders full of missing persons, just in Texas."

"Then we will do our best to cut off the source," Lotan said, looking at Cam with a frown. She shook her head, knowing he was thinking about their last resort option in the Nullius. But Cam wasn't willing to sacrifice Anya just yet. Not until they had no other option left.

"We'll cross that bridge when we get to it," Lotan said finally. "But first, we need to survive the day. Bael said he was going to be in Charleston at noon. The US is going to need all the help they can get."

"What about Mexico City?" Silvia asked.

"If things go the way we hope, Bael won't be around to send his army to Mexico City," Cam said. "But just in case, we shouldn't send everyone. I don't trust Bael not to pull something."

Charleston had already been alerted of the impending threat, thanks to Jack and George, and had requested all available forces to assist in the defense of the city. Marco and Silvia left to coordinate with El Divisiòn. Ana began making calls to the other countries in Central America who'd stood with Mexico against Bael's edict, to see if they had agents or help they could provide.

"We have willing agents, but they're spread out across Central and South America," she said, hanging up the phone and looking right at Lotan. "We'll need someone to stay here and help us reroute the portal to the different countries to bring them to Charleston. Lotan, maybe you could help?"

He furrowed his brow. "I'm going with Cam to Charleston."

Cam exhaled, putting her hand on his chest. "Maybe you should hang back a bit."

"And let you fight by yourself?" His brows rose, and a spark of anger lit in his gaze. "Are you *out* of your mind?"

Cam glanced at her mother, who'd ducked a smile, and looped her arm through Lotan's. "Come with me for a minute."

She practically dragged him out onto the veranda, as the sun was rising over the tops of trees. His face seemed set in a permanent scowl, which might've been adorable had they not been discussing life and death. When they were far enough away from eager ears, Cam turned on him.

"I'm staying with you, Cam," Lotan said. "You can't change my mind."

"Someone needs to stay behind," Cam said. "Would you rather it be you or me? And might I remind you that you aren't able to shapeshift into a huge wolf anymore."

Lotan pursed his lips. "Why does anyone have to stay behind? We'll just tell them how to use the portal to get the other agents. It's not that hard."

Cam swallowed, realizing that perhaps her mother didn't need him after all but was trying to protect him. "Because I don't want you in the thick of a demonic battle."

"I didn't give up immortality to let you walk onto a battlefield and forfeit your life," Lotan said. "At least with me by your side—"

"I'll spend half my time babysitting you," Cam said. "And we'll both end up dead."

Lotan's eyes widened and Cam regretted her words.

"Look—"

He turned away from her, folding his arms over his chest and looking out onto the treetops. Cam hated herself, but if it meant he would be safe…

"I've been through these sorts of things before—as a

human," Cam continued, needing to fill the silence. "It's not a place for…untrained people. You have to be able to fight and…" She winced, realizing she was making this worse instead of better. "I love you, and I don't want anything to happen to you."

He didn't respond, staring off into the distance. Tears welled in Cam's eyes, and she turned to leave, knowing she wouldn't be able to keep her mouth shut and keep herself from digging a deeper hole.

"I love you, too," Lotan replied quietly, turning around. He gently took her hand and pulled her toward him. She nestled under his chin and closed her eyes, inhaling his scent and listening to the sound of his heartbeat.

"This was much easier when I had no idea what was going on," Lotan said. "Just as soon as I have settled things here, I will be joining you. I may not be as competent with a sword, but I know how to use one. And I can shoot a talisman launcher." He tilted her chin upward. "You had better be in one piece when I get there. Understand?"

"Yes, sir."

Cam chewed her thumb as she hitched a ride to El División headquarters, Anya's portal in her back pocket. Lotan wasn't happy to let her go, but Ana promised they'd be right behind, once they finished gathering all the other agents. It was good news, at least, that they had more manpower coming, because the numbers waiting at El División weren't all that encouraging.

But more worrisome was Cam's underlying suspicion that

they were playing into some larger scheme of Bael's. It would be in character for him to challenge Anya to a battle, give her a time and place, then show up somewhere else and make them scramble. But it would also be a show of his own confidence if he showed up where he'd said. Cam wasn't sure which Bael they were dealing with, and it made her uneasy.

She pushed aside those fears for the moment, stepping into the bright morning in Charleston. The road leading to the ICDM compound was already filled with soldiers and agents, all of them holding anti-athtar talismans. It was a good showing, but something in Cam's gut said it wouldn't be enough to stem the tide.

When Cam arrived at headquarters, she asked around until she got pointed in the right direction. Another ten-minute walk, and she reached the end of the soldiers. Farther beyond that stood Jack and Anya, the latter leaning against a parked car and staring out at the ocean.

It wasn't until Cam got closer to them that she realized why. The ICDM headquarters was still covered in anti-athtar talismans, so this was as close as Anya could get. As she approached, Cam noted the pallor of Anya's skin, and that her eyes seemed a little unfocused.

"Oh, hey," Jack said after she got their attention. "What did Mexico say?"

"We're bringing the cavalry," Cam said, handing him the second talisman launcher. "A few hundred strong. Lotan's gone with my mom to look for more in the other countries."

"Hundred?" Anya said. "Is that all?"

"They have talismans," Cam offered. "That has to be worth something."

She exhaled, leaning on her hands. "Yes and no. Bael may have said Charleston, but we don't know where in the city he's going to open a portal. We know it's not going to be here with all this anti-athtar magic. I'm barely able to keep my breakfast down."

"We've sent scouts to all corners of the city," Jack said.

"Do you have control over the time river?" Cam asked.

Anya shook her head. "I thought about it, but... Bael wouldn't show then. If we want a chance at him, he has to feel he has the upper hand." She paused. "But we also don't want him to slow time and massacre our army before we even get started."

"Would he do that?" Cam asked.

"I don't know," Anya said with a defeatist shrug. "Depends on how confident he's feeling when he woke up this morning."

"The only thing to do is wait until he shows up," Jack said. "And once we know what we're dealing with, we'll react. The important thing is for Bael to want to show up and gloat. Once that happens..." He pulled the talisman launcher from his waistband. "Bang."

"Right." Anya leaned on the car hood and hung her head. "And hope he doesn't know something's up."

They fell into a tense silence, with the distant sounds of the agents in the distance carried on the breeze. Cam shifted from one foot to the other, checking her watch. It wasn't even ten in the morning.

"Fuck me," Jack muttered, running his hand through his hair. "It's like waiting for Demon Spring."

"You said it," she muttered.

Jack glanced at his watch. "Two hours."

"At least we know when," Cam said with a half-smile to Jack. "We used to have to sit around and wait for him to decide to grace us with his presence."

"I mean, it's just common courtesy," Jack replied with that familiar smile of his.

"How can you two crack jokes at a time like this?" Anya snapped.

"Coping mechanism." Cam's phone buzzed. She reached into her pocket to pick it up. "Lotan?"

"Get here—*now*." Lotan sounded horrified. "We were wrong. He's starting in Mexico City."

CHAPTER FORTY-FIVE

It had happened just as the last ICDM agent they'd rounded up from South America walked through the portal, and Lotan was ready to step through himself. Something tickled the back of his neck, that familiar sensation of nox magic. And kappa, lilin, eloko…athtar.

"Lotan…" Silvía tugged at his sleeve, and he slowly turned.

A small black schism, not unlike the one Lotan's mother had created, appeared ten steps from where they were standing. It grew slowly, and as soon as it was big enough for a man to walk through, the first arrow came flying out, landing in the chest of a nearby agent.

"Take cover!" Lotan bellowed, knowing full well the cars

they dashed behind wouldn't do much except delay the inevitable. He'd called Cam straightaway, but hung up as soon as the first demon emerged from the schism. She looked human. But for the sweet scent of flowers on the air, Lotan would've thought her harmless.

"Wait," Silvia said, putting her hand up to still the ICDM agents. "I know her. She's... She's family. I don't know how she..."

Lotan exhaled. Bael truly was sick. "She won't be the last."

Another came through, this time an eloko, and based on the reaction of another agent, it was another familiar face. Was Bael going to force everyone gathered to kill their own family?

"Steady," Marco called, coming to stand next to Lotan. "Are we ready if Bael shows?"

Lotan jumped; the talisman launcher was still in the car—twenty feet away.

But as soon as he thought to grab it, the schism burst open wider and a flood of demons came running from the dark void beyond into the streets, surrounding the agents in moments. Lotan had nothing but his two fists and was very quickly swept away by the initial stream. He pushed, but his human muscles were no match for demonic ones. If it weren't for the talismans painted onto his body, he would've been suckered.

He finally broke free of the river, landing against a building and finally able to catch his breath. The schism was still visible from this distance, and the stream of human-looking demons pouring out seemed unending. Even if they had every División agent back from Charleston, they would be overwhelmed in seconds.

In the midst of the demons, the ICDM jackets were few and far between. Lotan pushed himself upright, shaking himself. The talisman launcher was his only goal—it needed to be in his hands just in case Bael made his appearance.

He turned toward the schism, trying to find his bearings, but there was nothing familiar anymore, least of all the car. Even the building he stood against was strange.

"Lotan!" Silvia's voice rang out as she cut through the chaos. "You need to get out of here."

"I need to get to Marco's car," he said. "Where is it?"

She gave him a once-over. "Cam would want—"

"Cam will tell me what she wants when she gets here," Lotan said, irked that *everyone* seemed to think him weak. "Now find me a weapon."

Silvia pulled the second sword from the sheaths around her hips and handed it to him. "Are you sure?"

In one move, he pushed her out of the way, and sliced the head off an incoming nox demon who'd been approaching from behind. "Let's go. I don't want to be empty-handed if Bael makes his appearance."

Lotan led the way back into the fray, but it was hard to move. The order for the moment seemed to be to push into the city not necessarily fight. Those who did engage him in a fight went down quickly, as they were only a week or two turned. But an army of neophytes was still formidable, especially in their numbers.

"Where is that damn car?" Silvia grunted. "I don't see anything familiar—"

"Of course you don't," Lotan replied, recognizing the dampness on his skin for what it was—kappa magic. "They've put a glamour on this place."

He had a hunch the launcher, especially with the Nullius sand, would be hard to miss, but he needed to get higher to see it. He found a streetlight and climbed up the pole, scanning the crowd until he saw it—the demons seemed to be avoiding a certain spot about a hundred feet sunward. That had to be the spot.

"Did you see it?" Silvia asked.

He nodded. "We'll need to fight our way through to it."

Easier said than done. The volume of demons threatened to push them off their path, and every time Lotan looked up, it seemed the kappa glamour had changed, along with his perception. It was as if Bael knew exactly what they were planning and gave orders to the belus to prevent them from doing it.

Lotan scowled. That was probably *exactly* what was going on. The bastard was probably sitting in the time river a second behind present time, watching everything happen.

"You won't win," Lotan said, pushing back a pair of lilins who'd run into him. "Not today."

The crowd had pushed him off course, but still near enough to the car that Lotan could see where the demons parted around it. The kappa magic hadn't been able to change the look of it, which boded well for them. As long as they could get to it—

"Almost there," Lotan called to his newfound partner. "After that—"

Silvia let out a strangled cry, and Lotan turned quickly. The lilin—her cousin—had run a spear through Silvia's chest. Silvia gasped, staring at the sky as blood trickled from her mouth. The lilin tossed her to the ground, a gleeful look in her eyes.

"I always hated her," she said.

Lotan held his sword ready. "Where is Bael?"

"You must be the former nox prince," she said, her eyes growing white. "I've been given explicit instructions to leave you be."

A shot rang out, and the demon fell, dead before she hit the ground. Behind him, holding the smoking talisman launcher, was Marco. His face bore several scratches and cuts, and his jacket was ripped, but he was the best thing Lotan had seen all day.

"Looking for this?" Marco asked, turning the gun around to hand him the barrel.

"How many bullets have you used?" Lotan asked.

"Just the one," he said. "I would've used my blade, but this was faster." He nodded to Lotan. "What will you do with it?"

Lotan looked at the schism. "I may have to bring a gift to the so-called King of the Underworld. As long as that schism remains open, we have a way to get to him. Once I'm there, I'll find him and take him out."

Marco nodded. "I will help carve you a path."

"So I take it you like me now?"

"I didn't say that."

Lotan just cracked a smile. "I hope you know I'm planning to ask her to marry me as soon as I see her again."

Marco didn't respond right away, and Lotan realized he probably thought Lotan wasn't going to see Cam again. And considering the chaos, and the unknown of what he might find when he went through Bael's portal, he might not make it three feet before he was struck down.

But he had to try.

"Ready?" Marco asked.

"Lead the way."

They walked into the fray, swinging blades and cutting a path. With the Nullius sand in his back pocket, the demons were less eager to fight, but some still tried their luck. It didn't seem to be doing much good, not with hundreds of demons replacing the few they'd slain every second. The schism remained in clear view, but it seemed they would take one step forward and three steps back.

"I don't know if this is possible," Marco said.

"He'll have to run out of demons eventually."

"*Here* you are."

Lotan's heart dropped to his stomach, and not in a good way. Silvia stood before them, holding two new swords, her eyes dark with newly transformed nox energy. Bael must've taken her body, revived her, and transformed her—as he'd done with

María.

"Uncle," she said to Marco before turning to Lotan. "You look surprised to see me, prince."

"I'm not your prince," Lotan said. "And I'm not afraid to kill you if need be."

She smiled and ran for them—unable to transform into a fully grown nox so young. But her speed made her a formidable foe, her blades coming quick. She didn't seem bothered by the talisman launcher in Lotan's waistband, but perhaps her maker was egging her on, much like the ewû in the Nullius had ventured into the sunlight.

"Arg!"

Marco cried out as her blade slid across his chest. Lotan watched helplessly as he fell backward, clutching himself and gasping as blood stained from his shirt. The future flashed before Lotan's eyes, and his heart jumped a beat—it was one thing for Cam to have to fight Silvia, but her own father... And he wouldn't put it past Bael to do something like that, either.

"What are you doing?" Marco gasped, holding the gash in his chest. "Go!"

"No," Lotan said. "I'm not doing that to Cam. We will find another way."

The fighting quieted, and the crowd parted. Bael was giving Lotan a free path into the schism. But he would have to leave Marco behind and take Cam's father's only protection with him.

"Fuck you, Bael," Lotan snarled, standing over Marco. "Is this what you want me to do? I'll choose Cam every time."

Marco exhaled, his breaths shorter. "Who are you talking to?"

Lotan turned behind him, wishing he had a hotline to Anya. "Just stay with me. Cam would never forgive me if something happened to you."

"Leave me and take that Goddamn thing into the schism," Marco barked, his skin growing paler. "Cam is strong."

Not that strong. Lotan held steady. "Trust me when I say, death is not the only thing waiting for you if I leave."

But as he turned back around to face the crowd, he realized that Bael must've given new orders. Silvia had been joined by a thick ring of demons holding all manner of weapons. Silvia wore a cruel smile on her face, holding the sword that still had Marco's blood on it.

"Well?"

Lotan exhaled. Maybe it wasn't just Marco who needed to be concerned about death and what might happen. Bael would take perverse glee in turning *him*, too—so he owed it to Cam to stay alive. If that was even possible.

"Fine," Lotan said, lifting the launcher.

A loud crack drew every head south. Another schism had opened—and out came a few hundred US Division agents, as well as the Mexican agents who'd gone ahead. But Lotan's high hopes soon sank when the rush of humans ended—and the demonic one continued. They were still woefully, hopelessly outnumbered.

"Back to you," Silvia said, stepping forward. "You know, I

can't imagine why you'd give up this demonic magic. I've never felt so free in my life."

"It's overrated," Lotan said, his palms sweaty as she advanced. The new agents were too far to help, and Marco's breathing had become even more shallow as blood pooled around him. This was certainly not the way he'd expected to go.

Silvia lifted her sword and Lotan readied his, but before she could strike, she stumbled forward and fell, a bullet wound in her shoulder. Behind her, Cam stood, her face ablaze with fury.

"I don't know what the fuck is going on," she said, stuffing the launcher in her back pocket. "But I'm really glad I found you."

Lotan nearly dropped his sword as she rushed over to him, flinging herself into his arms and whispering prayers of gratitude that he was okay. But she was barely in his arms before she noticed her father lying on the ground and a cry of fear rose from her chest.

"*Dad!*"

"Don't worry. I've got him." Anya appeared out of the fray, kneeling next to Marco. She concentrated, holding her hand over his chest and wincing until the skin knitted closed. Then, they both disappeared and Anya returned, nodding to Cam. "He's safe."

"Can you control the time river?" Jack asked, hopefully.

"For a brief moment. Perhaps he's offering some mercy," Anya said with a scowl. "Have you seen him?"

"No, but he's keeping tabs on things," Lotan replied, turning to Cam, who was staring at Silvia's body with an ashen expression. "He's bringing people back from the dead and turning them. I couldn't let him take your father."

Cam lifted her gaze to look at him. "Thank you."

"No time for making out," Jack said. "What's our play here?"

"I was taking the talisman launcher to the schism," Lotan replied.

"Then we'll just have to try harder," Jack said, looking to Anya, who nodded. "Can you carve me a path?"

"I'll do my best."

They took off, and Cam turned to Lotan again. "Thank you for protecting my dad."

He looked at her, still shaken from his near demise and the knowledge that this fight wasn't over. It had never been so clear to him, his mortality. The brevity and beauty of a human life. He'd still been living by the rules of knowing he had years and years to do what he wanted.

But no longer.

"Lotan?"

"Marry me," Lotan said.

She blinked. "I'm sorry, what?"

"It's not the proposal I wanted," he replied, looking around at the chaos. "But I don't know if we'll get the moonlight and roses I'd been envisioning. So before we waltz off to almost certain doom, I need to ask if you'll be mine for however long we both shall live."

"Lotan, this is *not* the time," Cam barked in true Cam fashion. "We are literally—literally—in a battle against a huge army of demons. And we are *very* much outnumbered."

"There's no better time," Lotan said, taking her hand. "I haven't yet found the perfect ring, but I hope you'll accept me nonetheless."

"Lotan—"

"Camilla Lucia Macarro," Lotan began, having nothing prepared for this moment but hoping his heart would speak for him. "From the moment I first saw you at La Madriguera, then," he cracked a wry smile, "when I first saw you again in the Nullius, I knew, in my soul, that we were meant for one another. I have never met another who has made me so content with life, whose mere presence brings me unimaginable joy, and who still manages to excite and engage me intellectually and spiritually at every turn. To fight and die by your side would be an honor, but to know I would be the one you'd call husband would make me the happiest man alive."

"For as long as you *remain* alive," Cam said, but his words seemed to have gotten through to her, as her eyes shone with tears.

"Say yes," Lotan said, squeezing her hand. "Please."

"No," Cam said, sniffing back tears and yanking him off his knees to his feet. "Not now. Because we're not going to die today, and I want a real proposal with a ring and not with dead bodies as witnesses."

There was a lightness in her tone, but he could sense her real reason. "Cam…"

She wiped the tears from her cheeks. "No."

"Look at me." He smiled. "I love you."

Her lip trembled, and a rare show of fear reflected in her eyes. "If I tell you yes, that means you'll die today. Or I'll die today. So let's just put it off, okay?"

Lotan sighed. "Tell me."

She shook her head. "No. I refuse."

He leaned in to kiss her, whispering her name as a soft prayer. His stubborn love was as infuriating as she was intoxicating. But if this was what she needed to be brave…

"Then we will join our friends in battle," Lotan said. "And then we will get you the correct proposal."

CHAPTER FORTY-SIX

Bael, master of the Underworld, Lord of the Mountain, emperor of all he surveyed, the original athtar demon, watched his armies pour into Mexico City, amused at the humans' futile attempts at fighting back. They were hopelessly outmatched, even with that damn former demon prince gathering potential allies from around the world and sending them into the city. When they looked like they were getting somewhere, Bael would send more to the fight, overwhelming them. Even Anat was starting to tire. The Lady of the Mountain was not as powerful as she made herself out to be.

He heard her calling to him, daring him to show his face. But he'd become wise to their plans to kill him. Anat seemed to have forgotten that, although he could no longer set foot in the lands that used to be his, he could move at his leisure in the time river, listen to every conversation, watch every time that damn human put his hands on her. It helped Bael's rage, and his resolve, to watch her so happy with him. Her joy was an affront to every gift he'd ever given her, to the moment he'd chosen her to stand beside him for all time.

Now the ungrateful bitch thought he could be fooled into allowing her to kill him. But it would be impossible, now that he knew her true colors. And it was laughable that she would even think she could get close to him. He would remain in his newly formed Underworld, in his castle, until every human who dared defy him was under his control—and Anat was dead.

CHAPTER FORTY-SEVEN

Without the ability to move time, Anya was starting to see why Lotan's attempts to reach Bael's schism had been in vain. She'd known that this would be an uphill battle, but she'd never been in such a one-sided fight before. She wasn't even sure…

"Anya?" Jack said, three steps ahead of her. "C'mon."

She nodded. The talisman launcher in his waistband was a constant drain on her magic, but she'd become somewhat acclimatized to it, at least enough to fight. The demons were nothing, barely a week old. Bael certainly made up for their lack of strength in numbers—perhaps his strategy. He certainly didn't care if they lived or died.

Jack didn't seem to care, either, hacking and slicing through the crowd and heading toward the schism. Anya followed, her motivation a little less kill and more moving them out of the way. Bael would delight in her having to kill neophytes and watching her wrestle with that decision. The same way he'd targeted Cam's father. At least he was safe at Abuela's house.

They moved slowly, but steadily, their combined efforts making good time. The schism loomed large, with athtar magic flowing out from the void beyond. Anya didn't know what they would find once they crossed the threshold, but she was ready for anything.

"Almost there," Jack said, looking back at her. "I—"

The schism collapsed on itself, snapping shut and disappearing into nothing.

"What... What the shit?" Jack's shoulders fell. "Anya—"

"It's gone."

Anya's breath left her chest as she stared at the space where it had been, reaching her magic to search for a door, a sign, *anything* she could use to follow the trail to get to Bael's Underworld. But there was nothing. It was as if it didn't exist at all.

She turned back to the chaos behind them. From this angle, this was an impossible battle to win. She couldn't even see any of the ICDM agents they'd brought with them. There seemed to be nothing but demons as far as the eye could see—and they were winning. Their side was running low on ammo, on help, on time. The demons would soon overwhelm the humans. Mexico City was on the precipice of complete and total annihilation.

"Jack," Anya said, turning to him. "It's time. He's not coming."

Jack stared at her and shook his head. "Anya… There may be another way."

"People are dying," she said, lowering her weapon. "Bael can stay in his castle until every human is dead—present company included—and I won't have any way to get to him." She shook her head and looked around. "Jack, there's only one way this ends well."

"Not for you," he said.

"Let me do this."

"Absolutely not," Jack said, walking over to her. "There will be some other way. Some magical solution that appears at the last minute."

"We have one," Anya said, sadly. "You have to let me go."

"Anya, you can't be serious—"

She held Jack's face, staring deeply into his eyes and hoping one day, he'd understand. "I love you, Jackson Grenard. And I always will."

She leaned in to kiss him, imprinting this in her mind. And then her magic pulled her away to the Underworld.

Anya landed in Ath-kur, outside the home she'd constructed for herself and Jack. It had been her first attempt to show him that she hadn't changed, that she was still the same person, even as the most powerful creature in the universe. Looking at it now, it was nothing compared to the real thing back in Seattle. She wished she could've seen their home one more time.

She licked her lips, tasting Jack on them, and her heart broke into pieces at the thought of him suffering yet another loss. Hot tears fell down her cheeks and she let herself feel this emotion, this despair. To rage against the unfairness of this world and how bullshit it was that she and Jack would never get to know what it was to spend more than a few stolen peaceful moments together.

And like a new flower bud rising from broken concrete, Anya reached toward that deep magic that had so far been unreachable on command. The time river ground to a halt and the sensation of the talismans faded in her chest. She opened her eyes to the battlefield. Letting her tears fall freely, she stepped across the sand, walking confidently through the silent field until she found them—the last remaining weapon Lotan and Cam had hidden, laden with anti-talisman bullets.

Don't do this.

That voice—the Bael-like voice in her mind that had been gone since the real Bael had made his appearance—whispered in her mind. She'd once been afraid it would drag her down into darkness, that it would eventually turn her into Bael himself. She'd clung to Jack in hopes that he would keep her from succumbing to her worst instincts, thinking she would always need a safeguard.

But in hindsight, and having been reminded just how depraved Bael really was, she perhaps hadn't needed Jack after all. As powerful as this magic was, it could never fundamentally change her. She could never do the things Bael did, not if she lived with the magic ten thousand years.

The world slipped beneath her again and she landed on the border between Ath-kur and the Nullius. The sands were still, even though a wind clearly rippled through them. She took a step out onto the sand, then another, and another. Her magic remained firmly inside her bones, her steps solid. She chanced a skip across a dune, then another—all the way until she found herself at the mouth of the cave.

Her pulse grew more rapid as she stepped down into the darkness, knowing what she would find and already second-guessing her decision. Would she die quickly? Would this cave collapse and bury her for eternity? Or would she simply revert to human without a way home?

Faint light was visible at the bottom and her hands shook. She thought of Jack, perhaps frantically looking for a portal to find her. Cam, she hoped, was talking reason into him and reminding him that once Anya became human, all portals back to the human world would disappear. Anya hated that Cam would have to pick up the pieces of Jack's broken heart, once again. Perhaps this time he might be stronger than when he'd lost Sara—taking some comfort in the purpose of Anya's death.

She came to the bottom, face-to-face with the Abbunatu. It was still, so perhaps the pulsing power was all in her mind. The source for all demonic magic in the entire world, right here. And she held the key to destroying it.

She hoped.

"So. This is what you'll do."

"You can't stop me," Anya said, lifting the talisman launcher.

Bael appeared in front of the barrel, pressing his chest to the tip. "I suppose not. But are you willing to lose *everything* you've worked so hard to build? An end to yourself and thousands of years of demonic magic? This is ancient magic. And you would do away with all of it."

"I didn't have to," Anya said, hesitating with her finger on the trigger. "Didn't want to. You've given me no choice."

"There's always a choice," he said with a smile. "Isn't that what your Jack said? Would you be so quick to leave him to mourn you? Do you think he'll survive mourning two of his greatest loves?"

Goddamn this demon for always knowing her deepest, darkest fears and playing on them. Anya's finger trembled on the trigger as his words sank into her heart.

In her moment of weakness, Bael wrenched the launcher out of her hand. It bounced harmlessly across the stone floor. Anya stared at it for a moment before she noticed the blade coming for her. She pulled hers and met it, finding Bael's gaze and narrowing her eyes. He swung his sword with expertise, proving he wasn't as useless with a blade as she'd anticipated. Anya couldn't do anything but fight back—with her grip on the time river, any slack would result in the both of them succumbing to the Nullius—or Bael claiming control for himself.

"I can't let you destroy this magic," he said, bearing down on her. "You have no idea what it even means."

"I don't care what it means," Anya said.

She shot out her foot, kicking him in the shin and knocking him off balance, and in the moment's grace, she dashed across the cave and scooped up the launcher, turning it on the Abbunatu again. But Bael was once again standing in her way.

"Anat, please…" Bael fell to his knees. "You can't do this. You'll die. We'll both die. I will call off my attacks. The demons will return to the Underworld. The belus, too. Everything will go back the way it was. Just please, *please* leave this magic intact." His eyes shone with unshed tears.

They were lovely words, and once upon a time, she might've believed him. The voice in her mind that had been begging her to reconsider her plan was promising that *this time* Bael would keep his word. She was powerful enough to force him. She could remain a demon and protect humanity, just as she'd intended.

No.

That wasn't her plan for herself. She'd wanted to become human, to grow old by Jack's side and see what it might've been to lead a normal life. This magic had been trouble since the moment she'd taken it. And at the end of the day, Jack had been right—she *didn't* need it. She never had.

"Please," Bael whispered. "I promise things will be different."

"You've said that before."

She lifted the talisman launcher and fired before she knew what she was doing. The bullet penetrated the blob, sending a wave of energy backward as her grip on the time river loosened then fell completely. Anya landed in a heap against the wall.

"What have you done?" Bael asked, his eyes wide.

"Ended it," Anya said, gingerly coming to her feet as the world trembled—or perhaps it was just her legs. "Forever."

"You stupid bitch," he snarled, lunging for her, but he only made it a few steps before he fell forward, bracing himself on his hands. "You've ruined everything."

"Good."

The Abbunatu was writhing, and Anya didn't know if it could feel pain, but she knew the sensation acutely. And as it slowly died, the magic that lived in her bones evaporated like mist off a lake. She fell to her knees, struggling to grab hold of it, to transport herself to the human world, to stop or slow time. But it was leaving too fast, dying on the vine.

It was almost poetic, she thought, looking at Bael who was screaming and frantically trying to save the demonic energy. She felt his magic grasp the time river, but it wasn't strong enough to hold it for long.

After all this time trying to get away from him, her final resting place would end up being right next to him. But at least he wouldn't ever hurt anyone ever again. Demons would disappear from the world entirely. Jack would be safe.

Jack.

She smiled, closing her eyes and reliving every fleeting moment they shared together as huge chunks of the cave broke off from the ceiling. It was unfair, that they should have to sacrifice what could have been—what *should* have been—for the good of humanity.

But as she thought of him, recalled the touch on her skin, his whisper in her ear, the way she'd felt so safe with him. The sound of his laugh, the sparkle of his eye. The way he steadfastly remained by her side, even when old habits made her run. And to her surprise, she felt the last gasps of her power flicker to life —drawn from that same well of power that allowed her to stop time.

She opened her eyes, watching Bael's horrified expression, and knew that she deserved more. She deserved life and love and to never, *ever* have to worry about him darkening her door again. And she deserved to save herself for once, leaving him behind for good.

The world slipped beneath her, out of the Nullius, across the divide between the human and demon world, all the way to the spot where Jack, Cam, and Lotan stood in front of the portal in Mexico City. All around them, demons had fallen to the ground, now human. The humans who'd once been their intended victims were in something of a state of shock, amazed that what had once been a lost cause was now a miracle.

But as her body arrived, all was decidedly not well with her friends.

"*Do* something!" Jack said, frantically.

"I can't, Jack. The portal isn't working!" Cam cried. "Lotan?"

"She must've done it, I—" He straightened, turning to catch Anya's gaze behind them. "Anya?"

"Hi," she said, a little weakly. She took one step forward and fell, landing in Jack's arms.

"Anya?" He touched her face. "Are you… What happened? Where's Bael?"

"I came back to you, just like you said," she said. "I…"

Her mind went completely blank for a brief moment. Then, like waking from a dream, it came back to her. The cliffside in Lisbon, the nox who'd taken Cam, Jack's hateful words after Doroteia had betrayed them.

"What… What are you doing here?" She jumped from his arms, her gaze switching from person to person with wild abandon. "Cam, you were kidnapped, weren't you? And Lotan? How did you escape from Yaotl? And Jack, you… You just…"

Their amused faces stopped her wild stammering.

"I feel like I missed something," she said, after a moment. "What did I miss?"

"It'll come back, eventually," Lotan said with a big grin.

Anya looked at Jack, her heart pounding in her chest as he approached her, a wide, loving smile on his face. He'd never looked at her that way before. So confident, so sure of himself. So much love. It was how she'd always dreamed it.

"Jack?"

"Don't freak out, okay?" Jack said, before gathering her into his arms and planting a deep kiss on her lips. "Because we're not wasting time ever again."

CHAPTER FORTY-EIGHT

"Quit fiddling, you'll ruin your makeup," Jack said, swiping Cam's hand from her mouth. "Do you need another shot?"

"No," Cam said, resting her manicured hand on her pristine white dress. "How much longer?"

"Five minutes," Jack said, checking his watch. "But it's your day, so you make the rules."

Cam snorted and picked at her nails, acrylics with French tips. She'd been complaining about them since getting them the day before, but when Jack had asked why she didn't just *remove* them, she'd gone on a long tirade about wedding photos and close ups, how her hands were already calloused to hell and—

Basically, Jack was having some serious flashbacks to his own wedding.

But he sat next to her, keeping her nails from getting chewed off and acting as a calming presence, as he had during the past three days of wedding preparation. Although it had been almost a full year since the last demon disappeared from this world, humanity still bore the scars of the attacks. Cam had rejoined the US Division to help transition agents from the now-defunct agency into other government entities and rework treaties and alliances as ICDM was sunset. The process was still ongoing, and would probably keep her busy for the next decade, but she seemed to enjoy it when she wasn't wedding planning.

She'd mentioned an elopement, not wanting to seem macabre for celebrating so soon after so many had died. But her parents, grandmother, Jack—hell, even those she worked with at ICDM—all insisted that she and Lotan do it up. After all, what better way to show off that humanity had prevailed than to celebrate something as beautiful as love?

Cam looked up as her father walked in, and Jack dipped his head to hide a smile as Marco's eyes watered at the sight of her. They'd already seen each other ten times, but Marco seemed unable to hold it together.

"It's time," he said.

Jack stood next to Lotan, awkwardly trying to remember how the photographer had told him to hold his hands so they would look good in the photographs. No fewer than two hundred of Cam's family and various ICDM agents had packed into this large church outside Mexico City. In the front row, Juana sat wearing a large hat and an even bigger grin, and Ana sat next to her mother. Jack's own parents sat three rows back, holding onto each other as Karen wiped her eyes.

Behind them, there were so many missing, and no number of flowers could erase the gigantic loss experienced by those in attendance. But for today, there was a lightness back in the face of those gathered, and it was the first time Jack felt normal in an age.

The soft music swelled, and a couple of Cam's younger cousins walked out, throwing flower petals and earning the appropriate amount of "awws" from the audience. Jack had to admit, their white tulle dresses were adorable, and the youngest, barely three, took so long her mother had to come scoop her up.

Jack looked up as the doors opened again. Anya stood in a beautiful lilac dress, her hair swept to one side. She'd allowed Cam's mother to convince her to wear makeup for the occasion, though it was muted and not at all necessary ("Except for pictures!" Ana had exclaimed). She'd privately admitted to Jack that she was nervous to stand in front of everyone but made him swear not to mention it to Cam. Even so, there was a little fear in her gaze as she stepped out.

But all that fear melted away when her gaze met his, and her nervous smile widened.

It had taken a little while for her full memory to return. Although she believed every word Jack said in the interim, she still had gaps in her memory about her time as an athtar belu.

Jack had been relieved when she'd wholeheartedly accepted his suggestion to seek therapy, both solo and with him. She'd made so much progress in the past year, finding a peace that had been missing before.

They'd even hit a milestone the month before—their first real, healthy fight. That Anya hadn't spiraled was a testament to how hard she'd worked to keep herself steady. Jack couldn't have been prouder of her.

She reached the end of the aisle and turned to the other side, holding her small bouquet and keeping Jack's gaze. But before long, everyone's attention was drawn to the back of the church again. The doors had opened, revealing Cam and her father.

Someone had touched up her makeup, but she glowed like Jack had never seen her before. She walked confidently, smiling but keeping her gaze on Lotan. Jack snuck a look at him and hid a smile—the big softie was teary-eyed. But so was the rest of the crowd. Even Anya had a little dew in her gaze.

Cam reached the front of the aisle, and Marco kissed her cheek as she took her spot next to Lotan. Her father joined his wife in the front row and blew his nose, wiping his eyes with the back of his hand.

"Please be seated," the officiant began.

"Do you want to get married?" Jack asked as he rocked Anya around the dance floor. There hadn't been a slow song the entire night, as the instructions to the DJ had been to party hard. Anya might've been an expert fighter, but a dancer she was not, and

Jack enjoyed how she let him dance her around the tile floor.

"Do you?" she replied.

Jack shrugged. "It wouldn't be anything like this, for sure. Been there, done that." He paused. "I just didn't know what you were thinking."

Anya glanced at Jack's parents, who'd been watching them all night. "Do you think your parents want us to get married?"

"I'm not asking them, I'm asking you," Jack said. "Well?"

She grinned, almost as if she were hiding something. "It's not necessary. But if you want to, it could be fun to have a small ceremony."

Jack pulled her back to him, sliding his fingers through hers and kissing her knuckles. "If you want small, we'd have to keep it a secret. Otherwise, we're getting round two of this."

She laughed. "This isn't so bad. A room full of love and happiness. I can't imagine anything more wonderful."

"You didn't see Cam before the ceremony." He released her to spin her once again before pulling her back to him. "But I'm happy to see her so happy."

Anya cleared her throat and stiffened in Jack's arms. "Jack, I have something I need to tell you."

"Oh?"

She nodded, looking a little nervous. "Been waiting for the right moment."

"As long as you don't have any more demonic energy up your sleeve."

She laughed as he twirled her under his arm then pulled her

back close to him. "Not exactly. But it depends on your definition of demonic energy."

With an enigmatic smile, Anya pulled Jack's hand to rest on her lower abdomen, her eyes full of promise and happiness. Jack shook his head, confused for just a moment before realization dawned.

"H—Are you serious?"

She nodded, her eyes sparkling. "I found out last week."

He'd been joyful before, but there was nothing like the feeling that swelled in his chest. They hadn't been trying, but they hadn't really been too careful either way. Just enjoying the peace that came with their quiet life in Seattle.

"Is this okay?" Jack asked.

"I don't know. Is it?" She giggled, pulling herself away from him and lifting his arm to twirl underneath it as he stared at her, shell-shocked.

"You can't just..." He shook his head, unable to wipe the grin from his face before he found her hips, pulling her close and planting a kiss on her lips. "It's wonderful."

She pressed her forehead to his as the song finally changed to something slow. They swayed for a moment, enveloped in their own private bubble of happiness. Jack couldn't even find the words to express his feelings, except that he was absolutely, unbelievably happy.

The DJ spoke over the music, reminding him that it wasn't their day today. "Let's not tell anyone just yet," he said, lifting his head from hers to spot Cam and Lotan at the head table, finishing their dessert and talking with a never-ending stream of people. "I don't want to steal Cam's thunder."

"Are you kidding?" Anya snorted, following his gaze. "She knew the moment she saw me."

Cam took that moment to catch Jack's gaze. She winked and raised her glass, and, if possible, looked even happier than she had before.

"Of course she did," Jack said, turning back to Anya and sliding his hand to her lower back. "What do you think? Girl or boy?"

"My heart says girl," Anya said, tilting her head and biting her lip. "We could call her Sara, if you wanted?"

"You wouldn't want to honor Asherah?" Jack asked.

"It's not a very modern name," Anya replied with a shake of her head. "And…Asherah will still be her sister forever."

Jack nodded. "We'll make sure she knows all about her. I promise." He twisted her under his arm again. "But what if it's a boy?"

"I know it's a girl. I knew with Asherah, and I know now."

"Who am I to argue?" Jack said. "Mother athtars never change their stripes, I guess."

"Even when they're human."

ACKNOWLEGMENTS

First and foremost, thank you to my husband, for cheering me on, listening to my thorny plot points, and coming up with the wildest twists that somehow lead me to the ones that actually make sense to the story. Marrying you was the best decision I ever made.

Special thanks to Dani, my line editor, for catching my grammatical mistakes and non sequiturs. And thanks to my typo checker Lisa, who somehow always finds things I miss.

Finally, thank you, dear reader, for continuing on this journey with me. I'm so pleased that I was able to continue this story and bring real closure to Jack, Cam, Anya, and Lotan. Please consider leaving a review at any of your favorite bookstore websites to help spread the word.

ALSO BY S. USHER EVANS

THE MADION WAR TRILOGY

He's a prince, she's a pilot, they're at war. But when they are marooned on a deserted island hundreds of miles from either nation, they must set aside their differences and work together if they want to survive.

The Madion War Trilogy is available in eBook, paperback, and hardcover. Download the first book, The Island, for free on all eBookstores.

Empath

Lauren Dailey is in break-up hell, but if you ask her she's doing just great. She hears a mysterious voice promising an easy escape from her problems and finds herself in a brand new world where she has the power to feel what others are feeling. Just one problem—there's a dragon in the mountains that happens to eat Empaths. And it might be the source of the mysterious voice tempting her deeper into her own darkness.

Empath is a stand-alone fantasy that is available now in eBook, paperback, and hardcover.

ALSO BY S. USHER EVANS

The Razia Series

Lyssa Peate is living a double life as a planet discovering scientist and a space pirate bounty hunter. Unfortunately, neither life is going very well. She's the least wanted pirate in the universe and her brand new scientist intern is spying on her. Things get worse when her intern is mistaken for her hostage by the Universal Police.

The Razia Series is a four-book space opera series and is available now for eBook, paperback, audiobook, and hardcover. Download the first book, Double Life, for free on all eBookstores.

The Lexie Carrigan Chronicles

Lexie Carrigan thought she was weird enough until her family drops a bomb on her—she's magical. Now the girl who's never made waves is blowing up her nightstand and no one seems to want to help her. That is, until a kind gentleman shows up with all the answers. But Lexie finds out being magical is the least weird thing about her.

Spells and Sorcery is the first book in the Lexie Carrigan Chronicles, and is available now in eBook, paperback, audiobook, and hardcover.

ABOUT THE AUTHOR

S. Usher Evans was born and raised in Pensacola, Florida. After a decade of fighting bureaucratic battles as an IT consultant in Washington, D.C., she suffered a massive quarter-life-crisis. She decided fighting dragons was more fun than writing policy, so she moved back to Pensacola to write books full-time. She currently resides with her husband and two dogs, Zoe and Mr. Biscuit, and frequently can be found plotting on the beach.

Find her on the internet:

www.susherevans.com

www.facebook.com/susherevans
www.twitter.com/susherevans
www.instagram.com/susherevans